ALAMAT : BOOK 3

TAGUWASI

ᜆ ᜄᜓ ᜏ ᜐᜒ

ALAMAT: BOOK 3

TAGUWASI

ᜆ ᜄᜓ ᜏ ᜐᜒ

By:

Herbert De Leon

Poems and Narrative Translation by:

Dr. Honrado F.V. Palugod, MD

Book Cover by:

Become Ocean

Edited by:

Sara Miller

Imprint: Independently published

For Che, Caelin

and to my beloved late

Uncle Raul, Auntie Cynthia and

Auntie Marsha

Table of Contents

Preface

In this third book in the Alamat Series, I am introducing the reader to a relatively unknown epic hero called Taguwasi. The Negrito or Agta epic of *Taguwasi and Innawagan* like all other pre-colonial Filipino epics were originally passed down through the generations primarily through word of mouth.

But unlike the other more renowned epics that have seen ink to paper during the Spanish colonization of the Philippines, the story of Taguwasi had not been recorded as anything tangible only until the latter part of the 20th century. It was a University of the Philippines professor by the name of *Ernesto Constantino* who, back in 1977 met with an old Aeta woman called Marcela Tumbali *aka* Baket Anag, and recorded for the first time, the epic of Taguwasi and Innawagan.

Professor Constantino transcribed his recordings of Baket Anag's chanted song about Taguwasi in a book titled Endangered Languages of the Pacific Rim, *"Nanang: I Taguwasi Anna I Innawagan"* back in 2001. The translation of the song into English was done in such a way that it preserved the style of the original song. Something which I must admit had difficulty deriving the narrative from.

But with a great deal of help from my longtime friend and collaborator in this series, Dr. Honrado "Honey" Palugod, MD who took great lengths in unraveling the story of Taguwasi and Innawagan, we finally piece together the complete narrative of this ancient Agta epic.

But just as I did with my previous books, I am doing a re-telling of this timeless epic and incorporating it into my own literary universe while still basing its foundations on the original tale. As always, I would like to take my readers into the pre-colonial world of the Agta people as I blend it into my fictionalized world of the Lakandians.

-- Herbert De Leon

Prologue

A great change is taking shape across the mortal realm of *Kalupaan*. The dark machinations of the Yawàs continue to plague the world of man through their emissaries of death and destruction, the *dalaketnon*.

But as the dalaketnon continues to cause havoc in an otherwise hapless world, the scales of fate have a way of maintaining balance in a world in turmoil. The *Lakandians*, champions of the immortal realm of *Kaluwalhatian* as well as Kalupaan, are emerging at an increasing rate as the need for them arises.

Either through fate, destiny, or just happenstance, that the benevolent spirits of Kaluwalhatian called *enkantos* discover more and more of the *Angkang-Dian* whose divine bloodlines serve as the tree of life that bears the Lakandian fruit. But just like any other kind of fruit, Lakandians vastly differ in personalities and priorities much like how some fruits are sweet and some are sour.

It is through the same twists and turns common to every soul in the branches of fate that a Lakandian grows and comes into their own. Sometimes, it takes a storm to shake the fruit off a tree and what befalls the fruit will determine whether or not it will take root and grow or if it will simply rot and be forgotten in time. This is one of those stories.

Gampao (Map)

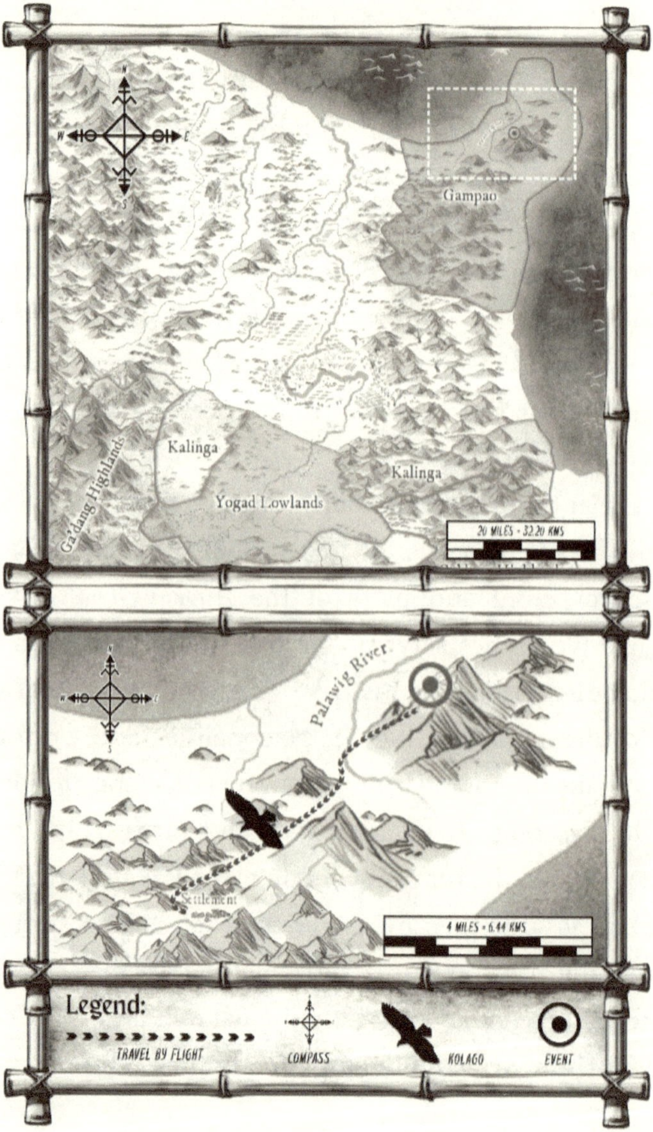
Gampao
Kalinga
Ga'dang Highlands
Yogad Lowlands
Kalinga
20 MILES = 32.20 KMS
Palawig River
Settlement
4 MILES = 6.44 KMS
Legend:
TRAVEL BY FLIGHT
COMPASS
KOLAGO
EVENT

Chapter 1
Lakandians

On top of an unnamed mountain in the heart of the Gampao region in the Northeastern part of the known land, an unprecedented event is taking place. For the first time since their kind came into being, two *Lakandians* (demigods) are in the same place and conversing with each other.

On a flat stretch of rock near the summit of the mountain stood the Ga'dang hero Lumalindaw. He stood there in awe along with his *bannog* (a giant eagle) and his *katiwala* (trusted companion) Kidul, an *anito* (male enkanto) trapped inside an *ayoding* (tube zither) for disrespecting the Poons. They were all looking up at a dark-skinned Aeta man who hovers above them, suspended in midair.

The Aeta man is called Taguwasi. He was born amongst the mountain-dwelling Agta people of the north. Like others of his kind, Taguwasi was a bit shorter and of darker skin compared to the other peoples and tribes of the land. He had short curly hair that he regularly cropped and wore a red and white *beg* (loincloth) tied around his waist by a string made from rattan. He also had *biskal* (armbands and leglets) on his arms and ankles made from rattan, wooden beads, and boar hair.

He carried a white, ivory-looking *pusot* (bamboo quiver) with seven white feathered arrows strapped to his waist by a thick beaded cord that stretched across the broad expanse of his chest. He also carried a white four-foot-long hunting bow with a golden string on his left hand at the ready.

Much like Lumalindaw, Taguwasi is a Lakandian. And much like Lumalindaw who has the power of the *Voice*, Taguwasi had the power to control the wind itself.

His mastery of the wind is so absolute that he can command it to carry him in its currents as easily as a mother would carry her baby in her arms. This makes Taguwasi the fastest being to ever take flight. In fact, he could fly so fast that he could put a bannog like Kolago to shame.

Aside from the gift of flight, his mastery of the wind also gives Taguwasi a second powerful ability. He calls this ability his *dinatal* (explosion). He can summon the strength of a *buhawi* (tornado), compress it in his chest, and release its concentrated power outwards like a giant invisible fist that can knock down trees and part the waters of a lake for hundreds of feet. But as powerful as this ability is, it does take a toll on him, limiting his use of his dinatal to only a few times a day before rendering him unconscious.

Less than a few moments ago, Taguwasi was on his way home to his family when he was suddenly accosted by a thundering sound that almost knocked him out of the air as he flew. The sound came from Lumalindaw who used his own power and accidentally struck Taguwasi as he flew. After reeling from the power of the *Voice,* Taguwasi gathered himself and flew toward the source of the attack. He was expecting to find an enemy as soon as he got to the mountaintop, but to his surprise found a disheveled-looking man and a giant bannog to be the culprit.

Seeing that the strange man and the bannog hadn't noticed his arrival, Taguwasi took his time to assess the strange visitors who wandered into his protected lands. The man was tall and looked quite disheveled. Though not too familiar with the other mountain tribes farther south from his own, Taguwasi did recognize that man's colorful albeit torn beaded clothes that he was in fact from the southern mountain tribes.

The bannog on the other hand was something completely new to Taguwasi's eyes yet not unheard of. He was in fact told of their existence by another magical bird from Kaluwalhatian. Being told about these giant blue, green, and red eagles was one thing, but seeing one in person was quite another thing entirely. Suddenly the stranger and the bannog were alerted to his presence and looked directly up at him.

"Do you mind keeping it down?! These are my lands and those are my birds you are frightening. Though I see you have a bird of your own, and a big one at that!" Taguwasi told the strange man whose voice was so powerful that he thought it might rival his dinatal.

The man said something to him in a language that was completely alien to him. Suddenly, an ethereal voice came from the strange-looking object next to the mysterious man.

"*Masampat e abi-abi* (Good Morning) Lakandian." the voice said.

Taguwasi was caught by surprise again! It was an anito that spoke to him in his Dupaningan Agta tongue. "Anito?! What are you doing inside that... thing?"

"That is a story for another day. Let me see if I can bridge your minds so both of you may understand each other," The anito said.

From the strange tube-like thing with golden strings came a soothing, otherworldly tune that felt like a refreshing drink of water on a hot summer day. His heart and mind were completely enthralled by the melody. In that instant, Taguwasi somehow felt connected to the strange man as if their spirits could speak freely to each other.

"Greetings." Taguwasi greeted the stranger.

"Greetings to you as well," Lumalindaw answered back. "I am sorry if I disturbed you with my outburst earlier. I'm having a hard time with my dilemma lately. My name is Lumalindaw of Nabbobawan."

"I'm sorry to hear that you are in distress Lumalindaw of Nabbobawan. My name is Taguwasi. Maybe I can help?"

"I seriously hope you can. I am looking for a *nalaing* (witch) who cursed me with blood magic. Her curse prevents me from going near my wife and children. I need to find her and force her to recant her curse upon me." Lumalindaw said as his eyes started tearing up after mentioning his family.

"Unfortunately, I have nothing to offer you as far as news of this nalaing that you seek. These lands have been blessedly free of such evil for many months now.

"Even the flying aswang or others of their ilk know better than to fly over these mountains lest I shoot them down from the sky," Taguwasi answered.

"Then it appears that I need to move farther west and try my luck there," Lumalindaw said with a sigh.

"I am sorry I cannot help you with your quest to find this creature but let me at least help you by giving you a meal and some *bilon* (provisions). My *bertan* (family group or familial settlement) is not too far from here," Taguwasi said as he felt sorry for Lumalindaw.

Suddenly a bizarre-looking *karat* (hawk) came flying in from out of nowhere. It was huge and white but seemed otherworldly at the same time. Its feathers had an illuminating sheen about them, and its eyes were a bright and golden yellow. It circled Taguwasi and spoke!

"Lakandian, your katiwala has a message for you. He said a fellow Lakandian is here and..."

But even before the bird could finish, Taguwasi held his hand up to silence it and then pointed toward Lumalindaw. "I know," Taguwasi said.

"Oh..." was all the bird could say.

"This is Dundunan, one of the *kumaw* from Kaluwalhatian. She is also my wife's *agom* (companion), much like our katiwala," Taguwasi said. "Which reminds me, I forgot to ask what your name is anito."

"I am Kidul from the Kingdom of Nanolay," Kidul answered. "And on behalf of my dumbstruck Lakandian charge, we graciously accept your offer of food and provisions."

"Hey!" Lumalindaw protested. "You do not speak for me Kidul!"

"Given that the last of your rice and fish are all but gone, would you rather continue your search tired and hungry, or do you want to take a break for a day and regain your strength?" Kidul asked Lumalindaw.

As Lumalindaw's stomach growled loudly at the mention of food, all he could do was meekly answer, "Yes. I would like to take you up on your offer of food and provisions."

"Good!" Taguwasi exclaimed. "Please follow me. I promise you, it's a very short flight to my home. I have some questions I wish to ask you given that you are the only other Lakandian that I've ever met."

*****

A few minutes later they were in the air. Taguwasi led the way as Lumalindaw followed close behind him on Kolago's back. Taguwasi tried his best to slow down knowing the bannog wasn't nearly as fast given its size and the fact that it had a passenger.

They headed southwest for a few minutes until they reached the mouth of a small branch of the Cagayan River. Taguwasi's bertan had settled near the river and farmed a small field of flat land next to it. It consisted of six huts that were lived in by five members of Taguwasi's immediate family and one for the *puyang* (shaman) that devoted her life in service of the Lakandian.

"You can land your bannog on that clearing near the vegetable farms. We cleared it for planting come summer but should be a safe enough distance, so he doesn't knock over our huts." Taguwasi told Lumalindaw as he pointed to the clearing.

Taguwasi landed first and used his powers to disperse the wind created by Kolago's wings as the bannog descended to the ground. As soon as Kolago's feet touched the earth, he heard an all too familiar voice scream at him from behind.

"Taguwasi! You left me behind again!" the ethereal voice said from behind him.

"I'm sorry Bago," Taguwasi apologized as he turned to face his katiwala, the anito Bago. "I didn't think anything exciting was happening today, so I went out on patrol by myself."

"Is that him?" Bago asked Taguwasi. "Is that the Lakandian?"

"That's him all right. In all his disheveled glory." Taguwasi answered.

Bago, like all other enkantos, whether they be the male anitos or the female diwatas are pure spirits in the mortal realm of Kalupaan. So, to Lakandians like Taguwasi and Lumalindaw as well as those sensitive to the presence of spirits, Bago would look like something between smoke and water but with the shape of a man.

Lumalindaw dismounted Kolago and approached Taguwasi and Bago. "*Macasta a fuwab* (Good Afternoon) anito. I am Lumalindaw." He greeted Bago.

"He speaks Ga'dang. How is it that you two can understand each other?" Bago asked puzzled.

"That would be my doing," Kidul answered from within the ayoding. "My name is Kidul from the Kingdom of Nanolay and katiwala to the Lakandian Lumalindaw."

"The imprisoned one!" Bago blurted out in astonishment, to which Kidul felt embarrassment and simply held his proverbial tongue.

"Bago! They are my guests!" Taguwasi exclaimed. "At the very least, treat them with respect!"

"Please forgive me Kidul," Bago apologized. "It's just you are well known amongst our kind, not just for what happened to you. But for your great deeds as well when you were a *punong alagad* (alagad commander) of the armies of the Kingdom of Nanolay. Especially after the Battle of Nabuangan Forest!"

"Let's leave the past where it is," Kidul answered as he played another tune to connect the minds of everyone in the vicinity to Lumalindaw's to make all understand each other when they spoke. "Let's focus on this present moment when two Lakandians are in the same place at the same time, for the first time. Unless of course, Taguwasi has already met the first Lakandian Lam-ang."

"I've only heard mention of his name from my late hama," Taguwasi answered. "He said he was in Garao close to ten years ago I believe when Lam-ang came to vanquish the deranged Tikbalang Sildado. Hama even said he and his friend even helped load Lam-ang's boat with supplies after they traded supplies for baskets of fish with them. But in all my three years as Lakandian of these mountains, I've never seen another one of our kind until this morning when I met you."

Then a woman's voice came from behind them, calling out Taguwasi's name. "*Kabanga!* (Spouse!) You're back! And who is this with you? And what is that giant bird?!"

"Lumalindaw. Let me introduce you to Innawagan, my wife with a thousand questions." Taguwasi said with a smile as he wrapped his arms around his wife.

Innawagan like her husband was of the Agta people. She was about the same height as Taguwasi with the same dark skin and same curly hair. Albeit her hair was longer and a little less curly and covered the back of her neck to her shoulders. Both husband and wife had small button noses and fuller lips which were common traits amongst their people. But where Taguwasi's face has hard and chiseled, Innawagan's face was soft and feminine and fair to a man's eyes, especially with her round eyes and thick eyelashes.

Innawagan wore a short wrap-around skirt around her waist called a *taloktok* which was made from the dried bark of a *Tangisang-Bayauak* (Red Stem Fig) tree. She wore no other form of clothing except for a small, beaded necklace around her neck and a few *beklow* bracelets made from local plant material. Her breasts were fully exposed which made Lumalindaw a little skittish given that he was Ga'dang, a people known for their highly stylized and beaded clothing.

"Kabanga, this is Lumalindaw. Lakandian of the Ga'dang people in the south. And that kabanga, is a bannog!" Taguwasi continued as he introduced his guests to his wife.

"Good afternoon Innawagan." Lumalindaw greeted Innawagan as he took her hand and placed his forehead on the back of her hand to perform *mano* (an act of respect and greeting).

"Please, I am only eighteen years of age and much too young for you to treat me as an elder." She half-jokingly said as she pulled her hand back.

"My apologies, Innawagan. I meant no disrespect. It's just that I myself am only six years old. Aside from your husband over here who is only three years younger than me, I believe; I always assume everyone around me is an elder by comparison." Lumalindaw said and smiled, feeling a little bit embarrassed by the whole thing.

"Come Lumalindaw," Taguwasi interjected. "I've spoiled your breakfast, let me at least make it up to you by feeding you boar meat, rice, and *habu* (honey)."

"You have my thanks for your generosity and hospitality," Lumalindaw said. "Let me just tell Kolago to go out and hunt for his food while I join you and your wife for a meal of my own."

"*Hapu* (title of respect) Innawagan," Dundunan said. "Should I go to Dalawesan and inform them that you have guests?"

"Yes, go my friend. And please tell my siblings to hurry home as well." Innawagan answered the magical bird.

As Kolago, the bannog took off to hunt the nearby mountains for a meal, Lumalindaw followed the couple into their settlement. The first thing Lumalindaw noticed was the strange half-finished huts made of bamboo and palm leaves erected like a sail but no taller than six feet in height. "What are those strange-looking huts?" Lumalindaw asked Taguwasi.

"Those are called *pinanahang* (lean-to structures). We usually set them up as shade when we settle into open areas like this one during the months when we plant fruits and vegetables," Taguwasi answered. "We're actually going to sit, rest and chew some betel nuts under that one next to my hut." He said as he pointed to a pinanahang next to a hut.

"My siblings should be back shortly from the bertan of Hapu Baket and her family just down the river with the boar meat. They joined her *apuku* (grandchildren) for the hunt this morning and should be back with their share of the meat." Innawagan said as she handed her husband and Lumalindaw some *butag* (betel nuts), *ikmo* leaves, and *apog* lime to chew on as they waited.

"Do you mind if I ask why you shouted 'Muwan ' earlier?" Innawagan asked Lumalindaw as she sat down and started rolling her butag in the ikmo leaf in her hand. "I honestly dropped the bananas I was carrying when I heard you. The sheer power of your voice was frightening."

"I'm sorry if I frightened you earlier," Lumalindaw said apologetically. "Muwan is the name of the witch who cursed me and forces me to be away from my wife and children. Out of frustration and anger, I lashed out against the empty sky. I know hearing the *Voice* for the first time can be quite daunting to some, and for that I truly am sorry."

"It's actually not the first time any of us have heard you use your... *Voice* before," Taguwasi said as he chewed on the *amman* (the chewing concoction made from betel nuts). "I think it was almost a year ago when we heard you say the exact same word as it thundered throughout the mountain ranges."

"You both heard that?" Lumalindaw said in surprise. "All the way from here?"

"Not too far from here, but yes. Though not as deafening as this morning's outburst, but clear enough to hear you say the nalaing's name out loud," Taguwasi answered. "Normally, I would have flown over to where you were as soon as I heard you, but during the time, I too was preoccupied with my own battle."

"I suppose that answers the next question of how you heard about Lumalindaw," Kidul suddenly interjected. "But it's not like we've never encountered mention of your name as well."

"Just how do you mean?" Bago asked.

"Is that his katiwala?" Innawagan asked surprised.

"Your wife can hear spirits?" Lumalindaw asked surprised as well.

"Yes," Bago answered. "She and her brothers are all sensitive to spirits which is why they have kumaws as friends and companions."

“Then allow me to introduce Kidul. And yes, he is my katiwala.” Lumalindaw answered. “I have heard of you from Poong Ofag himself when he came and blessed me and my wife on our wedding night.”

Lumalindaw took a bite from his amman and continued, “Lam-ang on the other hand, his exploits were already renowned even before I was born. Though admittedly, I have never met either.”

“It would seem between the two of us, there are vast mountains of tales to tell and learn from. Let us wait for my *patepag* (in-laws) to return so we might all enjoy the stories together.” Taguwasi said as he offers Lumalindaw some bananas to eat.

Chapter 2

Feasts and Tales

Innawagan and the two Lakandians stayed under the shade of the pinanahang for another two hours, ate fruit, and chewed amman. Lumalindaw asked them about their people and their way of life, which the couple was more than happy to share with their guest.

At the height of the second hour, two large birds flew over them and began circling them. One was white as rice and the other one was as black as a *duhat* (black plum). Lumalindaw recognized the white bird as the kumaw Dundunan, the black one he assumed was her brother.

Both hawk-like birds were almost identical except for the obvious color difference. They both had the distinct four protruding feathers atop their heads much like a bannog's head although the kumaw's feathers were the same color as all their other feathers.

The kumaws were also rather big compared to the other raptors that normally reside in the jungles of Kalupaan, yet still not as big as Kolago and other bannogs that even the fifteen-foot Poons could ride.

Dundunan landed next to where Innawagan sat and said, "Your *papatwadi* (siblings) are here Hapu Innawagan. And they brought back quite a feast of boar meat, sweet potatoes, and rice with them!"

"I'll go start a fire so we can start cooking the boar meat right away," Innawagan said as she stood up.

"No need *wadi* (younger sibling)," said a man that came out of the jungle holding a large rattan basket in his hands. "Hapu Baket insisted that we skin, clean, and roast the boar right then and there. Though we did take some home that still needs to be prepared for tonight and tomorrow's meals."

"That's why it took us so long to get back," said another man that came behind him, holding a similar basket. All in all, three men and two women came out of the jungle holding different size baskets of food. They were all armed with hunting bows strapped to their backs and a pusot of arrows to their sides.

Taguwasi and Lumalindaw stood up as Taguwasi introduced the newcomers to his guest. "Patepag, allow me to introduce you to the Lakandian Lumalindaw."

Lumalindaw nodded to each person as a sign of humility and respect. They in turn reciprocated the gesture.

"Another set of three brothers. This seems all too familiar." Kidul whispered to Lumalindaw.

"This is Talimannog," Taguwasi said as he motioned toward the man to his left. "He is the oldest of my wife's siblings and the woman next to him is his wife Sinag who also happens to be my older sister."

"Welcome to our bertan Lumalindaw," Talimannog greeted Lumalindaw as he placed the basket on the ground. "You are welcome to join us in quite an abundant feast."

Talimannog was the tallest of the group and even taller than Taguwasi. In fact, he was almost as tall as Lumalindaw, which was quite tall for an Aeta man. His face has sharp features that projected to those who did not know him that he was a serious man as well as the head of this family unit.

Like all the other males which included Taguwasi, Talimannog wore nothing more than a beg loincloth tied around his waist by a piece of string and a few biskal accessories. Sinag, his wife who stood next to him was as modestly clothed as Innawagan with only a short taloktok around her waist and nothing else to cover her plump breasts. In fact, everyone there except for Lumalindaw was hardly wearing anything.

Sinag had sharper features on her face compared to Innawagan which indicated that she was a bit older than Taguwasi's wife. Her hair was shortly cropped, almost like the men's which did not diminish her beauty as her eyes seemed brighter and seemed to glisten with the rays of the sun itself.

"Welcome to our home Lakandian Lumalindaw," she greeted him as she gave him a warm smile and seemed to marvel at his colorful albeit tattered clothes.

Lumalindaw smiled at her graciously and nodded his head. *She is a Lakandian 's sibling. I wonder if she also had the potential to be like us.* He thought to himself.

Next to Sinag were Innawagan's other two brothers Ammani and Anibo; the twins. Lumalindaw was astonished as soon as he noticed that the two were completely identical. They had the same face, build, and exact length of their bushy long hair. The only difference between the two was the color of the begs they were wearing. The one closer to Sinag was wearing a yellow beg whereas the one farther away was wearing a green one.

"These are the twins, Ammani and Anibo," Taguwasi said as he pointed to each brother respectively.

"I'm Anibo!" said the first brother.

"And I'm Ammani!" said the second brother.

"My apologies," Taguwasi said slightly embarrassed. "As you can see, I still can't tell them apart."

" We apologize as well," both brothers said in unison as they chuckled and placed their baskets on the ground.

"I actually am Ammani." the brother in the yellow beg said.

"And I actually am Anibo." the one in green smiled and said.

"We just like playing tricks on our patepag from time

to time," Ammani said as he placed his right hand on Lumalindaw's left shoulder as a sign of welcome.

Anibo followed suit and placed his left hand on Lumalindaw's other shoulder. "We are pleased to meet another Lakandian. Tell us, can you fly as well?"

"No. Not without Kolago whom I sent out to..." Lumalindaw was saying when the last of their party interjected. "There is time for stories when we begin eating. Please forgive my annoying wadi twins Lumalindaw. I am Alig, second sister to Talimannog. We are pleased to meet you, and you are welcome to stay with us to rest and eat."

Alig was taller than Innawagan and Sinag. She was somewhat statuesque in the way she stood, spoke, and moved which said to Lumalindaw that other than Talimannog, she was also in charge of their little bertan. Her hair was the longest amongst everyone in the group which she tied to the back of her head. Given the fact that she also had very curly hair, tying it at the back made her hair puff out around her head making it look like a black halo.

Alig's face had a serious look much like Sinag's. But whereas Sinag looked relaxed and understanding, Alig's face was more discerning, and her eyes were always moving as though she was always thinking and analyzing everything.

"*Akka* (older sibling)," Alig addressed Talimannog. "Can you tell your agom to call upon Puyang Anag, so she can join us in our meal? I think she is up the river by the riverbed trying to catch some fish."

"Dalawesan!" Talimannog called out to the black-feathered kumaw that flew around them.

The large kumaw landed next to Talimannog and stood next to him on its two feet. At that moment, Lumalindaw saw exactly how big the kumaw actually was. On both feet and standing perfectly erect, Dalawesan was only an inch shorter than Talimannog, meaning it stood somewhere near five feet in height.

"Is there something you need Hapu Talimannog?" Dalawesan asked.

"Yes, can you please fly to the end of the river and tell Puyang Anag to return home and eat with us? Please tell her our guest has arrived." Talimannog asked of the kumaw.

"Very well, Hapu Talimannog. I'll return shortly after I give the Puyang your message." Dalawesan said and flew off towards the river.

"Is it only you and your siblings that live here?" Lumalindaw asked. "Or are there still others coming?"

"Other than those you see here, we have no other family members to speak of," Talimannog answered. "Our parents were killed by Kalinga headhunters as were

Taguwasi and Sinag's parents and Puyang Anag's husband and son."

"Our hena was the puyang of our settlement when we were children. She was a very gifted healer and could see spirits, something she seemed to have passed on to all her children." Anibo said.

"I'd rather we not talk about how they died akka," Innawagan interjected. "It was sad and it was tragic, let's just leave it at that."

"Honestly, at this point, we are all the family we need," Innawagan continued as she turned her attention to Lumalindaw and held her husband's hand. "Unless of course Sinag or I become pregnant, or Alig finds herself a husband."

*****

A few moments later as the members of Taguwasi's bertan prepared the cooked food and laid it on the ground on top of banana leaves, a middle-aged woman in her mid-thirties arrived via the riverbed. She wore the typical taloktok and peculiar-looking headdress made of rattan and hemp and adorned by black and white feathers that looked like they came from the kumaws. She was bare-chested and quite muscular from years of farming, hunting, and fishing.

She clutched a string of three large *burasi* (carp) river

fish in her right hand and on her left hand was a bow and a few several *barot* (spiked) fishing arrows tied along across the bow itself. “It looks like we’ll have to save these fish for dinner then,” she said as she approached the group. “It would seem the hunt went splendidly by the amount of meat you brought back.”

“Puyang Anag! Come join us!” Talimannog called out to the newcomer. “Come and meet the Lakandian Lumalindaw.”

“*Masampat a apon* (Good afternoon) *Apo* (Ga’dang word similar in use to Hapu) Anag,” Lumalindaw greeted Puyang Anag as she approached.

“Apo? Kalinga or Ga’dang?” Puyang Anag asked with a hint of suspicion and trepidation in her tone.

“Ga’dang Apo,” Lumalindaw answered. “I come from Nabbobawan, and we do share land and neighbor with some of the Kalinga.”

“Relax, Puyang! The Kalinga he neighbors with are not the same that have wronged us.” Taguwasi told the old shaman, trying to alleviate the sudden tension her questions arose.

“She’s their *makamong* (Ga’dang shaman) Lumalindaw. Best to not infuriate her and get cursed on top of the one you already have.” Kidul told Lumalindaw.

“What is that?!” Puyang Anag exclaimed when she heard Kidul speak. “Is that an anito trapped in whatever that thing is?"

"Yes. This is Kidul, my katiwala. He is currently imprisoned in the ayoding," Lumalindaw answered. "If the next question is why then I suggest we all sit down and begin our meal because it is quite a tale."

"I agree with our guest," Alig said as she gestured for Puyang Anag to sit next to her. "It seems we have the entire day to listen to the tales of our esteemed guests. I suggest we start eating now so we can enjoy the rest of the day listening to their tales over some amman and cool river water."

They all sat squatted in a circle around the food laid out on the ground and began feasting on the boar meat, rice, and sweet potatoes. It wasn't long after they began eating when the questions started coming to Lumalindaw. To no one's surprise, it began with the twins.

"Is that a Raniagad (Blade of light) weapon?" Anibo asked as he simultaneously pointed at the white-hilted weapon on Lumalindaw's side and shoved a hand full of meat and rice into his mouth.

Lumalindaw licked the food off his fingers, reached for the Raniagad bolo at his side, and unsheathed it. The blade glowed white as it left the scabbard, leaving everyone speechless at its grandeur.

"This is my Raniagad bolo given to me by Poong Ofag

on the day of my birth," Lumalindaw said as slowly brandished the weapon in front of everyone. "It has served me well over the years against many enemies, including the dalaketnon."

"I'm sorry to interrupt you Lumalindaw but something you said caught my attention and now questions are nagging at my mind," Taguwasi interrupted Lumalindaw, who then put the Raniagad back in its sheath.

"Go ahead and ask your question."

"You said you received the Raniagad on the day of your birth, but it is my understanding that Lakandians such as ourselves must first earn the right to even wield such a weapon," Taguwasi began. "So, my question is, how was it that you were deemed worthy right away?"

"The answer is, I was not. It took me a year and a half to finally achieve *Pananglaw* (The state of illumination of a Raniagad weapon where it can cut through anything). I had to fully accept my role as Lakandian as I fought a nest of *aswang* (night creatures: vampires and viscera suckers) that were plaguing a neighboring *barangay* (village)," Lumalindaw began his answer. "I was only given the weapon because with the blade came its first owner, my katiwala Kidul."

"But what good is a weapon to a spirit?" Anibo asked quizzically.

"Since everyone here is sensitive to spirits and can hear me, which is something I have never thought I would see, I will answer the young man's question," Kidul replied. "Before I was imprisoned in this ayoding, I was an *alagad* (warrior anito) in Kaluwalhatian. And in the immortal realm, spirits such as myself and Bago, have a physical form and can wield weapons."

"I see," Taguwasi said as he pondered Lumalindaw's answer. "I suppose the same truths hold similar to mine as well."

"Show him your Raniagad weapon kabanga," Innawagan said excitedly.

"Wait, you have a Raniagad weapon as well?" Lumalindaw asked in astonishment. "Forgive my surprise but I was told by Poong Ofag that you and Lamang have yet to receive your Raniagad blades."

"When did the Poon tell you this?" Sinag asked.

"On my wedding day, close to two years ago," Lumalindaw answered.

"Then what he told you was true. Wadi did not receive his weapon until about a year ago. He was given his Raniagad when he rescued Innawagan and her brothers from their captors." Sinag said as she looked to her brother to continue.

"Also, my Raniagad weapon is not a blade like yours," Taguwasi said as he reached for his white hunting bow. "I don't know if you've noticed earlier, but my bow isn't made from the common wood like that of any others you may have seen before.

"This particular bow," Taguwasi said as he handed his bow over to Lumalindaw. "This is made from *gansagat* which is the wood taken from the balete trees in Kaluwalhatian. It is stronger than any wood that can be found in Kalupaan and the power behind it increases the longer the bow is drawn."

Lumalindaw drew the golden string of the bow and immediately felt the tension increase as he held on to the drawn weapon.

"My friend Mamlindao back in Kaluwalhatian also has a weapon similar to this one," Kidul said.

"I have heard of your friend as well," Bago said in response to Kidul's comment. "In fact, all of your deeds, including your sister's was quite known to us in the Kingdom of Mah-nongan. Especially during the Battle of Nabuangan Forest."

"I want to hear about that!" Ammani blurted out. "Tell us about the Battle of Nabuangan Forest!"

Suddenly, a small piece of bone from the boar's ribs came flying at Ammani and struck him in the chest. Everyone's attention then turned to Innawagan who threw the rib.

"Let my husband finish his tale and don't rush our

guests into starting theirs! That's just rude!" she said half-jokingly and a little furious at her brother's impatience. Everyone fell silent for a brief second then burst out laughing a second later.

"As I was saying," Taguwasi continued. "The bow isn't the Raniagad weapon given to me by Poong Kedes (Goddess of the Hunt). Aside from the bow, she also gave me these arrows with shafts made from the same gansagat wood, fletching made from the feathers of kumaws, and arrowheads of varying shapes, all made from *lawanag steel* forged from *punlanag seeds* (seed of the balete tree), all of them Raniagad." Taguwasi said as he unsheathed a total of seven arrows from his ivory-white pusot. All seven arrows glowed as white and as brightly as Lumalindaw's Raniagad bolo in Taguwasi's hand.

He handed the arrows to Lumalindaw which continued to glow in Lumalindaw's hands as he inspected each arrowhead up close. Two of the arrowheads were long and narrow, designed to penetrate deep into the flesh or pass through it completely. Another two had barbs that Lumalindaw assumed were meant to remain stuck within the flesh where the barbs were designed to cling to the muscles to prevent the arrow from being dislodged. Another two had wide-bladed arrowheads that looked like the tip of a sword.

"What do these do?" Lumalindaw asked Taguwasi.

"Those were designed to slice deep into the flesh and lacerate as much of it as possible," Taguwasi answered.

Finally, Lumalindaw looked at an arrowhead with a small, almost needle-like shape with a hollow tubular space in it. He had to squint his eyes a bit to focus on the hollow space inside the arrowhead.

"I don't know what this does either," Lumalindaw commented.

"Those are very similar to the *palagad* (poison-tipped arrows) my people use in combat when we have to defend ourselves from raiders and headhunters. Using the palagad in the heat of battle guarantees a kill as long as you can pierce your enemy's skin and inject them with poison that we usually harvest from certain tree saps," Sinag said as she answered Lumalindaw's question.

Lumalindaw handed the Raniagad arrows back to Taguwasi and took in another mouthful of rice and boar meat dipped in habu. "Do you mind if I ask another question about your Raniagad weapons?" he asked as he tried to talk and chew at the same time.

"Go ahead and ask," Taguwasi answered.

"You only have seven Raniagad arrows, are you not worried about losing some of them if you fail to retrieve them after a fight?"

"For anyone else experienced in fighting with bow and arrows, losing arrows is a very common thing that can happen even in a hunt. They are either lost or broken," Taguwasi began explaining. "For anyone else, even a Lakandian such as yourself, fighting with Raniagad arrows will almost guarantee that you will eventually lose one, or if the fight is a big one then you will definitely run out of them. But for someone who can control the very wind..."

In a movement so fast that even Lumalindaw almost missed it, Taguwasi nocked an arrow on his bow and let it soar towards the trees. It glowed brightly as it flew which made it seem like a beam of white light or a lightning strike. The next thing Taguwasi did was purse his lips as though he was whistling though no sound came from them. He then made a series of quick gestures with his fingers and waved them in quick frantic gestures in the air.

"Look up there," Innawagan told Lumalindaw as she pointed out to where the arrow was zipping through the trees as it was piercing branches, trunks, and leaves alike. After a few more seconds, the arrow zipped back to Taguwasi who caught it in his hand.

"How did you do that?!" Lumalindaw asked in astonishment.

"I can summon the wind and take control of the arrow and guide it as easily and accurately as though I were holding it in my hands," Taguwasi answered.

"I understand that part," Lumalindaw began. "But what I do not understand is how the arrowhead maintains its state of pananglaw after the arrow has left your touch."

Taguwasi looked at Lumalindaw puzzled for a short while. He didn't know what Lumalindaw meant. Finally, it was Talimannog who spoke up to clarify their guest's inquiry.

"Do you mind showing what you mean through example? Can you use your own Raniagad weapon to make your inquiry clearer?" Talimannog asked.

Lumalindaw unsheathed his Raniagad bolo for a second time and just like the last he did the last time, it glowed white and felt a little warm to those close enough to feel it. The next thing he did was hand over the weapon to Talimannog. As soon as the weapon left Lumalindaw's touch, the light waned almost instantly and all that was left was a bolo that appeared to be made of bone.

"It happened so fast with his bolo!" Innawagan exclaimed.

"Why did the pananglaw fade off so quickly?" Anibo asked.

Lumalindaw was perplexed by everyone's reaction to his Raniagad weapon.

Taguwasi finally understood what Lumalindaw meant by his inquiry and spoke, "Here patepag," Taguwasi said as he handed one of his glowing Raniagad arrows to

Talimannog who took it with his other hand.

The glow of Taguwasi's arrow did not wane in Talimannog's hand. In fact, it stayed in the pananglaw state for almost a minute before the glow started waning slowly until the arrowhead looked like the same bone-like material the bolo was made of.

"I do not know why my weapons stay in the pananglaw state much longer than yours. Maybe it has something to do with the size, maybe the magical light is more potent in the arrowheads than it is in your bolo?" Taguwasi said as he pondered the possible answer.

"Would you know Kidul? Amongst everybody here, you alone have used a Raniagad weapon the longest." Lumalindaw asked the anito in his ayoding.

"I have no answer to provide any of you either. When I used the bolo in the many battles I fought in Kaluwalhatian, the concept of Raniagad weapons losing their light was unheard of," Kidul answered. "But let's not dwell on this. The fact that there are two Lakandians in our midst that are proven worthy of wielding such powerful weapons is enough reason to celebrate."

"I agree with the anito," Puyang Anag said in continuation. "It matters not how the two Lakandians wield their mighty weapons, all that matters is that they are here to wield them against the evils that lurk in the dark and those whose hearts are darkened by evil."

Everyone agrees, dismisses the matter entirely, and continues with the feast. After a good long while and when everybody was full and satiated, Alig and Puyang Anag begin distributing amman to everybody as they all sat, chewed, and relaxed under the shade of the pinanahang.

"I cannot begin to tell you how much I appreciate this deliciously abundant meal you shared with me today," Lumalindaw said as he squeezed some apog lime on his betel nuts wrapped in ikmo leaves. "It's been many, many moons since I've been this full.

"If there's anything I can do to thank all of you for what you've shared with me, all you need do is ask," Lumalindaw said in gratitude.

"Well… we do love a good story." Anibo started saying when Alig started to shush her younger brother. But Talimannog swayed his sister's hand and spoke, "I'm actually also looking forward to your tales and adventures as Lakandian. Would you mind telling us your stories as we chew amman and digest the hearty meal we all just ate?"

"I would be more than happy to tell you my stories," Lumalindaw said as he spat out some orange spit and betel nuts. "Mind you that my tale is unfinished and will unceremoniously end in tragedy. But for clarity's sake, I should let Kidul tell you his tale first as it does intertwine with mine."

"Other than Bago and Lumalindaw, no one in Kalupaan knows what happened to me before I was imprisoned in this ayoding by *Poong Maykapal* (Grand Steward) Dasal all those years ago," Kidul began his tale. "It all began in the *Dakong Torogan* (Grand Castle) of Kalekay in the Kingdom of Nanolay…"

The Balete Tree (Map)

ᜀᜅ᜔ ᜊᜎᜒᜆᜒ

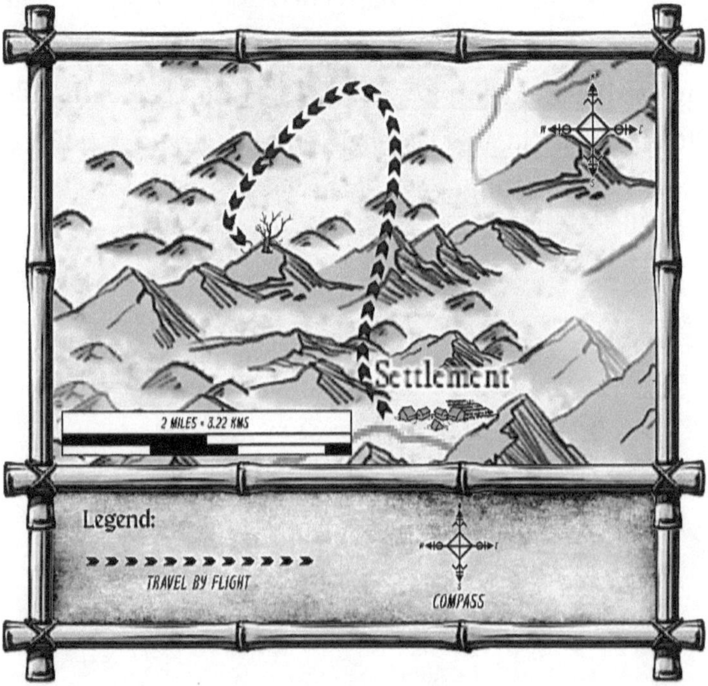

Chapter 3

Reflections

Kidul finished his tale by late afternoon. Taguwasi and the rest of his family were so completely enthralled by this that as soon as he finished, the twins couldn't contain their excitement and began asking questions almost immediately.

They wanted to know everything Kidul knew about the immortal realm of Kaluwalhatian; from the trees of gold, the *Bulawanong Taaw* (The Golden Seas), Kalekay, the Poons, the *Bukang Karimlan* (The Five Pits; The Bottomless Tranches), the Great Bird Manaul, etc. Kidul was more than happy to answer all their questions. He had never experienced having this large an audience that could naturally hear him before and found the experience quite enjoyable.

"It looks like it will be another while before Lumalindaw can tell his tale to anyone," Taguwasi said as he stood up. "Would it be acceptable to everyone if Lumalindaw and I talk among ourselves in private? I have… questions of my own that I wish to ask him."

"Take him up to the hill where the balete tree grows," Innawagan said as she grabbed Taguwasi's hand. "And take Bago with you, I think he is still upset that you left him again this morning."

"Very well. Lumalindaw, would you mind joining me for a few moments?" Taguwasi asked.

"That would be fine. I'll leave my ayoding here so you can continue conversing with Kidul. I'm sure he's enjoying the company of others after almost a year of being alone with only myself and my woes." Lumalindaw said as he stood up to join Taguwasi.

"And get some mangoes on your way back," Sinag told her brother who just as quickly turned her attention back to Kidul.

"Shall we go?" Taguwasi asked Lumalindaw.

"You lead the way. Mind you Kolago has not returned yet so you may have to wait for me to catch up. Climbing mountains does take longer if you have to trek up them."

"Let me worry about that," Taguwasi said as he gestured for Lumalindaw to follow him away from the pinanahang. They walked a little closer to the riverbank where Taguwasi suddenly stopped and turned towards Lumalindaw.

Bago was hovering next to them and asked, "Should I go on ahead and meet you at the balete tree?"

"Yes. You should go now, and we'll meet you there shortly." Taguwasi answered.

"This will feel strange at first, but you have to put your trust in me when it begins," Taguwasi said as he raised both of his hands towards Lumalindaw as though he were holding an invisible basket between them. "Don't fight it and don't resist. Be like a leaf carried by the wind."

"What wind?" Lumalindaw asked puzzled.

"This wind," Taguwasi said when all of a sudden, a gust of wind came from out of nowhere and started encircling Lumalindaw like a tiny cyclone.

Lumalindaw panicked at first but remembered Taguwasi's advice to not fight it. So, he relaxed his body and left the wind to do as it pleased. The air around his body felt like a soft gigantic hand that had him in its grip. A moment later, the hand started carrying him.

Lumalindaw felt his feet leave the ground as his body went up and up and then passed the trees. Taguwasi was right beside him as they went higher and higher. "Remember, don't fight it. Let the wind take you and you'll be fine."

"I'm not fighting it. I'm actually enjoying this," Lumalindaw said with a great big smile across his face. A smile that has been absent from it for almost a year at that point. "Can we go faster?"

"Then you best hold on to that cape around your shoulders!" Taguwasi said with a smirk as they suddenly shot up toward the sky even higher and faster.

They reached a height where the north and eastern seas were but one ocean and the far reaches of the great Cagayan River stretched out to the southern horizon and disappeared into vast mountain ranges. Though not unfamiliar to Lumalindaw, seeing the world at this height, he had never actually looked at it without a giant bannog under him. Looking down at nothing but the green mountains under his feet, made him a little bit fastidious about the whole flying without a bannog thing.

The winds at such a height were strong and loud in addition to the sound of the wind that Taguwasi was already controlling to keep them falling back to the earth. Before he spoke, Taguwasi calmed the winds around them to give their voices a chance to be heard. "From this far up and beyond the confines of the ground, the world looks so big and so small at the same time, does it not Lumalindaw?" Taguwasi asked.

"It does. It makes one think of how precarious the safety of our world and loved ones are knowing the kind of evil that is out there seeking its demise," Lumalindaw answered. "Being here, right now, knowing that only a few beings like us can actually see the world like this, gives me a clearer perspective of how much rests on our shoulders to keep it like this against the dalaketnon and their night creatures."

"The dalaketnon… this is actually one of the reasons I chose to speak with you alone. I heard you say that you have faced them before, do you mind telling me about them?" Taguwasi asked.

"I am actually surprised that you've never crossed paths with them before. From what I've heard about the Lakandian Lam-ang as well as my own experience, they seem to be very active up here in the north." Lumalindaw said.

"If you are willing to tell me what you know of them, then we should return to the ground and meet up with Bago by the balete tree," Taguwasi said to which Lumalindaw nodded in agreement.

*****

They landed near a large gangly balete tree on top of a steep hill near where Taguwasi's bertan had settled. From the hilltop, Lumalindaw could already see the others as they remained gathered under the pinanahang and listened to Kidul's tales.

As soon as they came within a dozen feet from the balete tree, both Lakandians felt the magic emanating from the tree at the same exact time. They felt quickened by it as though it connected the *balaang nakar* (holy pearl) that resides within their bodies to the realm from which it came.

By the foot of the tree stood the ethereal form of Bago as he patiently waited for the Lakandians. As soon as he was only a few feet from the ground, the wind that carried him dissipated as quickly as it came. Lumalindaw landed on his feet a little less gracefully than Taguwasi who had obviously done it before and to a greater extent.

"It's been a while since I came this close to a balete," Lumalindaw said as placed his hand on the tree's trunk and closed his eyes. "I had forgotten how soothing these trees feel when we come close to them."

"I come here every day," Taguwasi said as he too placed his hand on the tree. "Not just to feel the magic of the tree, but to say a prayer to the Poons and thank them for the blessing they have given me and my family."

Lumalindaw felt a little ashamed after hearing Taguwasi's words. It felt like an entire lifetime ago since he felt anything to be thankful for. Wanting to change the mood and the topic, Lumalindaw asked Taguwasi bluntly what he wanted to ask of him. "Well, we're here. What did you want to know?"

"I need to know more about the dalaketnon," Taguwasi answered as he snapped out of his tranquil haze and removed his hand from the balete. "I need to know more about them. Especially since I pledged myself to Poong Kedes when she came to my aid almost a year ago."

"Did you not tell him anything about them?" Lumalindaw asked Bago.

"I've told him all that I know about the dalaketnon. But you must understand, unlike Kidul, I was never an alagad. I never fought in the *Kanibusanan* (The Great War of Kaluwalhatian)," Bago answered Lumalindaw. "I was an anito of the jungles and that was all I was until the day I found his *hama* (father); until I accidentally stumbled upon the *Angkang Dian* (Dian Bloodline)."

"Very well, tell me what you've told him," Lumalindaw said.

"The only thing I was told of the enemy was that they used to be night creatures; aswang to be more precise. They were then taken to Kasanaan, possessed by the *Aninas* (the living shadows of Kasanaan), and turned into the dalaketnon," Bago said.

"He also told me that, unlike night creatures, the dalaketnon are not weakened by the sun but only mildly irritated by it. They are intelligent, cunning, and extremely fierce warriors." Taguwasi continued for Bago.

"Did he tell you about the Lalad?" Lumalindaw asked.

"No," Taguwasi answered. "Who or what is the Lalad?"

Lumalindaw looked at Bago to see what his reaction was. Though he could not really discern what Bago's expression was given that even to Lakandians, an anito or diwata's features were murky at best; he could see that Bago was also perplexed at what he said.

"I find it strange that those in Kaluwalhatian have not told you of the Lalad as of yet," Lumalindaw said. "Well, to begin with, your knowledge of the dalaketnon is accurate but incomplete. They are what you say they are. They are amongst the most dangerous of our enemies, and the most intelligent.

"Having said that, to Lakandians such as ourselves and from what I've heard of Lam-ang's deeds, they are a challenge but nothing we cannot handle," Lumalindaw said as he removed his *tapet* (cape) from around his shoulders. "And then there are the members of the Lalad. They are the few dalaketnon to whom the Yawàs have granted special abilities and powers. Powers that may rival our own. I know of this because I faced one of them in battle a few years ago. It was a dalaketnon named Nabunab with the ability to transform her body to smoke. She also gave me this scar."

Lumalindaw showed Taguwasi and Bago a huge scar on the right side of his chest that crossed his collarbone. The scar looked like any other one would receive from a stabbing except for the edges that looked as though they were scarred from a burn.

"What in all of the three realms could leave a scar like that?" Taguwasi exclaimed. "Even the fact that you scarred the way you did is unbelievable!"

"Such a mark should not even be possible for Lakandians," Bago said. "Your kind heals so quickly that receiving scars is a rarity on its own."

"The weapon that left this mark on my flesh was a *Hartadem* (Shadow Blade) spear," Lumalindaw answered. "Do you know what a Hartadem weapon is?"

"Yes," Taguwasi answered. "When Poong Kedes bestowed upon me my Raniagad weapons, she spoke of the only thing in all the three realms my arrows cannot cut or pierce, a weapon made from *harandok* (decayed punlanag), a weapon of darkness; the Hartadem."

"I have seen only two dalaketnon in my lifetime," Lumalindaw said as he fastened his tapet back on. "One as I mentioned earlier was Nabunab, the other was a male dalaketnon that seemed to be her underling. The male did not carry a Hartadem weapon.

"Kidul and I suspect that only the Yawàs and the Dalaketnon carry these very dangerous weapons. They might be as rare as our Raniagad weapon since they both come from the balete trees in the other realms. Which is a good thing I suppose. If we were ever to face off against a *sangkawan* (horde) of dalaketnon wielding Hartadem blades, then we might as well hand over the *Likum* (the hidden ones; the sleeping Dians) and be done with it."

The mention of the Likum took both Taguwasi and Bago by surprise. Hearing Lumalindaw mention it out loud was daunting, to say the least.

"You know the Likum as well?" Taguwasi asked softly and very carefully.

"Of course, I do," Lumalindaw answered very nonchalantly. "Isn't the whole point of our existence is to protect them and all of humanity?"

"I... I know but... To say it out loud like that..." Taguwasi was finding it hard to find the words. "You see when Poong Kedes told us of... of the Likum, she was very adamant about keeping their existence a secret.

"Her exact words to me were, *'one cannot reveal a secret that one doesn't even know exists.'* I haven't even told my wife about them. Only my sister is aware of them and only because she was there with me when I was told," Taguwasi said.

"I understand all of that. That is why even *we* are unaware of their exact locations or how many of them are actually here," Lumalindaw said assuring Taguwasi of what they must do. He placed a hand on Taguwasi's shoulder and looked him in the eye.

"We came here because you wanted to know what I know about the dalaketnon. I told you they are dangerous and what they are capable of. But remember this, we are far more dangerous than they ever hope to be because there is one undeniable difference between us and them. We have people we are fighting for out of love and that alone makes us dangerous.

"Do not overthink what our existence means or what our duties to Kaluwalhatian are. Just simplify everything down to two truths. We are protectors and we are destroyers. Protect those we love and kill every evil thing you come across. Though at times you may find yourself questioning yourself on which role you should fulfill, trust that the goodness in your heart will lead you to the right decision all the time."

"You are a wise Lakandian," Bago said approvingly. "Though you Lakandians are very young beings, I am happy to know that wisdom comes to you just as fast as you grow."

"I thank you Lumalindaw," Taguwasi said as he too places a hand on Lumalindaw's shoulder. "I will take your words to heart and use them as a guide throughout the many, many years I have in this world."

"You are quite welcome Taguwasi," Lumalindaw responded. "But if you really want to thank me, do you mind telling me how was it that you only came into a Raniagad weapon so late into your life?"

"The story of how I came into my Raniagad weapon will have to wait as it is a very long one," Taguwasi answered. "But I think we have time to tell you why I came to it late. But to do so, I think it would be better if Bago was the one who told it. He is the only one here who was actually there before I was even born."

Lumalindaw turned to Bago and looked at him intently as he awaited the tale to begin.

"Very well, I will tell the tale," Bago answered. "Though I suggest sitting down for it as it may not be particularly long, but it's not that short either…."

Garao to Gabur Falls (Map)

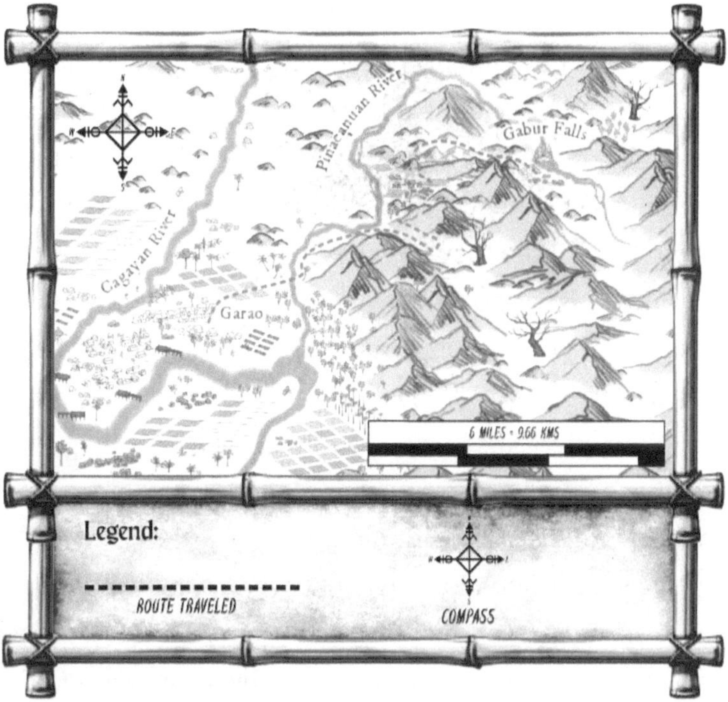

Chapter 4
Bago's Tale

The jungle anito Bago was near the edge of the jungle near the eastern banks of the Cagayan River only a few miles north of the busy barangay of Garao. He usually frequents this area of the jungle to help lost travelers find their way should they lose it in those dense jungles.

Since Garao is a barangay frequented by a great number of people from different tribes that cohabitate the Great Cagayan River, Bago had always been a busy anito for the better part of two hundred years. Nothing ever really changed for him though a great many things have changed in the world around him.

He simply kept doing what he was tasked of him to do by Poong Kedes when she made him, and everything stayed the same. Not even the Kanibusanan affected the carefree anito though he did return to Kaluwalhatian from time to time. But everything changed for Bago on one particular night when two young Aeta men found themselves lost on the way home.

The two had just come from Garao and each carried a basket of fish strapped to their backs that they got from a group of Ilocano fishermen they had met in Garao. One of the young men was called Kabug, he was a burly young man with wide shoulders, an even wider chest, a head full of long bushy hair, and a wide infectious smile that heavily showcased his white glistening teeth.

The other one was called Taruban. Unlike his cheerful friend, Taruban was a bit more stoic and serious. He was skinnier in comparison to Kabug yet still very muscular through years of hard labor as both hunter and fisherman. He had a short crop of curly hair on top of his head and a thin bristle of facial hair above his lips and across his jaw that he kept at that length as it pleased his wife to see him have it.

Taruban had been married for almost two years at that point and had a young daughter whom he cherished and loved above anybody else aside from his wife who was named Aran.

"Those Ilocanos were extremely generous giving us all these fish for a few pots of rice, vegetables, and fruit," Kabug said with a large grin across his face. "Though I couldn't really understand a word he said, I kind of liked that... what was his name? Gulungan?"

"Gibuan," Taruban retorted. "His name was Gibuan."

"Right! Gibuan! As I was saying, he had a very pleasant demeanor about him that I really liked. Unlike that his big muscular friend, what was his name?"

"Shush!" Taruban silenced his friend. "This is where we start walking northeast toward the *tapaw* (waterfall) right?"

The two men look around as they try to find their trail marker made of branches and vines to show them their way back. But unbeknownst to them, a hunting party of Itawit hunters found their marker earlier during the day and discarded it out of spite against the Agta tribes.

"Isn't it a little farther up the river?" Kabug asked.

"I honestly thought it was in this area," Taruban replied. "You know what, let's just start going northeast anyway. I'm sure we're bound to see something familiar that will take us back to the bertan."

About an hour later, the two friends found themselves in unfamiliar surroundings. "I don't know those farms and I don't know where we are!" Kabug started to panic.

"Just keep your calm Kabug, we're bound to find our way sooner or later," Taruban said, trying his best to calm his friend. "There is a small settlement over by the farm near the edge of the jungle. Let's ask if they know the way to *Gabur Tapaw* (Gabur Waterfalls)."

"They can also be headhunters Taruban! Did you think about that?" Kabug protested.

"Look around you, what do you see?" Taruban asked rhetorically. "Farms! Whoever lives in those settlements are most likely farmers."

The two friends reached the settlement and quickly noticed that it was an Itawit settlement. Luckily, Taruban spoke a little Itawit and was confident he could communicate enough with them to get directions.

They saw a large, unelevated hut with light coming from the inside. Several shadows were dancing from the hut that they assumed might be a family supping there.

"Napia nga gabi (Good evening in Itawit)," Taruban greeted as he stepped through the doorway. But to his surprise, it wasn't a family of farmers that looked back on him but rather a trio of Itawit headhunters sharpening their axes on whetstones. One of them was even polishing a human skull with a piece of rag.

"Run," Taruban said calmly at first. Then he looked at Kabug and yelled out, "Run! Start running, now!"

The two ran as fast as they could back to the jungle to try and lose the trio of headhunters that chased after them. They had reached the jungle first but the fish they carried on their backs were slowing them down and the headhunters were starting to catch up.

But unbeknownst to the two, the anito Bago had been following them since he found them wandering around the jungle earlier. Bago felt something different about one of them and decided to follow them to investigate.

But when he saw that they were in danger, he decided to help them out. The first thing he needed to do was to guide them to safety and help them lose their pursuers. He usually approaches those who are lost and implants a magical suggestion in their thoughts to help them find their way.

But as Bago, approached Taruban to imply his magical suggestion, Taruban suddenly looked at Bago directly and screamed out loud. "Yaaagh!"

Taruban suddenly stopped in his tracks at the sight of Bago, causing Kabug to slam right into him. Both men fell on the ground along with their baskets of fish.

"What are you doing?!" Kabug exclaimed. "They're right behind us!"

"There...there is a spirit looking directly at us," Taruban said in a quivering voice.

"You've always been able to sense these things!" Kabug said as he picked up his friend by the shoulders. "But right now, those headhunters should be our primary concern. They will kill us and mount our heads on spikes!"

"Listen to your friend," Bago told Taruban. "Drop your baskets and follow me."

Taruban told Kabug to leave the fish as he followed the anito into the jungle.

"Hide behind those trees," Bago told Taruban. "I will lead the headhunters away from you."

The two of them waited behind the trees for a good long while. None of them spoke as they waited patiently for the headhunters to give up their pursuit. Finally, after what seemed like an eternity of waiting, Bago returned and told them to come out.

"The spirit is back," Taruban whispered to Kabug. "He says they're gone."

"Greetings, my name is Bago. I am an anito of the jungle."

"Uhm… Greetings?" Taruban replied perplexed.

"Are you talking to the spirit?" Kabug asked. "Tell him or her that we appreciate the help, but I really need to get those fish back. It's the whole reason we went to Garao in the first place."

"The Itawits had unfortunately taken your fish back to their settlement," Bago said.

"Don't bother with the fish," Taruban told Kabug. "Bago, the anito, said they took them."

"*Agay!* (An expression of surprise) What a waste!" Kabug cried out in frustration.

"Do you mind telling me if you are the Puyang of your bertan? The reason I ask is the fact that you can see and talk to me."

"No, I am not. Our Puyang is our childhood friend Puyang Anag," Taruban answered. "Though I have always been sensitive to spirits."

"I see," Bago said as he focused on the magical essence he feels in Taruban. "Would it be acceptable if I guided you and Kabug back to your settlement?"

"Sure…?" Taruban answered, yet still unsure why an anito would take so much interest in him.

*****

It took them until a little past midday, the next day when they reached Taruban and Kabug's settlement near the Gabur Waterfalls. The settlement itself was a bertan composed of three large families.

There was Taruban's family composed of his elderly hama, his wife Aran, and his twelve-year-old daughter Sinag. Then there was Kabug's family, consisting of both his parents and three siblings, each with a family of their own. Kabug's family comprised of fourteen members which made up the majority of the entire bertan.

And then there was Puyang Anag's family, made up of her husband Bananayo and her five-year-old son Kabugnayan. Puyang Anag was quite young to be an actual Puyang. She was just in her late twenties whereas most Puyangs would be in their late thirties or older. But Puyang Anag had always been a gifted healer and sensitive to the presence of spirits; much like Taruban and his daughter were.

"Don't tell anybody about Bago," Taruban whispered to Kabug as soon as they got to the settlement. "I don't want to start a panic and I don't want Puyang Anag to start chanting like a bird."

"Fine," Kabug answered. "Just as long as you don't mention to anyone how we lost the fish. Remember, we were attacked by at least a dozen headhunters and had to abandon the fish after we killed four of them with our bare hands."

"I'm sure everyone will believe that," Taruban said sarcastically. "I'll see you later tonight."

Taruban went straight for his hut as Bago followed him around like a puppy. "Why are you still here?" he asked the anito. "I am grateful for all you have done for us and for getting us home safely, but should you still be here? Don’t you have other wayward travelers to help?"

"I should. I know I should," Bago answered. "But there is something very different about you and I feel like I should know what."

As soon as Taruban entered the hut, he was greeted with a warm welcoming embrace from Aran as well as a good peppering of kisses.

"What took you so long to get back?" Aran asked as she continued to kiss her husband. "The trip to Garao shouldn't have taken you more than two days. It's been almost four days now."

"It was a long unproductive trip kabanga," Taruban said exhaustedly. "I'll tell you all about it later. But right now, I want to see my darling little girl. Where is Sinag?"

"Humph!" Aran grunted. "She is outside playing with the other children."

"Don’t be angry kabanga, I promise I'll make it up to you tonight," Taruban said as he gave his wife a passionate kiss.

"I'm counting on it!" Aran said as she stepped out of the hut. "I'll go and get some vegetables from the garden. I'll call you when it's time to eat.

"Sinag! Your *hama* is home!" Aran called out to Sinag.

"Hama! Hama!" Sinag cried out and jumped into her father's waiting arms. "You've been gone so long! What took you so long to get…"

Sinag was in the middle of saying something when her eyes darted to the ethereal figure of Bago standing at the corner of the house. "Hama… there… there is a spirit standing over there," Sinag said as she pointed at Bago.

"Don't be afraid *asang* (daughter), his name is Bago. He was the anito that helped me get home." Taruban said.

"Whatever it is that you have, she seems to have it too," Bago said softly as he approached them. "This goes far beyond being sensitive to my kind."

"What do I have? Am I going to be sick?" Sinag asked worriedly.

"Nothing to worry about little one," Bago said, trying to reassure Sinag that all is well with her. "What you and your hama have is a gift.

"I must take my leave now and I promise I will never bother you or your hama again. Though from time to time, I might check up on you. But only from a distance. Goodbye little Sinag and Taruban."

Kuta Salakan (Map)

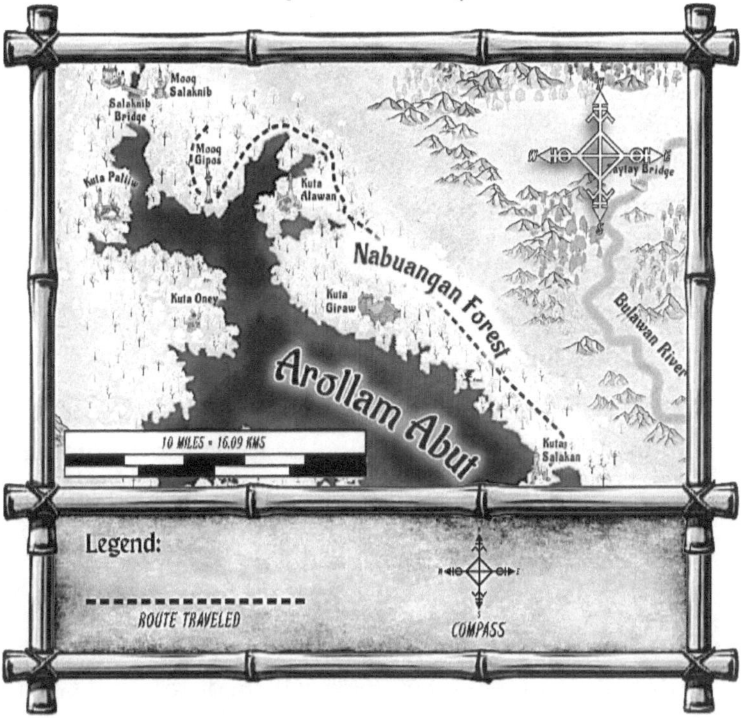

*****

Bago left the settlement and immediately sought out the nearest balete tree he could find. After finding one a few hours later, he returned to Kaluwalhatian in search of Poong Kedes.

He emerged near the edge of the northeast corner of Nabuangan Forest; somewhere between Moog Salaknib and Moog Gipos, the watchtowers of the north. It took him a good moment to realize where in Kaluwalhatian he was, but as soon as he saw the sapphire-encrusted rooftop of Moog Gipos to his south, he knew exactly where to go.

The first thing he needed was to reach Moog Gipos and get some clothes. As is with all enkantos who return to Kaluwalhatian from the mortal realm, they are physical in form and completely naked. The last thing Bago wanted to do was present himself to his Poon creator with nothing on.

It didn't take him long to reach the watchtower and borrow a set of clothes from one of the alagad warriors stationed there. The next thing Bago had to accomplish was to find Poong Kedes. He knew she was usually stationed at *Kuta* (Fort) Salakan, at the southeastern corner of Nabuangan Forest which was a good twenty miles away.

But if Poong Kedes had returned to The Grand Torogan of Paslakop, then his journey would be more than two times as far. But Bago wasn't in a hurry. In fact, he actually wanted to walk all the way to Paslakop. He has not been home for more than eighty years and had missed the calming and soothing effect that the light from the balete trees had on him.

After a long and relaxing trek through Nabuangan Forest, Bago had finally reached the gold and marble fortress of Kuta Salakan. At the gates of the Kuta, Bago was greeted by an old friend of his, the Alagad warrior, and Punong Alagad Anlabban.

"Bago!" Anlabban cried out as he saw Bago approach the gold and marble archway. "I haven't seen you in a while. What brings you back old friend?"

"I need an audience with Poong Kedes. Is she here?" Bago asked as he gave his old friend a hug.

"She is inside as she usually is," Anlabban answered. "Do you mind telling me what it is all about?"

Bago gave his friend a suspicious look as it was very uncommon for enkantos to meddle in the business of others, especially if it concerns the Poons.

"I'm sorry if I seem intrusive Bago, but there has been much excitement going around ever since Sarangay and her kawan returned from Kalupaan after they finally vanquished the cursed tikbalang Sildado," Anlabban said and realized how rude he was being. "But it's really none of my business what you have to tell your Poong creator. She's inside, go right ahead."

Bago entered the fort and went straight for the *bulwagan* (Court or Throne Room) where he found Poong Kedes giving instructions to several alagad warriors. Bago stood quietly at the corner and waited for them to finish. The meeting itself didn't sound important. It sounded like the typical instructions the alagad usually gets, like running patrols and lookIng out for enemy burrows.

When the meeting finally broke and all the warriors were dismissed, Bago approached Poong Kedes and bowed before her. The Poon stood and bid Bago approach. Like all Poons, Poong Kedes stood at a towering fifteen feet tall. Light emanates from her eyes and skin as effortlessly as it would from a star.

She had long flowing white and silver hair held to the back of her head by a *dungdung* headband on top of her head with a golden carving of the figure of Dian Mah-nongan. She wore a white *baruwasi* (blouse) patterned with gold and studded with multicolored gems. She had a similarly fashioned wrap-around skirt around her waist that stopped just above her knees. Her arms, wrists, and ankles had bracelets, armbands, and anklets made of silver, gold, and other precious stones.

"You may stand Bago," Poong Kedes said as she motioned for the anito to arise. "What brings you home? What is so important that you need to seek an immediate audience with me?"

"I found something... someone very strange my Poon," Bago replied. "Something I have never seen or felt in all my long years in Kalupaan."

"Yes, go on." Poong Kedes said as she noticed him pause and gather his thoughts.

"I saw a human with dormant magic lurking inside him, my Poon," Bago told Poong Kedes.

"But humans have been dabbling in magic for thousands of years Bago. Some are even so naturally attuned to it that they can see and hear you. This is nothing new." Poong Kedes said.

"The magic I speak of is old magic my Poon. Very, very old and powerful magic. Like... like the type of magic I... I feel in the Dians themselves."

"Stop!" Poong Kedes immediately ordered Bago. "I will ask you a series of questions now and I need you to answer them clearly and precisely, do you understand?"

"Y...yes my Poon," Bago answered but was confused as to what was happening.

"Did you tell anybody else about this human that you've found?" Poong Kedes asked first.

"No. I spoke with Anlabban when I arrived but mentioned nothing about it to him."

"Good. This human, she is a woman I assume."

"No, my Poon. The human is an Aeta man named Taruban of the Agta people."

"A man?" Poong Kedes said puzzled. "Is he a young man?"

"He is of age my Poon," Bago answered. "He is married and has a twelve-year-old daughter. In fact, his daughter also has this strange magic in her as well."

"He already has a child!" Poon Kedes said surprised. "It is very important that he bears another one."

"Would you mind me asking why my Poon?"

"What I am about to tell you is a secret of the utmost importance do you understand Bago?" Poong Kedes said softly as she knelt in front of the anito so that they were able to speak at near eye level.

"Y...yes my Poon. You can trust me."

"I am going to tell you about powerful beings that can bring the Kanibusanan to an end and win the war for us. How to produce them and how we will move forward after I tell you. After which you shall spend every moment of your existence watching over Taruban and his future progeny."

Agam (Poem)

ᜀᜄᜋ᜔

Pakinggan mo ang dalamhati ko
Dito sa paanan ng mga ulap.
Lumalim ang katahimikan
Tila naglaho ang alingawngaw.
Ang tinig ng mga nag-uusap
Ang masasayang hiyaw
Naglalarong mga bata
Yabag ni Ama sa kanyang pangangaso
At kaluskos ni Ina sa loob ng kusina.
Isasalaysay ko ito sa inyo –
Damhin ninyo ang pangamba ko Ama
Dito sa paanan ng mga ulap
Nakahimlay ang kanilang katawan
Sa lupa na basa ng hamog na dugo
Kidlat ang bilis, Kulog ang pighati.
Lumalim ang katahimikan
Naglaho ang alingawngaw.
Nasaan ang mga salita mong nagtuturo?
Nasaan ang mga brasong nagkukubli
Laban sa daigdig ng pangamba?
Nasaan ang sulyap na nag-aaruga?
Ang palad na nagmamahal?
Malalim na katahimikan
Wala ni alingawngaw
Dito sa paanan ng ulap.

Moving (Map)

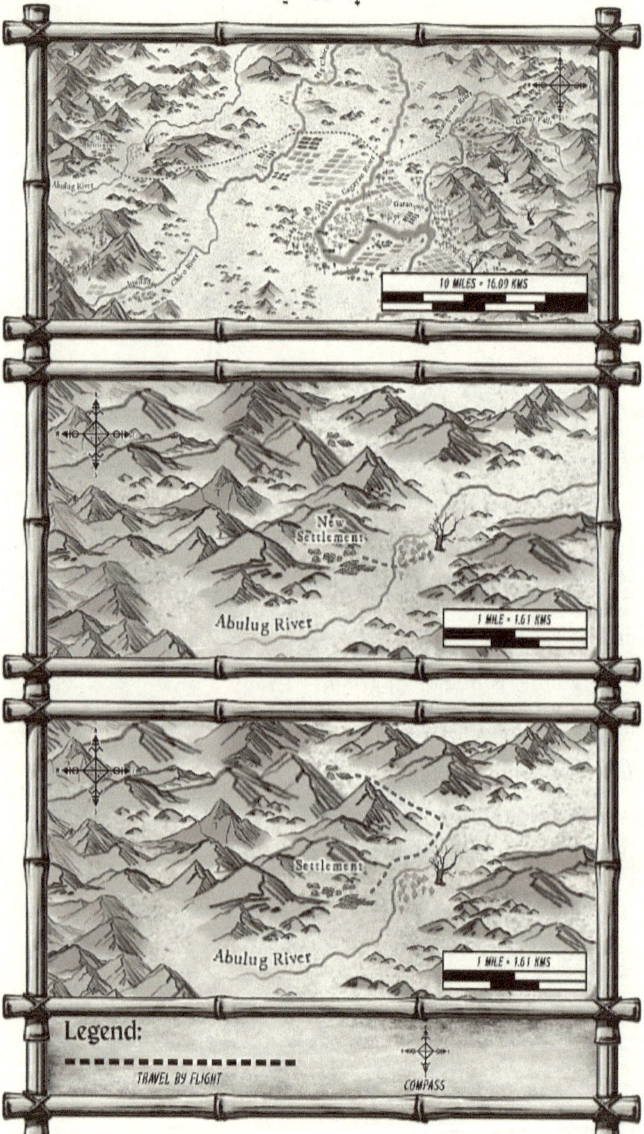

Abulug River
Chico River
Cagayan River
Gattaran
10 MILES = 16.09 KMS
New Settlement
Abulug River
1 MILE = 1.61 KMS
Settlement
Abulug River
1 MILE = 1.61 KMS
Legend:
TRAVEL BY FLIGHT
COMPASS

Chapter 5

Taguwasi, The Lakandian

ᜆᜄᜓᜏᜐᜒ᜵ ᜇᜓ ᜎᜃᜈ᜔ᜇᜒᜌᜈ᜔

After returning from Kaluwalhatian, Bago spent the next seven years watching over Taruban and his bertan. Though he did his best to hide his presence from them, both Taruban and Sinag did catch him lurking from afar a few times.

As it was common amongst their people, Taruban and his bertan moved settlements back and forth across the Cagayan Valley. They have even tried setting up a settlement near the eastern sea like some of the other Agta tribes.

Near the end of Bago's seven-year watch over the bertan which by then settled by the banks of the Abulog River, the moment he had been looking out for had finally arrived; Aran had conceived a second child.

The moment Taruban and Aran's next baby was conceived, Bago felt its presence right away. The feeling of ancient magic increased by one and just as he was instructed by Poong Kedes sever years ago, Bago immediately returned to Kaluwalhatian.

Two days later, Bago returned to the bertan and spoke to Taruban and Sinag as they ate lunch. Taruban, Sinag, as well as Aran, were seated comfortably on the floor of their hut as they ate boiled sweet potatoes and roasted river fish along with some rice.

"Masampat a udto, (Midday greeting)" Bago greeted them as he entered their hut. Taruban and Sinag were a bit surprised by his abrupt presence but felt Bago approaching even before he showed up. But what really surprised everyone present, including Bago, was Aran's reaction. She almost choked upon seeing and hearing the anito.

"You can see him?!" Sinag exclaimed. "Since when?!"

"Why are you both so calm?!" Aran screamed as she spat out a piece of sweet potato on the floor. "You know this spirit?"

"His name is Bago," Taruban said as he handed his wife a coconut shell with water in it to drink. "I met him many years ago during one of my return trips from Garao. He is a good spirit... I think. But ever since then Sinag and I have been feeling his presence following us everywhere we've moved."

"I am sorry to interrupt your lunch," Bago said apologetically. "I have come bearing news from Kaluwalhatian that involves all of you."

"Hold on for a moment!" Aran interjected. "I know I am very new to this entire seeing spirits... thing?! But will someone explain to me why I am suddenly seeing an anito?"

"You are right, I apologize," Bago said. "I am Bago,

anito of the jungle. The reason you are seeing me right now is that you are pregnant and carrying Taruban's second child. But the child you carry is no ordinary one. But in order for all of you to know more and understand, I ask you all to please meet me later at sundown across the river where the bamboo stalks grow.

"There, you will meet someone who can explain everything to you and tell each one of you exactly what is in store for you in the immediate future. But please keep all of this to yourselves. Secrecy is of the utmost importance." Bago concluded and left hoping that they would consider heeding his message.

*****

Bago patiently waited for Taruban and his family by the bamboo grove. He chose that particular spot because of the balete tree that grew less than a mile from there. As the sun started to dip into the western horizon, Taruban arrived with Aran and Sinag.

"We are here Bago," Taruban called out to the anito. "Please show yourself."

"I am here," Bago answered as he stepped out from behind a cluster of bamboo trees.

"The sun has set; would you mind telling us what you couldn't earlier?" Taruban asked.

"I am not the one whom you shall be listening to

tonight," Bago answered. "Please do not be afraid when she arrives."

"Who is coming?" Taruban asked.

"Hama!" Sinag suddenly exclaimed. "Something is coming! The presence is so strong!"

Suddenly, a flash of light appeared out of nowhere and blinded the family temporarily. "Agay!" Aran exclaimed as she clung to her husband's arm.

"Do not be afraid Aran," a soft, calming voice came from within the light. "I am Poong Kedes from the Kingdom of Mah-nongan, and I bring glad tidings for you and your family."

When the light dimmed and as their eyes adjusted it, all three of them saw the tall, magnificent visage of a deity standing before them. At once Taruban and his family fell to their knees and bowed before the Poon.

"There is no need for such gestures of reverence towards me," Poong Kedes said. "I am the one who actually came here to ask something from all of you. Though it would have been nice had you kept your word and mentioned nothing of this meeting to anyone."

"But we didn't say anything to anyone my Poon," Taruban said as he felt both surprised and somewhat hurt by the Poon's accusation.

"Whomever you are hiding behind the shrubbery, please make yourself known to everyone here." Poong

Kedes commanded.

"Please forgive my intrusion my Poon!" A young middle-aged woman suddenly came out from behind a bush. "It wasn't my intention to spy on anyone."

"Puyang Anag?!" Sinag said, surprised to see the shaman jump out from behind the bush. "What are you doing here?"

"Please do not punish Taruban and his family my Poon," Puyang Anag said as she too dropped to her knees. "He speaks the truth when he said that they told no one of this gathering. I saw the anito enter their hut earlier and had followed him here." Puyang Anag explained.

"Well since you are already here, I suggest you stay quiet and listen to what the Poong Kedes wants," Bago told Puyang Anag. "Poong Kedes is a benevolent and forgiving Poon."

"I need everyone to sit and make yourselves comfortable," The Poong said. "I am going to tell as well as show you through my light magic, the history of the three realms, our eternal enemies, the Angkang-Dian, and the Lakandians."

Poong Kedes ended her tale hours later. She told them everything she could tell them and at the same time omitted things that they did not need to know at that point.

Aran was given the *balaang nakar* (holy pearl). She held

it in her hand and just stared at it for a while. She looked at her family and then at Poong Kedes. She was torn between swallowing it and obeying the will of Poong Kedes or returning it to the Poon and continuing to live their lives as they always had.

Sinag finally broke the silence with a question to the Poon, "Poong Kedes, I understand that the realms need a Lakandian. But seeing *Hena's* (Mother's) apprehension, would it be possible for me to take the balaang nakar instead and be your Lakandian?"

"Unfortunately, it won't," Poong Kedes answered. "To be a true Lakandian, one must be given the power of the balaang nakar while still developing inside their mother's womb. Had it been given to you all those years ago when Aran was pregnant with you, then you would have been a Lakandian. But now that you are a young adult, then it is far too late."

"Don't concern yourself too much with this burden asang," Aran said as she hugged her daughter. "The world will have its Lakandian and we... all of us, will help give it one that it needs."

Aran swallowed the balaang nakar and gave the realms another Lakandian.

*****

On a particularly windy afternoon seven months later,

Aran went into labor. Bago felt the baby's arrival as soon as Aran's water broke. "He's here!" Bago said. "Your brother is on his way."

"Brother?" Sinag who was with Bago outside the hut said. "How do you know it's a boy? It could be a girl you know."

"Believe me I know," Bago replied. "I'll go check on your mother. Could you go and tell your hama and call Puyang Anag as well?"

Sinag nodded and ran to the vegetable farms where Taruban, Puyang Anag, and most of the bertan were busily harvesting what they could before the storm hit.

"Bago!" Aran cried out when she saw the anito enter their hut. "The baby is coming! Please go and tell my kabanga."

"Sinag is already on her way. I felt his presence as soon as your water broke."

"You know my baby is a boy?"

"I've suspected as much since yesterday; I just wasn't sure," Bago replied. "Are you in pain?"

"Yes!" Aran answered. "My water is gone, and my contractions have started."

"Let me relieve you of your pain," Bago said as he went behind Aran and placed his hands on her head. "A while back, I ran into a wounded farmer who was attacked by a boar. I masked his pain from his mind without him knowing it. I believe I can do the same for you."

Moments later, Taruban, Sinag, Puyang Anag, and a young girl of thirteen years, one of Kabug's nieces entered the hut.

"Kabanga!" Taruban called out to his wife as he ran toward her. "How are you feeling?"

"Much better now that Bago made my pain disappear," she answered with a slight smile.

"Who is Bago Hapu Taruban?" the young girl asked.

"Don't get distracted *madiket* (young woman)!" Puyang Anag snapped at her. "Focus on the task at hand. See if you feel the contractions on Aran's belly."

"I suggest sending her off as soon as the baby arrives," Bago told the group. "Though I have never seen a Lakandian before, I can feel the unbelievable power residing in his tiny little body. Something otherworldly will definitely happen."

"The baby is a boy?" Sinag asked as she handed her mother a bamboo cup with a herbal decoction of leaves and roots commonly given to women during childbirth. "I'm going to have a brother?"

"How do you know the baby is a boy?" The young girl asked again.

"What did I say?!" Puyang Anag snapped at her again. "If you don't focus on what you're doing, I'm going to tell your *botay* (uncle) that you are not even trying to be useful in delivering his best friend's baby!"

"I am sorry Puyang Anag. I will focus from now on."

"Good!" Puyang Anag said as she turned her attention to Aran. "Aran, you've done this before. Push when I tell you to push. I can see the baby's head starting to come out."

It didn't take long for Aran to give birth to her second child. The whole process seemed normal to the young girl. She only thought of three things that were out of the ordinary. One was the absolute lack of pain from Aran's reactions. The second was the fact that every time Aran tried to push the baby out of her, the wind would suddenly howl as though the air itself was the one giving birth. And finally, she noticed the wind suddenly die down the very second Aran's baby boy was born.

"Give me the bamboo to cut the *pusad* (umbilical cord)," Puyang Anag told the girl. "Now go out and tell everyone it's a boy. And tell Bananayo to make sure our hut is secure before the storm hits."

As soon as the girl left, Aran's baby boy did what all Lakandians do the moment they were born. He opened his eyes and told everyone his name; Taguwasi.

*****

Taruban's family, along with Puyang Anag, and the anito Bago decided then and there that to keep Taguwasi a secret, Taruban, and his family will have to move and separate themselves from the bertan. As the son of the former *Rupos* (male leader) and *Moden* (female leader) of the bertan when both his parents were still alive, Taruban still held a bit of sway with the bertan, and they would respect his wishes. The decision came easily enough especially when they found out that Taguwasi will grow at an exceptionally fast rate.

But not wishing to completely isolate themselves from the other families, they did not venture out too far. Especially since they knew that Kalinga tribes lived not too far at the foot of the mountains where they too dwelled.

At three months old, Taguwasi was physically that of a ten-year-old boy. He was strong for a child and quite fast. But above all, he had almost mastered his powers to summon and control the wind.

The entire family taught Taguwasi everything they knew about archery and hunting. They taught him the ways of the jungle including how to track prey, read signs left by other Agta people, and how to avoid headhunters.

Taruban still visited the bertan every now and then, especially since he missed his best friend Kabug whom he went out hunting with at least once a month. Though Kabug and the others begged him to tell them where they moved to and wanted to see the other members of his family, Taruban constantly came up with excuses to avoid telling them anything.

Their move was especially hard for Sinag who as a young woman at the time and had already missed her friends dearly, including one of Kabug's nephews whom she secretly admired. But knowing what her younger brother was and what his purpose would be to the realms, Sinag was mature enough to recognize the importance of her sacrifice.

Puyang Anag, the only other person outside of the family who knew of the Lakandian Taguwasi, would secretly visit them from time to time to check up on them. She came frequently, in the beginning, to help nurse Aran back to health after giving birth. She also spoke to Bago for her if Taruban and Sinag were out hunting since she had lost the ability to see spirits after Taguwasi was born.

At six months old, Taguwasi, who had the body of a young man in his late teens, had learned how to use the wind to fly. He would often soar as high as he could and spend hours at a time in the one place that only he and the birds were privy to. It was also the one place where Bago could not follow. Though Bago had always hovered above the ground and never really set foot on it, the ability to free himself from its pull was beyond that of any enkanto. A fact that Taguwasi exploited whenever he wished to escape Bago's lectures and lessons about magic and magical beings.

Those first six months were both a boon and a burden for Taguwasi and his family. But overall, Taruban and Aran could not be any happier. Their family was closer than ever, and they couldn't be any more content. But it all came crashing down the day Poong Kedes returned to Kalupaan.

*****

One afternoon, as Taguwasi and his family were carving up a deer they had hunted earlier in the day, Bago was suddenly alerted to the presence of another enkanto. "Someone is coming!" Bago exclaimed.

"I feel it too," Taguwasi seconded. "Is it an enkanto like you?"

"Yes," Bago answered when a spirit came from the jungle and approached them.

"Masampat a apon Bago and Lakandian. I am the diwata Mamiyo." The diwata introduced herself.

"Mamiyo!" Bago greeted her as soon as he recognized her. "I have not seen you for more than a century. What brings you to Kalupaan?"

"Poong Kedes has sent me to tell you that she wished to speak to the Lakandian later tonight. She said she would meet the Lakandian and his katiwala alone by the balete tree where you saw each other last."

"Why does the Poon want to speak to our son alone?" Taruban asked.

"She did not say," Mamiyo answered. "But it must be of the utmost importance if she was willing to inform me about the Lakandian Taguwasi and his whereabouts."

"Please tell Poong Kedes that the Lakandian and I will meet her tonight at the bamboo grove near the balete tree," Bago told the diwata. "Thank you for relaying the Poon's wishes."

As soon as Mamiyo left, Taruban, Taguwasi, as well as Sinag, gave the anito a stern annoyed look. "Since when do you speak for me Bago?!" Taguwasi exclaimed. "I am more than capable of answering and deciding for myself."

"I am sorry if I spoke out of place..." Bago was apologizing when Taruban cut him off.

"Yes, you spoke out of place, and this will be the last time that you do so, especially where my family is concerned! I am still the head of this family, Lakandian or not! Do you understand anito?"

"You are right Taruban, it will not happen again," Bago said apologetically.

"Good!" Taguwasi seconded.

"And since we all seem to agree that Bago does not speak for all of us, I am coming too!" Sinag interjected.

"But Sinag, Poong Kedes said..." Bago was saying when Taguwasi cut him off. "She is coming with us Bago, and that's that."

Just before sundown, Taguwasi and Sinag set out to meet with Poong Kedes by the balete tree. Still a bit annoyed with Bago from earlier, Taguwasi used his power to command the wind to take both him and Sinag up into the air as they flew to where the meeting was to take place. He left Bago to get there on his own even though either of them could have carried him on their backs.

Taguwasi and Sinag waited in the bamboo grove for about twenty minutes before Bago arrived. Bago was silent when he arrived. He was a little hurt being left behind by Taguwasi but knew he deserved it. But at that point, Taguwasi and Sinag were already past their anger and couldn't help but snicker at Bago.

Suddenly, a flash of light appeared out of nowhere which heralded the arrival of Poong Kedes. All three of them fell to their knees and bowed their heads on the ground.

Taguwasi was both excited and nervous at the same time. This was the first time he would get to see a Poon in person. He had heard of that fateful meeting between Poong Kedes and his family almost a year ago before he was born. But that was all that it was; a story.

"I thought I made myself clear that my audience was to be the Lakandian and his katiwala alone," Poong Kedes said as soon as she saw Sinag. "Did Mamiyo not mention this fact when she told you of my summons?"

"She did Poong Kedes," Bago answered but remembered what happened earlier and rethought his next response. "Perhaps, the Lakandian would like to explain it himself."

"Your diwata messenger did mention your intentions when she visited us earlier my Poon," Taguwasi began. "But my sister Sinag will be a part of my life as the Lakandian for as long as we are together. Whatever you need to tell me should be known to her as well.

"Had Bago found my hama before Sinag was born, then she would have been the Lakandian. So, the way I see it my Poon, there should be no reason not to trust Sinag with any information you see fit to tell me." Taguwasi said with as much confidence as he could muster. Though truth be told, both he and his sister were second-guessing their decision at that very moment.

After a long pause as she contemplated Taguwasi's words, Poong Kedes finally spoke. "Very well Lakandian, I will trust your sister. Though both of you must understand that what I am about to tell you will be of the utmost importance and a sacred trust. If you should find yourselves in a situation where you will have to choose between divulging this information or death, then I hope you would choose the latter."

Both brother and sister sat up and looked at each other as the magnitude and seriousness of the situation started to dawn on them. But both Taguwasi and Sinag were naturally courageous as well as curious individuals, so they nodded to each other and then turned their gaze to Poong Kedes. "We understand and accept the responsibility," Sinag said.

"Very well. When I first appeared before you and your family Sinag, I told all of you about your bloodline, the Angkang-Dian as well as the Lakandian. Now I will tell both of you about the dalaketnon, the Yawàs, and above all else, the Likum..."

An hour later, Poong Kedes ended her tale and concluded with one final lesson for Taguwasi. "In a few months' time, you will have reached your physical peak and will be in your perpetual prime. But to be a true Lakandian and unlock the full potential of your powers, you must commit your very existence and soul to serve the will of the Kaluwalhatian and the protection of the Likum.

"The only way to truly know that you are a true Lakandian is to wield a Raniagad weapon," Poong Kedes said as she handed Taguwasi a white arrow as long as a spear. The arrowhead glowed as brightly as the Poon herself. But as soon as Poong Kedes handed the arrow to Taguwasi, the light of the arrowhead slowly started to wane and faded; leaving only an arrowhead that looked like it was made of bone.

"That is one of my Raniagad arrows Taguwasi," Poong Kedes explained. "When it glows, the Raniagad arrowhead is in a state of pananglaw, the state when a Raniagad weapon is at its most powerful and can destroy almost anything the wielder wants it to destroy.

"But to achieve such a state, the wielder must be completely devoted to Kaluwalhatian. And as you can clearly see Taguwasi, you are not ready. Even for a Lakandian, you are still young. One day, you will find yourself yearning to be complete. On that day, you must relinquish your worldly bonds and submit yourself to the will of Kaluwalhatian and its Poons. When that time comes you must ask yourself only one question, are you truly ready to be a true Lakandian?

"If your answer is sincere and true, then I will seek you out and bestow upon you a Raniagad weapon. But until then, you must learn and train. Be the warrior that the spirit realms and the mortal realm need you to be.

"But above all else, the both of you must keep the secret of the Likum. Tell no one, not even your parents about them or what you know of them for one cannot reveal a secret that one doesn't even know exists." Poong Kedes concluded and disappeared just as quickly as she came.

*****

Taguwasi, Sinag, and Bago returned to their family's settlement less than an hour later with a thousand questions running through their minds. But as soon as they landed, they were greeted by a frantic and frightened Puyang Anag. "Taguwasi! Taguwasi! They need you! They all need you now!"

"Hapu, please calm yourself," Sinag said as she held the crying shaman in her arms. "Who needs us? What is going on?"

"They attacked the bertan! They came just before nightfall!" Puyang Anag continued to wail. "The Kalinga headhunters from the foot of the mountain found us! Bananayo told me to find you and ask for your help."

"What?!" Taguwasi said in shock and horror. "Where are our *daddakal* (parents)?"

"Taruban and Aran told me to stay here and wait for you while they ran back to the bertan to help," Puyang Anag said. "I asked them to tell me where you were, but they wouldn't tell me."

Taguwasi ran into their hut and came out with a bow in one hand and all the arrows he could carry. He also had a bolo tucked into his beg. "Stay here with Puyang Anag," he told Sinag. "I'm going after them and see if I can help."

"Be careful wadi," Sinag said.

"I'll be back with Hama and Hena as soon as I can,"

Taguwasi said and took to the air.

*****

It was a little past midday when Taguwasi returned. He had a defeated forlorn look on his face and was covered in blood from head to toe. "Wadi!" Sinag shouted out as she ran to her brother.

"What happened? Where is Hama? Hena?" she asked, though from the expression on her brother's face, she knew what the answer was.

"They're gone akka, they're all gone, " Taguwasi said as he fell to his knees and cried on his sister's shoulders.

"Poons save us. Tell me what happened. Are you hurt?"

"Lakandian!" Puyang Anag said as she came out of the hut and ran towards the siblings. "What happened to our bertan? Did you see my family? Did you see Bananayo and Kabugnayan?"

"They killed everybody Hapu," Taguwasi said as he continued to cry. "They killed Hama, Hena, Hapu Bananayo, they even killed the children, including your son."

"No! No!" Puyang Anag fell to the ground crying and pulled at her hair. "Kabugnayan! Kabugnayan! My baby boy!"

"Why are you covered in blood wadi?" Sinag asked, as

she too cried her eyes out but did her best to remain strong for her baby brother.

"It's not my blood akka," Taguwasi said as he stared at his bloodied hands. "It's the blood of the Kalinga that did this to us! They were still taking heads when I got there. So, I killed them all! Every last man and woman that attacked the bertan!"

"I am tired now," Taguwasi continued. "Tomorrow morning, as soon as the sun rises, I'm going down the mountain and killing every single Kalinga that I find! I will go from settlement to settlement, and I will..."

"You will do no such thing," A voice suddenly interrupted Taguwasi. It was Bago who had just returned from the slaughter right after Taguwasi. "Your vengeance against those who did evil to your family was justified and the blood that those headhunters spilled was replenished with their own. But to kill those who had nothing to do with the slaughter is evil as well.

"Those whom you killed today were evil to their core. Even their own people despise them. But doing as they did is not what Poong Kedes would want of her champion." Bago said, trying to talk some sense into Taguwasi.

"Anito," Puyang Anag said as she knelt in front of Bago. "Please go to Poong Kedes and beg her to return our slain loved ones to us. Surely a Poon can do this, especially for her champion."

"I am sorry Puyang Anag, but Poong Kedes cannot resurrect the dead," Bago regretfully replied. "Even if she could, resurrections are prohibited as a general rule and will require the permission of all the..."

"Had Poong Kedes not called us to go to her secret little gathering, I would have been here and both our daddakal would still be alive!" Taguwasi snapped at the anito. "Do not talk to me about what Poong Kedes wants Bago! Just don't!

"The Poons have failed to protect my family even though I am their so-called champion which all but tells me everything I need to know about their uncaring and self-serving nature! I am done with them and their precious war! Tomorrow, I will have more of my vengeance and..."

"No wadi, you won't," Sinag said as she wrapped her baby brother in her arms. "Bago is right. Justice was done. Doing an evil deed will not make another evil right. It just makes more of the same. But you might be right about the capricious nature of the Poons. Only time will tell us the truth and that goes for you as well anito. You may stay with us if you wish but you are forbidden to speak of Poong Kedes or any other Poon whilst in our company.

"Tomorrow, when the sun rises, we will bury our daddakal as well as Puyang Anag's family, and all the others. Then we will move on from this place and go where you are needed and do good. For it is only in doing good do we truly remove the stains of evil. Doing good is how we make Hama and Hena proud of us." Sinag concluded.

*****

After Bago's tale, the two Lakandians then turned their attention to the west where the sun was beginning to set past the great valley, the Cagayan River, and the western mountains. “We should return to the others,” Taguwasi said as he wiped the tears from his eyes.

"I don't know what to say," Lumalindaw said as he too was already tearing up. "Why is it that the lives of the two most powerful beings in Kalupaan are mired in sadness and tragedy?"

"Maybe because it is only in the muck of tragic events where a truly good person emerges," Bago answered. "Like a flower growing from a crack in the stone."

"We should really head back now," Taguwasi retorted. "They're all probably looking for us at this point."

“Don’t forget the mangoes your sister wanted you to get.” Lumalindaw reminded him.

They arrived back at the settlement just as Kidul was finishing his tale. They landed near the pinanahang each with armfuls of mangoes wrapped in banana leaves.

"We're back!" Taguwasi called out just as his feet touched the ground.

"And we have mangoes for everybody," Lumalindaw said as he landed right next to Taguwasi. "Did Kidul bore you with his long-embellished tales of Kaluwalhatian?"

" I'll have you know that every single one of these people enjoyed every word I told them!" Kidul corrected him. "Even the birds loved them!"

"We are kumaws Hapu Kidul, not birds." Dalawesan protested. "But I must confess that my sister and I did enjoy your tales. It has been quite a while since I've seen Kaluwalhatian, and I do sometimes miss it."

"Especially the *Lungog Masilap* (The Valley of Crystals) where we came from. How I wish I could show Hapu Innawagan our home with its mountains of colorful crystal with all the colors of the rainbow," Dundunan said right after her brother.

"I will see it one day after I have gone and my spirit travels to Kaluwalhatian," Innawagan said as she gently stroked the feathers on Dundunan's head. "And you can be my guide."

"Anyway, how was your talk?" Sinag asked her brother.

"It went well. I heard what I needed to hear and let's leave it at that." Taguwasi answered as he tossed a mango to his sister.

As the sun began setting and the moon began rising past the eastern mountains, Taguwasi's bertan began preparations for supper. They cooked more rice and boiled some additional sweet potatoes as the others roasted some of the raw boar meat that they had left.

"You have so much meat," Lumalindaw commented as he skinned the hairy flesh from what he believed to be the boar's hind leg. "I'm actually amazed how much meat the other bertan chose to part with just to share them with you."

"Sharing the spoils of a hunt or a harvest is actually very common among my people," Talimannog replied. "We call it *bahaginan,* it helps strengthen relationships between bertans, especially those that live close to each other. But tell me Lakandian Lumalindaw, will you be sharing your story with us tonight?"

"Are you sure you and yours are still up for another long tale on the same day after Kidul's?" Lumalindaw asked.

"We are honestly extremely excited to hear your tale and I was hoping you wouldn't make me beg for it in front of the twins," Talimannog said with a warm-hearted smile.

"Very well. After supper, I promise."

They all ate supper gathered around a bonfire in an open spot away from the huts and pinanahang.

Taguwasi's bertan was particularly careful about keeping the embers from reaching their very flammable dwellings.

They ate the exact same thing they had for lunch with the addition of the mangoes that the Lakandians picked for them, which was still a hearty meal. Even the kumaws were happily gorging on the fish that Hapu Anag had caught earlier in the day.

The twins Ammani and Anibo were already giddy with excitement ever since Talimannog told them that Lumalindaw was sharing his life's story with them that night. They were in fact, already debating whether or not Lumalindaw's story would top that of Kidul's. Of course, Innawagan and Sinag told them that Taguwasi's own epic tale could rival anyone else's.

After their meal amman was passed along for everyone to enjoy and get a little perk from. Puyang Anag seemed especially happy when she got her hands on some amman that Innawagan makes. She apparently has a mild addiction to it and feels quite invigorated every time she gets her hands on some.

"Should I begin?" Lumalindaw asked Taguwasi who was meticulously wrapping his butag in ikmo, being extra careful not to let any of the apog seep out.

"Yes please!" Ammani exclaimed.

"Yes please, I can't wait any longer!" Anibo seconded.

"Hold your tongues!" Alig snapped at her younger

brothers. "Let him begin when he is good and ready and not before!"

This made Lumalindaw smile uncontrollably. He missed this sort of family squabbling and arguing as he missed his own family. He missed his father's unending criticism of him, and his mother always trying to calm him down after. He missed the sound of his brothers-in-law arguing much like how Innawagan's siblings were arguing right now. But above all else, he missed his wife Menalam's head on his shoulders on nights like this one when they would share a fire with her brothers as their children slept in each of their arms.

"I was born in a barangay called Nabbobawan in the Ga'dang highlands far south of here..." Lumalindaw began.

Camiguin Island (Map)

Chapter 6

The Three Birds

Taguwasi awoke the next day just a little after the crack of dawn. Innawagan was still fast asleep and didn't look like she was planning on getting up anytime soon. He slowly sat up from their *abak* (sleeping mat) in their small hut and carefully crawled to the door.

Their room was elevated a few feet from the ground to prevent snakes and other animals from joining them in their sleep. The rest of the hut was at ground level, including the kitchen and a small storage room where they kept their tools, weapons, and food.

Taguwasi was still a little light-headed from all the amman he had the night before and all the food that they ate. The first thing he wanted to do was relieve himself, so he went down by the river to do exactly that.

The air by the river was cool and refreshing to the skin. As soon as his toes touched the cold water underneath them, Taguwasi's wits started coming around as his whole being started awakening.

"Masampat e abi-abi," Lumalindaw suddenly greeted Taguwasi. "Did you sleep well?"

Taguwasi was caught by surprise and jolted as he accidentally sprayed his urine all over the riverbed. "Agay!" Taguwasi exclaimed. "I didn't see you there!"

"I'm sorry," Lumalindaw said half chuckling. "I thought you saw me pissing here when you arrived."

"I slept quite soundly thank you," Taguwasi answered. "How was your night?"

"Honestly, a little terrible," Lumalindaw answered. "I slept between the twins and unfortunately for me, they are huggers!"

"Help! Help!" A voice suddenly cried to them. "Call him off Lakandian! He wants to eat us!"

They looked up and saw the kumaws Dundunan and Dalawesan flying frantically toward them.

"What?!" Taguwasi asked worriedly. "Who is trying to eat you?"

"The bannog!" Dalawesan cried out as he and his sister landed behind Taguwasi.

"It saw us this morning as we were hunting our morning meal and started chasing us," Dundunan said as her voice trembled in fear.

Suddenly a giant shadow flew right over them. They looked up and saw Kolago circling the riverbank and looking down on them.

"Is your bannog really hunting my friends, Lumalindaw?" Taguwasi asked.

"I wish I could say no...," Lumalindaw answered. "But don't worry, I'll put a stop to this. After taking a deep breath, Lumalindaw called out to Kolago using the *Voice.*

"Kolago! Mataqdig!"

Kolago shook his head, circled around, and landed next to Lumalindaw. "Are you trying to hunt these two?" he asked the bannog as he gently rubbed the feathers on Kolago's chest. Kolago shook his head and squawked disapprovingly.

"I think he just wanted to play with you?" Lumalindaw told the kumaws, trying to assure them that Kolago meant no harm to them.

"Forgive us for being cautious, but you must understand that even in Kaluwalhatian; birds eat other birds!" Dalawesan said with a bit of a sarcastic tone.

"Let's just all calm down," Taguwasi said. "I'm sure Lumalindaw can handle Kolago and make sure he doesn't do anything untoward, like eat you."

"*Squawk!*" Kolago said in a gesture of affirmation.

"There you go," Lumalindaw said. "He promises not to harm anyone here, whether they be human, Lakandian, or kumaw."

"Now that we've got that settled, I have an idea," Taguwasi said as he approached Lumalindaw. "Given that you've been gracious enough to tell me and my family all about your tragic tale, would you be willing to stay with us for another night so we might tell you ours?"

"That sounds really good, to be honest, but I really must be going. The longer it takes me to find Muwan, the longer it will take for me to see my wife and children again." Lumalindaw answered.

"But you don't even know where you are going next." Taguwasi protested. "Listen, last night before we slept, I had Bago go west to find any information he could from anyone who knew anything about anyone being cursed. He said he'll be back tonight. Please reconsider waiting for his return, before you fly off aimlessly in your search. If he returns with information, then that would save you days or weeks of wandering. If not, then you only would have lost a day."

Lumalindaw pondered this for a few moments. "Very well," he answered. "I graciously accept your offer. But you must let me help with your day's labor. I will not be a bother to you and yours."

"Then we'll do this… I have a taste for *karoykoy* (crabs) today and my sister absolutely loves them. Join me for a flight to the islands just north of here. The people who live there always have karoykoy and other large fish that they are happy to trade for rice.

"They speak a different language from us but after seeing what Kidul can do in linking our minds, maybe we can get a better deal with the people there," Taguwasi said.

"That sounds like fun, but I do have one condition," Lumalindaw said.

“What is that?”

“I’m riding Kolago to the islands. Flying with you through your powers was exhilarating, but it was just all too strange for me.”

Taguwasi nodded in agreement.

“Good. Let me get Kidul and let’s be off.”

*****

A short time later, the two Lakandians were over the northern sea looking past the unending blue horizon. Taguwasi as always was flying through the use of his powers while Lumalindaw was on the back of the bannog Kolago. But for this trip, the two Lakandians were not alone.

Lumalindaw had Kidul with him, still trapped inside the enchanted ayoding, and with them was Innawagan. She insisted on coming along having a strong desire to ride Kolago. Alongside Kolago were the kumaw siblings Dundunan and Dalawesan. Dundunan who is Innawagan’s agom and did not want to leave her Hapu’s side, whereas Dalawesan was worried about his sister being that close to a bannog whom they thought wanted to eat them that morning.

They were still a few hours from midday when they arrived on an island closest to the mainland. They landed near a small settlement just past the beach at the foot of a large mountain that loomed over the entire island. Needless to say, the people panicked as soon as they saw Kolago. But Kidul quickly remedied the situation by playing a tune to calm their nerves as well as bridge the minds of the people to that of their party.

The people of the Babuyan Islands were called the Ivatan. They bore similarities to not just the Ibanag and Isneg peoples that populate some of the northern seaside sections of the mainland but share traits similar to those of the lighter-skinned peoples in the far north and west.

Lumalindaw found them quite intriguing as they were both familiar and different at the same time. They wore the typical abag or beg loincloths somewhat similar to both his and Taguwasi's people. Some wore vests like Lumalindaw's kuton as well as shell necklaces and bracelets. What the Ivatan people wore that was completely alien to Lumalindaw's eyes was their *vakul* headgear which most of them wore as protection from both the sun and rain as they labored outdoors.

The vakul headgear was made from a palm fiber from the *vuyavuy* palm. Atop their heads, the vakul looks more like a bushy mane of yellow-brownish hair that extends passed their shoulders all the way to their shoulder blades.

The settlement was made mostly of huts and houses made from bamboo and cogon grass yet constructed so sturdily that they were able to weather the storms that frequently pass by their islands. Rice was a little harder to grow on the islands which makes root crops such as yams, sweet potatoes, taro, garlic, ginger, and onion were common produce that they plant in their farms and gardens. They also raise some livestock such as pigs and cows in a communal pasture called *payaman*. But the real source of livelihood and nourishment for the Ivatan is the sea, which is what brings the two Lakandians to their shores, to begin with.

Having Kidul open and link their thoughts with the Ivatan, the visitors from the mainland were able to calm the islanders down when they began panicking after seeing Kolago. It also made trading with them much easier to accomplish.

Rice being a prized commodity, they were able to trade two large sacks of rice for several baskets of crab, fish, and lobsters. Innawagan was already famished at that point and told her husband that they should stay for a few hours as they sat under the shade of coconut trees and roasted some of the fish they received over a small fire. The kumaws were given several *dibang* (flying fish) to eat as Kolago stood by the beach and stared blankly at the waves that calmly crashed on his taloned feet.

As they ate the fish and some yams by the beach, Kidul asked the kumaw Dalawesan a question. "I have many of your kind in Kaluwalhatian when I was still of service as punong alagad. Your kind were great allies to the Poons and served as reliable messengers to them. Do you mind if I ask how you came about in service to Innawagan and Talimannog?"

"That is quite a tale," Dalawesan answered. "But to cut a long story short, we owe them a life debt."

"Both Hapu Innawagan and Talimannog saved our lives and for that, we have pledged ourselves to their service and protection for the rest of their lives." Dundunan continued.

Lumalindaw was confused by Dundunan's statement when she said *'the rest of their lives'*, to which Kidul quickly addressed having noticed his reaction. "Kumaws are *nilalang-lubong* (earthbound creatures). Like all others created by the Poons, they are mortals. But like all other nilalang-lubong, their lifespans will dwarf that of normal humans. Kumaws in particular can live for up to three hundred years."

Lumalindaw nodded and said, "I see. But since we're all just sitting here, I would really appreciate it if you told me this tale. I am always keen on hearing great fantastical tales. Anything that can distract me from…" he was saying and then abruptly stopped as he accidentally almost diverted the topic toward his own tragic tale.

Noticing this, Innawagan quickly interposed and said,

"You may tell him if you and your brother wish, Dundunan."

"Very well Hapu," Dalawesan replied. "Our tale happened close to five years ago and began in Kaluwalhatian…"

Ambush (Map)

The Tale of the Kumaws

Lungog Masilap, in the Kingdom of Mah-nongan. Flying across the emerald green plains surrounded by mountains of multicolored crystals were three kumaws.

They had just crossed the golden bridge of Taletay and were racing towards the Dakong Torogan of Paslakop where Poong Maykapal Liddum resides along with Poong Ampual, Wigan, and Sedsed.

The three kumaws were flying in a V-shaped formation where the lead kumaw was a particularly large, red-colored male called Ammalabukaw. Behind him were two other kumaws, Dalawesan to his left and Dundunan to his right. The three of them were messengers of the Poons. They served all the Poons and Poong Maykapal of Paslakop, and at that exact moment, they had just left Kuta Salakan and had an urgent message to deliver to the Poons.

"We still have around ten miles to fly before we reach Paslakop," Ammalabukaw told the Dalawesan, the older of the two kumaws behind him. "You and your sister better keep up! We need to tell the Poons what is happening in the north as quickly as possible!"

"Don't worry about us," Dalawesan replied. "My sister and I can keep up with an old bird like you anytime we feel like it!" he said as a jape.

The three kumaws fly past miles and miles of large barangays that house more than a hundred thousand human souls that have earned the right to spend eternity in Kaluwalhatian. After a few more minutes, they were within sight of Paslakop, the emerald citadel of the east.

Paslakop, like all other Dakong Torogans, is a gigantic structure topped with the typical *diongal* (apex roof) commonly seen in all torogans. Surrounding the main torogan are a few smaller ones that serve as residences for the six Poons in the Kingdom of Mah-nongan and a tower that dwarfs all other buildings where Poong Maykapal Liddum resides. All the structures in Paslakop are made of gray and white marble and are topped with apex and domed roofs made of green, shimmering emerald.

The citadel rests at the foot of one of the crystal mountains that wall its northern section while three defensive walls of gray marble protect its west, south, and eastern sections. Each of these walls has an elevated gate accessed by a flight of steps only ten feet wide. Towers and battlements garrisoned by alagad warriors and nilalang-lubong serve as sentinels on each wall and gate ensuring the security of Paslakop and the sleeping form of Dian Mah-nongan himself enshrined inside the heart of the main building.

The three kumaws began flying lower and slower as they reached the high walls of Paslakop to let the archers know who they were and not to shoot them down.

"Should we just go in unannounced?" Dundunan asked Ammalabukaw.

"Considering the urgency of the news we carry; I don't think the Poons would mind if we barged into the Grand

Bulwagan," Ammalabukaw answered.

They enter through an open window and land in the middle of the Grand Bulwagan. The bulwagan itself was an immensely large rectangular room with walls made of green and blue crystals and the floor was white polished marble. Along its length were golden torches hanging from the crystal walls. The walls were decorated with carvings that depict the history of Kaluwalhatian. From *Maykapal* (the One God of all) lifting the lands from the depths of the golden seas to Dian Mah-nongan creating Uvigan and Bugan, the first Aeta man and woman, and down to the Kanibusanan.

On the far end of the room was an elevated platform and, on that platform, sat Poong Maykapal Liddum flanked by Poong Ampual, Pawi, Sedsed, and the beautiful Poong Wigan. The fifteen-foot Poons all sat on the floor of the platform on silver mats with their legs crossed. Finally, behind the Poons was a colossal stone figure of Dian Mah-nongan himself, sitting in the exact same fashion as the Poons.

The Poons all had white glowing hair that matched their glowing florescent skin. Their eyes were white and shone brightly as the light of their magical souls manifested itself in them like beacons. They all wore garments common to the Agta and Ifugao people since they were the ones who first taught these humans to weave them.

The male Poons wore beg-style loincloths, vests, and other accessories made of gold, silver, and other gems. Though similar to the style of human clothes, the material from which they were made was where the stark difference lies.

The clothes they wore were made from a material called *sulaga* (woven light). These were made from the fibers harvested from the gansagat from balete trees. Though they flow like regular fabric, the sulaga can also serve as light armor since they are quite sturdy and cannot easily be pierced or cut. They also amplify light which makes them all that much brighter if worn by a Poon.

The three kumaws bowed their heads and waited to be addressed. "What brings three messengers to the Grand Bulwagan of Liddum so abruptly and unannounced?" Poong Wigan asked.

"Forgive us for entering your Grand Bulwagan my Poons but we come with urgent news from Poong Kedes herself," Ammalabukaw began. "I don't know if you are aware but the forces of Kasanaan have opened several small burrows near the edges of the Nabuangan Forest."

"We are aware," Poong Wigan responded. "In fact, Poong Puwok along with a few hundred alagad warriors and nilalang-lubong left a few hours ago to join the coalition army at the behest of Poong Maykapal Dasal."

"But what you may not know is what Poong Kedes ordered us to tell you," Dundunan interjected. "She had just recently returned to Kuta Salakan with her *hukbo* (army) from scouting the banks of the Bulawan River. She found an even larger army led by Gat Yawà Asuang himself assembling from a very large burrow east of the Taytay bridge."

"Whether they are marching towards Kalekay or Paslakop remains uncertain," Dalawesan continued. "But Poong Kedes told us to come here and inform all of you of what is happening and to prepare for an attack from the north if Asuang does intend to march south with his armies."

"Poong Kedes was very adamant about making sure Paslakop gets this information that she even sent all three of us to deliver it in the unlikely event that a night creature might intercept a single messenger," Ammalabukaw concluded.

"We are thankful for the information that you have brought to us," Poong Maykapal Liddum told the kumaws. "Now go and return to Kedes and tell her that I will order the armies of Paslakop to prepare for a possible attack. And do what you can to help her secure our western borders and our section of the *Arollam Abut* (The name of the northernmost Bukang Karimlan)."

"As you command," the three kumaws answered in

unison.

They left Paslakop and headed back to the forest stronghold of Kuta Salakan as quickly as they could. Tired as they were, they knew that tensions were high and that this was a serious and dangerous situation that the kingdom was in. If there was one thing kumaws are known for, it was their dedication and absolute loyalty to those to whom they owe their lives to. Having been created by the Poons, the three kumaws are loyal to the Poons of Paslakop to a fault.

As the three flew past the Lungog Masilap, they began nearing the Taletay Bridge that crosses over the Bulawan River. They already felt their wings aching, but they sojourned forward as their loyalties would not let them surrender.

Suddenly, something dark whizzed past them. The three gave a start and looked around below them. That was when they saw them. A small group of *danag* archers (aswang variant) crossing the Taletay Bridge.

The danag looked frail and gangly as they always did, only this time, they actually seemed worse. They were fully exposed to the light of Manaul, the great bird, even though Manaul was several miles from their location. But weakened as they were, the danag were still fully functional as archers, and as soon as they saw the kumaws heading their way, they started nocking arrows to their bows.

Arrow after arrow was loosed. The kumaws did everything they could to avoid them. “Look out!” Dalawesan screamed at his sister as an arrow narrowly passed by her left wing.

“Get to the forest!” Ammalabukaw yelled at the siblings. “We need to take refuge behind the balete trees! They cannot follow us there!”

Whoosh! Whoosh! These were the only sounds they heard as arrows continued to fly past them. Dundunan, who was the faster flyer among the three flew as fast as she could towards Nabuangan Forest. Her brother flew right behind her followed by Ammalabukaw.

They tried to fly higher but that only made it take longer to reach the forest. “Keep heading straight to the forest!” Ammalabukaw yelled again. “They will shoot us down before we even reach a safe distance. Our only chance is to reach the balete trees!”

“Go, Sister! Go, faster! We are almost there! I can already see the trees!” Dalawesan encouraged his sister.

Dundunan looked down and saw the danag giving chase and continued to lose arrows as they did. She looked ahead of her and to her relief, the crystalline visage of the balete trees was already visible. “We’re almost there!” Dundunan exclaimed. “We’re so close!”

She looked back to assure the others but saw only her

brother. "Where is Ammalabukaw?!" she screamed.

"They got him! Don't think about that now! Just go!" Dalawesan replied just as an arrow struck his left wing and he began to fall.

"No! Dalawesan!" Dundunan screamed in horror. She was about to turn and dive for her brother when she suddenly felt a jolt on her right wing. There was no pain at first. She simply felt her wing stiffen and found it unresponsive. She looked at it and much to her horror, she saw what she was dreading to see. A black arrow was embedded deep in her wing. The arrow had gone through her white feathers and flesh and by the sudden onslaught of pain she felt when she tried to move her wing, the arrow had also grazed her hollow bones.

Dundunan was falling. She knew she was about to die. As she fell, she cocked her head to where she last saw Dalawesan and see if he somehow survived, but alas she couldn't find him. The wind was rushing all around her as she fell. Dundunan was counting the seconds before the inevitable end then she felt something hit her body. She closed her eyes and waited for oblivion.

It felt like forever had passed yet seemed like a series of fleeting moments. She opened her eyes and saw only darkness. And then she felt something strange touch her entire being. It was water. It was raining!

As it never rains in Kaluwalhatian, she couldn't make

out what was happening. She tried to move, but the pain in her wing was still there. *Where am I?* She thought to herself.

It was dark yet not so dark that she couldn't see anything. As the lighting flashed across the stormy night sky, Dundunan saw the silhouette of trees all around her. The rain was pouring constantly, and water was seeping in through the spaces between her feathers. *I'm in Kalupaan. I must have fallen through a landanan* (a door of light in the trunk of balete trees) *when I fell.* She was thinking as exhaustion started getting the better of her and the sweet embrace of sleep began to pull her under.

*****

Dalawesan opened his eyes and couldn't understand what he was seeing. Everything around him was green. From the leaves in the trees, the bushes, and the grass; the forest he was in was not made of bright glowing crystalline things. "Poons save me, I'm in Kalupaan!" he exclaimed upon realizing where he was.

How did I get here? And why am I still alive? he thought to himself. *I must have fallen through a landanan...*

"Dundunan!" he suddenly blurted out upon realizing that the same thing might have happened to his sister. "Dundunan! I'm alive! Are you out there?"

Suddenly, he heard a rustling sound coming from a

nearby bush to his right. He turned his head and saw something move behind the foliage. It was gray and hairy with black spots. *What is that?* he thought.

Rescue (Map)

The creature's head suddenly popped out from the foliage. It was feline in nature, with rounded ears, big round eyes, and a small round nose at the tip of its short snout. Its fur on its neck and down to its chest made a striped pattern of grayish brown and black. "A *madipa* (a type of civet)!" Dalawesan said as he recognized the intruder. Though the madipa was a larger-than-average cat at around two and a half feet long, it wasn't big enough to take on a kumaw.

"Move along cat!" Dalawesan yelled at the madipa as he tried to roll and get to his feet, but the arrow that was still embedded in his left wing prevented him from rolling plus the fact that the pain was excruciating.

"You better leave and forget about me!" he yelled again as the hungry predatory look in the cat's eyes started to make him nervous. "You are not big enough to kill me madipa and if I catch you with my beak and talons then you will be MY prey!"

Suddenly, he heard another rustling sound coming from the foliage to his left. Another madipa popped its head from the bush and hissed at him. Then another madipa appeared next to the second one and then another by his feet.

Against one jungle cat, Dalawesan felt confident with his chances, but against four, he knew he was the prey. The family of madipa approached him cautiously. They crept down low as they approached their intended prey and flexed their hind legs in readiness to pounce on Dalawesan. But just as the first madipa was about to pounce on him, an arrow suddenly whizzed from somewhere in the jungle and embedded itself right in the jungle cat's neck.

The madipa leapt and screeched uncontrollably which frightened the rest of its clowder as they ran away. "I got him!" said a voice from somewhere in the jungle. "I got him with one arrow!"

Human! There's a human here! Dalawesan thought. *He speaks the tongue of the Aetas.*

The hunter appeared from behind some trees with a small knife in his hand as he planned to slit the madipa's throat. But as soon as he saw Dalawesan on the jungle floor, he dropped his knife and scrambled for his bow strapped to his back. "Agay!" The hunter exclaimed.

"*Uppunan-moy-bas hikan. Uppunan-moy-bas hikan.* (Please help me.)" Dalawesan said over and over, hoping the hunter was able to understand him and might take pity on him. Dalawesan spoke several human languages since this was not the first time he was in Kalupaan. The Poons would send him, his sister, and other kumaws to the mortal realm on a few occasions to spy upon humans, night creatures, or nilalang-lubong for reasons unbeknownst to them.

The hunter was Talimannog and as soon as he saw Dalawesan, the sight of a giant karat laying on the jungle floor startled and frightened him. He scrambled for his bow and managed to nock an arrow and took aim. He was a split second from losing his arrow when he realized that the giant karat was talking. "You...you speak?"

"Yes. I mean you no harm, so I ask the same in return," Dalawesan responded. "I am a kumaw from Kaluwalhatian. I am hurt and in desperate need of your help."

The hunter redrew his bow and fastened it back on his back. He slowly walked closer to Dalawesan and saw the black arrow embedded in his wing. "Did another hunter do that to you?" he asked.

"It wasn't a hunter who shot me with this arrow, it was a servant of Kasanaan; an aswang," Dalawesan answered.

The mention of the word aswang gave the hunter pause. Apprehension started building up in him again as he started looking around in fear of finding one of the night creatures lurking in the jungle.

"Do not fear. The aswang that shot me is back in Kaluwalhatian. It cannot cross the realms in the same way I did."

"I believe you," the hunter said as he knelt by Dalawesan's wounded wing. "Would you like me to remove it so you may return to the spirit realm?"

"If you would please, I would forever be in your debt. But as far as returning home, I do not think I would be capable of accomplishing that in my current condition."

"Then let's remedy your predicament one problem at a time. First, I need to remove this strange-looking arrow from your wing. This will be painful so promise me you will not harm me as I attempt to remove it."

"I promise," Dalawesan said as he extended his left wing as far as he could. "Oh, I do not recommend that you touch the arrow with your bare hands. It was made in Kasanaan and might cause you harm simply by touching it."

The hunter took his knife and cut some large heart-shaped leaves off a nearby bush and carefully wrapped them around the arrow's shaft. Dalawesan winced in pain as the arrow's shaft shifted inside his flesh.

With one quick snap, the hunter broke the shaft in half and threw away the end with the fletching. "Now comes the really painful part," he told Dalawesan. "I'm going to carefully pull the arrow out of your wing. I imagine the pain will be terrible, so please don't harm me when I do so."

"You have my word...," Dalawesan was saying when he realized he didn't know the human's name. "What do I call you?"

"I am Talimannog."

"You have my word Talimannog. You can call me Dalawesan, and you may begin when... SQUAWK!" Dalawesan was saying when Talimannog pulled the arrow out in one swift motion.

The pain left Dalawesan dazed as the jungle canopy started spinning above him. He was about to pass out when he heard Talimannog say, "I have some *bayobang* (guava) leaves I carry with me when we go hunting. I'm going to apply this to your wound to stop the bleeding."

"Ammani! Over here!" Talimannog continued to say when the sweet embrace of sleep took Dalawesan.

*****

Dalawesan was awakened by the crude bobbing motions his body was experiencing as well as the voices of humans conversing. He opened his eyes and found himself on a makeshift sled made of several long branches and jungle vines.

Two male humans were carrying him. By his head was the man named Talimannog whom he recognized while the man by his foot was unfamiliar to him. *Are they planning to cook and eat me?* Was the first thing that came to his mind but was just as quickly dismissed as soon as he realized and thought, *then why keep me alive?*

"You're awake. That's good. I stopped the bleeding in your wing with the bayobang leaves so now we just need to take care of you while you heal," Talimannog said. "That is my younger brother Ammani over there. We are heading over to where my other siblings are, so we all go home together."

"You have my thanks Talimannog. It would seem that I am in your debt. But please tell me, did you by chance happen to run into another one of my…" Dalawesan was saying this when he was interrupted by a woman's voice.

"*Dekka!* (Older siblings!) Dekka!" The woman's voice cried out. "Over here! Quickly, I found… something in the jungle. Hurry!"

"Forgive me for interrupting Dalawesan, but that is my sister Innawagan calling for us," Talimannog said. "Ammani, let's set him down here."

"Stay here giant bird," Ammani said in his cheerful, unpretentious voice. "We'll just see what wadi wants. This won't take long."

"I found something in the jungle as I was tracking an *ogsa* (deer) a while ago," Innawagan told her brothers. "Don't be frightened when you see her."

"Her?" Talimannog asked.

"It's… she's definitely female… she was injured, and I helped her… just come and see," Innawagan said as she fumbled her words in trying to find the best possible way to explain what she meant.

"Dundunan," Dalawesan whispered. "Thank the Poons you're alive."

*****

The next morning, Alig and Anibo were gutting some brown feathered ducks that they caught earlier in the day. They were currently settled by the Pared River in an area called Baggao. Their bertan settled there during those rainy months as it was close enough to the hills should they suddenly need to take refuge on higher ground if the river ever flooded. It's been two days since the last time it rained, and the last downpour didn't last too long which meant that they could remain near the river for the foreseeable future.

"Shouldn't they be back by now?" Anibo asked Alig as he plucked off the feathers on a headless duck's body.

"They should be back soon wadi, they didn't go too deep into the jungle to hunt this time since ogsa has been spotted not too far from the river. Just focus on cleaning the ducks so we can cook them already. I'm hungry as a..." Alig was saying this when she suddenly stopped when she spotted the rest of their siblings coming out from the jungle. "They're here!"

Anibo turned around and saw the rest of his siblings emerge from the jungle carrying something big in a makeshift sled. "What is that?!" he asked, looking puzzled. "It doesn't look like an ogsa. What did they hunt?"

As soon as Alig and Anibo saw what their siblings were carrying with them, they dropped the ducks along with their jaws. "I guess we won't be eating ducks tonight," Alig said with a bemused grin on her face.

But when the kumaws started moving couldn't help

but scream. “Agay!” they said in unison.

“What are those things?!” Anibo asked both screaming and pointing at Talimannog.

“Relax wadi,” Talimannog said as they carefully laid down the sled. “They are kumaws and our guests. Now get over here and help us.”

*****

The kumaws stayed with Talimannog’s family for several weeks as they healed and recuperated. The siblings built nests made of various twigs, vines, and other plants for each kumaw to act as their cot as they rested.

Since they were the ones that found the kumaws, Talimannog and Innawagan took care of each kumaw that they found. They would clean their wounds and feed them whatever meat they could hunt as well as fetch them water to drink and clean them. When the kumaws regained some of their strength and could walk freely of their own volition, though moving their injured wings was still too painful, they would walk with Talimannog and Innawagan to the river and help them catch fish. When the family needs to leave and hunt, which could last up to two days at a time, they always made sure that someone was left behind to keep the kumaws safe.

Over time a bond had developed between the kumaws

and the members of Talimannog's family. They had for all intents and purposes, became like family to each other and were now a bertan. The connection between Dalawesan and Talimannog as well as that of Dundunan and Innawagan had grown to a point that the kumaw siblings felt that what they owed the human siblings was beyond that of a simple debt. They knew that they will not be returning to the service of the Poons, especially on the day that they regained the ability to fly.

*****

"I've known of the extreme loyalties the kumaws have for the Poons, as well as the ones that followed the Yawàs to Kasanaan during the times of the *Kanulo* (The days of betrayal)," Kidul said after hearing the tale of the kumaws. "But I've never heard that your loyalties can be given to another. Which is ironic I suppose."

"The loyalty we feel to those whom our souls choose to serve is absolute," Dundunan replied. "Though we do not control to whom our soul gives this loyalty to."

"I suppose ironic is the word best used to describe our kind," Dalawesan continued. "We are, after all, nilalang-lubong, or those created by the Poons and given the gift of free will much like the gift humans were given when the Dians created them. Yet we cannot freely choose to whom we bestow our loyalties."

"Yes, we truly are an irony made manifest in flesh and feathers. But this I am sure of, and I am sure I speak for my brother as well when I say, our loyalty to Talimannog and Innawagan was born of gratitude and love and will continue to endure until death breaks it asunder." Dundunan concluded.

Innawagan could not help but kiss Dundunan on the head and stroke the back of Dalawesan's head. She was truly overcome with joy and love that she felt for the kumaws who had given her, and her brother more than she felt they deserved.

As they sat there finishing what was left of their meal, a middle-aged man and a woman who appears to be his wife approached the Lakandians and their party. Both the man and his wife were wearing the shaggy vakul headgear, beg loincloths, and several beaded necklaces made of shells around their necks. The man had a small basket of dried salted fish and gestured for Taguwasi to take it.

"We have nothing more to trade for this Hapu," Taguwasi told the man.

"My name is Timban, and this is my wife Hagsa. You misunderstand my intentions great Lakandian. We give you and the other Lakandian this basket of salted dibang freely and as tribute." The man named Timban said as he handed the basket to Taguwasi.

"We thank you for your gift Hapu, but we do not ask for tribute," Taguwasi said as he tried to return the basket to Timban.

"He speaks the truth," Lumalindaw chimed in. "We are here for fair trade and that is all. What we do as Lakandians is done freely and as a duty to the Poons. We ask no payment for them."

"Yet I remember your hama asking tributes from others when you were younger..." Kidul said when Lumalindaw give him a resounding slap on his ayoding prison.

"Then take them as a sign of our appreciation for your dedication to your duties," Timban's wife Hagsa finally said. "Many years ago when I was a budding youth, my hama and sibling were killed by a monstrous creature of the deep called the Berbakan. It was a monstrous *iyu* (shark) that devoured many of our people.

"For many moons, none would dare fish the seas in fear of the Berbakan. We ate most of our livestock and could not grow roots fast enough to sustain and nourish ourselves. We were on the brink of starvation. We prayed and gave tributes to the Poons and the enkantos to save us and rid us of the Berbakan.

"Then on one faithful day, Kaluwalhatian answered our prayers. They sent the Lakandian called Lam-ang to save us. It was said that he along with the aid of the merfolk of Sirokdanum killed the Berbakan and returned the gifts of the sea to our people." Hagsa said as she handed the basket of fish back to Taguwasi.

"This is why we give you tributes," Timban said. "You are Lakandians. You are the gifts that the Poons of Kaluwalhatian have bestowed upon humanity. Your existence whether you yourself, believe it or not, is the answer to everyone's prayers even before they ask for it."

The two Lakandians were left speechless. Never before were they given such reverence by anyone from anywhere. All that they could do was humbly accept the basket of dried fish and thank the couple.

"We should really make time to find Lam-ang," Taguwasi said as he handed the basket of fish over to Innawagan. "I would wager that he, being the first among us would know a little bit more about protecting the *you know what*."

"I actually know where to find him," Lumalindaw said which caught Taguwasi by surprise.

"Agay! Really? Why didn't you tell me this before?"

"There are a few things that I might have omitted when I spoke with Poong Ofag on my wedding night," Lumalindaw said. "I wasn't sure if you were ready to hear them yesterday."

"Now my curiosity is piqued!" Taguwasi exclaimed. "Let's start with Lam-ang. Where is he and why haven't you gone to him yet?"

"He is in a place called Nalbuan in the Samtoy Nation. The reason I haven't gone to see him yet is that my focus right now is to find Muwan and end my curse."

"Very well. I understand. What else did the Poons tell you?"

"He said that someday, the first true Lakandian will come and lead all of us in a great war against the dalaketnon."

"First true Lakandian? That doesn't make sense. Poong Kedes already told me that I am a true Lakandian." Taguwasi asked puzzled by Lumalindaw's statement. "And if there was such a thing as a first true Lakandian, wouldn't Lam-ang be the one?"

"I honestly don't know. Poons speak in riddles to us as you are probably well aware having spoken to one yourself," Lumalindaw answered. "All I know is, it's not Lam-ang."

"How would you know that?"

"The first true Lakandian is a woman," Lumalindaw answered and grinned at Taguwasi.

"What?!"

The Lagoon (Map)

Chapter 7
Innawagan's Abduction

They returned to their settlement a few hours later. They landed by the banks of the river and unloaded their baskets of fish and crabs from Kolago's back.

"Where is everyone?" Lumalindaw asked as he looked around and surveyed the empty settlement.

Innawagan looked around and pointed towards some branches embedded in the ground with a rope tied around them. "They went out to hunt by the foot of the hill. They had left not too long ago so they shouldn't be back until later in the afternoon." Innawagan told Lumalindaw with such certainty.

"How would you know all of that just by looking at those branches and rope?" Lumalindaw asked puzzled.

"Our people use such markers to leave messages to one another," Taguwasi answered as he helped unload the baskets and set them near the pinanahang. "I see that Talimannog used branches pointing to the nearby hills which tells me that's where they all went. The rope they used is barely the length of my forearm which tells me that they left a short time ago."

"We also use leaves as signs for either information or warning," Innawagan continued. "It all depends on the message we intend to leave. We usually use these forms of messaging during hunts. It lets the others in our bertan as well as other families hunting on the same grounds know what the prey is and where we will be."

"That is a useful skill to learn," Lumalindaw retorted. "Can you teach me more about them before I depart tomorrow?"

"It would be my pleasure," Taguwasi replied. "But right now, I think I want some amman to chew while we wait for the others."

Kolago went back out to hunt for his meal while the two kumaws stayed and fed on some of the fish they received from the Ivatan. As they chewed amman while waiting for the others, Bago returned from the jungle to greet them.

"You're back!" Bago said as he hovered towards them. "And I see you've been successful with your trade with the Ivatan."

"I hate to brag..." Kidul was saying this when Lumalindaw suddenly interjected. "Yes, you do!"

"Humph! As I was saying, had it not been for me bridging everyone's thoughts with my magic, then our bounty would have been far less."

"Please excuse Kidul," Lumalindaw excused Kidul in a jovial manner. "Unfortunately for everyone present, his imprisonment has done nothing to temper his arrogance."

"Bago," Taguwasi interjected. "How was your trip this

morning? Did you find out anything that can help our guest? Any information no matter how small could be pertinent to help Lumalindaw."

"I spoke to several puyangs and other healers that can see spirits from several settlements and tribes, all of which had nothing significant to offer. But on my way back, I met an Isneg man who told me that his akka heard something about a cursed woman. And apparently, his akka knows of Puyang Anag.

"Unfortunately, his akka is also a bit fearful of the Agta. Something about an unfortunate incident involving unwanted beheadings. But he will be visiting Puyang Anag later today but insists that he will speak with only her." Bago said, trying to be as accurate with his answer as possible.

"I'm glad to hear you took the time to include all the pertinent details in your story," Kidul said sarcastically.

"Kidul!" Lumalindaw snapped at his obnoxious katiwala.

"Your katiwala certainly seems to be in high spirits considering his predicament," Taguwasi said, feeling a bit annoyed at Kidul's attitude.

But after saying what he said to irritate his fellow enkanto, Kidul suddenly realized there was a detail in the Kumaw's story from earlier that was missing.

"Dalawesan, Dundunan," Kidul called to the kumaws

who were eating their fill of fish. "Do you mind if I ask a question about the story you told us earlier?"

"By all means, Hapu Kidul ask," Dalawesan answered.

"In your story, you mentioned a third kumaw who was with you when the danag ambushed you. Whatever happened to Ammalabukaw? Did he survive as you and your sister did?" Kidul asked as an eerie silence suddenly fell before everyone present.

It was Dundunan who finally answered, "Yes. He survived. And like us, he also fell into a balete tree and was transported to Kalupaan."

"This is the part of the story where all our fates intertwined as well as how I met the love of my life," Taguwasi continued. "For this first part, maybe it's best to start with my wife and the two *manulib brothers*."

"Manulib? Are they a tribe that I haven't heard of before?" Lumalindaw asked.

"Manulib is but one of their many names," Innawagan answered. "The Ivatan call them *mamakaw* or *manulib*. But I believe your people call them..."

"Nalaing!" Kidul interjected.

At the sound of this word, Lumalindaw tensed all over and felt an invisible hand squeeze his heart.

"Calm yourself Lakandian," Innawagan said softly. "The manulib brothers were not the same creature that you hunt. Here, have some water and let me tell you all about them. It all happened around a year ago…"

*****

The kumaws, Dalawesan and Dundunan had been living with Talimannog's family for close to three years at that point. Due to the increasing number of Kalinga and Itawit headhunters encroaching near their settlement by the Pared River, Talimannog and Alig decided to move their settlement farther east.

They followed a branch of the Pared River that led northeast. The journey took them almost four days going up and down mountains which were not without their small brushes with danger. Once, they ran into a small band of Itawit headhunters that tried to kill them and take Alig and Innawagan. Though slightly outnumbered, Talimannog and his siblings managed to fight off and kill several members of the headhunter band in no short part to the kumaws.

They did meet other Agta bertans along the way who was more than happy to trade whatever they could with them as well as those that were generous enough to provide them with bilon. Again, in no short part to the kumaws whom they showed off to the Agta families who were more than willing to pay tribute to them.

There was a night when a small bertan of their fellow Agta invited them to stay and exchange *nanang* (chanted tales) by the fire. Alig chanted the comedic tale of Mandaripan from which they all shared a laugh as they enjoyed each other's company and some amman. After an hour or so of Alig's nanang, the elder of the host's bertan, an old woman, chanted a tale about an Aeta man who could enslave the wind and fly like a bird. The man was also exceptionally strong and summon an invisible arrow from his beg that can vanquish any enemy.

After the old man finished his nanang, Innawagan said, "Surely such a man does not exist. Only the Poons and enkantos can possess such power."

"Yet here you are with two talking kumaws from Kaluwalhatian..." The old woman replied.

Near the end of the week, they reached a point where the river trickled down to a stream. There were several open grounds near the stream where the soil was dark and rich and ideal for planting root crops.

"The soil here is rich dekka," Innawagan inferred as she dug her hand into the dirt.

"The water is clear, but not too many fish swim up here," Ammani said as he crouched near the stream.

Talimannog surveyed the area and approached the edge of the jungle. Alig joined him as they looked for tracks and other signs of big game. "I see tracks akka. Ogsa and boar by the looks of them."

"This looks like a good area to settle for the summer,"

Talimannog said as he turned and addressed the rest of his siblings. "We should stay here and settle for the summer and maybe even when the rains come. Other than the lack of fish in the stream, I think we should do fine. There is game in the jungle and the area seems high enough that we don't need to worry about flooding when the rainy months hit us."

"Dundunan," Innawagan called to her agom. "Can you fly up and follow the stream farther into the mountains? I want to know if there are any other settlements in the area."

"Good idea wadi," Talimannog said as he called out for Dalawesan. "Can you do the same as your sister? Only go north and east from here. I especially want to know if there are Kalinga settlements in the area. Please return here after an hour."

"As you wish Hapu," Dalawesan and Dundunan replied.

Dalawesan went north for twenty minutes and circled back south for another twenty. He covered somewhere close to ten square miles and only found two other small settlements of small Agta families and didn't consider either of them as a threat.

Dundunan followed the steam northeast for a few miles. The stream meandered a few times and flowed into the jungle where it spilled over to a small, clear watered lagoon. The few fishes that swam up the stream ended up being trapped in the lagoon where they began spawning in great numbers. On the other end of the lagoon, Dundunan saw water being fed into the lagoon from a few small waterfalls from a series of unground caves.

There is not much space to plant crops in this area, but at least now we know where we can find fish. Dundunan thought to herself. *I better return to Hapu Innawagan and tell her the good news.*

Just as Dundunan took off, little did she know that there were two sets of eyes watching her from within the cave. "Not yet my friend," said a voice from inside the cave. "We'll watch them for now and see who they are and why they've come."

*****

The siblings worked diligently over the next few days. They built their huts, cultivated a patch of level earth, and planted their root crops. The game, as Talimannog and Alig predicted was plentiful in the nearby jungle. Ogsa, wild pigs, and madipa frequented the stream to drink, which made hunting them all that much easier.

On the fourth day of their stay, when most of the work in the new settlement had already been done, they all decided to explore the lagoon that Dundunan found a few days earlier. They all followed the stream through the jungle and emerged a mile away where it opened up to a clearing and the lagoon.

"Agay!" Anibo exclaimed when he saw the lagoon. "Look at all the fish that ended up trapped in there!"

"I guess fishing is not going to be a problem after all," Alig said as she walked to the edge of the lagoon to wade her feet.

"Do you suppose there are crocodiles in there?" Ammani asked.

"I don't think so," Talimannog answered. "If there were we would've seen them by now. Given how many fishes are in the lagoon, I suppose it would be easy to speculate that nothing except birds are probably feeding off them."

"That's good enough for me!" Ammani exclaimed as he stripped off his beg and jumped in the water.

"Me too!" Anibo cried as he followed his twin into the clear, bluish-green water of the lagoon.

Talimannog followed soon after and then Alig. Innawagan had set her bow down and removed her taloktok and beg. As soon as she was naked and was about to jump into the water, she suddenly felt an eerie sensation that someone was watching her. Someone with dark intentions. She looked around the jungle and saw neither animal nor man hiding in the foliage.

"Dundunan." she called her agom. "Would you mind

if I asked you and your brother to fly around the lagoon a few times and see if we're alone out here?"

"As you wish Hapu," Dundunan agreed. "If don't find anything, can my akka and I catch some fish afterward?"

"Of course," Innawagan said as she thanked Dundunan.

"Are you jumping in or what?" Alig called out to her sister.

"Yes! I'm coming." Innawagan said as she walked over to the edge of a large rock near the bank of the lagoon. She was about to jump when she caught a glimpse of something glistening in a small cave at the other end of the lagoon. There were two of them and looked like eyes.

What was that? Innawagan thought to herself. She strained her eyes to see past the dark opening of the cave but whatever it was she thought she saw was gone. Having circled the lagoon twice, Dundunan returned to Innawagan to assure her that they were in fact alone. Thinking that whatever she thought she saw was nothing more than a figment of her imagination, Innawagan jumped in the water and joined her siblings.

*****

It wasn't until a week later that strange occurrences began happening in their settlement. They would see footprints around their settlement that don't belong to anyone in their group, and some of their root crops would be dug up but not taken. They would sometimes see a man standing in the jungle from the corner of their eye, but as soon as they turned their head he would disappear.

Talimannog and his siblings had always been sensitive to those from the spirit world. Seeing a jungle spirit or river spirit is nothing new to the siblings. Most of the time, these spirits don't even pay them any heed and go about their business. On rare occasions, they would run into a mischievous spirit like the *tayaban* that caused travelers to lose their way. The siblings were already familiar with handling spirits such as these and had never really had a problem with them. And with the addition of the kumaws who could outright communicate with enkantos, the spirits of the jungles and the mountains have all but left them in peace.

But this invisible prowler that stalked them at night had the siblings worried. "Dalawesan, Dundunan, are you sure you found no traces of anyone or anything near us the past few nights?" Talimannog asked the kumaws.

"Nothing Hapu," Dalawesan replied. "We found no traces of human, spirit, or any other being near the settlement."

"There is a balete tree five miles north of here, but it is just too far for those crossing from it to even find us." Dundunan continued after her brother.

“Whomever this being is, it’s been getting bolder and bolder the longer we stay,” Alig said as she pondered their situation. “It started from the fringes of the settlement and now we see its footprints within the settlement itself and next to our huts.”

“We should have at least one person awake and on guard with a kumaw at the ready,” Talimannog said. “I’ll keep watch tonight, Dalawesan will be up alongside me and keeping watch.”

This went on for a few more nights as each sibling took turns watching the settlement at night with at least one kumaw at their side. So far, Talimannog’s little plan seemed to be working. They experienced no strange visitations nor was their settlement intruded upon. But that didn’t last long.

On the fourth night as Innawagan slept in her hut, the intrusion from the mysterious stranger had escalated to an all-new level. It started as a low rumbling sound that Innawagan heard as she slept. Innawagan then felt a hand softly run its fingers across her body. It started with her hair and slowly came down to her cheeks. It went down her neck and started touching her bosom. This was when she opened her eyes and saw a strange-looking man with bright yellow eyes laying down next to her. She heard the intruder whisper, “So lovely.”

Innawagan screamed and swung her fist at the man’s

face as she did. To her surprise, she hit nothing but air. Innawagan got to her feet and searched the darkness of her hut for the intruder but found nothing but an empty hut.

A second later, Dundunan poked her head into Innawagan's window and asked in a panic, "Hapu! Hapu! What happened? I heard you scream!"

"He was here! The intruder was inside my hut!"

The siblings along with the kumaws gathered outside Innawagan's hut. Alig had her arms around her younger sister as she tried desperately to console her.

"Wadi, take this water and try to calm yourself," Talimannog said as he handed her a coconut shell with water from the river. "The twins and Dalawesan are circling the settlement as we speak. Whomever that intruder was, he is not coming back tonight unless we find him first."

"Wadi, can you talk about what happened?" Alig gently asked her sister.

Innawagan took a sip of the water and tried her best to compose herself. "He, or whatever that thing was, looked like a man," she began. "It was dark but there was enough moonlight coming through my window for me to recognize that he wasn't one of us. He wasn't Aeta."

"What did he look like?" Talimannog asked.

"He... he looked like one of the Ivatan. His face was a

little older than yours dekka, and his hair was long… tied behind his head. His eyes were narrow… Ivatan like I said, and they were… they were… yellow?"

"Akka, do you think it was an anito or some mischievous forest spirit?" Alig asked Talimannog.

"I'm not sure. I've never heard of spirits actually touching someone physically. The stories I've always heard were always about spirits either guiding you through the jungle if you were lost or of them causing you to be lost." Talimannog answered.

"Maybe it was an aswang?" Alig asked again.

"I… I don't think so," Innawagan answered, still trembling. "For one, I am not pregnant. Also, it did not try to kill me."

"There is nothing out there!" Anibo said as he and his twin came up to the rest of their siblings.

"We circled the settlement twice and Dalawesan searched above the trees twice as much as us," Ammani said following Anibo. "We didn't find a trace of anything!"

"The lagoon," Innawagan retorted. "Tomorrow, when the sun is out, we should all go to the lagoon."

"Why the lagoon?" Anibo asked.

"I felt something or someone watching us when we first came there to swim," Innawagan answered. "It all happened really fast, so I just passed it off as my imagination."

"Tomorrow then. We'll go when the sun is at its peak." Talimannog said.

*****

At midday the following morning, the siblings reached the lagoon armed and ready for anything. Dundunan and Dalawesan circle the area just above the lagoon, ready to sink their massive talons into anything that might endanger their respective agom.

"There's nothing here," Talimannog who was in the lead said once they had investigated the perimeter of the lagoon. "Did anyone see anything?"

"Nothing akka," Anibo answered. "No tracks. No signs of anyone dwelling anywhere near the lagoon."

"The cave," Innawagan interjected. "I felt or saw the presence in one of those caves that feed the waterfall."

"We'll explore the caves. Everyone sticks together." Talimannog ordered his siblings. "Be ready for anything once we reach the mouth of the cave."

The siblings reach the mouth of a cave where Innawagan felt the presence of the stranger. They all had nocked arrows that they used for combat rather than hunting, which included the poisonous palagad that Alig liked using.

The siblings were crouched low and quiet as they

entered the cave. The kumaws landed behind them and followed them on foot as there wasn't much room for them to use their wings inside.

Water ran in the middle of the cave floor that flowed out to the lagoon. Where the water came from initially was a mystery to them, but that didn't concern them at the moment. There was a slight elevation on the sides of the cave floor that they could walk on. The water eroded most of the dirt and rocks in the middle of the floor that created a natural canal from where the water flowed freely.

They explored a little deeper into the caves and found a labyrinth of tunnels that seemed to run deep into the mountain's bowels. The tunnels ran so deep into the mountains that after a short while, seeing anything through the ever-growing darkness was becoming a problem.

"Should I go out and make *sulus* (torches)?" Ammani asked in a low whisper.

"No," Talimannog answered. "It's only getting darker and narrower as we move deeper into the cave. If we are attacked here, we're doomed."

"I agree with you Hapu Talimannog," Dalawesan interjected. "We should leave. There is something wrong here."

"What do you mean?" Alig asked.

"Our eyes can see far better than yours and our sense of smell is also just as keen," Dundunan answered her. "Dalawesan is right; something is not right with these caves. We can smell bat droppings on the cave walls and floor but most of them are dry and old. But what we don't see are the bats. There should be bats hanging in the ceiling, yet we don't see a single one."

"Did something scare the bats away?" Innawagan asked.

"Yes," Dundunan answered her agom. "That or something has been feeding on them."

They stepped out of that first cave and explored the other smaller ones. All of which yielded the same result. Finally, they abandoned the thought of exploring the caves and reconvened by the lagoon.

"It's too dangerous to go in deeper," Talimannog began. "Whatever it is we are facing is not worth dying for. We should break the settlement tonight and move farther north.

"Alig and Innawagan, gather as many root crops as you can and pack up our belongings. The twins and I will help gather the weapons and whatever meat we have left. Since it's already late, we should stay another night before leaving out, but together in one hut. We'll leave at first light."

The siblings returned to their settlement and began

making preparations for their departure. They gathered whatever food, weapons, and supplies they'll need and gathered them all next to the twins' hut where they all planned to sleep together and leave at the first light of dawn.

They took turns as lookouts as the rest slept. All except Innawagan in whom the stranger seems to have taken an express interest in. Alig was the fourth sibling whose turn it was to watch over the group when the stranger returned to their settlement.

She was looking into the bonfire that they kept burning when she heard a rustling sound to her left followed by the same low rumbling sounds that Innawagan described. Compared to the rest of her siblings aside from Talimannog, Alig was smart and cunning. From the corner of her eye, she saw the light of the fire reflect on two sets of yellow eyes lurking in the bushes to her left.

Without letting the intruders know she was aware of their presence; she slowly nocks an arrow on her bow while pretending to be sleepy. As soon as she feels the arrow securely in place, she makes her move. In one swift, fluid motion, she aims the bow toward an intruder, draws the string, and calls out to her siblings, "They're here!"

Alig lets her arrow loose as it flies toward one of the intruders. But to Alig's surprise, the intruder waves his hand in front of the arrow as something round and golden yellow appears out of thin air and blocks the arrow before it reached him.

Alig nocks another arrow and shoots again. The exact same thing happens. By this time, all the siblings were up and awake.

This time though, Alig had time to take a better look at their enemies. Innawagan was correct in saying they looked like the Ivatan. One of them even had the vakul headgear on him. They had brown skin like the others of their people except that theirs seemed eerily different somehow. The intruders 'skin seemed to have a sheen to it as though they were somehow metallic. But what made them especially frightening were their eyes.

Their eyes reflected the firelight like a cat's, and they glistened yellow in the dark. "*Dangpiran!* (Attack!)" Talimannog's voice rang out as he commanded his siblings to loose their arrows.

"Shoot the other one!" Alig followed Talimannog's command as she already saw what the other one can do.

The siblings loosed their arrows in unison and sent several arrows hurtling toward the other intruder. The second intruder stretched out his arms as an uncanny warp or ripple happened to the air in front of him. It was hardly visible, but everyone could see it was there. As the arrows reached this ripple, they up and vanished right before everyone's eyes.

"Poons save us! What just happened?!" Anibo exclaimed. "Where did my arrow go?"

"Stop thinking about it and nock another one!" Ammani told his twin.

The kumaws who were circling the settlement heard the commotion and were already diving down to attack the intruders. All the siblings nocked arrows on their bows and prepared for another volley. But as they did, the two intruders did something unexpected. They turned around and ran back into the jungle laughing as if goading the siblings to follow and chase them.

"Stop!" Talimannog said as he raised his bow as a signal to halt. "Follow them!" he commanded the kumaws. He then turned to Alig as if to confer their next action.

"Go after them with the twins and the kumaws," Alig said. "I'll stay here with Innawagan to keep her safe."

Talimannog nodded and said, "We won't go too far out. We'll be between them and the settlement. Ammani, Anibo, come with me and keep an eye out for the kumaws."

The three brothers ran into the jungle and disappeared into its depths. The two sisters kept vigilant and right next to each other with an arrow nocked and ready for anything.

"Stay close wadi and be ready," Alig said as she did

her best to survey the surrounding darkness of the jungle around them. "If anyone who isn't our brother jumps out of the foliage, stick it with your arrow."

"How long do you think they'll be gone?" Innawagan asked. "Shouldn't we just make a run for it when they return? I don't think going after those... those things is the best idea."

"We can't make a run for it wadi. Especially at night when I suspect they have a better advantage against us."

"I know, but still, the risk of going after them..." Innawagan was saying when a strong gust of wind suddenly came from out of nowhere. Then a shadow suddenly flew over them, blocking the light of the moon for a split second.

"What was that?!" Alig exclaimed as both sisters looked up. "Did you see it?"

"No. It was too fast." Innawagan answered back, anxiously searching the skies.

"Was it one of the kumaws?" Alig asked again as she raised her bow to the night sky.

"I don't know," Innawagan answered as she too raised her weapon. "It seemed big though. Maybe too big."

"We should go inside and ..." Alig was saying when suddenly another powerful gust of wind blew at them from behind. They turned as fast as they could to face whatever it was that was coming for them.

Alig managed to draw her weapon, but even before she could aim it, something big and powerful slammed into her and knocked her back several feet. She hit her head on one of the clay pots that they had laying around.

The pot shattered as her head collided with it which caused Alig to lose consciousness. As her eyes started to close and everything around her turned black, the last thing she saw was an enormous red bird that had Innawagan clutched in its talons.

Dalupiri Island (Map)

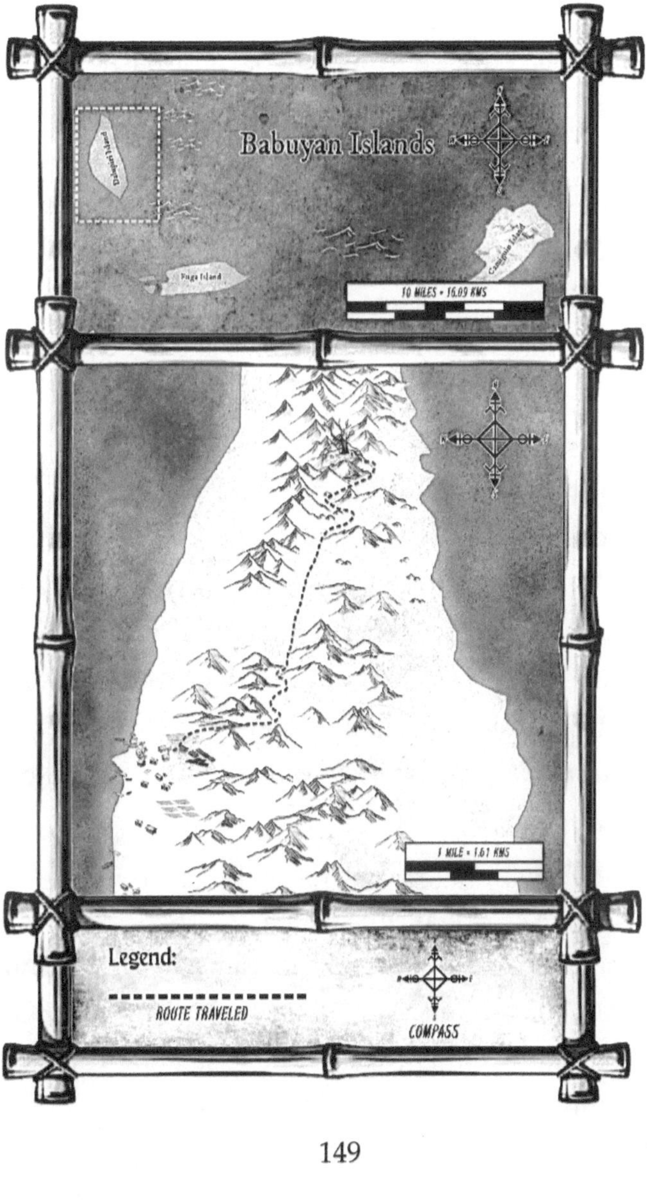

Chapter 8
The Manulib

Innawagan drifted in and out of consciousness as soon as the creature slammed into her and dragged her up to the sky. The whole ordeal was so violent and sudden that she couldn't make sense of any of it or even tell how long she had been in the air or how long she had been unconscious.

When Innawagan finally awoke, she noticed that she was in a dark place. Yet not so dark that she couldn't see. There were small torches on the walls that gave off a faint light as their fires waned but never died down.

The ground she was on was hard like stone but smooth. The air around her was chilly, but the air felt humid as though she was in a fog. Innawagan stood up and fell back down in a wave of dizziness that washed over her as soon as she got to her feet.

I must have hit my head harder than I thought. she thought to herself. *I wonder if Alig… Poons save us!*

"Alig! Alig! Are you there?" Innawagan called out to the darkness. "Where are you akka?"

Then from out of the darkness came the all too familiar low rumbling sound. A voice suddenly came from behind her that startled Innawagan, "Your sister is not here *mavid* (beautiful)."

Innawagan instinctively rolled on the ground, away from the voice. She got to a crouched position and tried her best to fight past her dizziness.

"There's no need to be frightened mavid… Innawagan yes?" The voice said. "I mean you no harm."

Innawagan looked at the man who spoke and knew from the sound of his voice that it was the same intruder who had been in her hut earlier that evening. Though the room they were in had some light, it was still too dark for Innawagan to clearly identify what her abductor looked like. All she could see were his yellow glistening eyes and his shadow-covered silhouette that told her he was tall.

"Who are you and why have you taken me from my family?" Innawagan asked as bravely as she could.

"Please forgive me for not introducing myself," The stranger said in a deep, low-pitched voice. "I am called Pane Kalimangalnuk."

The torches on the wall suddenly got brighter and Innawagan could see everything around her much clearer, including the stranger himself. She was in a circular room made entirely of stone from the domed ceiling down to the floor. Around the room were five doors and between each door was a torch that illuminated the threshold.

Pane Kalimangalnuk was exactly as she remembered seeing him earlier; tall and dressed like the Ivatan with his colorful loincloth, seashell necklaces, and the vakul on his head that extended down his back. His skin was brown, though it was closer to copper in tone than a typical Ivatan man. His body was heavily muscled, and his face was hard with sharp features. Finally, Innawagan was drawn to his eyes which are narrow and had a menacing look to them though he tried his best to make them look as calm and docile as he could. The whites of his eyes were extremely white and had no visible veins. His irises were golden yellow and reflected light like those of a cat; just as she remembered seeing them earlier.

"I don't care who you are!" Innawagan exclaimed as she ran out the door closest to her.

The passageway she was in was dark but very short. She immediately saw the exit and ran straight for it. But to her utter surprise, she ended up right back in the same room she was just in.

"There isn't any point in running Innawagan." Pane Kalimangalnuk said with a chuckle as he stood there, seemingly amused by what was happening. "You will always end up in the same place every single time."

Innawagan ran through another door and the same thing happened again and again. After four attempts at making a run for it, Innawagan decided to just attack the being that imprisoned her. Without skipping a beat, Innawagan lunged at her abductor in an attempt to drive her fingers into his eyes.

But just as quickly as she lunged at Pane Kalimangalnuk, something hard grabbed her by the waist and held her mid-jump. She looked down and saw a gigantic yellow hand, pop out from the stone floor and just held her in place.

From the door behind Pane Kalimangalnuk came another being with his right hand extended forward in a fist. The newcomer displayed similar traits to Pane Kalimangalnuk though the other man was a bit shorter and wearing the same type of clothes as Pane Kalimangalnuk. He was also wearing a vakul which immediately told Innawagan that he was Ivatan as well.

"Let me introduce you to my younger brother, Pane Nagdombilan," Pane Kalimangalnuk said as he introduced his brother. "Forgive him for grabbing you like that; he is a bit protective of me for some reason."

"Release her *kakteh* (brother). She has about as much of a chance of harming us as a fly would."

Pane Nagdombilan dropped his hand and almost instantly the yellow hand that held Innawagan disappeared like smoke. "Forgive my brash actions… patepag is it? That is how you say it in your tongue yes?" Pane Nagdombilan asked.

"Why would you call me that?" Innawagan asked puzzled. "I am not married, nor am I married to your brother!"

"Not yet mavid. But soon." Pane Kalimangalnuk said and laughed.

*****

Alig stirs awake and sees her brothers and the two kumaws looking down on her with fear and worry in their eyes. "Wadi! Wadi, wake up! What happened?" Talimannog said over and over as he shook his sister awake.

"Where is Hapu Innawagan?" Dundunan asked worriedly.

"I... we... something... something attacked us." Alig tried to say as she tried desperately to get her bearings. "It was big. Fast! We couldn't even defend ourselves fast enough when it came at us."

"What? What attacked you?" Talimannog asked as his tone changed from worried to agitated.

"It was... a bird. It was a kumaw!" Alig finally answered as she sat up and shook her head to clear her thoughts. "It attacked us from behind. It rammed me with its head, and I saw it... I saw it take Innawagan and fly off with her."

The brothers then all looked at Dalawesan and Dundunan as if expecting an answer from them. The two kumaws looked just as shocked and puzzled by what Alig had just said as the brothers did.

"We don't know any other of our kind to stay and dwell in Kalupaan other than ourselves," Dundunan said. "As far as I know, we are the only two kumaws to ever owe a life debt to a human."

"Hapu Alig, do you mind if I ask what color the kumaw was that took Hapu Innawagan?" Dalawesan asked.

"Red. It was big and red! Much bigger than you and your sister," Alig answered.

As soon as everyone heard what color the kumaw was that took Innawagan, the same thought entered everyone's mind.

"Didn't you mention a red kumaw that was with you the day you were ambushed in Kaluwalhatian?" Ammani asked the kumaws.

"Ammalabukaw. His name was Ammalabukaw," Dalawesan answered.

"But didn't you say you saw him fall after being struck by the danag?" Dundunan asked her brother.

"I did. I saw him get struck by three arrows. One in his left wing and two on his body. The last thing I remember of him before I turned my head and flew for dear life was the image of him falling," Dalawesan said with a sad tone in his voice.

"Could it be possible that he fell through a balete tree

just like you and your sister did?" Talimannog asked his agom.

"I can't see how Hapu," Dalawesan answered. "We were not too far from Nabuangan Forest, but he was struck first. He would've had to walk to the balete trees with three arrows stuck in him."

"Why are we just sitting around here doing nothing!" Anibo exclaimed suddenly. "Wadi is out there, and we know where that Amma...bakulaw... or whatever his name is, took her. Let's just go in those caves, lose some arrows in him and get our sister back!"

"We'll go. But it's still dark out and Ammalabukaw is not alone. Remember there are still those two strangers out there," Talimannog said. "We'll wait by the edge of the lagoon and as soon as the sun rises, we go in.

"Dalawesan. You and your sister fly around the lagoon and see if you can spot anything that might help us. Any information we can get might help us save wadi all that much sooner.

"Alig. Your head has a cut, and you are still wobbly from the ordeal. Stay in a hut and rest. But make sure you are armed. We'll be back with Innawagan soon, I promise." Talimannog concluded.

The siblings nodded in agreement to their eldest's plan. They gathered what weapons they could which included three *pinahig bolos* (short swords), three headhunter axes, and an assortment of arrows. The two kumaws flew ahead to scout the lagoon as Alig waited impatiently in a hut with a bow in her hand as she prayed to the Poons for her family to return to her safely.

*****

"If you're going to feed on me then at least kill me already!" Innawagan screamed at her abductors.

"Why would I feed on you when I said I wanted to make you my wife?" Pane Kalimangalnuk said as he laughed at Innawagan's suggestion. "Besides, Kakteh and I are not aswang or some revolting night creature. We are men, just like your siblings, albeit a little bit more."

This caught Innawagan's attention for a second and piqued her curiosity. *I need to know what manner of men these two are if I want to kill them and escape.* she thought to herself.

"If you are not aswang then what are you?" she asked nonchalantly.

"Our people call us the manulib," Pane Nagdombilan answered. "Though in other tongues, men, and women like us are known by many names. People in the Samtoy Nation call us mangagauay or tamay, the Kalinga call us nalaing, even as far as the Tagalog lands where they call us the mangkukulam."

"Ultimately, we are just people who understand how

to use magic. Whether it be spirit magic like what the enkantos use or dark magic used by the dark ones, we know how to use them as best as any human can," Pane Kalimangalnuk continued.

Pane Kalimangalnuk approached Innawagan and held her in his arms. He held her body close to his and began smelling her hair and neck. "But enough about us. I've desired you ever since I saw you bathe in the lagoon when you and your siblings first came here. I've been watching you sleep every night since then. Now that I have you, you are now my wife."

Innawagan could not budge from his embrace. His strength was immense, and his skin and flesh were hard like an animal's. She could feel his desire growing as he held her body close to his. She saw his brother smile a hideous grin as he watched. She knew what was going to happen next and that there was no physical way she could get out of it. So, she tried another approach to delay the violation that was about to happen.

"Wait. Stop," She insisted. "If I am to be your wife then at least let me know more about my husband-to-be."

This seemed to have worked as she felt Pane Kalimangalnuk's arms loosen around her. He stepped back and stared at her intently.

"You can force me to be your wife, but would you rather not have a willing wife than one that was taken against her will?" she asked and silently prayed that he went along with her ruse.

"Are you saying that you are willing to be my wife of your own volition?" Pane Kalimangalnuk asked a bit intrigued by her unexpected reaction.

"Only if you woo me as any real, brave man would do," Innawagan said with a hint of hope in her voice. "Well, are you? Are you truly a man as you said you were?"

"You are testing me then? Well, this is quite an unexpected turn of events. Something that has piqued my interest greatly," Pane Kalimangalnuk said with exuberance as he crossed his arms across his chest. "Go ahead, ask me what you wish to know, and ask me what you want to be done."

Innawagan was beside herself as she could not believe that her desperate ploy seemed to work. She did know that she couldn't show her abductors that she was pleased that they fell for it. *I need to be coy about this. I need them to waste time so that my siblings will be able to find and save me.* she thought to herself.

"You said you are not aswang and that you intend not to feed on me. You said you are manulib, though I do not know what that even means," Innawagan said as confidently as she could. "Please explain to me who, and what, you and your brother are; just to put my mind at ease at the very least."

Pane Kalimangalnuk and Pane Nagdombilan looked at each other for a moment as if silently conferring if they should indulge Innawagan's request for an explanation. Pane Nagdombilan slowly shook his head in disagreement, but Pane Kalimangalnuk being the older of the two had the final say in the matter.

"To truly understand what we are, you must first know who we are. We were born around eighty years ago on the island of Dalupiri far north of here," Pane Kalimangalnuk began his tale. "Like you and your siblings, my kakteh and I are sensitive to the presence of spirits and the enkantos.

"We were born and raised in a small fishing *idi* (village) on the northwestern side of the island where our *āmang* (father) was the *mangpus* (chieftain). Ours was a small community of around twelve families and unlike the other idi in the islands east and north of us, we were quite poor.

"We traded what we could and fished whatever we needed to eat. Our people planted root crops and other vegetation as well. I remember growing up relatively happy in our simple yet content existence on the island.

"As I said earlier, we could see spirits. Atop the highest peak in the northern part of the island, which by the way was quite humble in height compared to the mountains in these lands, was a gigantic balete tree.

"We often visited that tree whenever our chores were done, and we would see all manners of spirits and enkantos use the balete to pass through. They came in and out of our world as they pleased and most of the time, they paid us no mind.

"Then there were the rare occasions that an anito or diwata would stop and notice that we could see them. They would engage us in conversation and be about their way. On even rarer occasions, we would run into beings that were not spirits. Kapres, tikbalangs, kumaws, and other such beings. We stayed away from them as much as possible for these are beings that can truly harm us if they choose."

"Kakteh," Pane Nagdombilan protested. "Why go through all these pretentious diatribes? You have her here with us. Why not just take her as I told you from the beginning?"

Pane Kalimangalnuk suddenly turned and glowered at his younger brother. "I do this because I want to do this!" he exclaimed. "Do not interrupt me again or I will expel you from my *rakuh* (dwelling)!"

Pane Nagdombilan backed down and stepped away from his brother. Innawagan saw this and took note of it in her mind. *There is tension between them. Maybe it's something I can exploit when the time comes.* she thought.

"Where was I mavid?" Pang Kalimangalnuk asked as he was just about to continue his tale.

"Before you continue, you said a word I am not familiar with. You said 'rakuh', what do you mean by it?" Innawagan interjected.

"Rakuh means dwelling or domain," Pane Kalimangalnuk answered dismissively. "But I will get to that later. As I mentioned earlier, Kakteh and I would often see and sometimes interact with beings from the spirit world when we visited the balete tree. We would visit it as often as we could; except on moonless nights.

"On nights that the moon was absent or hidden behind clouds, we knew better than to be near the balete tree. Because it was on nights like those that the dark ones pass through it. It was on nights like those that the aswang sometimes come.

"Āmang being the mangpus of our little idi, would have everyone inside their homes, armed and ready on nights such as those. I remember when my āmang or some of the men of the idi would encounter a night creature, hunt it down, and kill it. Dangerous as those creatures might be, they posed no real threat if the people knew when they were coming and prepared accordingly.

"Those days went by fast for us. The simple uneventful days were very much welcomed by my people, and everything was peaceful. Or at least it was until the bandits arrived."

Pane Kalimangalnuk looked at his brother again and placed his hand on his brother's shoulder. Pane Nagdombilan had his yellow eyes closed and his fist clenched tight. The mention of the bandits triggered a dark reaction from him as Pane Kalimangalnuk tried to soothe his brother's anger.

"As you can see, the mention of those despicable bandits unearths painful memories for my Kakteh," Pane Kalimangalnuk continued. "On one particularly sunny day, my āmang, kakteh, and I were tending to our nets near the shore when one of our neighbors whose name has been lost to me, came running down the beach with blood streaming down from his head.

"He ran to Āmang crying and wailing as he warned him that bandits attacked their boat when they were near the shore, took their cargo of rice and yams, and killed his son and kakteh. He told my āmang that they looked and sounded like the Chinese people from the far west. He asked Āmang for justice and vengeance.

"Āmang gathered anyone willing to go and managed to gather eight men and three women including Kakteh and myself to go after these bandits in three fishing boats. We searched the seas until it was near dusk but found no trace of them. We did this for the next two days which resulted in the same outcome. We didn't see or hear anything from these foreign bandits for the next two weeks and everything eventually returned to the way that it was.

"But that all changed one dark moonless night. The moon was nowhere to be found, probably hiding behind some distant cloud. Just like we've always done on nights like these, we kept to our homes and stayed vigilant should an aswang or something undesirable decide to pay us a visit from the balete tree.

"Suddenly in the dead of night, we heard screaming from one of the nearby huts. I remember our *ānang* (mother) cowering in fear as our āmang peeked through the window of our house to see what was happening outside. As soon as he lifted the flap of the window, a bright yellow-orange light came flooding into our home. It was a fire!

"The hut of one of our cousins was ablaze with his entire family trapped inside. We quickly sprang into action and joined our neighbors in doing what we could to put the fire out. But as soon as we all gathered outside, instead of contending with a blazing inferno, we were met with a continuous volley of small featherless arrows.

"It turns out, the bandits had returned in the dead of night, and it was they who started the fire in an attempt to lure us out of our huts. Āmang was struck in the chest by one of these small arrows and fell to his knees along with some of the other people gathered there. Kakteh and I were some of the lucky few that managed to evade the ambush by ducking behind a hut or a tree.

"We managed to pull Āmang behind the hut where we hid and removed the small arrow from his chest. Luckily, aside from being featherless, the arrow was barbless as well. Our āmang, though bleeding and in pain still maintained his wits about him and ordered us to grab some kalasag shields, weapons, and whatever men we could find to go after the bandits.

"We obeyed Āmang's wishes and with much difficulty, managed to do as he commanded. Armed with shields, bolos, and spears, Kakteh and I along with five men went after the bandits.

"The bandits ran for the hills as we gave chase. Much to our surprise, there were only four of them. Though we greatly outnumbered them, defeating them was much more difficult than we ever imagined. They were armed with strange cross-shaped bows that loosed these small arrows at an unbelievable rate.

"As we gave chase to them, the bandits would suddenly stop, mount another attack, and run farther up the hill. They did this a few times and every time that they did, another member of our party died.

"We finally caught up with them near the balete tree. We got close enough to render their weapons inept, and they were forced to fight us with blades up close. By the time we dispatched all four of them, only three of us survived.

"We beheaded them and planned to take their heads back to the idi. But as I hacked away at one of the heads, I saw a dark shadow-like figure emerge from the balete tree. My kakteh and I being the only ones who could see spirits, froze as we looked at this ominous being just standing there and observing us. We were well aware that spirits could not harm us in any way that actually mattered so we decided to just brush off the spirit. We didn't even bother telling our last surviving companion about it.

"As we headed back to the idi with our trophies, we noticed the dark spirit following us. It followed us as we trekked down the hill. It followed us when we stopped to mark the spots where the bodies of our fallen lay so that we could return in the morning and give them a proper burial. It even followed us all the way back to the idi where all hope was stripped away from us as we watched the entire idi up in flames and everyone we ever loved was slain.

"As it turned out, the four bandits that attacked us were merely a diversion to thin out our warriors. As we chased after the initial four bandits, another twelve swept in and killed everyone that we knew and loved. We were beside ourselves with rage and the desire for revenge. All three of us dropped the heads we took and were about to charge the bandits and take out as many as we could before they eventually killed us.

"We were prepared to die, and we accepted the fate that the Poons have given us. But just as we were about to attack, the dark spirit appeared before us and spoke. It introduced itself as the mamaw Munduntug and offered to aid us in our mission of vengeance.

"We stopped our companion from jumping into the fray and told him what was happening. Munduntug told us to hold off on slaking our bloodlust for another night and to return to the balete tree. He would meet us there the following night and give us the means to exact our vengeance against the bandits.

"All three of us returned to the balete tree the following night. A storm had arrived during the day and continued its onslaught into the night. All three of us waited drenched in rain as we anxiously awaited the arrival of Munduntug.

"When Munduntug did arrive, he told us that for him to help us, there were certain conditions that we had to meet. The first thing he needed was a human heart. It didn't matter if it was dead or alive. Another thing we needed was gold. Luckily for us, those things were not difficult to obtain. After the fight with the bandits the previous night, human hearts were quite abundant. The gold took us a little longer to obtain but one of the bandits had rings of gold on one of his hands.

"The torrential rain continued as the night progressed. After obtaining the hearts and the gold, we all stood in front of the mamaw and awaited further instructions. He told us to bury each of them in the ground, one heart and one ring for each of us. To bind the items to our souls, we needed to offer it our blood.

"We passed along a knife to each other and cut our palms on each of our small mounds where we buried the heart and gold. Then Munduntug told us the last thing we needed to do to gain the thing we needed to have our revenge; we needed the lifeblood of a human sacrifice to enact the magic.

"I told the mamaw that we needed to go back and kidnap a bandit to sacrifice. But he told us that we didn't have enough time to do that. He said that if we left, then he would leave.

"The three of us stood there confused and panicked. We were faced with an impossible situation. But as the seconds passed and confusion gave way to paranoia, the third man in our little group whose name escapes me, suddenly realized that his life was in danger.

"I cannot recall how it began, and Kakteh will not speak of it to this day, but all of a sudden, blades were unsheathed, and a fight began. I recall defending myself with my own bolo. I remember losing my footing and slipping on a muddy patch of grass and falling. And then I recall the man's face frozen in complete shock with his eyes wide open and his mouth agape.

"My dear younger kakteh stabbed him in the back again and again with a knife as he lay there dead and bleeding atop the mounds. I recall hearing Munduntug laughing as he chanted words in a language completely alien to me.

"Kakteh reached down to pull me up and as soon as I stood on my feet, two bright bolts of lightning shot down from the night sky and struck the ground next to us. All I can remember was the deafening sound of thunder exploding in my ears and a white blinding flash of light. "Pane Kalimangalnuk said and then paused for a brief moment as an expression of regret came over his face.

"I don't know how long I lay there unconscious. It might have been for only a few moments, or it might have been an hour. The next thing I remember was the rain splashing endlessly on my face and the voice of the mamaw telling me to get up and take it.

"My ears were still ringing when I opened my eyes. Munduntug was standing over me and yelling at me to get up. I remember standing up almost at the same time as my kakteh. We were both still reeling from the effects of the lightning bolt when we saw Munduntug standing over a crater where the lightning struck and where the exploded body of our neighbor used to be.

"Munduntug was telling us to come over and pick it up. At first, we didn't understand what he meant, but when we walked closer to the shallow crater, that's when we saw them. Two small golden beating hearts no bigger than a chicken's heart. He told us that they were magical and called them *agimat* (magical items).

"Kakteh and I each picked up the agimat and examined it closely. They really were what they seemed to be; small beating golden hearts. The mamaw told us that if we swallowed these hearts, it would grant us magical abilities that we could use to vanquish our enemies.

"But Munduntug also warned us that these agimats came with a price and the price to be paid was an oath to do a task that the mamaw needed doing. We give the oath to the mamaw and the promise to fulfill it in exchange for the power to exact our vengeance. Having come that far and having done the unthinkable in the murder of our neighbor, my kakteh and I agreed and swallowed the golden hearts.

"The pain that followed was excruciating. Every muscle and vein in our bodies felt like boiling water was running through them while every inch of our skin was freezing cold. I can remember screaming in pain. The pain was deafening while everything else spun around uncontrollably. But just as quickly as it began, the pain suddenly stopped and everything about us changed.

"We became what you see before you now. Our flesh became something other than flesh and our eyes turned yellow as though they were cast in gold. We felt the very muscles under our copper-tinged skin ripple with strength as the world seemed to change yet stay the same.

"Munduntug approached us and told us that other than the physical changes that we received from the agimat, we were also given a magical ability that reflected our underlying personalities. Pane Nagdombilan, being the more fervent warrior and protector, received the *tagaliwas* agimat. It gave him the power to create solid objects out of thin air.

"He can create weapons and shields; even disembodied yellow hands as you saw earlier when you tried to attack me," Pane Kalimangalnuk said as he placed his hand on Innawagan's belly where the giant golden hand still held her in place. "Me, being the controlling older kakteh that I was... or rather am, received the *tagrakuh* agimat.

"It gave me the ability to create rakuhs, spirit rooms, or territories. It basically means that I can alter small spaces around me and control almost every aspect and condition within the rakuh.

"Take this room you are in for example. You see a small circular room with five doors. You can see the torches on the walls illuminating everything you see. What if I tell you that you are not actually in here? What if I told you that you are actually deep inside a system of caves that you and your siblings tried to explore once?

"With but a whim, I can change this rakuh from a stone room into something a little more familiar," Pane Kalimangalnuk said as the entire room suddenly changed into the visage of the lagoon outside.

"Agay!" Innawagan exclaimed. "Are we outside?"

"No, you are where you were but a moment ago. You never left the cave."

"Then this is all false. Nothing of what I see, smell, or hear is real." Innawagan said as she tried to grasp the reality of her surroundings.

"Yes and no," Pane Kalimangalnuk answered. "But what is real? Is real something you can see? Is it something you can hear or smell? Or touch? In my rakuh, reality is whatever I want it to be."

Innawagan took a moment to process everything that Pane Kalimangalnuk had told her up to that point. Knowing the extent of the creature's powers might be the means for her to escape. She knew she had to keep probing him for information, but she didn't want to be too obvious. Innawagan knew she had to be subtle, but she had to keep him talking.

"You mentioned earlier that the dark spirit held you and your brother to an oath. An oath to do a task. What was the task?" Innawagan asked.

"Ah yes… the task," Pane Kalimangalnuk said under his breath as he looked at his brother. "I'll let you know after I tell you what happened to us next.

"Munduntug instructed us for a few hours on how to use our newfound abilities. Learning how to use our powers came naturally to us as it reflected heavily on our personalities. As soon as we learned enough, we returned to our former idi to claim retribution.

"It was about an hour before sunrise when we arrived. The bandits had moored their boats on the beach close to the idi and had completely taken over our old home. There were more of them now, probably closer to twenty-five based on the six boats moored on the beach. I didn't really count.

"Most of them were sleeping in what used to be our huts and houses, while some stayed up and stood guard. The bodies of our friends, neighbors, and family were strewn in a pile by the beach. They were probably going to burn the bodies but were delayed on account of the rain.

"Kakteh wanted to just charge in and slaughter everyone being the hot-headed youth he once was. But I wanted our revenge to be slow and deliberate. I wanted them to be afraid and begging before we sent them to Kasanaan.

"With my newly acquired powers, I created a rakuh that engulfed the entire idi. Within this rakuh, I poured out my hate, anger, rage, and loss. I wanted the bandits to see how I felt, and how they made me feel after all the evil that they have done. I made the bandits see fire and what it feels like to be engulfed in its destructive embrace!

"The first thing I did to them was to awaken all of them from their restful slumber. I began with smoke. The smell of burning wood was the first thing that alerted the bandits as they slept. Then came the visions of dark clouds of smoke seeping in through every door, window, and crack on the floor.

"Everyone bolted up and ran out of the huts that used to belong to my people. Everyone yelled and screamed in panic which included their wives whom they brought along with them. As soon as they stepped out of the huts, the first thing that they saw was the endless tongues of flame shooting out from the very ground beneath their feet.

"As soon as anyone stepped foot outside a hut, a fire would shoot up at them and singe their feet and clothes. Others were completely engulfed in flame and fell to the ground screaming and rolling as they desperately tried to douse the fire that wouldn't die.

"You see the fire that burned them and shot out from the ground wasn't real, nor were they really burning. Anything and everything inside my rakuh are illusions. But the sensations that everyone perceives are quite real; at least in their minds. Which of course includes the feeling of smoke entering their lungs and the sight of their flesh burning and all the pain that goes with it.

"The others who never left the huts stayed in them and cried and prayed to whomever gods they worshiped, while others decided to just take their own lives than subject themselves to a slow and painful death. Those who burned outside kept running around screaming and pleading for death to take them, but for most, it didn't come. Those that did, died because their bodies simply gave out or their minds just couldn't cope with the pain.

"Now since that was the first time I had used my power to such an extent, I couldn't hold on to the rakuh and eventually succumbed to exhaustion. That was when Kakteh stepped in and collected his pound of flesh. With relatively emotionless proficiency, my little kakteh impaled the survivors on golden spikes across the beach.

"By the time he finished dispatching the last of the surviving bandits, the sun was already rising past the hills. And much to our surprise, our newly acquired golden yellow eyes were quite sensitive to its rays. We quickly took shelter in one of the huts and stayed there for the duration of the day."

"And what of your oath to the dark spirit?" Innawagan asked.

"Oh yes, I almost forgot to tell you," Pane Kalimangalnuk chuckled. "As soon as the sun set that day and we were finally able to leave the hut, we found Munduntug waiting for us outside. He congratulated us for achieving the revenge we wanted and told us that it was time that we give him what he was owed.

"The mamaw wanted us to scour the vast mountain ranges of the lands far and wide and find for him and his ilk hidden beings called *those who sleep in the mountains.* He told us that one of the benefits that the agimat he gave us was that we will never grow old or die unless we are killed by powerful beings and the agimat is taken from within our chests. So that gave us all the time that we will need to accomplish his bidding which unfortunately for us, we have not yet been able to do."

"But why must you do what Munduntug asks of you?" Innawagan asked. "Why not just ignore him and do what you will?

"Because until we accomplish this task, Kakteh and I cannot die?" Pane Nagdombilan answered with a bit of anger in his voice. "And after almost a hundred years of this existence, we want to die!"

"Please excuse my kakteh's hot-headedness," Pane Kalimangalnuk said as he placed a hand on his brother's chest. "You see, there is another aspect to being a manulib that I failed to mention. Ever since that fateful night when we consumed the agimat, we have not and cannot eat any food, nor could we drink a drop of water. As soon as anything passes our lips, they disappear without a trace. We have been famished and thirsty for decades!"

Innawagan was aghast by what she heard and felt a little sympathy for the two brothers. "That's what I've been hearing all this time!" Innawagan suddenly exclaimed as she understood. "That rumbling sounds I've been hearing all this time are your bellies! Your perpetually hungry bellies!"

"Ah! You see Kakteh! I told you she was special!" Pane Kalimangalnuk cheered, to which his brother simply shrugged.

"But please answer me this," Innawagan said. "If you and your brother are suffering so much, why not just end it? Why must you subject yourselves to this torture?"

Pane Nagdombilan chuckled wryly and said, "Maybe she's not so smart after all Kakteh!"

Pane Kalimangalnuk creased his brow in annoyance and turned to Innawagan. "Were you not listening? The only way we can be killed is if we die and someone rips out the agimat from our hearts. Our flesh has gotten stronger over the decades to a point that no one other than ourselves or someone stronger can kill us."

"Believe us when we say that we have fought tikbalangs, kapres, and other monstrosities hoping that at least one of them had the power to kill us. But to this day, no one has even gotten close to doing so." Pane Nagdombilan said somberly.

"One of us could kill the other," Pane Kalimangalnuk said. "But alas, in doing so one of us will have to endure this curse alone. And we just cannot bring additional torment to our otherwise miserable existence. So, we take solace in the small things that give us pleasure."

Pane Kalimangalnuk approached Innawagan once again and opened his arms and take her against her will. Innawagan's mind raced as it became horrifyingly obvious that she was out of time.

But at the last moment, just before the unthinkable was about to happen, something caught Pane Kalimangalnuk's attention. He stepped back and turned his head in the opposite direction.

"Someone has entered one of my rakuhs," Pane Kalimangalnuk said. "It seems your siblings are here looking for you."

Chapter 9

The First Rakuh

The afternoon was coming to a close when Talimannog and the rest of the bertan returned from their hunt. They managed to track and bring down a young buck which would be more than enough to feed them for at least three more days. And with the crabs and fish that Taguwasi and Innawagan received from the Ivatan, they were all set for at least five days before they needed to go out again.

"You're back!" Ammani exclaimed as he and his twin placed the deer carcass on a large slab of stone that they used to carve meat on. "What did you get from the Ivatan?"

"We got a few small baskets of fish, crabs, and squid," Innawagan replied. "I see you got a good one as well. Did you have to track it down long?"

"Not too long," Alig answered. "Sinag saw fresh tracks this morning right after you left. We followed them into the jungle and back out into the river again by midday. There were three of them, a doe and two of her fawns. We took down the smallest one."

"It looked like we interrupted something," Talimannog said as he sat next to Taguwasi who handed him some amman. "What were you talking about?"

"I was telling Lumalindaw about the manulib brothers," Innawagan answered. "You guys look hungry. I'll start boiling some potatoes and some of the crabs that we got from the Ivatans. You can continue the story if you'd like."

"Where did you leave off?" Talimannog asked.

"I stopped at the part when you first reached the caves when you guys came to rescue me," Innawagan said as she stood up and grabbed the basket with the crabs.

"Ooooh, I love this part!" Ammani said excitedly. "Can I tell Lumalindaw the story?"

"No!" Talimannog and Alig answered in unison.

"You'll exaggerate the details like you always do when you tell the story. Let akka tell it so it comes out truthful." Alig told her younger brother.

Talimannog spat out some betel nuts and started wrapping another amman in his hands. "So, there we were at the mouth of the largest cave by the lagoon. We all had a bow in hand and an arrow ready to loose at a moment's notice."

*****

"I'm taking the lead," Talimannog said as he slowly entered the mouth of the cave. "Once inside, I'm switching to my pinahig bolo so I can carry a torch. You two be ready to launch a volley at anything or anyone that's not our sister."

At around fifteen feet into the cave, the daylight was already starting to wane. Talimannog stopped, strapped his bow to his back, and set fire to his torch. It lit easier than he expected given how wet and humid the cave was.

Behind Talimannog were the twins that stood guard over him with their bows nocked and ready to loose. Dalawesan and Dundunan, moved ahead of Talimannog to scout farther into the bowels of the cave as they were able to see that much better in the dark.

"Everything is clear up ahead Hapu," Dalawesan said. "It is as it was the last time we were here; empty."

Talimannog stood and raised his torch over his head with his left hand and held his pinahig bolo tightly in his right. "Let's keep going," he said. "The longer it takes to find our sister, the more dangerous it gets for all of us."

A few minutes later they arrived near the spot where they had stopped a few days earlier. "This is it," Talimannog said. "This was as far as we dared venture a few days ago."

"Who cares akka?!" Anibo exclaimed. "Let's just go already, Innawagan needs us to find her."

So onwards they went. Deeper and deeper into the dark expanse of the caves. The light coming from the mouth of the cave was all but a distant memory as the air became thick and moist and the simple act of breathing was starting to become a chore. Suddenly, Dundunan called for a sudden halt.

"Stop!" Dundunan cried out. "There is something in front of us. Something… something that hints of magic."

"What is it?" Talimannog asked. "What do you see?"

"There is a ripple in the very air," Dalawesan said as he too spotted what his sister had seen. "It is the ripple you spoke about when you and your siblings attacked the intruder last night."

"Can we get past it?" Ammani asked.

"It extends to the very walls and ceiling of the cave," Dundunan answered. "We cannot go around it."

"Then we go through it," Talimannog said as he brushed passed the kumaws and disappeared through the ripple.

*****

"I'll take care of them kakteh," Pane Nagdombilan assured his brother. "This shouldn't take long."

Upon hearing this, Innawagan jumped in front of Pane Kalimangalnuk and fell to her knees. "Please don't kill them! I beg of you!"

Amused by her sudden change in demeanor, Pane Kalimangalnuk signaled for his brother to stop. "Why shouldn't I let him kill your siblings?" he asked Innawagan. "Just last night they tried to kill us with their arrows."

"They only shot at you to defend ourselves," Innawagan pleaded. "Please spare them. I love them just as much as you love your own brother. If you spare their lives, then I will willingly love you and be your dutiful wife and remain with you for as long as you want me."

Pane Kalimangalnuk was intrigued by Innawagan's proposal and took a moment to consider them. Meanwhile, his brother was getting impatient and began to storm off to dispatch Innawagan's siblings.

"Stop!" Pane Kalimangalnuk commanded his brother who all but ignored him and went through one of the five doors. But to his surprise, he ended up back in the same room as Pane Kalimangalnuk and Innawagan.

"What?!" Pane Nagdombilan bellowed in frustration. "What do you think you're doing kakteh? Don't tell me you're actually thinking of sparing these foolish humans for the sake of their whimpering sister?"

Pane Kalimangalnuk calmly approached his brother and gave him a thunderous slap in the face that sent Pane Nagdombilan sprawling to the floor. Seeing the shock and anger in Pane Nagdombilan's expression, Innawagan thought the brothers were going to fight and this might be her one and only chance to escape should the brothers succeed in killing each other.

But Pane Kalimangalnuk turned out to be more than

just a man of violence and avarice as Innawagan thought him to be. He was apparently a man of cunning intellect as well. A man who could influence his brother just as easily as he would his rakuh.

"Calm your heart kakteh," Pane Kalimangalnuk said as he took his brother in his arms and embraced him tightly. "Please bear with me and let me have this. Ours has been a life of misery and hunger for almost a century. Why not entertain ourselves from time to time? Please indulge my simple need for love from this exquisitely beautiful woman. I beg this of you brother."

With that, Pane Nagdombilan's tense frame relaxed as his brother's words calmed his indignant heart. "Very well kakteh, what would you like to do?"

Pane Kalimangalnuk stood and turned towards Innawagan saying, "We shall test them kakteh. We shall see if they are warriors that can serve us and even go so far as aid us in our search for the beings that sleep in the mountains."

He crouched down to where Innawagan was kneeling on the floor and lifted her face up by her chin so that their eyes might meet. "If they are worthy enough warriors, they get to be with their sister and become family. But should they fail, then I will lock them in a rakuh so small and narrow that all they can do is stand. There will not be enough room to kneel, sit, or lay down as they slowly die from starvation or go insane; whichever comes first."

"Do you think it a fair arrangement mavid?" Pane Kalimangalnuk asked Innawagan.

Knowing how cruel and evil his intentions might be, it would still be better than letting her brothers die outright. It might also give her enough time to think of a way to escape and save them if she could. So, with great reluctance, Innawagan answered, "Yes."

*****

Ammani was the last to emerge from the ripple. Before stepping through, Ammani saw his older brother Talimannog step through followed by the two kumaws and then by his twin Anibo. He was apprehensive at first but the shame of being labeled a coward by his siblings was something he could never bear. So, with his eyes closed tight and a deep breath he held in his chest, Ammani took a step forward and stepped through.

Ammani felt a strange sensation on every surface of his body. The feeling felt similar to someone who accidentally ran through a spider web they didn't notice. Having felt no pain, Ammani opened his eyes and exhaled. But what he beheld; he could not comprehend.

In front of him stood his brothers and the kumaws. But what lay in front of them was nothing short of otherworldly. They all stood outside in the open air but in a place that they have never been before. They were at the bottom of a deep chasm surrounded by a waterfall that spread all around them. The water fell into an even deeper crevasse and disappeared into a mist.

No more than twenty feet in front of them was a tower of stone that had hundreds of steps carved along its face. The steps looked slippery and led all the way up to the surface of the hole.

"Where are we?" Ammani asked under his breath. "How did we end up outside?"

"I have no idea wadi," Talimannog answered. "Dalawesan, could you and your sister fly up and see where exactly we are?"

"As you wish Hapu," Dalawesan answered. "Dundunan, let's go."

The kumaws flew up towards the opening of the crevasse as quickly as they could. When they neared the very top, they saw a ledge where the steps ended, and on the ledge was a massive golden door. The door was shaped like an arch that tapered to a point in the middle. Inside the arch were double doors made of the same metallic gold-like material. Both the arch and the doors were smooth in texture and bore no visible markings of any kind.

"What is that brother?" Dundunan asked.

"I don't have the slightest clue," Dalawesan answered.

"I have never seen a golden door in Kalupaan, nor did I know they existed in this realm. Let's keep going up and see where we are."

But as the kumaws flew past the ledge and mouth of the chasm, they felt a familiar sensation of passing through something that blocked their path. Then just as quickly as they could blink, water started splashing all over them. To their surprise, they found themselves flying past the bottom of the crevasse where the brothers stood!

The kumaws were disoriented and confused. They couldn't understand what was happening, so they landed back where they began; right beside where the brothers stood.

"What happened?!" Talimannog asked perplexed. "I saw you fly up and vanish into thin air. How did you end up back here in the bottom?"

"We don't understand it as well," Dalawesan answered. "The sky got brighter as we got higher. And as soon as I blinked my eyes, I found myself flying up from the crevasse below."

"Did you see anything when you were up there?" Anibo asked the kumaws.

"The steps stop at a ledge just before the opening of the chasm," Dundunan replied. "And on the ledge is a door made of gold."

"I don't see anywhere else we could go through to

leave this place," Talimannog said. "I suppose we must all go through that door. Dalawesan and Dundunan, you have to carry us up there. It would probably be safer if both of you carried us up there one by one."

"But that would be cheating," A booming voice suddenly shouted out to them from atop the ledge.

"It's them!" Ammani exclaimed. "They took our sister!"

"Dalawesan! Dundunan! Attack them!" Talimannog commanded the kumaws who took off even before Talimannog finished his command.

"Where did you take Hapu Innawagan?!" Dundunan cried out to the manulib brothers as she flew straight at them. "Give her back to us, now!"

"Attacking us here in my rakuh is a very bad idea kumaw," Pane Kalimangalnuk said as he just calmly stood there by the edge of the ledge. "Don't kill them kakteh. At least not yet."

Pane Nagdombilan nodded to his brother and stepped forward. As soon as the kumaws were only a stone's throw away from them, he raised both his hands in front of him. Suddenly, two golden chains sprang forth from out of thin air behind the kumaws and spun straight for them. The chains wrapped themselves around the kumaws and hurled them against the face of the tower and buried each of its ends into the rock.

The kumaws gave a thunderous squawk as their bodies slammed against the tower's hard surface.

"Dalawesan! Dundunan!" Talimannog cried out in horror as he witnessed what befell their kumaw agoms.

"Do not fret Talimannog," Pane Kalimangalnuk said in his thunderous voice. "The kumaws are well and will stay so if you and your siblings can pass my challenges."

"What challenges?!" Talimannog exclaimed. "Where is Innawagan? What do you want from us?"

"I already have what I want Talimannog. I have your exquisitely beautiful sister and she will be my wife soon enough. What I am doing to you and your siblings right now is because of Innawagan. Call this my wedding gift to her if you wish."

"We don't understand," Ammani said quizzically. "What is going on? Is our sister well?"

"Hay!" Pane Kalimangalnuk sighed in exasperation. "You must be the stupid one then. Allow me to explain. The first thing you must know is our names. I am Pane Kalimangalnuk, and this is my younger sibling Pane Nagdombilan. We are manulibs which automatically makes us far superior to you in strength, powers, and abilities. This ultimately renders the possibility of you killing us next to impossible, so do not waste time even trying it.

"As I mentioned earlier, I am making Innawagan my

wife. For even attempting to kill us with your arrows last night, we should just dispatch all of you right now. But fortunately for you, your sister begged that we spare all your lives, both as a favor to her and as my servants.

"Hence the challenges. I told my wife to be that if you and your siblings pass my challenges then I will allow you to live and be our servants. But failing them on the other hand is something I wouldn't recommend. Failing will warrant all of you a fate worse than death."

"Worse than death? How could anything be worse than death?" Anibo asked dumbfoundedly.

"Failing any one of my challenges would mean imprisonment," Pane Kalimangalnuk said and grinned. "Imprisonment by me means that each of you will be trapped in a dark room only big enough for you to stand but too small for you to sit or lay down. There you will stay for as long as I wish, away from the freedom of death. You will live, suffer, starve, and thirst for years until your mind shatters into a thousand pieces."

Pane Nagdombilan could not help but chuckle at his brother's cruelty.

"But what will we get if we succeed and pass your challenges?" Talimannog asked.

"You get to be with your sister at our side and in grateful servitude to our every whim," Pane Nagdombilan finally spoke. "But whether you succeed or not, all of your lives now belong to us."

"Then it seems my siblings and I have no other choice but to succeed. Explain what this first challenge is and what we have to do." Talimannog asked the manulib brothers.

"Good, good! It is good that you understand the futility of doing anything else," Pane Kalimangalnuk said with a triumphant smile. "This first challenge is very simple; this is a speed challenge. All you have to do is reach my kakteh's *sakbawan* (golden door) at the top of this ledge and pass through it. You may use the small steps carved at the face of the tower to get here."

"Pane Kalimangalnuk, may I ask something of you before you begin the challenge?" Dundunan asked as she struggles from the grip of the golden chains.

"Speak fast kumaw," Pane Kalimangalnuk said, a bit annoyed at the interruption.

"Might I ask that you release my siblings and I from these chains? We promise not to interfere with your challenges and provide no aid to the brothers whatsoever. I would also ask if I may join Hapu Innawagan wherever she is being held. You see I am bound to her and every moment we are apart is an agony I needlessly endure."

"Very well," Pane Kalimangalnuk replied. "Kakteh, release the kumaws."

Pane Nagdombilan was a little hesitant at first but

knowing how consumed his older brother was with Innawagan at that point, he did as he was told without question.

The kumaws flew toward the manulib brothers and landed next to them. Each kumaw stared at the two brothers intently for a few seconds. "You were human once," Dalawesan said as he eyed each brother. "Your magic was given to you; agimat!"

"You are quite observant kumaw," Pane Nagdombilan said begrudgingly. "Though I am not surprised that creatures as old as you two noticed that almost instantly."

"But it matters not," Pane Kalimangalnuk interjected. "Older you kumaws might be, we are still far more powerful. But since you've angered my kakteh, I am changing my decision concerning who gets to see my betrothed."

Both kumaws were taken aback by this. Dundunan opened her wings and looked at her brother for a second as if awaiting his signal to attack. But Dalawesan being the agom of Talimannog and not Innawagan's was a little more temperamental and level-headed than his sister. He shook his head slightly as if to say *don't do it, we will not survive a fight with them.* Dundunan eased herself and folded her wings back against her body.

"That was a good decision kumaw," Pane Kalimangalnuk said. "Had you and your sister decided to attack us then both of you would be dead right now. For being the smarter kumaw, I will allow you to go to my beloved Innawagan and tell her that I've kept my word and spared her brothers. Go through the sakbawan and do as I command."

Pane Kalimangalnuk pointed his finger at the golden doors which suddenly swung open. Dalawesan nodded and flew through them without hesitation.

"As for you," Pane Kalimangalnuk said as he turned his gaze toward Dundunan. "Go down to the brothers and give them my instructions."

*****

Dundunan flew down to Talimannog and his brothers. As soon as she landed on her feet Talimannog asked, "What happened up there? Where is Dalawesan?"

"And what of the challenge?" Anibo asked as well.

"Dalawesan was sent to Hapu Innawagan to be with her. I was left here to aid you in the challenge but not physically help any of you," Dundunan answered. "We don't have any time to waste. Please Hapu Talimannog, Anibo, and Ammani start running up those steps now!"

"I don't understand what's going on..." Ammani was saying this when suddenly he felt something cool wash across his feet. Everybody looked down and was surprised to see that the water from the waterfalls had suddenly filled the crevasse and was overflowing… fast!

"Run!" Talimannog said as he and his brothers instinctively knew what the challenge actually was. They needed to get up those steps or drown!

Anibo being the faster runner, reached the foot of the steps first. To his horror, he realized how arduous the challenge actually was when he saw the steps up close. Each step was a small, narrow slab of rock that stuck out of the rockface like a splinter of wood. They were only long enough to accommodate one person with an almost rounded surface which made standing on them even harder.

"Go! Stop looking at the steps and start running up them!" Ammani yelled at his twin. As soon as Anibo felt the water touch his feet again, he bolted up the steps as quickly as he could.

"Faster wadi!" Talimannog yelled out to Anibo as he was bringing up the rear and the person whose feet were constantly wet.

It was fortunate for the brothers that they'd spent most of their lives climbing up and down hills and mountains. This gave them impeccable agility as they traversed the slippery steps that led up to the ledge where the sakbawan was. But as fast as they ran up those steps, they couldn't outrun the rising water.

"Please hurry Hapu!" Dundunan yelled at the brothers

as she flew right next to them as they climbed. "The water rises as fast as you run! You must go faster!"

But as Dundunan flew by Talimannog, she suddenly noticed a shadow emerge from under the water and just below her feet. A split second later, a large snout and dagger-like teeth sprang from the water and tried to ensnare her in its mouth. But Dundunan was far too agile and managed to fly higher and avoid the predator.

"Crocodile!" Dundunan yelled out as she flew even higher to get a better view. "There are two very large crocodiles swimming in the water! Hapu Talimannog, run faster!"

Upon hearing Dundunan's cry of crocodile, Talimannog slowed down and started looking back at the water lapping at his feet. With absolute horror, Talimannog saw the second crocodile swimming toward him no less than five feet away. A heartbeat later, the crocodile lunged at him from the surface of the water!

Talimannog managed to leap out of the way of the crocodile's snout and rows of pointed teeth at the last second. He landed three steps in front of him and almost lost his footing as he did. Luckily, he managed to cling to a small indentation on the rock wall with his left hand and righted himself. But his sigh of relief was short-lived after only a few seconds as the water continued to rise and the crocodile reared its head towards him for another attempt to grab his legs. *Agay! I have to keep moving!* He thought to himself as he started running back up the steps.

"Don't stop Hapu Talimannog!" Dundunan yelled as she flew by him. "The second crocodile is coming as well, and I am not allowed to help you lest Pane Kalimangalnuk decides to punish all of you if I do."

"I understand!" Talimannog retorted in short gasping breaths. "Just tell me if they are closing in on me."

The journey to the top leading to the ledge was arduous and exhausting. All in all, there were five hundred and twenty slippery steps that the brothers had to pass through. They all slipped on more than one occasion but luckily managed to right themselves and continue. The pain in all their legs burned in every single muscle as their ribs ached and cramped as they persevered.

Almost an hour later, the twins finally reached the top of the steps and fell on the open surface of the ledge in exhaustion. Their entire body cramped and forced them to stretch out every fiber of leg muscle that they had just to get them to finally relax.

Talimannog, being the bulkier brother was still around twenty steps behind. For almost half an hour, the water kept catching up to his feet as he ran. The crocodile closest to him at the time almost managed to snag his legs on more than one occasion had it not been for Dundunan's warnings. Talimannog knew that exhaustion was only a few moments away from getting the better of him, but he also knew that he was only a few more steps away from salvation.

As his vision started to blur and everything was starting to get dark, Talimannog once again heard Dundunan's screams of warning ring out next to him. "Jump Hapu! It's right behind you!"

Without any real or conscious thought, Talimannog instinctively followed the kumaw's command and leapt forward and skipped a step.

The crocodile's gaping mouth missed Talimannog's left leg by a hair and instead accidentally broke off the step that he was on. The piece of protruding rock broke off and fell into the crocodile's gullet and began choking the beast. The crocodile swam off as it thrashed its head violently trying to dislodge the piece of rock.

Though fortunate yet again in avoiding yet another attack, Talimannog's luck finally ran out as soon as his feet landed on the step he leapt to. For the first time since he began running up the steps, Talimannog was unable to grab hold of anything to steady himself. He lost his footing and fell into the rising water with one more crocodile left that swam straight toward him as soon as he splashed down.

"No!" Talimannog heard Dundunan scream as soon as

he hit the water. And when the cold icy water enveloped his hard burning leg muscles, both his legs cramped up, and the act of treading water simply to stay afloat fell to his arms alone.

My legs hurt too much! He thought to himself. *I'm going to drown.* But when he turned his head to his left and saw the crocodile's mouth open less than three feet away his next thought was. *Maybe not.*

But just when all hope had left Talimannog, as he accepted his fate to be devoured by a crocodile, an arrow flew from out of nowhere and struck the beast in the right eye! The crocodile veered its head away and instinctively dove down to the depths of the water.

He turned his head around and realized the water level had already reached the level of the ledge. And there on the ledge stood Ammani with a bow in one hand and the other reaching for another arrow. By Ammani's feet was Anibo on his knees with his right hand stretched out, calling out to him. "Akka! Grab my hand!"

A few moments later, each twin had their older brother by an arm as they dragged him out of the water. As soon as Talimannog felt the hard solid ground under him, he thought his brothers would stop and help him get the cramps out of his legs. But to his surprise, his brothers kept dragging him through the wet surface of the ledge.

"Stop!" Talimannog ordered his brothers. "Put me

down and…"

"No time akka!" Anibo interjected and continued to drag him on the ledge.

Talimannog was going to ask why his brothers wouldn't stop but then he saw Dundunan flying over them. "Don't stop! We're almost there! The crocodile is right behind you!"

Talimannog looked down past his cramped legs and saw the other crocodile who apparently managed to dislodge the rock in its gullet barreling after them. "Go! Go!" Talimannog yelled at his brothers as they reached the sakbawan that opened as soon as they reached it.

Ammalabukaw (Map)

ᜀ ᜋ᜔ ᜋ ᜎ ᜊᜓ ᜃ ᜏ᜔

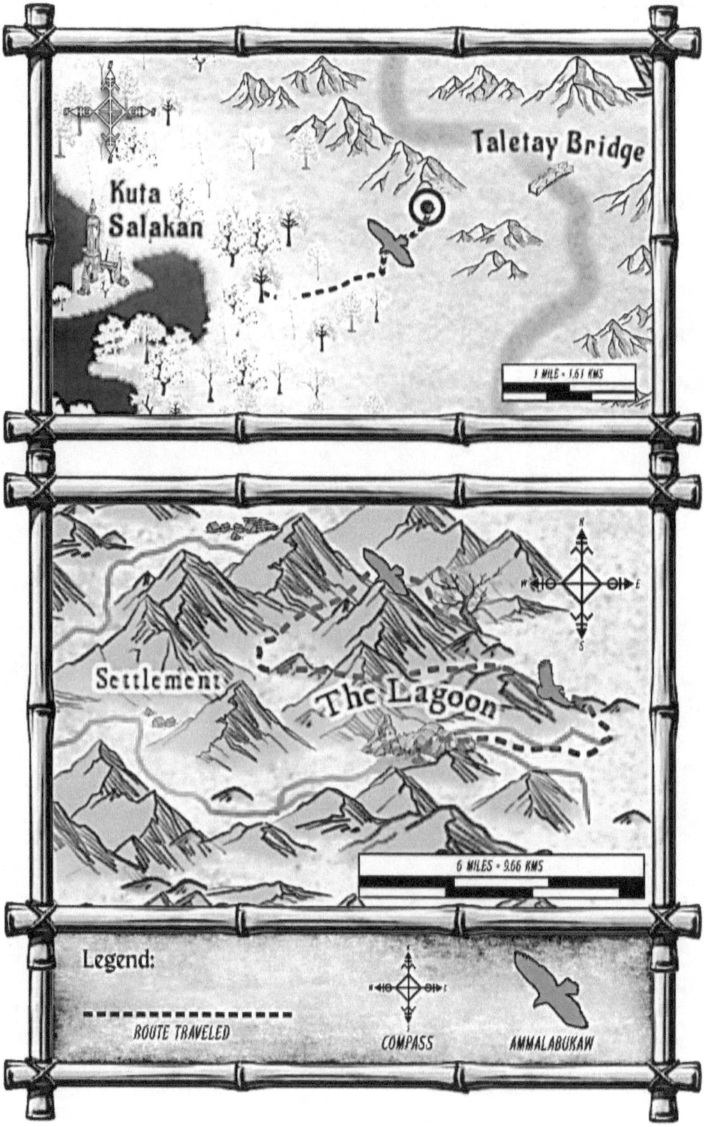

Chapter 10

Ammalabukaw

ᜀᜋ᜔ᜋᜎᜊᜓᜃᜏ᜔

As soon as Dalawesan entered the sakbawan, he found himself passing through a dark, narrow tunnel. Fortunately for him, the tunnel was wide enough to accommodate his wings which allowed him to continue flying.

He saw a yellow light from a torch that marked the end of the tunnel. He flew towards it and exited into a large stone room with four other doors and a high domed roof. In the middle of that room stood Innawagan.

“Hapu Innawagan!” Dalawesan exclaimed and landed next to her.

“Dalawesan! Thank the Poons! Is that really you?” Innawagan said as she wrapped her arms around the neck of the kumaw.

“Yes, Hapu it is I,” Dalawesan answered. “I came here with your siblings and my sister to find and rescue you.”

“Just my brothers? Where is Alig? Did something happen to her?” Innawagan asked worriedly.

“Your sister is fine. Hapu Alig hit her head when you were taken. Hapu Talimannog told her to stay behind and recuperate as we went out in search of you,” Dalawesan answered. “How are you? Are you hurt? Did the manulib do something to hurt you?”

"I am unharmed, for now. Pane Kalimangalnuk wants to take me as his wife against my will."

"I've heard him tell us as much before I left the others behind to come to you," Dalawesan said.

"Left behind? Please tell me what happened. Are my siblings alive and well? Why isn't Dundunan the one who came to see me? Not that I mind your presence which truly brings hope." Innawagan asked.

"You brothers are currently going through a challenge set before them by Pane Kalimangalnuk. A challenge apparently requested by you," Dalawesan said.

"It was either that or Pane Nagdombilan would kill all of you outright," Innawagan said in her defense. "The challenges buy us more time. Time we might be able to use to find a way out of here."

"Then all you did was prolong their deaths and made them suffer needlessly," a hoarse guttural voice suddenly said. "For there is no possible way for you to leave."

Innawagan and Dalawesan looked up to where the voice came from and to their astonishment, a large red kumaw descended on them from above. Dalawesan instinctively shielded Innawagan with his wings as the red kumaw landed and stood next to them.

"That's him!" Innawagan exclaimed. "That is the kumaw that attacked me and Alig! That's the kumaw that abducted me!"

As soon as Ammalabukaw landed, Dalawesan turned to face him with his wings slightly opened and his head lowered and postured to attack. He immediately recognized his old friend and companion, but something was very different about him since the last time they met.

The first thing that Dalawesan noticed was the difference in Ammalabukaw's voice; it was very hoarse and guttural. Then he saw a large scar under Ammalabukaw's throat where the feathers stopped growing. Something horrible happened to his old friend aside from being shot down by arrows.

"Calm yourself Dalawesan," Ammalabukaw said as softly as his mangled voice could resonate. "I did not come here to do either of you any harm."

"You're alive! How is that possible?" Dalawesan asked without lowering his guard. "I saw you struck with arrows and fall to your doom."

"And as I did, I saw you struck down yourself. Yet here you are," Ammalabukaw replied.

"My sister and I fell into balete trees and were transported to Kalupaan. But you were struck even before we reached the forest. How did you survive such a thing? And why are you doing the bidding of these manulib humans?" Dalawesan asked as he slowly lowered his guard noticing that Ammalabukaw meant neither of them any harm.

"The answer to both your questions is a tale I am willing to tell you if you wish to hear it," Ammalabukaw answered.

"Yes, please," Innawagan answered for Dalawesan. "Dundunan spoke of you before, as did Dalawesan. From what they've told us, you were a close friend to them and served the Poons of Kaluwalhatian for many decades."

"You speak the truth Innawagan," Ammalabukaw replied. "I am... was very close to Dalawesan and Dundunan. We were loyal messengers to the Poons and served them well in the war. But that all changed when I fell and landed an inch away from death's door.

"As Dalawesan probably told you, we were on our way to Kuta Salakan to meet up with Poong Kedes when we were ambushed by the danag. As he probably told you as well, I was the first to be shot down.

"The first arrow struck me on my right wing, but luckily went right through it. The pain was horrendous, but I knew I would still manage to keep myself in the air. I was about to call out to you and your sister when another arrow struck me in the chest.

"That second arrow pierced one of my lungs and drove the wind out of me. Then another arrow struck me on my left wing and buried itself deep in the bone. That was when I started to fall from the sky. I even remember seeing you struck down as well when I turned my back just before I hit the ground. I was actually very lucky that I unconsciously turned the way that I did. Had I not, the arrow embedded in my chest would have hit the ground and buried itself deeper, killing me for sure.

"I passed out after that. The next thing I knew was feeling a hand grab my throat just under my beak and a sharp slicing pain running along my throat. I opened my eyes and saw a danag standing over me with its pale bald head and red eyes salivating as it sliced open my throat.

"I distinctively remember looking up and seeing Nabuangan Forest glowing brightly less than a couple of miles from me. I remember chuckling in my head as I thought how unfortunate I was to fall so close to salvation yet just far enough for oblivion to reach me. But just as I surrendered myself to the inevitable, something miraculous happened.

"An arrow suddenly struck the danag at the side of its misshapen head and killed it. I looked in the direction where the arrow came from and saw a small hukbo of anggitay and alagad warriors charging straight for the danag archers.

"In retrospect, I suppose I should also consider myself fortunate that the small hukbo just so happens to be patrolling that area at that exact time. A skirmish ensued as can be expected.

"As the chaos of the battle continued, I managed to get

on my feet and slowly walked away from the fight and headed towards the forest. The last thing I wanted was to be caught by a stray arrow or get accidentally trampled by an unsuspecting anggitay.

"I don't recall much of what happened as I walked. The trauma of everything that had just happened was taking its toll on my body. I do remember trying to call out to you hoping that you or your sister survived the fall as well. But the gash on my throat had done significant damage and all I could produce was the gurgling sound of my own blood.

"I honestly couldn't say who won the battle that I had just walked away from. Had the alagad warriors and anggitay succeeded in routing the danag, then why didn't they come to help? Had the danag won, then why didn't they finish me off? Ultimately it didn't matter.

"I reached Nabuangan Forest after a long, painful, and arduous trek. As I said before, much of my memory during that time was obscured by pain and suffering. I do recall walking up to a balete tree and resting my body next to it before I collapsed. The next thing I knew when I opened my eyes was being surrounded by greenery.

"I had awakened in a jungle in Kalupaan next to a balete tree. How long I was unconscious was unknown to me, all I knew was that it was enough to invigorate me enough to get to my feet again. After looking around and realizing where I was, my first thought was to return to Kaluwalhatian and hope an alagad or anggitay would find and help me.

"But the opening of the balete tree was too high up in its trunk for me to reach and the arrow embedded in my wing prevented me from doing anything except walk. So, walk I did, aimlessly through a dense jungle with no direction whatsoever. My only hope was to find help, whether it be from an enkanto or a kind-hearted human. But as night fell over the jungle, my fortunes changed very little.

"I kept myself nourished by feeding on small rodents or monkeys that were even more forlorn than I was, and I drank from a stream that had crossed my path. For three days and nights, I followed that stream hoping that it would eventually lead me to a human encampment and provide my aid. But for three days and nights, my unfortunate situation worsened.

"The arrows still embedded in my body weakened me with each passing day. It eventually got to a point where no matter how much I rested, ate, or drank my body would simply not get better. On the fourth day of my following the stream, I eventually ended up in a place where the stream fell into a lagoon.

"My heart sank faster than the water fell knowing that the lagoon meant the end of my journey. It was dusk when I stood at the edge of the rock face just above the lagoon. I was too weak and tired from everything that had happened and just decided to surrender my fate to the waters below.

"As I sank beneath the cold water, I saw something I could not believe. I saw two humans standing by the edge of a short ledge looking down on me as I sank. The humans had a copper tinge to their skin and yellow eyes. What followed next was darkness. The cold, empty, and comforting embrace of nothingness.

"When I opened my eyes next, I found myself inside a cave. There was a fire burning near me that provided warmth and the arrows embedded in my chest and wing had been removed. The wounds that they caused were covered in poultices and bandages. And there next to me stood the two strange humans with yellow eyes.

"They asked me questions when they saw me stir awake. They introduced themselves as Pane Kalimangalnuk and Pane Nagdombilan. They knew I was of Kaluwalhatian but were uncertain as to what I was. They apparently have never seen a kumaw before.

"We talked for several hours as Pane Kalimangalnuk gave me water to drink and fed me rodents, fish, and monkeys. I could tell Pane Nagdombilan wasn't too particularly fond of me, but his older brother somehow welcomed my presence.

"They asked me about the immortal realm of Kaluwalhatian, the Poons, the enkantos, and about all manner of beings. Pane Kalimangalnuk told me their life story and how they became manulib much like how he told you. Then they asked if I knew anything about *those who sleep within the mountains*. Unfortunately, I knew nothing of such beings. But if a mamaw is looking for such creatures, then it does not bode well for anybody.

"I told them about the Kanibusanan, the great war. I warned them that beings from Kasanaan were not to be trusted. Pane Kalimangalnuk said that it was too late for them and that they were beyond caring about the struggles of others. All that he and his brother cared about was being freed of the agimat that had claimed them.

"After more than a week of nursing me back to health, I had finally regained enough strength to leave the cave and stretch my wings. I took flight for the first time a day later.

"But like Dalawesan and Dundunan whom I assumed never returned to Kaluwalhatian, I developed a bond with Pane Kalimangalnuk and owed him a life debt. I pledged my loyalty to them and over the next three years, I helped them seek out caves and other subterranean entrances in their search for the sleeping beings.

"We would go out and conduct our search for months at a time. Yet every now and again, the brothers always return to this very cave and lagoon to rest when the pain of their hunger and thirst overwhelms them. Though I know you see them as evil beings who have taken you and your siblings against your will, should you ever see them hunched over and crying in pain, your heart would break for them as mine does every time it happens.

"Then one day from out of the blue, you and your siblings appeared at the lagoon. Pane Kalimangalnuk was instantly smitten when he saw you. He would have taken you and killed your siblings then and there had I not seen my fellow kumaws with you and your siblings. Just the knowledge that they were with you somehow told me that killing your siblings might not yield the most optimum outcome.

"So I begged Pane Kalimangalnuk to hold off taking you for a few nights. I begged him to let me spy on you as well as my fellow kumaws before he would take any action against you and your family. He agreed and for the next two nights, I flew over to your huts and watched."

"You were there?" Dalawesan asked puzzled. "How was it that my sister or I didn't see or hear you?"

"Pane Kalimangalnuk created a rakuh over your dwellings from where I could fly unnoticed and observe all of you," Ammalabukaw replied. "Then on the night that his desire for you reached its pinnacle, Pane Kalimangalnuk ordered me to take you. I asked him again to spare your siblings, especially Talimannog to whom I knew you owed your life debt. Pane Kalimangalnuk agreed, and you know what happened next."

"Then I have just one last question to ask you," Innawagan said. "Will you allow Dalawesan to carry me out of here and return to my siblings?"

"No," Ammalabukaw answered with certitude. "Though it is highly unlikely that you can escape this rakuh on your own, I was ordered to make sure you didn't escape."

A sudden tension filled the space between the two kumaws. After hearing Ammalabukaw's last statement, Dalawesan was already assessing his chances of besting his old friend in a fight to the end. Ammalabukaw noticed the change in Dalawesan's demeanor and said, "Please don't. You cannot win nor do I want to kill you."

After hearing this, Innawagan placed a hand on the back of Dalawesan's head and told the kumaw, "There is no need for that. Akka Talimannog will be greatly saddened if you died for nothing, and so shall your sister." To which Dalawesan responded by calming himself.

"That was a wise choice kumaw." Pane Kalimangalnuk suddenly said as he appeared behind one of the doors. "You would have surely perished had you acted brashly."

"What happened to siblings?" Innawagan asked.

“They are being tested, just as you wished them to be. Right now, it seems they are about to succeed in escaping my first rakuh.” Pane Kalimangalnuk said as he approached Ammalabukaw and petted his head.

“Please let me see them,” Innawagan begged. “Please let me see them as a token of your love for me.”

“As a symbol of my love mavid, I will grant you your request,” Pane Kalimangalnuk said as he waved his right hand to the floor in front of Innawagan and Dalawesan.

At first, Innawagan thought that the manulib was granting her an exit to go to her brothers. But that hope was short-lived when she saw a pool of water seep through the solid rock beneath her feet, appearing from out of nowhere. The small pool swirled into a perfect circle on the ground as images started appearing on the pool’s surface.

Innawagan saw Talimannog being dragged by his arms by the twins as they carried him across a flooded ledge. Behind them, she saw a large crocodile barreling after them. “Agay!” Innawagan exclaimed. “Is this real?”

“Yes, it is mavid,” Pane Kalimangalnuk replied. “You asked if you could see your siblings and so there they are. You can see and hear everything that is happening to them, but they in turn cannot hear nor see you.”

Pane Kalimangalnuk approached the pool and said, “Judging from what I see, it seems I am needed to present them with the second challenge.

"Pray to the Poons mavid, pray for your siblings," Pane Kalimangalnuk said as he turned and headed out one of the doors. "They will need them."

Chapter 11

The Second Rakuh

The brothers and the Dundunan emerged in a clearing surrounded by thick, uncompromising foliage. Just like it was in the first rakuh, they emerged from a ripple out of thin air with no visible way back to where they came from.

The overhead canopy was as dense and thick as the surrounding jungle that surrounded them. Flying over it was an impossibility for Dundunan, forcing the kumaw to fly no higher than a few feet above the brothers' heads. The only way forward was to follow a narrow path that led somewhere deeper into the jungle.

“Where are we?” Anibo asked as he let go of Talimannog’s arm. “Are we in another one of Pane Kalimangalnuk’s… what did he call it?”

“Rakuh,” Talimannog answered as he got to his feet. “He said these places that he creates are called rakuhs.”

“The canopy overhead is too thick to fly through Hapu,” Dundunan said as she inspected the jungle canopy. “Though I suspect that within these rakuhs, I can only fly to places that Pane Kalimangalnuk allows me to get to.”

“There is a narrow path through the jungle over there,” Ammani said, pointing to the path. “I don’t see another way through. I guess we don't really have a choice."

"Agreed," Talimannog said. "But be vigilant papatwadi, nothing is ever what it seems in a rakuh."

The brothers followed the narrow path which wound its way deeper and deeper into the dense jungle. The path itself was less than ten feet wide and in some places, only around five. The whole ordeal was confining at best, but luckily for them, small pockets of sunlight found their way through several small gaps in the jungle canopy that illuminated their way.

Their trek was uneventful at first but after a short while, they all started to hear a strange yet familiar sound coming from the trees and foliage flanking them. "What is that?" Ammani asked.

"It sounded like… like a croak!" Anibo said perplexed.

"They do sound like frogs Hapu," Dundunan said. "But whatever they are, we should not trust them to be safe. Not in a place like this. We should hurry forward."

"Go!" Talimannog commanded.

*****

Innawagan and Dalawesan stood over the magical pool and watched as their siblings hiked through the dense jungle. Pane Kalimangalnuk had left a few minutes ago, which left only Pane Nagdombilan with them as he stood guard.

"What are you doing to our papatwadi next?" Innawagan asked the stoic manulib that just stood over the pool motionless. "Answer me! I want to know what sort of demented game you and your brother have in store for our family this time."

Pane Nagdombilan did not respond.

"I said answer me!" Innawagan yelled again as Pane Nagdombilan continued to stand there unresponsive and unmoving like a statue.

"Agay! Just answer my question! What are you and your brother planning to do to them?" Innawagan raved as she picked up a small rock and hurled it at Pane Nagdombilan's face.

"Hapu don't!" Dalawesan cried out as soon as he saw Innawagan throw the rock.

But just before the rock struck Pane Nagdombilan in the face, something darted out from the darkness behind him and snatched the rock midflight.

"What was that?!" Innawagan gasped and fell back.

"Stay behind me Hapu!" Dalawesan said as he instinctively stood between her and the manulib with his wings spread out.

Pane Nagdombilan turned to the two and smiled at them. "You said you wanted to know."

*****

The brothers and Dundunan followed what seemed to be an endless path through the unrealistically dense jungle. They had to stop twice to rest and eat just to sustain themselves to go on farther. All the while the croaking sounds that followed them on their hike only got louder and louder as they went.

"I swear if I ever find those frogs, I will make a tasty meal out of them!" Anibo cried out in annoyance.

"But that's just it Hapu," Dundunan replied. "We can't seem to actually see them. I hear them following us in the bushes and behind the trees, but I too cannot seem to find them. Even with my keener eyesight."

"Maybe this is a test of patience *abeng* (brother)," Ammani retorted. "And if it is, then you are failing miserably."

"Try not to talk too much wadi," Talimannog told his younger brothers. "You need to conserve your strength and stamina. We still have no clue as to how far this jungle path goes. Dundunan, could you please fly ahead and see if there is any end in sight?"

"At once Hapu," Dundunan answered as she flew ahead of the brothers.

Dundunan only went ahead by a mile when something new finally came about from the jungle. She came upon an abrupt end to the jungle path that led to an open area of mangrove trees and a muddy swamp. *Poons save us! This swamp just came out of nowhere!* Dundunan thought to herself.

Unnatural as this place might be, at least the canopy isn't as dense. Dundunan thought as she flew over the mangrove trees. A star-filled night sky and an eerily large full moon greeted her as she passed the top of the mangrove jungle. It didn't take long for her to ascend before she noticed the rippling in the air blanketing the entire sky. *Best not to go past the ripple. I might not like where I end up if I do.*

She flew around the swamp for a short while until she saw something golden glinting about a mile or two from where she flew. She headed straight for it knowing that it was most likely the sakbawan that they sought and the exit that the brothers needed to reach.

But as she got closer to the door, the croaking sounds returned and in greater number. *It's those damnable frogs again!* She thought as she flew closer to the sakbawan. But with every foot that she flew closer to the golden door, the louder the croaking sounds became. So loud in fact, that by the time she could make out the details of the sakbawan, she could hear dozens, if not a hundred frogs croaking underneath the mangrove trees.

This is far enough. Dundunan thought as she turned around and headed back to the brothers. *I need to tell Hapu Talimannog and the twins what I saw.*

All three brothers were already near the edge of the jungle when Dundunan arrived.

"Where did this swamp come from?!" Anibo said perplexed as soon as they cleared the jungle.

"There akka," Ammani said as he pointed to their left. "I see Dundunan."

"Hapu Talimannog," Dundunan said as she landed next to the brothers. "I saw the sakbawan. I know where it is."

"Good. Can you fly us there one by one?" Talimannog asked.

"Unfortunately, I cannot," Dundunan regretfully answered. "It is close to two miles away. I do not possess the strength nor the fortitude to carry you or your siblings that far."

"And as I said before, that would be cheating!" Pane Kalimangalnuk said from behind the brothers.

Startled and completely taken off guard, all three brothers jump at Pane Kalimangalnuk's voice. But years of being experienced hunters as well as having won a few fights have honed their reflexes to instinctively draw their bows and take aim at the intruder.

"Loose those arrows at me and this entire game we are playing ends with all of you begging to die!" Pane Kalimangalnuk threatened the brothers without so much as moving an inch.

"Lower your weapons wadi," Talimannog commanded his younger siblings. "They serve us no purpose in this fight."

"Are you sure akka?" Ammani asked hesitantly.

"Do it!" Talimannog said with more authority. "He is beyond our skills and weapons."

"A wise choice Talimannog," Pane Kalimangalnuk said and grinned at the proud Aeta warrior. "Something your beautiful sister would appreciate very much."

"How is Hapu Innawagan?" Dundunan asked.

"Your master is quite safe and well," Pane Kalimangalnuk answered. "She and your brother are being kept company by mine as well as your old friend, Ammalabukaw."

"So, it was him who took Hapu!" Dundunan exclaimed. "How did he survive the danag?"

"That is a question I do not care to answer," Pane Kalimangalnuk said as he approached the brothers. "But I will answer the question that is currently buzzing around Talimannog's head as we speak."

"What do you want of us?" Talimannog said softly.

"Yes! Finally, a question of substance," he answered. "I want you to do the same exact thing you did in my last rakuh; reach my kekteh's sakbawan and make it to my next rakuh. The sooner you accomplish this, the sooner you get to see your sister and be our servants."

"But what you also said earlier was that you are testing us," Talimannog retorted. "What is the test?"

"Another good question Talimannog," Pane Kalimangalnuk said. "Earlier, I tested for your speed and agility. This time, I am testing your strength and resilience."

"And how exactly are you testing us this time?" Ammani asked.

"I won't actually," Pane Kalimangalnuk answered as he turned to the swamp water at his right. "But they will."

Bubbles started coming up from the water next to the manulib's feet. But even before anyone could say something, two gigantic toads emerged from the swamp. Each toad was as big as a dog with hideous warts and bumps covering their bodies.

One toad had a greenish hue while the other one was brown. They both had large bulging black and yellow eyes that looked at each brother intently.

"What kind of frogs are those?!" Anibo asked in horror and disgust. "They look like…"

But as Anibo stood there and pointed his hand towards one of the toads, the creature flicked its tongue out with lightning speed and ensnared Anibo's left arm! "Agay!" Anibo screamed as the toad tried to pull him in its gaping mouth.

As Anibo pulled against the monstrous toad,

Talimannog leapt into action and severed the creature's tongue with his bolo. As soon as the toad's severed tongue recoiled back in its mouth, Ammani loosed an arrow that struck the beast in the eye.

As all this unfolded, the second toad leapt forward and was about to flick its tongue at Talimannog. But the ever-vigilant Dundunan flew at the beast and caught its head in her talons. She buried her dagger-like talons deep into the toad's head and ripped it wide open.

As soon as the two monstrous toads were dead, they all turned their attention to Pane Kalimangalnuk in fear of what he might do to them for killing the toads. But to their relief, Pane Kalimangalnuk just smiled at them and slowly walked back toward the swamp. "Do what you must to get to the sakbawan," he said as he slowly sank beneath the water. "Kill as many toads as you wish. I even grant the kumaw permission to aid you.

"Pass through the golden doors, reach the next rakuh, and you pass this challenge. Anything else will mean eternity in a box." Pane Kalimangalnuk said as he vanished under the murky waters of the swamp.

"Whatever those frogs or toad creatures are, at least we know we can kill them," Talimannog said. "Dundunan, you can lead us to the sakbawan yes?"

"Yes Hapu," Dundunan answered. "It's not too far from here. But I must warn all of you that the closer we get to the sakbawan, the more of those creatures there are."

"Just what we need, more of these disgusting toad creatures!" Anibo complained as he pulled at the severed tongue still stuck to his forearm.

"Give me that!" Ammani exclaimed as he helped his twin brother unstick the tongue off of him."

"Agay! That hurt Ammani!" Anibo cried out as the tongue came off.

"We best prepare when we encounter these creatures when we reach the sakbawan," Talimannog said as he pointed to some mangrove branches. "Start cutting off a few vines and leafy branches. We need something to block those tongues from touching our skin."

*****

Less than an hour later, Dundunan and the brothers were on their way toward the sakbawan. All three brothers had managed to cover themselves with twigs and small branches that they gathered from the mangrove trees. They used whatever vines and roots they could get to tie their makeshift armor around their chest and back as well as substantial areas of their extremities.

"These are itchy akka!" Anibo complained.

"Stop complaining and focus!" Talimannog barked at his brother. "I can already hear those toad creatures up ahead. But I also think they are not the only creatures in this swamp."

They continued slowly along the muddy embankments, cautiously reacting to every sound and splash. Dundunan watched over them from above, ready to give them a quick warning as she too surveyed their surroundings as meticulously as possible.

They ran into a few venomous snakes along the way which they mostly stayed clear of. Once a crocodile came slinking up to them and tried to attack Anibo when he lost his footing and slipped into the water. Luckily, Dundunan saw the crocodile even before Anibo slipped and was able to kill it before it even got close to him.

Though the swamp was fraught with danger, the trio was able to skate unharmed. But that ended as soon as they were halfway to the sakbawan, and the croaking noises became louder.

"They're close!" Talimannog yelled out to his brothers as it was the only way they could hear him talk over the deafening sounds of the croaks that surrounded them. "Stick together! We need to watch each other's backs!"

"Akka! They're everywhere!" Ammani cried out when suddenly, a large sticky tongue flicked out from behind a shrub.

The tongue struck Ammani on his left shoulder which he, fortunately, was able to cover with some leaves and roots. The tongue had adhered itself to his leafy armor and ripped it off his body. "Agay!" Ammani exclaimed.

Upon seeing the tongue retract after it had stuck his brother's shoulder, Anibo was made aware of where the toad was hiding. He loosed one of his *patak* (arrow with a narrow iron arrowhead) arrows at the creature and killed it instantly.

"Over there!" Talimannog yelled as another toad leapt out of the water directly in front of him. He loosed a patak arrow of his own and killed the creature even before it had a chance to flick its tongue out at him.

But even before Talimannog could nock another arrow on his bow, another tongue struck him on his right arm and yanked his leafy armor off. This time, the creature was a gigantic version of a green treefrog clinging to the trunk of one of the mangrove trees.

The brothers had their backs to each other as more and more of the creatures came out of the woodwork and assailed them. They shot as many of the toads and frogs as they could but more and more kept coming. Dundunan tried her best to dive down and grab a toad or two, kill them between her talons, discard their bodies above the trees, and repeat.

But the sheer numbers of amphibians were beginning to overrun them. Though each arrow loosed killed one, they simply did not have enough arrows to win. "Run!" Talimannog commanded his siblings. "We need to make a run for the sakbawan! Now!"

The twins nodded in acknowledgment and complete unison, all three brothers started running towards the golden door. They tried their best to duck and dodge every tongue that assaulted them from every direction. But for every step they took, a piece of their leafy armor was being stripped away from them, twig by twig, branch by branch.

They only ran for about twenty feet when the first tongue finally made contact with bare skin. Talimannog felt something slam against his right calf muscle. A split second later, came a sudden jerk and Talimannog fell face-first into the mud.

He quickly anchored himself by grabbing onto a mangrove root and prevented himself from being dragged farther. He reached for his bolo and with one quick swing, Talimannog severed the tongue and jumped back onto his feet. He looked up and saw his brothers a dozen feet ahead of him. Without a second thought, he sprinted after them.

Anibo felt a tongue land on his back just below his right shoulder. It adhered itself to the root that tied several twigs that served as the coverings for his right shoulder. Though the tongue did not touch his skin, the root was securely tied to his chest. When the toad retracted its tongue, it sent Anibo spiraling down.

He felt himself being dragged toward the creature much like Talimannog was only a moment ago. Anibo was about to reach for his bolo when he felt a sudden slack in the tongue pulling at him. He felt strong hands grab him by the shoulders and hoist him up to his feet; it was Talimannog.

"Get up wadi!" Talimannog exclaimed as he lifted Anibo to his feet. "Pick up your bow and put it away. You'll need your bolo to cut away at those creatures' tongues!"

Anibo picked up his bow that he dropped in the mud and slung it to his back. "Akka, look out!" he cried out as he unsheathed his bolo and hacked at a tongue coming for Talimannog from an orange treefrog.

As the two brothers ran, they saw Ammani ahead of them get struck by two tongues from toads and a third tongue from a tree frog. Ammani was still on his feet as the three creatures dragged at him. One of the toads' tongues had Ammani by the wrist of his left hand while the second toad had him by the elbow on his right. To make matters worse, the tree frog had its tongue stuck to his neck. Try as he might, Ammani could not reach for his bolo and free himself from his predicament.

"Akka help me! Anibo!" Ammani cried out.

Though Talimannog and Anibo heard their brother's plea, they were still fifteen feet away and could not reach him in time before he got dragged into the water. But as luck would have it, Dundunan swooped in and buried her talons deep into both the toads' brains.

"I have them Hapu!" Dundunan said as she squeezed her grip even tighter, and a loud crack could be heard from the toad's skulls.

"*Pagyamanan* (Thank you)!" Ammani said as he reached for his bolo with his newly freed hand and severed the tree frog's tongue.

But just as Dundunan released her grip on the dead toads, three more tongues struck out from the water behind her and adhered to her back feathers. Two between her wings and one at the back of her head. Dundunan flapped her wings as hard as she could as she tried to free herself from the relentless creatures' grip, but spots along her body where the tongues pulled at her leeched the strength she could muster to take flight.

Suddenly, the tension from the tongues' pull gave way and shot Dundunan into the air with the severed tongues still stuck to her back. Talimannog and Anibo arrived and freed the kumaw. "Don't stay down here too long," Talimannog told her. "Swoop down, pick them up, and kill them in the air. You are too vulnerable this close to the ground!"

"Yes, Hapu! You have my thanks." Dundunan replied gratefully.

"How far are we from the sakbawan?" Ammani asked Dundunan.

"Not too far. It's a hundred feet or so behind that big tree." Dundunan answered.

"Let's go!" Talimannog barked. "There are a lot more of them coming!"

All three of them ran as fast as their tired legs could take them. All the while dodging, evading, and slashing through the increasing number of toads and frogs that were constantly attacking them. Talimannog and Ammani were once again struck by treefrogs as they approached the big mangrove tree but managed to sever the tongue almost as soon as it hit them.

As soon as they rounded the tree, they caught sight of the sakbawan less than a hundred feet away from where they stood. The golden door looked exactly as it did in the last rakuh they battled through.

"There it is!" Talimannog exclaimed.

"And there they are!" Ammani retorted as soon as he saw more than two dozen toads standing between them and the sakbawan.

"How are we supposed to get past all of them akka?" Anibo asked Talimannog.

Talimannog took stock of what weapons they had left. Though they somehow managed to hold on to their bows amidst the chaos, between them they only have eight arrows left. "Not enough to shoot our way through," Talimannog told his siblings.

"Can we circle around them?" Ammani asked.

"That would be unwise Hapu Ammani," Dundunan said. "There are hundreds more of them gathered on the outskirts of the sakbawan. Going straight through would be your best option in reaching the exit."

"We're going to get hit with more than one tongue once we get close to them, that much is a certainty," Talimannog said. "We could probably outpower three tongues at the most, but any more than that will surely mean we will succumb to the onslaught."

"Then we should combine whatever strength we have left against those abominable frogs!" Ammani said.

"How do you mean?" Anibo asked his twin. "How can we combine our strengths?"

"We gather as many vines as we can," Ammani answered. "We need to tie ourselves together by the waist. That way, if one of us becomes overpowered by those things, the other two can lend their strength to keeping that one on their feet. Also, we become a heavier weight to simply pull in."

"That is genius abeng!" Anibo lauded his brother's ingenuity.

"That's a good plan wadi," Talimannog said. "Enough talk and start cutting down some vines! Some of them already saw us!"

As the twins began cutting down some vines from the mangrove tree behind them, Talimannog and Dundunan faced off against the few toads that noticed their presence there. Moments later, all three brothers have vines looped around their waists as they tied themselves together back-to-back-to-back, forming a tripod of sorts with their bodies.

"Here we go!" Talimannog said as he took the lead. Anibo was facing his left flank while Ammani was to his right.

As soon as the toads saw them approach, they attacked them without hesitation. Tongues flicked out of their hideous mouths as they tried to subdue their would-be prey.

During the first few moments of the onslaught, Ammani's plan seemed to be working. All three brothers managed to intercept some of the sticky tongues that darted at them. Even though they did eventually get struck with multiple tongues, their combined strength held them upright and gave them enough time to react and sever their attacker's tongue.

Dundunan was also successful in her dive attacks on the toads. She already had racked up eight kills and was well on her way to getting more. It even got to a point where Ammani and Anibo were stuck at the same time and the pull of each toad's tongue actually countered the other one. Fortunate as they might have been, everything suddenly shifted and took a dark turn when they were only a dozen feet away from the sakbawan.

"Just a little more wadi!" Talimannog exclaimed as he sliced off another toad's tongue. "The sakbawan is very close! We're almost there!"

Suddenly, three toads struck Ammani and began pulling at him. Another two got to Anibo and one got to Talimannog on his right. Dundunan dove down and went straight for two of Ammani's attackers. But as she dove another six toads appeared from the murky waters close to Ammani.

One of the toads stuck out its tongue and struck Dundunan on her left leg just as she buried her talons into two of Ammani's attackers. She quickly let go of her two victims and tried to take flight before any more toads got to her.

This left Ammani wide open for an onslaught unlike any of them had experienced before. Seven toads had tongues that adhered to all of Ammani's extremities, two on his torso and one on his left cheek.

Talimannog and Anibo had already taken care of their attackers but the sheer force of the seven toads pulling at Ammani was pulling all three of them back as well.

"Aaargh!" Ammani cried out as he felt his very flesh

being slowly pulled and torn from his body.

"Wadi! Hold on!" Anibo cried out to his twin as he pulled against the giant toads. "Akka! What do we do?"

"We have to give in and attack the toads! We cannot overpower them!" Talimannog said as he too pulled against the amphibians.

"No! No!" Ammani said as two more toads appeared and struck him in both thighs. "There are too many of them! Aaaargh!"

"We give in and turn on the count of three!" Talimannog told Anibo who nodded in understanding.

"One!"

Ammani realizing what his brothers were planning realized what he had to do. He managed to bend his arm holding his bolo and reversed his grip on the blade so that the tip was pointed at him.

"Two!"

Ammani used whatever strength he had left and began cutting through the vine tied around his waist.

"Three!" Talimannog counted when suddenly the vine around Ammani's waist came loose and the sudden slack shot Talimannog and Anibo forward. They lost their balance and fell forward, rolling in the mud as they did. Both brothers ended up only two feet away from the sakbawan.

Anibo raised his head and saw his twin brother

grabbing hold of a mangrove root next to the edge of the swamp. "Ammani!" Anibo cried out as he tried to get to his feet only to slip on the mud and fall back on his knees.

Ammani saw Talimannog get to his feet and was about to run after him. He knew he was more than halfway submerged and was only a second away from being taken fully under.

So, with the last gasp of air and with all his strength, Ammani yelled out to his siblings, "Go!" Ammani let go of the root and disappeared from all sight, under the dark, murky waters of the swamp.

Anibo tried to go after him, but Talimannog grabbed his remaining brother by the waist and pulled him into the sakbawan. Dundunan who had just managed to kill the toad attached to her feet saw all of this unfold.

Hapu Ammani! No! she thought to herself as she circled the spot where Ammani disappeared from sight. But to her horror and sadness, no trace of Ammani could be found. *I am sorry for failing you Hapu. I am so sorry!*

Dalawesan's Escape (Map)

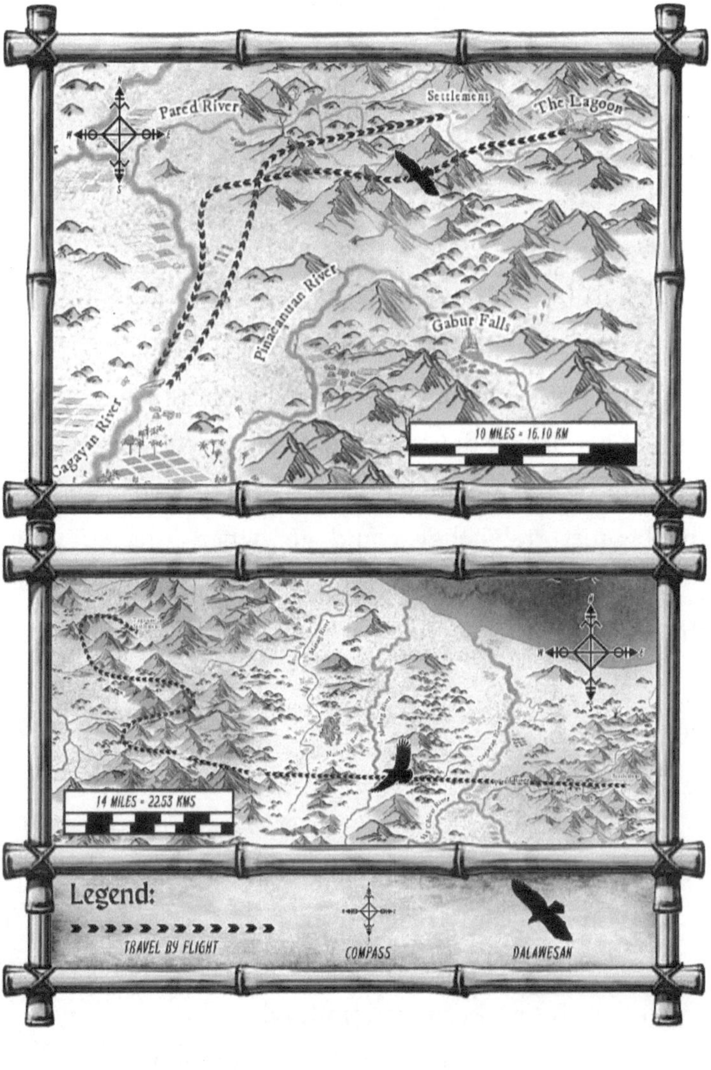

Chapter 12

In Search of Help

Dusk was nearing when Innawagan and Puyang Anag returned from the cookfires with some boiled crabs and potatoes. Talimannog has just finished the part of his tale when Ammani was taken by Pane Kalimangalnuk.

"It's time for supper!" Innawagan said as she placed the basket of hot, freshly boiled crabs in front of the men.

"Here are the potatoes as well," Puyang Anag said as she set her basket down next to the one with the crabs.

Anibo and Ammani were just about to dive in and take the biggest crabs they could get when Alig suddenly pointed a finger at her younger brothers and stopped them cold in their tracks. "Let our guest take the first crab! You two are worse than monkeys!" she scolded her brothers.

"Yes akka," The twins answered sheepishly.

"Lumalindaw, please take a crab before my patepag start fighting over them." Taguwasi told Lumalindaw.

As Lumalindaw reached in for a crab, he asked Ammani, "Wait. I am confused. You were taken by those frog creatures and dragged under the water, yes?"

To which Ammani nodded in affirmation.

"You obviously didn't die. So, what happened to you?"

Ammani and Anibo reached in and took a crab from the basket as Ammani answered, "Nothing at first. All there was, was darkness. I thought I would drown before I died, but as soon as my head disappeared under the murky water everything disappeared.

"When I open my eyes next, much to my surprise, I was still alive. I was trapped in a dark stone box that stood me up on my feet. It was so tight that I couldn't move much or turn my body around. I couldn't even reach up and touch my face. Sitting or lying down was out of the question. All I could see through the small window that exposed my face to the outside world was the dark shadows of stone and water.

"I was in a cave of sorts and some light from the moon or sun; I wasn't sure which, seeped through some cracks along the cave wall. But it wasn't much. I could hear small animals screeching and scurrying around. I shouted for my siblings but all I heard was the sound of my own echo. The manulib placed me in a prison designed to drive me insane." Ammani continued.

"Though I must attest, between the two of us you actually are the crazy one." Anibo joked as he cracked open his crab.

"Shut your mouths and let Lumalindaw eat in peace!" Alig scolded the twins yet again.

"Yes, akka," answered the twins.

"Actually, I wouldn't mind if you continued your tale while you eat," Kidul said. "I am very much curious about the agimat those manulib creatures used."

"Yes, me too!" Lumalindaw seconded. "Not about the agimat, but about what happened next."

"Well, let's see. Since this story takes place from different perspectives of the people here, who would like to go next?" Talimannog asked his bertan.

"I suppose I could go again," Innawagan answered as she sat down next to Taguwasi who handed her a cracked crab to eat. "And then maybe Dalawesan could continue after me."

"Go ahead and begin Hapu," Dalawesan answered who stood behind them with Dundunan as they watched them eat. "I will continue after you've said your part."

"Very well," Innawagan answered. "So, there we both were, Dalawesan and me as we looked down on the magical pool and saw Ammani taken by those things…"

*****

"No!" Innawagan screamed in horror. "Ammani! Ammani! You killed him!"

Dalawesan quickly wrapped his wings around Innawagan to hold her back as she was about to charge at Pane Nagdombilan. "Hapu, please calm yourself! You cannot do anything to help your brother. At least not right now."

"Listen to your bird patepag," Pane Nagdombilan glowered at Innawagan. "You cannot do anything to me nor help your brother. He was a stupid man and met his end as a stupid man usually does."

"Don't be cruel kakteh," Pane Kalimangalnuk said as he suddenly appeared through one of the doors. "Especially to someone who will be my wife in a very short while."

"You killed my akka you animal!" Innawagan growled at her captor. "Why would I ever consent to be your wife after what you have done?"

"Have you not been listening to anything I said mavid?" Pane Kalimangalnuk answered as he took Innawagan in his arms and started kissing her neck. "I promised you that I wouldn't kill any of your siblings, at least not outright did I not?"

"Ammani's alive?!" Innawagan exclaimed as she tried to push away from Pane Kalimangalnuk.

"Yes! Yes, he's alive!" he answered her. "I told you I will hold them in one of my rakuhs and keep them there as long as I want."

"Can I see him? Can I please see Ammani?" Innawagan said as she stopped resisting Pane Kalimangalnuk's advances and let him kiss and lick her face. "If you let me see my akka, then I promise to make it up to you on our wedding night."

"No kakteh," Pane Nagdombilan protested. "You have been far too lenient with these people. Don't you see that..."

"Very well mavid," Pane Kalimangalnuk interjected, cutting his brother off mid-sentence. "Just go through that door and you will see your brother. I will give you but a few minutes, after which you shall return here. Now am I not a merciful husband mavid?"

"Your act of mercy speaks loudly of your greatness as man and husband-to-be," Innawagan answered as she walked into the door.

Innawagan found herself walking through the same dark tunnel that she walked through earlier. She was half expecting to return to the same room just as it happened before. But to her surprise, the tunnel was much longer than it was earlier and seemed to be leading her somewhere.

Then she heard the sound of water. Like a whisper of a babbling brook, she heard the faint sound of a small stream in all that quiet nothingness. Then she heard him.

"Akka! Anibo! I'm here!" Ammani yelled.

" Amani! I hear you!" Innawagan cried out as she followed the sound of her brother's voice through the dark expanse of the tunnel.

"Wadi?!" Ammani answered back. "Is that you? I am

here wadi! Follow my voice! I am trapped and cannot get to you!"

Innawagan reached the end of the tunnel where there was very little to no light at all. But unlike the tunnel, light coming in through cracks in the cave wall provided some illumination.

"Ammani, I'm here," Innawagan called out to her brother. "Where are you?"

"I'm over here. Follow my voice."

Moments later, Innawagan found where her brother was being held. Ammani was trapped inside the cave's wall itself with only a hole exposing his face to let him breathe.

"Ammani!" Innawagan exclaimed when she saw her brother.

"Wadi! Are you well? Did those creatures hurt you?"

"No. At least not yet. Pane Kalimangalnuk wants to take me as his wife. I'm trying my best to stall for time hoping you guys can save me. But after seeing their powers and what they can do, I am now stalling to keep you alive."

"Can you get me out?" Ammani asked.

"You're trapped inside the cave wall. Even if I had tools, which I don't; it would take me a very long time to break through. Pane Kalimangalnuk only allowed me a few minutes to see you, so let's make the best of it."

"We'll need to ask for help," Ammani suggested. "Is Dalawesan with you?"

"Yes, he is," Innawagan answered. "But even if he can somehow escape and seek help, I doubt a hundred men would do us any good. The manulib are creatures with powers and magic. I don't think warriors will even be of any use to us."

"Then we need someone with powers and magic of their own," Ammani said.

"Forgive me for being skeptical akka, but the last time I checked, we don't know anyone with powers," Innawagan said sarcastically.

"But we do wadi!" Ammani said excitedly. "Do you remember when we were invited to stay a night with a bertan on our way up here? Alig sang the nanang of Mandaripan and then the head of their bertan sang a nanang about..."

"The flying man!" Innawagan interjected. "But is he even real? For all we know, he might be just as real as Mandaripan."

"One of the women there told Alig that she actually saw this flying man. She told Alig where she saw him last, but for the life of me, I cannot recall," Ammani said frustratedly. "If Dalawesan can fly to Alig and ask her where he can find this flying man, maybe he would agree to help us?"

"That's a lot of uncertainty to pin our hopes on," Innawagan replied. "But since we really don't have any other choice in the matter, I'll make sure Dalawesan escapes."

"That's quite enough time mavid," Pane Kalimangalnuk's voice suddenly came booming from out of nowhere. "Time to return to me."

Suddenly everything began spinning. Innawagan was disoriented as the entire cave spun erratically. All she heard was Ammani calling her name and just as quickly as it began, she found herself back in the room with the manulib brothers.

"I trust everything was satisfactory mavid," Pane Kalimangalnuk said. "You've seen and spoken to your brother, yes?"

"Yes. Yes, I have," Innawagan replied as she quickly collected herself and put on a brave face. "And I am truly grateful for your mercy and generosity."

"Humph!" Pane Nagdombilan grunted as he picked up on Innawagan's insincerity.

Pane Kalimangalnuk glowered at his brother's displeasure but quickly brushed it off. "Then I expect much satisfaction in return on our wedding night mavid. But right now, I have to attend to your other siblings and their third challenge.

"Come kakteh. I will need you for this third challenge."

Pane Kalimangalnuk said as he gestured for his brother to follow him through one of the doors.

As soon as the manulibs left, Innawagan rushed to Dalawesan's side.

"Dalawesan, I need you to listen to me carefully. We don't have much time," Innawagan said with urgency. "Do you remember the story we were told about the man who could fly?"

"Yes Hapu, I do," Dalawesan answered.

"Do you recall where the flying man can be found?" Innawagan asked again.

"No, Hapu. Hapu Alig was the only one who was told about the flying man. I thought it rude to eavesdrop, so I stopped listening."

"I need you to find a way to escape, go to Alig, find out where the flying man is, and seek his assistance. All our lives depend on it."

"And what makes you think I would allow such a thing to happen?" Ammalabukaw interjected as he swooped in from the ceiling though they did not see him there when they began talking.

"Why are you doing this?" Dalawesan asked his old friend. "We have known each other for more than a hundred years. Why subject me, Dundunan, and these humans to such cruelty?"

"You know why old friend," Ammalabukaw replied. "I

owe Pane Kalimangalnuk a life debt, much like you and your sister owe these humans one. And like you, I am bound to follow his commands down to the letter."

"Then it seems I have no choice but to go through you then," Dalawesan said decidedly as he readied himself to fight the bigger kumaw to the death.

"You will lose," Ammalabukaw retorted and readied himself to fight as well.

"Stop!" Innawagan exclaimed. "Please answer this one question before the two of you kill each other."

Ammalabukaw nodded.

"What exactly did Pane Kalimangalnuk order you to do?" she asked.

"He ordered me to keep an eye on you and prevent you from escaping," Ammalabukaw answered her followed by a few seconds of silent contemplation. "Which includes preventing Dalawesan from freeing you through the secret passageway on the very top of the domed roof."

Innawagan and Dalawesan were stunned to silence by Ammalabukaw's honesty. He had just told them about the one and only means to escape though he did not need to do it. But upon closer inspection of Ammalabukaw's expression, they both knew that Innawagan's question provided them with a loophole past Pane Kalimangalnuk's orders. He was only to prevent Innawagan from escaping. His orders did not include

Dalawesan.

Innawagan quickly turned her attention back to Dalawesan. "Go to Alig and find out where the flying man is. Go quickly! Please."

"I leave at once Hapu," Dalawesan replied. "If he is a human gifted with such powers, then I might have an idea of what he is. There were rumors of such beings to whom the Poons bestowed so much power and abilities."

"I have also heard of such rumors before we fell through the balete trees," Ammalabukaw said. "They are supposed to be the answer to the dalaketnon that the Yawàs have unleashed onto the world. If that is in fact what this flying man is, then it may be the answer to my master's suffering."

As Dalawesan was just about to take flight and pass through the secret passageway, Ammalabukaw approached him and gave him a stern warning.

"Though I may not have been ordered from preventing you from escaping, I would be remiss of my duties to my master if I simply let you leave unhindered," Ammalabukaw warned Dalawesan. "I will give you a few minutes head start after which I will go after you. If I find you, I will kill you. It is now midday in the outside world, if by sundown I fail to find you, I will return here and leave you be."

"I understand," Dalawesan replied. "Goodbye, old

friend."

*****

Innawagan stopped her tale as she sipped the fatty juices from the crab's shell she had in her hands.

"These crabs are excellent!" she exclaimed.

"I know." Taguwasi seconded as he too sipped the juices from his crab. "Aren't you glad we decided to visit the Ivatan kabanga?"

Innawagan nodded in affirmation as her mouth was already full of potatoes and crab meat. After chewing and swallowing her food, Innawagan turned to Dalawesan. "Would you mind continuing the tale? I think this next part should be taken from your perspective."

"I would be honored Hapu," Dalawesan said in his stoic fashion.

"I shot up as fast as I could. As I neared the dome ceiling of the room, I quickly noticed that the roof had a ripple on it, much like how the entrance to the rakuhs looked like..."

*****

Dalawesan closed his eyes and hoped for the best for a split second before colliding with the roof. But just like before when he crossed over from one rakuh to the next, all he felt was that faint sensation like passing through a spider's web.

When he opened his eyes, he was in a tunnel made up of thorny vines. Luckily, the tunnel was wide enough to accommodate his wingspan as it was meant to accommodate the bigger Ammalabukaw. The thorny vines were meant to prevent anyone else who did not possess the ability to fly from escaping.

The end of the tunnel led to one of the caves overlooking the lagoon. The mouth of the cave had the same rippling effect which meant that the tunnel itself was just another rakuh. A warm midday sun greeted Dalawesan as soon as he shot out of the cave.

Though it seemed they were only in those caves for a few hours, a whole day had passed in the outside world.

There is no time to relax. He thought to himself. *Ammalabukaw will be coming for me soon. He knows I am heading to Alig and will no doubt follow me. His eyesight is far better than mine so hiding from him in the clouds is out of the question. I need to hide and wait until sundown when he stops looking for me. I need to hide somewhere he least expects to find me. I need to get to the Cagayan River.*

Dalawesan flew as fast and as low as he could and headed straight for the great Cagayan River. A few minutes into his flight, he instinctively knew Ammalabukaw was already in pursuit of him. He had flown with his old friend for more than a hundred years in Kaluwalhatian and somehow knew when he was close by. *I'm not too far from the river. I just need to fly faster!*

After a few more minutes, he could see the light of the sun shining down on the surface of the Cagayan River. As soon as he reached the river, Dalawesan turned south and followed the river until he found fishing boats moored near the shore. He was already near the large settlement of Garao when he saw his first unmanned boat.

He dove down as fast as he could and breached the surface of the water with a gigantic splash. Though not particularly adept at swimming, Dalawesan managed to maneuver his body under the boat, and with his sharp talons, he anchored himself firmly beneath it. The only part of him sticking out of the water was the front half of his head.

The boat and Dalawesan moved slowly and aimlessly with the current of the Cagayan River for hours as he patiently waited for the sun to set. It was already near sunset when Dalawesan caught the unmistakable image of Ammalabukaw flying overhead. Dalawesan held his breath in anticipation as he silently prayed to the Poons to hide him from his old friend.

Ammalabukaw circled the area once and then began heading east, presumably to return to the caves. Dalawesan waited a few more minutes, and as soon as he felt secure enough, he let go of the boat and began floating on the water's surface. He flapped his wings a few times to clear the water off. A few minutes later, Dalawesan took to the air and started flying home.

The sun had not completely sunk below the western mountains when Dalawesan reached their home. Alig was lighting a bonfire in preparation for the coming night when he landed near her.

"Dalawesan!" Alig exclaimed as soon as she saw him. "What happened? Where is everybody?"

"They are all taken by the manulib," Dalawesan answered as he tried to catch his breath.

"What are the manulib?" Alig asked nervously. "Are my siblings alive? Are they well? Tell me everything that happened!"

"I am sorry Hapu Alig, but time is of the essence. But to put your mind at ease, everyone is still alive for the time being," Dalawesan assured Alig. "But right now, I need to seek out and ask the help of the man who flies. Do you recall the nanang sung to you by the woman from the bertan we ran into before settling here?"

Alig thought about it for a moment as she desperately tried to recall the tale. "Yes. I do believe I recall some of it," she answered.

"Hapu, do you remember if she told you where she saw him last?" Dalawesan asked.

"Yes!" Alig suddenly retorted as she recalled an important aspect of the tale she was told. "The woman said she saw him fly down to her and her parents when they were trading with some Isneg hunters. The flying man was hunting aswang and wanted to know if they'd heard of any sightings in their area.

"The Isneg hunters told the flying man that there were strange tales from their settlement nearby. You should go to the Isneg settlements in the western mountains!" Alig concluded excitedly.

"Thank you, Hapu Alig. I will go there right away." Dalawesan said.

"You look tired Dalawesan. Do you want to stay and rest first before you leave?" Alig asked worriedly.

"I am fine Hapu. But our siblings won't be the longer it takes me to find this flying man and get him to help us. Also, it would be wise to go into hiding once I leave. Though Ammalabukaw said nothing about looking for you, if he is ordered to by Pane Kalimangalnuk, then he will have no choice but to obey." Dalawesan answered and took off.

Though still feeling a bit nervous when he began flying towards the western mountains, his fears all but disappeared when the sky turned black. Having black feathers all over his body, Dalawesan was in all essence, invisible in the night sky. And so, on he went past mountains and rivers until he began encountering human settlements.

As much as he wanted to just drop in on unsuspecting humans and ask if they'd heard about a flying man, Dalawesan knew that doing so would probably get him killed so he thought better of it. He would spend the night resting and recuperating, probably catching a monkey or two to feed on. Come daybreak he would find and talk to isolated humans out fishing or foraging and hopefully, someone could point him in the right direction.

*****

The first person he encountered was a Kalinga woman attending her vegetable garden near her home. He landed next to her and greeted her. But as soon as she saw a black, five-foot talking hawk, she fell into hysterics and started screaming and running immediately. As soon as the men with bows and arrows showed up, Dalawesan took off immediately.

This is going to be harder than I anticipated. Dalawesan thought to himself.

The next person he found was an old man spearfishing by the river. Upon seeing that the old man had a spear, Dalawesan decided to speak with him from a good distance away in case he needed to evade an attack from the spear. So he perched himself by a tall tree and called out to the old man.

"*Macasta a daddaramat.* (Good morning)" he greeted the

old man.

The old man turned and looked around. "Who's there?" he asked when he didn't see anyone around.

"I am up here. Please do not be afraid," Dalawesan said as calmly as he could.

When the old man looked up, his eyes widened, and his lips began to tremble. The first thing that came to his mind was aswang, seeing a larger-than-normal, black-feathered bird. But when Dalawesan spoke again, the next thing the old man thought was *tigmamanukan* (a bird of omens), which gave the old man pause and tempered his fear.

"Are you a tigmamanukan?" the old man asked.

"No, I am not," Dalawesan answered. "For one, those creatures don't exist. I am a kumaw. My name is Dalawesan."

"Are you here to kill and eat me?"

"We do not..." Dalawesan was about to answer when he paused and said, "I've just eaten my fill of a man who would not answer my question truthfully. I do not mind having seconds so I suggest answering me with all the honesty you can muster."

Dalawesan did not enjoy frightening innocent humans, but he knew that time was of the essence and that he had very little of it to spare. Had he indulged the old man's curiosity, the conversation might trail off longer. So, for the sake of those he loved, he was willing to play the monster to get his answer sooner.

"Then ask, please. I will answer you honestly. Just please don't kill me." The old man answered as he shivered in fear.

"I am looking for the man who flies. I was told he dwells near these mountains. Do you know of him and where I can find him?"

"I have heard tales of him from the Isneg settlements in the Apayao mountains farther north from here. I have never seen him myself, but I've been told that he was the one who killed the Blood Serpent Laho," The old man answered and fell to his knees and started begging for his life. "That is all I know of this flying man whom you seek. Please spare me great bird!"

As the old man bowed and begged, Dalawesan simply took off and started heading north. *The old man has heard of the flying man from others. This is good news indeed.* Dalawesan thought to himself. *This proves that he exists somewhere in these mountains. I just need to go farther north.*

Dalawesan visited several Isneg settlements and tried the same tactic as he did with the old man. Unfortunately for him, his plan of scaring the people to answer only worked once for every five people he questioned. Most either ran screaming or started attacking him as soon as he spoke to them.

It was already late on the second day and on the third person that actually answered him, did Dalawesan finally get something solid he could work with. The information came from an Isneg woman who showed no fear upon seeing him, she told Dalawesan that the flying man was an Aeta man much like his Hapu Talimannog.

The woman told him that the flying man lived in a small camp only a few miles north with two women; one young and one old. Though she did not know their names, she knew of them when they drove off a horde of flying night creatures called *alàn* from the multiple Isneg settlements in their immediate area.

Dalawesan thanked the woman as there was no reason to subject her to any further subterfuge and took off north to finally see and talk to this flying man. *This has got to be it*. He thought. *Whoever this flying man is, I will finally get to see him and plead Hapu Innawagan's case and hopefully gain his assistance in freeing them. I sincerely hope he agrees to help us, otherwise, all hope is lost.*

Dalawesan visited three Aeta settlements and to his surprise, none of them showed any fear of him. They greeted him back when he spoke to them, and one even offered him a piece of deer meat as he looked hungry. But most importantly, they all pointed him in the right direction and gave him the name of the man who flies; Taguwasi.

Finally, Dalawesan reached a very small settlement made up of two small huts. There he found the two women that the others described as Taguwasi's bertan. There was a young, beautiful woman with bright eyes who was busy blowing air through a piece of bamboo as she set the cookfire ablaze. Not too far from her was an old woman sitting next to one of the huts stringing a freshly carved bow. But much to his disappointment, there was no sign of Taguwasi.

Not wanting to waste any more time as he was already tired from his search, Dalawesan landed close to the two women and greeted them in the Agta tongue.

"*Masampat a abi* (Good evening)," He greeted the women as calmly as he could. "Please do not be afraid. I am..."

"A kumaw!" the old woman suddenly interjected. "A messenger from the Poons of Kaluwalhatian! I never thought that I would ever get to see one of your kind while I still dwell in the mortal world. Whatever message the Poons want you to tell us, tell them we are not interested!"

The old woman's reaction caught Dalawesan by surprise. Not only did the old woman know about his kind, but she also seems to have a grudge against the Poons.

"I was a messenger from Kaluwalhatian many years

ago, but that is not why..." Dalawesan was trying to answer when the old woman interrupted him again.

"Is it about the Lakandian? Is it about Taguwasi?" the old woman asked.

"Yes. I was wondering if he is by chance..." Dalawesan again tried to answer.

"If Poong Kedes wants something of Taguwasi, tell her to come here herself! Tell her to give me back my..." the old woman interrupted him again, only this time the younger woman interjected before she could finish.

"Puyang Anag! Control yourself and let the kumaw answer at least one of your questions!" the younger woman yelled at the old woman who bowed her head in surrender.

"Hapu kumaw, please excuse Puyang Anag. She is old and quite excitable. I am Sinag, sister of the Lakandian Taguwasi. I assume he is the reason you are here?"

"Lakandian? I am seeking the man who flies through the air like a bird. Is he the Lakandian you speak of?" Dalawesan asked perplexed as he had never heard the word Lakandian before.

"Wait. So, you've never heard of the Lakandian? The champion of the Poons? The one chosen to defend the mortal realm?" Sinag asked suspiciously.

Dalawesan paused and processed this new information before he answered. *Does she know of Poong*

Kedes? Lakandian? That must be what the rumors were about. The weapon that the Poons created. This Taguwasi must be one of these so-called Lakandians. If he is, then he is surely powerful enough to save everyone from the manulib. I must be forthright if I wish to gain favor from the Lakandian's family.

"I shall be honest with you, Hapu Sinag. I have never actually heard of the Lakandian until you spoke of him a moment ago. Though I did hear of a weapon the Poons have created before I left the immortal realm," Dalawesan began. "But I do seek the one called Taguwasi because I need his help. I need him to help me free my human family and my sister from the clutches of two powerful manulib.

"Do you know where I can find your brother? Time is unfortunately not on our side. The longer it takes for help to arrive, the deadlier the peril that awaits them." Dalawesan concluded.

"My sibling has been out fighting an endless horde of flying aswang called alàn for the past four days," Sinag answered. "The last time we saw each other was two nights ago. All he said was he was doing his best to drive them south and away from our mountains.

"But before we tell you where to find my wadi, I do need to ask something of you. I want you to tell us what became of you. How you've come to the mortal realm and how you've become endeared to a human family.

"If we find your tale honest and sincere, then we will tell you where to find Taguwasi. But be warned, Puyang Anag can smell out a lie like rotting meat. She will know if you are lying." Sinag demanded of Dalawesan.

"I beg your forgiveness, but as I mentioned earlier, I really don't have much time to spare. If you would only..." Dalawesan was saying when Sinag cut him off.

"I beg your forgiveness as well, but you must also understand that being the Lakandian, makes my wadi a target for every deceitful and evil being in the world. He is far too important to everyone in all the realms. So, I must insist that you convince me to trust you myself."

"Might I also remind you that looking for the Lakandian in random places anywhere south from here will actually take you longer than convincing us to trust you," Puyang Anag seconded. "That is of course if you have something to hide."

Finding himself backed into a corner and presented with no alternatives, Dalawesan agreed to the two women's terms and told them his tale and how he and his sister developed a life debt with Talimannog and Innawagan.

Though he tried to tell them his tale as quickly as he could, it still took him almost most of the night to finish. When he finally concluded his tale at the moment he left the caves, the two Aeta women looked at each other and nodded. In an unspoken agreement, both women knew that Dalawesan was truthful and sincere.

"If you wish to find him, you best start looking in the Itawit lands southeast from here," Puyang Anag said. "The Lakandian said the alàn suddenly seemed to be heading south all on their own. It was as though someone commanded them to do so. Taguwasi just wanted to make sure he kills as many of them as possible before they leave our mountains."

"I thank you for this information. I'll leave for the Itawit lands right away and hopefully convince the Lakandian to help us," Dalawesan said as he turned and spread his wings.

"Wait!" Sinag called out. "When you do find my wadi, he will need some convincing that he can trust you. As good as a man as he is, he is a bit untrusting of others, especially after what happened to..." Sinag was saying when she abruptly stopped.

"Wait here, you need to prove to wadi that you've spoken to us and that we have given you our trust," Sinag said as she rushed inside one of the two huts.

When she came out, she held a small pouch made of deer hide in one hand and a long string of hemp in the other. She approached Dalawesan and said, "When you see him, tell him that I've sent you to him to plead your case. If he does not believe you, which he probably won't, offer him this pouch."

Sinag tied the pouch securely on Dalawesan's right foot and spoke to him again. "This pouch contains some amman betel nuts that he loves to chew on. This will show him that you are a friend. And to truly gain his trust, tell him to smell the pouch itself. I dosed it with some of the fragrant sap I extracted from the *surob* plant. I use this very sap on myself and that will let him know that it is truly from me as soon as he smells it."

"Once again, I thank you Hapu Sinag and Hapu Puyang Anag. I am in your debt. I only hope that I find your brother in time to save my family," Dalawesan said right before he flew off in his desperate search for Taguwasi.

Dalawesan's Search (Map)

Chapter 13

Master of the Wind

Taguwasi belched a loud and obnoxious burp that suddenly broke the somber attitude brought about by Dalawesan's tale. Everyone around the fire looked at him and were stunned silent for a brief second before bursting out into gregarious laughter. Even the kumaws chuckled even though it was harder to tell if they were smiling or not on account that they don't have lips.

"Kabanga!" Innawagan called out her husband.

"I'm sorry," Taguwasi apologized. "I couldn't help it. It just came out."

"Don't apologize to me!" Innawagan said. "Apologize to Dalawesan whom you've rudely interrupted."

"You have my apologies Dalawesan," Taguwasi apologized yet still half laughing. "I'm sorry I've ruined your tale. Please continue."

"Your timing couldn't be more perfect Hapu," Dalawesan replied. "I was actually about to ask you if you'd like to continue the story. There's nothing much else for me to add. You should start with our first meeting and what you were doing that night."

Taguwasi got another crab from the basket and cracked it open. He took another mouthful of the crab's juices before cracking the crab in half and took a large chunk of white meat from inside the crab and popped it into his mouth. As soon as he swallowed, he began. "Very well. Where were we? Oh yes, I remember that night fairly well.

"I had been chasing down the horde of alàn that had been pestering the different mountain tribes for two days and nights at that point. I was in a small Itawit purok that night and had just finished shooting down those beasts when I first saw Dalawesan..."

*****

Taguwasi was locked in a battle with several alàn night creatures in a barangay called Daraga. The barangay itself was to the west of a small river that branches off from the Abulog River from the north and was settled mostly by the Itawit people, though some of the population also included Kalinga and Isneg.

Daraga was but one of the numerous mountain settlements that these night creatures have plagued over the course of the last two months.

"How many more are there?" Taguwasi called out to his katiwala Bago as he dodged an alàn attacking him from below. He twisted his body just before the alàn made contact, spiraled in midair, and loosed a regular *pinaeknod* (barbed) arrow at the alàn's nape just as the creature passed him.

"Less than a dozen I think!" Bago answered as he hovered a foot above the roof of a hut, completely invisible to the people of Daraga that hid inside their homes. "I see three coming at you from behind!"

Taguwasi turned and saw the three night creatures gliding toward him with evil intent. The three were only a few feet away from him which didn't give him enough time to nock another arrow. So, Taguwasi flew down and let the three alàn follow him. Unlike the night creatures whose leathery flaps only allowed them to glide through the air, Taguwasi commanded the winds which allowed him to move through the open air much like how a fish moves through the water.

As he fell to the ground, Taguwasi commanded the wind to stop and let gravity do its work as well as allow the alàn to catch up to him. At the last second, Taguwasi commanded the wind, to pick him up just before he reached the ground. But that last second made all the difference for Taguwasi. All three alàn crashed to the ground and broke several of their bones whereas Taguwasi was left unscathed. All that was left for him to do was draw his short pinahig bolo and slash each of the alàn's throats, effectively ending the threat.

"Where are the rest?" he asked Bago who came up to him as he cut open the last alàn's throat.

"I lost track of them when I saw you plummeting,"

Bago answered. "I'll look near the river and see..."

"No! My son!" A woman's voice suddenly cried out and interrupted Bago.

Taguwasi and Bago looked towards the direction of the woman's voice and saw the last five alàn grab a little boy of around five years of age from his mother's arms and attempt to glide off with him. "Let him go!" the mother cried. "Lakandian help me!"

"Another child," Taguwasi said as he nocks a patak arrow on his bow. "No children will die tonight. Not while I can do something about it."

Taguwasi made sure to take careful aim and loosed the arrow. The arrow flew straight at the alàn that was clutching the boy's right arm. But just before the arrow struck, Taguwasi commanded the winds and pushed the arrow forward even faster! The arrow passed straight through the alàn's neck, almost decapitating the night creature.

He then made a series of gestures with his right hand and commanded the wind to take the arrow and bring it around. The arrow spun in midair and buried itself in the head of the alàn holding the boy's left arm.

With no one holding him, the boy began to plummet to the ground. But with another series of gestures, Taguwasi utilized the wind to catch the boy and gently return him to his mother's waiting arms.

The last three alàn try to escape by landing on the thatched roofs of the huts and leaping from roof to roof, building up speed as they attempted to make it to the jungle. Taguwasi reached for the pusot to his side, immediately searching for another arrow to nock but finds it empty instead.

"They're getting away!" Bago cried out.

"Not from me," Taguwasi replied as he took to the air. He flew a few feet above the unsuspecting alàn and waited for them to clear the houses and glide toward the jungle. But as he did, he called upon the wind and collected its strength into a small spot between his chest. He holds his breath and then allowed the power to build.

As soon as the three night creatures cleared the vicinity of the huts and took to the air, Taguwasi unleashed the built-up power of the wind into a small concentrated funnel of air that slammed down on the unsuspecting alàn with the power of a small tornado. All three alàn didn't know what hit them.

They were sent spiraling beyond their control as they crashed into the jungle trees at incredible speed, breaking every bone in their bodies. Death was quick and came with a splat and cracking of bones. Such was the power of Taguwasi's dinatal!

"I'm heading up to see if there are any more," Taguwasi said as he commanded the wind to take him up another thirty feet.

It looks clear. Taguwasi thought to himself as he surveyed the barangay. *I think I got them all. I better move on to the next...*

Suddenly, a thundering sound echoed from the south and startled Taguwasi as he surveyed the area. *Muuwaannn...* was what the thunder sounded like. "What was that?!" Taguwasi exclaimed.

"Bago did you hear..." Taguwasi was saying when he found himself surprised again when he saw a massive black bird flying by the edge of the barangay near the river. It seemed to falter as it flew as though it were exhausted. It landed awkwardly near the river to drink and probably rest.

Was that where that sound came from? Is that another type of aswang? Taguwasi asked himself. *It's definitely unnatural and does look dangerous. I better make sure and just kill it to be on the safe side.* Taguwasi thought as he silently flew down to the creature with his bolo drawn.

The big black bird was completely unaware of his presence. All it felt was a sudden gust of wind as Taguwasi got closer. He raised his bolo and was about to deliver the fatal blow when Bago suddenly came barging in and started screaming at him. "Stop! Don't kill him! He's not an aswang!"

Both startled by Bago's sudden outburst, Taguwasi

and Dalawesan both jumped and recoiled. Dalawesan instinctively opened up his wings and tried to attack Taguwasi with his talons.

"Agay!" Taguwasi exclaimed as he moved out of the way of Dalawesan's talons and dashed directly above him and gave him a quick kick in the head. Dalawesan was knocked out cold.

"Poons strike you dead Bago!" Taguwasi snapped at his katiwala as he slowly descended to the ground. "Are you sure it's not another type of aswang? A garuda maybe?"

"No! No! That is a kumaw. A messenger from the Poons," Bago answered swiftly.

"Then what is it doing here?" Taguwasi asked. "Do you think it is another attempt by the Poons to get me to do their bidding?"

"Probably," Bago answered. "Which is why I am still urging you to reconsider giving them your oath."

"I'm not in the mood for this right now," Taguwasi answered. "Should I tie it up? It might attack me again when it wakes up."

"There's probably no need to," Bago said. "Just take it up to the mountain, away from these people. The last thing they need is to see another strange flying thing pestering them."

"Hey! I'm a strange flying thing!" Taguwasi retorted as

he approached the kumaw to take a closer look.

*****

Taguwasi was sitting by a fire as he calmly sharpened some arrowheads on a flat piece of stone when Dalawesan started coming to. The kumaw looked at the strange man that knocked him out and immediately got to his feet.

"Where am I?" Dalawesan asked alarmed.

"Take it easy kumaw," Bago said as he approached Dalawesan. "You are safe."

"Anito?" Dalawesan asked perplexed upon seeing Bago. "Why are you here? Why am I..."

"You are safe," Bago assured him again. "I am Bago from the Kingdom of Mah-nongan, and that is Taguwasi, the Lakandian. What is your name kumaw?"

"I am Dalawesan, and I have been looking for Taguwasi for two... no, three nights now. I desperately need your help!"

"Were you sent by Poong Kedes?" Taguwasi asked nonchalantly as he continued to sharpen his arrowheads.

"I was one of her messengers, many years ago but I have not been to Kaluwalhatian for just as long."

"Then what is it that you need Taguwasi for?" Bago asked.

"I need him to..." Dalawesan was saying this when he abruptly stopped and stepped toward Taguwasi. He bowed his head to the Lakandian and continued. "I am begging you Taguwasi, the Lakandian of the Poons, to help save my human family and my sister from evil humans."

Taguwasi stopped and looked at Dalawesan curiously. "Why not save them yourself?" he asked Dalawesan. "Surely a powerful magical bird like you can take care of a few evil humans?"

"These humans I speak of have great magical powers taken from an agimat. They were gifted these agimat talismans by a mamaw," Dalawesan answered.

"You say all of this to me but tell me why I should even believe you?" Taguwasi asked.

"Taguwasi! He is a kumaw. He is an ally of Kaluwalhatian and..." Bago spoke up but was cut short by Taguwasi holding a hand in the air.

"He says he is of the Poons yet here he stands apart from them," Taguwasi argued. "Did you betray the Poons or just decided not to do their bidding anymore? Whatever your reasons are, I don't trust you."

"I understand your reluctance, Taguwasi. I truly do," Dalawesan replied. "But I am not a traitor. Even creatures with free will such as myself do not openly denounce the Poons lest we find ourselves destroyed or banished. The anito can attest to this.

"Quite the opposite can actually be said about my kind.

We are loyal to a fault to whom we serve or to those we owe a life debt. These humans that I speak of, I consider them family as I and my sister, owe Hapu Talimannog and Innawagan life debts."

"Hapu? Is your human family Agta like me? Are they Aeta?" Taguwasi asked.

"Yes, they are," Dalawesan answered. "Please Lakandian, I need you to trust in me. As your sister, Sinag trusts in me."

"You know my sister?!" Taguwasi was surprised by the sudden revelation.

"Yes. I met her yesterday. She was the one who told me where I could find you." Dalawesan answered.

"You see Taguwasi. He knows of your sister," Bago spoke up again, and again he was cut off by Taguwasi.

"How do I know that you didn't harm Sinag to get the information? I am sorry but the mere mention of my sister's name doesn't automatically gain you my trust."

"Hapu Sinag told me you were a little untrusting," Dalawesan replied. "This is why she told me to give you this pouch she tied around my leg," Dalawesan said as he pointed to the small pouch tied to his right leg.

Taguwasi untied the pouch and smelled it. It definitely had his sister's fragrance. He opened it and found the amman Sinag placed there for him.

"Hapu Sinag said you liked chewing on those things,"

Dalawesan said. "Much like how Hapu Talimannog and his siblings do."

Taguwasi took some of the amman and placed it in his mouth. *This definitely came from Sinag.* he thought to himself. *Definitely made by Puyang Anag.*

"Very well," Taguwasi said. "I believe you. Now tell me of your bertan and these manulib beings."

"I beg your forgiveness Hapu Taguwasi, but we really don't have time to spare. The manulib might do something despicable to the others, especially Hapu Innawagan whom he desires to be his wife." Dalawesan pleaded.

"I am not about to fly into a fight without knowing anything about my enemy or those whom I'm supposed to save. Dawn is coming soon, and we will leave then. But not before. So, start talking and talk fast." Taguwasi demanded as he spat out some betel nuts and continued working on his arrows.

Having no other option but to tell his tale, Dalawesan agreed and told Taguwasi everything about his family, Ammalabukaw, and the manulib. Though he did not admit it, those few short hours before dawn gave him the much-needed rest he craved, especially for the long flight back.

*****

As soon as the sun was up, Taguwasi and Dalawesan were in the air heading east towards the rising sun. Bago hovered on Dalawesan's back and was quite pleased that Taguwasi decided to include him instead of sending him back to Sinag.

Dalawesan was still a little tired from his multi-day search which slowed down Taguwasi at first. So, to speed them along, Taguwasi commanded the winds to carry the kumaw just so he could keep up with the Lakandian.

"Tell me more about the powers these manulib brothers possess," Taguwasi asked of Dalawesan. "I want to be as prepared as possible when I face them."

Chapter 14

The Third Rakuh

The bertan of Lakandian Taguwasi along with their distinguished guest had finished supping on the crabs and potatoes when Taguwasi ended his tale. Sinag and Alig had already started distributing the amman to everyone as they all relaxed and digested their large meal next to a roaring fire.

"I must say, even when I was home, I have never had quite such a satisfying meal," Lumalindaw said as he stretched his legs out on the ground in front of him and patted his full belly.

"It has been a while for us as well," Taguwasi answered back with a sated smile. "I think the last time we ate this well was when my sister and I got married together to Innawagan and Talimannog."

"You and Sinag were married at the same time?" Lumalindaw asked surprised.

"Yes," Talimannog answered. "That was quite a night and worthy of its own nanang if you asked me."

"We would love to hear that story as well," Lumalindaw said as he started chewing on his amman.

"All in good time Lakandian," Sinag spoke. "That would be jumping way ahead of our tales. And believe me, there are many more tales to be told before we get to our weddings."

"Then by all means, please continue," Kidul said from deep within the ayoding. "As much as we enjoy all of your company, Lumalindaw and I will need to continue our search for Muwan very soon."

"Should I continue or should someone else go first?" Taguwasi asked and looked at all the faces gathered around the fire.

"Can I go next akka?" Anibo said as he looked at Talimannog. "I'd like to tell the story of the third rakuh we faced."

"Very well wadi," Talimannog replied to his younger brother. "I'm still too full to start talking anyway."

"Yes!" Anibo said excitedly. "So, there we were, akka Talimannog and I. We had just crossed the sakbawan and entered the third rakuh..."

*****

"Ammani!" Anibo continued to cry out as he struggled to free himself from Talimannog's arms around his waist. But they had already crossed the sakbawan and all that stood in front of him was the rippling distortion in the air and a vast green field of *ruot* (tall grass) as the sun glared brightly above them.

"Anibo stop!" Talimannog said as he tried to calm his baby brother. "Ammani is gone. He sacrificed himself to..."

"No!" Anibo yelled as he freed himself from Talimannog's grip and punched his elder brother in the face, knocking him down. "No akka! Just no! We could have gone back for him! We should have gone back!"

"And then what?!" Talimannog snapped back at him. "I would have lost two brothers if we did! And had we all perished in that swamp, what would become of Innawagan then?"

Anibo fell to his knees and cried. "He was my twin akka. I didn't just lose a brother you understand. I lost half of myself!"

Talimannog knelt beside Anibo and cried with him as they both mourned the loss of their sibling.

"What are they doing kakteh?" Pane Nagdombilan asked as the sudden sound of his voice made Talimannog and Anibo jump to their feet.

"It looks like they are crying kakteh," Pane Kalimangalnuk answered his brother. "As to why they are crying, I have no idea."

"You piece of filth!" Anibo cried out as he jumped at Pane Kalimangalnuk.

But even before Talimannog could stop his brother, Pane Kalimangalnuk simply swatted Anibo like a fly and knocked him to the ground.

"Control your brother Talimannog or the next time he

does something stupid, you will truly have lost one of your siblings!" Pane Kalimangalnuk threatened Talimannog.

"What do you mean by your words?" Talimannog asked as he held Anibo by his shoulder to steady him. "And where is Dundunan?"

"They are truly stupid people kakteh. Why do we even bother letting them live?" Pane Nagdombilan said with an air of superiority.

"Do none of you even remember what I told you before?" Pane Kalimangalnuk asked in frustration. "Your brother Ammani lives, just as I promised my wife-to-be. He is imprisoned in one of my rakuhs for failing the last challenge. Whether or not he continues to live, only depends on if the two of you can survive three more challenges."

Talimannog and Anibo look at each other and recall the manulib's words from the first rakuh. They nod to each other and stand, facing the copper-skinned manulib, and looked them directly in their yellow eyes.

"Ah, they finally seem to remember kakteh." Pane Nagdombilan said and grinned at Anibo.

"And what about Dundunan?" Anibo asked. "What befell our kumaw friend?"

"Dundunan was sent to your sister to keep her company," Pane Nagdombilan answered. "Her presence in this rakuh will give the two of you too much of an advantage in this challenge to let her stay with you."

"Please tell us what this next challenge entails so that we can be better prepared," Talimannog requested of Pane Kalimangalnuk after realizing that Ammani was still alive and hoping to change the mood to give him and Anibo a chance to fight for their lives.

"Good choice Talimannog," Pane Kalimangalnuk said in appreciation as he turned around and showed Talimannog and Anibo the rest of the landscape. "As you can see, you and your brother are in a field of ruot that stretches for miles all around you.

"If you look over behind me, toward that distant hill, it is there where you will find my kekteh's sakbawan. Just like before, all you and your brother have to do is reach it and cross over to the next rakuh. Pretty simple, yes?" Pane Kalimangalnuk said and smiled at Talimannog.

"Nothing is ever as simple as you say manulib," Talimannog scoffed. "What lays in wait for us behind the tall ruot? What sort of strange animal stalks us?"

"No animals, I promise," Pane Kalimangalnuk replied. "No more animal hunting for you and Anibo. What hides behind the ruot are Kalinga headhunters. This time you are the hunted."

"Fight your way through and reach the sakbawan!" Pane Nagdombilan said. "Don't bother to reason with the headhunters for they are not real men. Kill as many as you can."

The two manulib brothers turned and disappeared into the tall grass, leaving Talimannog and Anibo to face the challenge.

"What do we do?" Anibo asked Talimannog.

"Keep your voice down," Talimannog whispered. The hill where the sakbawan is located is quite a distance away. We need to be stealthy and try to avoid headhunters."

Talimannog and Anibo crouched and kept low as they slowly traversed the sea of ruot that kept everything, and everyone shrouded from each other. A few times they heard movement from people rustling through the grass around them. But being experienced hunters, the brothers were not unfamiliar with keeping silent yet being able to communicate effectively in the field.

Talimannog was hoping they would be able to avoid detection and reach the sakbawan without incident. But that hope quickly faded when a headhunter accidentally bungled between them.

The Kalinga headhunter was armed with a two-foot headhunting axe and a short kalasag shield. The headhunter just stumbled between them and stopped as soon as he saw Anibo. He raised his axe and was about to attack Anibo when Talimannog shot him with an arrow to the back of his neck.

The headhunter fell and died almost instantly, but not before another pair saw him fall. Anibo saw the other two coming at them and quickly drew his bow and aimed at the one closest to him. At the same time, Talimannog dashed for the kalasag that the fallen headhunter dropped when he died.

Anibo's arrow struck the headhunter in the neck, but to his surprise, the Kalinga kept running towards him with his axe raised high in the air. Anibo had to draw his bolo and parry his attacker's overhand blow. The Kalinga headhunter kept coming at him which forced Anibo to be defensive. Finally, after his attacker's third strike, signs of fatigue from his wounded neck finally manifested in the Kalinga. Anibo noticed this and quickly went on the offensive. With one telegraphed horizontal swipe of the headhunter's axe, Anibo was able to quickly dodge the blow and stab his attacker in the chest.

As Anibo buried his bolo even deeper into the Kalinga's chest, he noticed his opponent's eyes look at him without any fear, emotion, or even concern for his own life. *Something is wrong with this man.* he thought to himself. *He has no emotion, no soul.*

To his further surprise, as soon as the body of the Kalinga headhunter fell to the ground, the earth beneath the body started to shift almost immediately. The ground itself opened up and began swallowing the dead body as though it fell on deep soft mud. Within moments, all that was left of the body was his axe.

What is going on?! Anibo thought as he became panicked and confused.

While all of this was going on, Talimannog was busy with his own headhunter assailant. His opponent was armed with a bow and arrow of his own. The Kalinga shot two arrows at Talimannog, both of which he was able to block with the kalasag shield he took from the first headhunter.

After the first two arrows, the Kalinga dropped his bow and proceeded to attack Talimannog with his axe. Talimannog had to drop his own bow and draw his bolo. Compared to Anibo, Talimannog was the better fighter with blades and was able to end his fight quickly with a quick upward thrust of his bolo under his opponent's chin. But just like Anibo, Talimannog noticed the utter lack of emotion in his enemy's expression as he died.

"Akka! More are coming this way!" Anibo told Talimannog as he picked up his brother's bow and handed it to him.

"Then we better start running," Talimannog said as he took his bow and both brothers started running for the sakbawan.

"Did you see the ground swallow up those men's

bodies?" Anibo asked Talimannog as if trying to confirm that he wasn't seeing things.

"I did. But put that thought behind you. We are not out of danger yet." Talimannog responded.

"Something is very strange about these men akka," Anibo said as they ran. "They don't have any feelings or emotions. Did you notice that?"

"I did, I suspect they're not really alive to begin with," Talimannog answered. "Nothing in this place is real. The only thing real here is us and the sakbawan."

"Then why are we even running?" Anibo asked.

"Because whatever happens to us will have real results. Now save your breath and keep running." Talimannog told his brother as a couple of arrows zipped past their heads.

*****

Their unending skirmishes in the tall grassy plains lasted for hours. Luckily for the brothers, their emotionless adversaries were all fighting at a disadvantage since they lacked the basic instincts a warrior needed to be cunning in battle. They usually attacked as soon as they spotted the brothers, which made them predictable.

But as predictable as their opponents are, the sheer number of them was starting to take its toll on

Talimannog and Anibo. Though the brothers have collected arrows and kalasag shields from their fallen enemies, they were getting very tired and weary from the constant fighting. Hunger and thirst were starting to weigh them down and weakness was already beginning to weigh heavily on their muscles.

"Akka... I don't know how long I can keep this up. How far are we from the sakbawan?" Anibo asked as he gasped for every breath of air he could pull into his starved lungs.

"I'm not sure wadi," Talimannog replied. "Let me take a look."

Talimannog stood up to his full height, which was a good three inches above Anibo, and looked toward the direction of the hill where the sakbawan was supposed to be. But as soon as he got his head up past the height of the grass, an arrow came straight at him.

But Talimannog was already aware of these attacks and was able to block the arrow with his hole-riddled kalasag. "We are still a good two miles away from the hill," he told Anibo. "To your left, one attacker."

Anibo drew his bow from his crouched position and aimed his arrow pointing diagonally upwards to his left. A few seconds later, another headhunter barreled through the grass. Anibo loosed his arrow and struck the attacker in the middle of his chest and pierced his heart.

"Two miles?!" Anibo complained as he pulled his arrow out of the dead Kalinga's chest. "I don't think I can make it that far."

"Maybe we don't have to," Talimannog retorted. "I saw a mound a few hundred feet to my right. I saw some large rocks sticking out from atop the mound. Maybe we could go there and see if we can get some rest.

"The rocks should give us cover and the elevation will help us see our enemies as they come. Keep low and follow me." Talimannog said as he gestured for Anibo to follow.

They reached the mound without incident and true enough, it had several large outcrops that they could hide behind. "Rest here for a while wadi," Talimannog whispered. "I'll take a look around and see exactly where we are and how many are still out there."

He slowly peered over an outcrop and just as he suspected, the mound's elevation gave him a better view of his surroundings. The first thing he noticed was the distance to their destination. Getting to the mound led them a little farther away from the hill, but at the rate they were going, he doubted that they would've made it to the hill anyway.

The next thing Talimannog noticed were the Kalinga headhunters searching for them in the tall grass. Their movements were quite visible as they disturbed and bent the grass in front of them as they moved. From where Talimannog was, the Kalinga looked like fish swimming near the surface of the water, making small visible cuts along the surface.

"There are five of them out there right now," Talimannog whispered. "None of them are close which gives us ample time to rest."

"Good," Anibo said in relief. "I could really use the rest, but my mouth is parched. I don't suppose you see a stream or brook out there?"

"I'm thirsty as well wadi, but I don't see anything resembling water from here."

"That's not good," Anibo said as he closed his eyes to rest. "Is it just me or had the sun not moved in the last few hours? I swear I remember it being high noon when we first started, and it still looks like noon right now?"

"It hasn't moved an inch wadi," Talimannog answered. "Not even the sun is real in this place. Now be quiet and rest. I'll keep watch."

As far as resting his eyes and dozing off was a welcome relief to Anibo, but unfortunately for the brothers, the respite didn't last long. "Get up! They saw me!" Talimannog cried to the sleeping Anibo.

Anibo jumped to his feet and quickly nocked an arrow on his bow. "Where akka? Where are they?" Anibo asked as he tried to gather his wits about him.

"One is coming in from my left!" Talimannog said as he raised his kalasag and blocked an arrow aimed at his head.

Anibo dashed to his brother's left and saw a headhunter running through the grass and nearing the foot of the mound. He waited until the Kalinga passed the tall grass and shot him in the chest as soon as he had a clear line of sight.

But just as soon as the headhunter fell, Anibo saw another one ascending the mound farther to his left. This time he saw that it was a woman headhunter and that his line of sight was already blocked by rocks. So, Anibo drew his bolo once again and hid behind an outcrop he knew the headhunter would pass through on her way to him.

His wait didn't take long. The woman passed by the outcrop with her axe held high and headed straight for Talimannog who was busy aiming at his own opponent. As soon as the woman passed Anibo, he grabbed her by her long hair and pulled her head back, exposing her neck. He ran his bolo across her neck and felt it slice clean through the woman's throat.

Anibo looked up at his brother and saw him loose an arrow at his enemy. But unbeknownst to Talimannog, another headhunter came up behind him with a bolo of his own. Anibo had to act quickly.

He had dropped his bow on the ground before he

ambushed the woman and didn't have time to pick it back up. Having only his bolo in his hand, Anibo flipped it over and threw it at his brother's attacker. It struck the Kalinga at the side of his stomach and buried itself deep in his bowels, knocking him down to the ground. This gave Talimannog enough time to turn around and react.

Talimannog stomped his foot squarely on the headhunter's jaw and broke his neck. Anibo, thinking that the danger had passed was about to walk over to Talimannog when he saw his brother's eyes widen. Anibo turned around and saw another attacker coming at him from behind. This new Kalinga headhunter had his axe raised high and was a second away from burying it in Anibo's skull. But even before the Kalinga could swing his axe down, an arrow flew just above Anibo's head and struck the Kalinga in the left eye, killing him instantly.

"Grab what you can! I see more coming! We need to go now!" Talimannog barked at Anibo.

The brothers ran as fast as they could through the tall grass and toward the direction of the sakbawan. They were tired beyond anything they have felt before with only the instinct to live keeping them on their feet.

"Where are we heading akka?" Anibo asked as he panted.

"The sakbawan," Talimannog answered. "There is nowhere else to go. That mound was probably the last refuge we could hope for. Keep strong wadi, it won't be long now."

*****

Against all odds and with a tremendous amount of luck, both brothers neared the edge of the grassy plain that opened up to the foot of the hill. They only had one skirmish on the way in the form of a headhunter whom they quickly dispatched with an arrow shot to the back of the neck.

"We're here akka," Anibo exclaimed as soon as he saw the hill above the grass as they approached. "I can't believe we made it."

"Hush!" Talimannog suddenly hushed Anibo. "Get down."

Talimannog gave Anibo the hand signal to get down on his hands and knees. He then gestured for them to be quiet and observe the space between the edge of the field and the hill.

At first, Anibo thought more headhunters were coming from behind them. But just as he was about to turn around and see, he heard footsteps crunching on dry earth coming from ahead of them.

They slowly crawled closer to the edge of the field and carefully peeked through the tall grass. That was when he saw them. Seven headhunters, five men, and two women were walking in the open space between the field and the hill. Three of them had bows and arrows while the other four were with axes and shields.

Talimannog slowly approached Anibo and whispered in his ear, "Do you see where we need to go?"

"No. Up the hill I assume?" Anibo whispered back.

"Look over there," Talimannog whispered and pointed to a narrow slit on the side of the hill. "We'll let them pass us and then we'll make a run for that narrow pass. There's only around twenty feet of open space we need to cross."

"Are you sure akka?" Anibo asked, uncertain of his brother's plan. "How do you know that's not a dead end? Why not just climb or look around for another place to go up?"

"We'll be too exposed if we climb," Talimannog explained. "And I don't think there is another way up. Look at that hill. It's mostly rock and earth. I don't see any slopes we can easily traverse to reach the top and find the sakbawan. Just trust me wadi. We'll wait for them to pass us, and we'll just sneak up there without them noticing."

So Anibo silently waited there with Talimannog as they watched each of the seven headhunters walk past them. Everything seemed to be going their way as the last headhunter's legs walked past the brothers. Anibo was thinking they only need to wait for another minute, and they should be beyond hearing range.

But as he crouched there, Anibo suddenly heard the sound of grass rustling from behind them. He turned to look and to his horror, he sees a headhunter standing behind him with a bow and arrow in hand. What happened next was a blur of confusion and chaos that lasted a few seconds but seemed to last forever for Anibo.

Seeing that the bow was aimed directly at him, Anibo reflexively jumped at the Kalinga and pushed the bow upward to avoid getting shot by the arrow. The arrow was accidentally loosed and flew off to Anibo's left. As soon as he saw what was happening, Talimannog jumped at the Kalinga as well as drove his bolo right under the headhunter's chin which killed him instantly.

But even before the body of the headhunter was swallowed by the earth, much like what happened to everyone they killed in that field, whatever hope the brothers had of stealth and subterfuge disappeared. An arrow from one of the seven headhunters that had just passed them struck Anibo on the right shoulder. The seven were alerted to their presence when the recently dead Kalinga's arrow shot out of the field and struck the ground next to one of the seven.

"Aaargh!" Anibo yelled out as the arrow buried itself behind his right shoulder. "Run akka! Run!"

The brothers ran as quickly as they could to the narrow slip that ran in the middle of the hill's face.

Arrow after arrow flew at them as the headhunters loosed them. Talimannog caught one on his kalasag as he tried his best to shield Anibo that ran ahead of him. But luck was still on the brothers' side as the headhunters were still about a hundred feet away from them and couldn't get an accurate shot.

"Get to the pass wadi!" Talimannog barked at Anibo. "I'll shield you from the arrows."

The pass itself was only about three feet wide and in some sections barely two. Due to the narrow corridor that they had to traverse, the arrow protruding from Anibo's shoulder started hitting the side of the walls and began ripping at Anibo's shoulder blade.

"Akka! You need to pull it out! I can't move with this thing sticking out of me!" Anibo screamed in pain.

"But you might bleed out if I pull it out without bandaging it," Talimannog said worriedly.

"I can't make it through this pass with this in my back! What do you think will happen next?!" Anibo protested.

Seeing as there was no other alternative, Talimannog decided to pull it out. "Hold firm wadi, this will hurt."

"I know," Anibo said as he bit down on his bow and nodded to Talimannog to show that he was ready.

With one quick pull, Talimannog pulled the arrow out of Anibo's shoulder blade. Talimannog was relieved to see that the arrow was similar to their patak arrows which were straight and barbless. But the wound left behind was deep and began bleeding profusely.

"You're bleeding bad wadi," he said as he tried to cover the wound and staunch the blood flow with his hand.

"That's the least of our worries akka," Anibo said as a sudden clinking sound came from behind Talimannog. It came from another arrow! "They're here! Run akka! Run!"

With the arrow removed from Anibo's back, the brothers moved much quicker through the narrow corridor that ran through the middle of the hill. As it zigged and zagged between two narrow rock faces, they noticed that the ground elevation started climbing. They prayed to the Poons that the pass will lead to the top of the hill where they suspected the sakbawan would be and not to a dead end.

They would hear the ever-present sound of arrows clinking as they struck the sides of the wall every time the headhunters would miss. As nerve-racking as the situation is, hearing some of the arrows zipping past their ears did not help alleviate the tension.

But as grueling and exhausting as the trek through the pass was, Anibo was still somewhat appreciative of it. Even though he knew that the headhunters were directly behind them, he was at least confident that he knew exactly where they were as compared to the uncertainty that the grassy field offered.

"I think we're near the top akka!" Anibo yelled out as he ran. "I think the air is getting cooler at this point."

"Stop thinking wadi and keep running!" Talimannog responded as cautiously brought up the rear. "They're gaining on us!"

It only took the brothers a few more minutes of running before they reached the end of the pass; with only a few more narrow bends and turns. As abruptly narrow as the entrance to the pass was, the end of it was no different. Though the angle in the incline of the path drastically increased as they neared the exit, the end of the path opened up to a wide-open space on top of the hill.

At the other end of the space, at about eight hundred feet away, stood the sakbawan. The brothers were now faced with a decision to make on how to go about their next move.

"Akka, should we make a run for it?" Anibo asked. "Should we make a run for the sakbawan? I see it right there."

"Those headhunters are not too far behind us," Talimannog replied. "If we both run, they will catch up to us the moment they exit the pass. You are wounded, start running. I'll hold them off here as long as I can. I'll be running behind you in a few moments."

"But akka, I can't leave you..." Anibo was about to argue with his older brother's plan when Talimannog cut him off.

"Go! Just go! They're here!" Talimannog yelled at Anibo and drew his bow.

After hearing his older brother's command, Anibo started running for the sakbawan without question. It was only in the open space atop that hill that Anibo actually realized the extent of his wound. Having enough space to swing his arms in conjunction with his legs, Anibo had just realized that the puncture wound behind his right shoulder blade made the use of his arm extremely limited. And that was on top of the excruciating pain he felt.

His legs felt like there were rocks tied to them given how tired they were from the non-stop running they'd been doing since they entered the rakuh. But Anibo tried his best to fight through and ran as fast as he possibly could towards the sakbawan that seemed so close yet felt so distant from him.

*****

Talimannog had shot and killed the first Kalinga headhunter that turned the last bend of the path and headed up the steep incline that led towards him. The first one was a woman armed with a bow, probably the same one that had been shooting at them since they reached the narrow pass.

The second one that followed her was a man with a

kalasag shield raised in front of him. Talimannog's first arrow struck the shield which caused him to curse under his breath. Talimannog checked his pusot and discovered that he only had three arrows left.

Talimannog turned around to check on Anibo's progression and sadly saw his brother almost limping toward the sakbawan. *Damn it wadi, run faster!* Talimannog thought to himself as he drew a *ginilat* (bladed arrowhead with barbed thorns on the shaft) arrow and nocked it on his bow.

Talimannog took careful aim and targeted the left leg of the Kalinga headhunter. The kalasag shield being long and rectangular in shape, provided the headhunter superior protection from Talimannog. But the grooves at the shield's bottom section did give Talimannog a small sporadically moving opening that he could exploit.

As he drew his bow and aimed, Talimannog took a deep breath and held it in his lungs. He focused all his energy on that small moving opening and waited for his moment. As soon as he saw his opening, Talimannog exhaled and loosed the arrow from his bow.

As if guided by the Poons themselves, Talimannog's ginilat arrow passed between the grooves of the kalasag and buried itself deep in the Kalinga's thigh, down to every single barb.

The headhunter fell to his knees, effectively blocking

the path of the others behind him. He tried to pull the arrow out, but the barb of thorns clung to his thigh muscles as a fish to a hook. Talimannog saw this as his opportunity and started running after Anibo.

"Run wadi! Run faster!" Talimannog yelled as he ran behind Anibo. "We only have a few moments!"

Talimannog was only able to run a couple of hundred feet when he instinctively turned his head and saw the rest of the headhunters emerge from the pass and immediately run after them. The ones with bows and arrows start lobbing arrows at them as they ran after the brothers.

Talimannog thought about using his own kalasag shield to protect himself but quickly realized that he had left it on the ground next to the pass when he loosed arrows at their pursuers. So, to avoid getting struck by a wayward arrow, he started running in a zigzag pattern as he desperately tried to catch up to Anibo.

Arrows started landing to his left and right as he ran. Talimannog's legs were already starting to burn from fatigue and exhaustion, but he knew he had to power through for the sake of his siblings Anibo and Innawagan. He saw that he was more than halfway to Anibo and in a few more seconds, he would catch up to his brother. But as he turned his head once more, he also saw the headhunters gaining on him as well. These false people apparently don't get tired at all.

"Run faster wadi!" Talimannog yelled at the top of his lungs. "They're right behind me!"

After a few short moments that felt like forever, Talimannog eventually caught up to Anibo. He considered turning around and shooting back at the headhunters to give Anibo more time but reconsidered after he saw that the sakbawan was less than twenty feet away from them.

"We're almost there!" Talimannog yelled as he forced the last remaining ounce of strength he had left, to push his tired burning legs to last a few more seconds. Less than ten feet away from their objective, he heard Anibo call out to him as he passed his younger brother. "Go akka! I'm right behind you!"

Talimannog leapt at the last second and passed through the sakbawan and let his tired body fall through the emptiness of nothing for a few short seconds before emerging on the other side.

*****

Talimannog, who had taken over telling this part of the tale fell silent and looked blankly at the roaring flame in front of them.

"Then what happened?" Kidul asked inquisitively.

"And then I fell on the ground, stood up, turned

around, and waited for Anibo to pass through the ripple in the air," Talimannog said solemnly. "I waited and waited, but wadi never came."

"Wait! You didn't make it?" Lumalindaw asked Anibo, surprised. "But you were only a few feet away from Talimannog!"

Then Anibo spoke up to break the suspense, "The very second that I saw akka pass through the sakbawan, I felt a sharp stabbing pain run through my left calf muscle.

"I fell on the ground face first, only two feet away from the sakbawan," Anibo said as he recalled what befell him. "I knew an arrow had struck my leg, but I could practically reach up and almost touch those golden doors. I tried to crawl to them but as soon as I did, another sharp stabbing pain struck me in the small of my back. That one I think damaged my spine as I had lost all feeling in my legs. Gone was the burning of the tired muscles and the sharp piercing sensation of the arrow.

"The next thing I saw were the headhunters standing next to me as I felt the earth beneath me start to rumble and shift. I was about to experience what those dead headhunters went through after I killed them and to this day, I have never been as scared as I was at that moment.

"As the earth took me, I waited for the sweet release of death, hoping that my spirit would take me to our daddakal in Kaluwalhatian. But imagine my surprise when I suddenly felt my body encased in rock with hardly enough room to move.

"There was a small hole in front of my face and all around me was darkness as my eyes started to adjust to the gloom," Anibo said.

"*Where am I?* Was the first thought that came to my head. Then I called out for akka but all I heard was the sound of my own voice echoing all around me. And just then, the strangest thing happened. I heard someone speak in the darkness, "Anibo? Is that you?"

"That was me by the way," Ammani said.

Chapter 15

The Lull Before Bedlam

So now we're at the part where almost everything is happening all at once," Taguwasi said as he stood up to stretch his arms and legs that were starting to fall asleep. "Who is going to tell the next part of our story?"

"If none of you mind, I have heard this tale before and it is getting very late," Puyang Anag said as the old shaman got to her feet. "I will meet this Isneg man whom I suspect is my old friend Namandiyanin and hear what he has to say. Besides, the elderly such as I need as much rest as we can get. Will I still see you tomorrow Lakandian Lumalindaw?"

"Rest assured, I will say my goodbyes to you before I leave Puyang Anag," Lumalindaw answered. "I will also need that information your old friend tells you, so I at least know where to search next."

"Then, I am off to meet with him then," Puyang Anag said as she turned to go to her hut. "Masampat a abi to all of you."

"Masampat a abi Puyang Anag," Innawagan greeted the old woman back as she left.

"There is still a good amount of story to tell Lumalindaw," Taguwasi said. "Do you want to continue, or do you want to retire for the night like Puyang Anag?"

"I want to hear the end of this story," Kidul spoke up before Lumalindaw could answer. "If you say you want to sleep before they finish their tale then I swear no one will get any sleep. I'll make sure of it."

"Then I suppose I don't have any choice in the matter," Lumalindaw chuckled. "So who would like to go next?"

"I suggest we don't waste any time choosing who gets to go next," Alig said. "Let's just start and see the tale through to the end."

"I agree with akka," Innawagan said next. "Ready yourself for a long night Lumalindaw. We're going to finish this tale even if it takes us 'til dawn..."

*****

"Is he alive?" Innawagan asked Pane Kalimangalnuk. "Is Anibo with Ammani?" She tried her best to hide her horror as she watched her younger brother get struck down by arrows.

Pane Kalimangalnuk approached Innawagan who stood at the other side of the pool. He wrapped his arms around her as a lover would as if to console her for her troubles. Troubles that he, in all irony, caused to begin with.

Dundunan, who had been allowed to join Innawagan fought every instinct in her body to defend her Hapu from the manulib's advances. But after seeing the kumaw struggle, Innawagan shook her head ever so slightly at Dundunan as if to tell her not to do anything.

"Of course, he is alive mavid," he said as he kissed her neck. "He is safe and unmoving with his twin contained in my rakuh."

Fighting the revulsion that crept its way up to her throat, Innawagan tried her best to brush it off and ask, "Would you allow me to visit Anibo as well? Just as you did when you allowed me to go to Ammani."

"You've already seen my mercy and my honesty when you saw Ammani earlier," Pane Kalimangalnuk said as he released Innawagan from his embrace. "I honestly don't see the reason to go back there just to see Anibo."

Innawagan stood silently for a moment as she contemplated what her next move should be. She needed to stall for time. She needed to do something to help Talimannog as well as give Dalawesan enough time to find the flying man.

Suddenly she heard wings flapping just above them. She looked up hoping to see Dalawesan with their rescuer finally arrive. But Innawagan's heart sank as she saw Ammalabukaw descend from the domed ceiling above.

The gigantic red-feathered kumaw landed in front of Pane Kalimangalnuk and bowed his head. Pane Nagdombilan approached Ammalabukaw with anger and disappointment burning bright in his eyes and asked,

"Did you find him? Did you find the black kumaw whom you let escape yet?"

"No, Pane Nagdombilan, I have not. For the last two days, I have searched every settlement in the western mountains that I could find and have found no sign of Dalawesan." Ammalabukaw answered in frustration.

"Which brings me back to the question I have asked you before kakteh," Pane Nagdombilan said as he turned to his brother. "Why should we let this treasonous creature live after he betrayed us?"

"I have not betrayed my master!" Ammalabukaw snapped back at Pane Nagdombilan. "I simply followed his commands down to the letter. I owe Pane Kalimangalnuk a life debt. If he so wishes to kill me for this transgression that you speak of, then I will gladly accept my fate as payment for my life debt. But I do not owe you anything Pane Nagdombilan!"

"Stop it!" Pane Kalimangalnuk commanded. "Both of you! This bickering will not resolve anything nor does the entire thing actually merit any concern to us.

"Kakteh, think about it. What can one kumaw do to us? So Ammalabukaw allowed Dalawesan to flee. So what? What can he do? Who can he ask assistance from?" Pane Kalimangalnuk said as he tried to soothe his brother's bruised ego.

"And what about this flying man whom the kumaw

seeks?" Pane Nagdombilan asked his brother. "What if he finds him?"

"First of all, dear kakteh, no such person exists," Pane Kalimangalnuk said as he tried to make his brother listen to logic and reason. "He is nothing more than a myth! Secondly, even if he did exist, what could he possibly do to us?"

"What if this flying man is the one that killed the blood serpent? Would you not find him dangerous?" Pane Nagdombilan insisted.

A loud grumbling sound came from Pane Kalimangalnuk's stomach as the stress of it all began manifesting in his torturous hunger. "Enough with the what-ifs!" he finally snapped.

Pane Kalimangalnuk then turned to Innawagan with a scornful, angry expression on his face which made Innawagan run to Dundunan's wings and cower at the sight of him. "For the last time mavid, where did Dalawesan go? What did you tell him?"

"I told him exactly as Ammaḷabukaw said I did. I told him to go to my sister and find out where the flying man lives," Innawagan answered as her voice quivered in fear. "I told him to ask for help. That is all."

"The sister! Did you find her sister?" Pane Nagdombilan asked Ammalabukaw.

"No. I visited their camp and found it empty. Wherever

Alig is right now, she is definitely in hiding." Ammalabukaw answered.

"Yyyaaarrgh!" Pane Nagdombilan screamed in frustration as golden spikes suddenly shot up from the ground and hovered perilously in the air around the manulib.

This sent everyone in the room other than Pane Kalimangalnuk into a state of panic. Both kumaws who had no life debt to Pane Nagdombilan suddenly felt threatened and instinctively took a defensive posture.

"Kakteh, stop it," Pane Kalimangalnuk said calmly. "There is no point in venting your frustrations out inside this rakuh. Talimannog on the other hand is waiting for us in my other rakuh. I think it's time we visit him and vent some of your frustrations out on him instead."

After hearing what the manulib brothers had planned for Talimannog, Innawagan knew she had to act fast. She knew she could not allow the manulib brothers to go to Talimannog angry and frustrated. She needed to calm them down, especially Pane Kalimangalnuk.

"If you go to akka Talimannog as you are now then you have just proven to me that you are not a man of your word!" Innawagan cried out in desperation. "And if there is one thing that I despise the most in a man, it's dishonesty!"

The manulib brothers were just about to enter a door

leading to where Talimannog was when Pane Kalimangalnuk suddenly stopped and turned back towards Innawagan. "Now is not the best time to test my patience mavid," he said as threateningly as he could.

"Your patience?" Innawagan asked rhetorically. "Your patience is the reason why I am calling you out in the first place."

Pane Kalimangalnuk started approaching Innawagan with anger and fury conveyed with every step. Dundunan instinctively jumped in front of Pane Kalimangalnuk as soon as she saw the evil intent in the manulib's face. But as intimidating as an angry kumaw might be to anyone unfortunate enough to encounter one, to someone like Pane Kalimangalnuk, Dundunan was nothing more than a nuisance. Something he only needed to swat away to be rid of, which was exactly what he did.

With a quick slap from his left hand, Dundunan went flying across the room and crashed on the floor right in front of Ammalabukaw. Dundunan was about to get up and attack Pane Kalimangalnuk when she felt something heavy pin her down to the ground. It was Ammalabukaw who held her down with one of his gigantic feet, "Stay down old friend," he whispered to her ear. "There is nothing either one of us can do for your Hapu."

"What are you doing?!" Innawagan yelled at Pane Kalimangalnuk, with all the courage that she could pretend to muster. "Why are you pouring out your anger at those who have done you no wrong?"

Even before the manulib could do anything, Innawagan gave him a thundering slap across the cheek. The audacity of Innawagan had somehow shocked Pane Kalimangalnuk into stillness. He wasn't expecting her to be so aggressive. For the first time in almost a century, Pane Kalimangalnuk was dumbstruck.

Innawagan noticed the manulib's confused reaction to her outburst and quickly followed up on it. "I was the one who told Dalawesan to go and seek help from this flying man who may or may not even exist! I was the one who convinced him to leave! After seeing how you've been treating me and my family, could you really blame me for trying?

"You promised to test my siblings as warriors to see if they are worthy of serving you and in return, I agreed to be your wife willingly did I not? But you weren't really giving them a fighting chance. Talimannog is all that is left for you to test, yet you won't even give him a chance to rest and regain his strength.

"And because you were angered by my actions, which to be honest, will most likely not bear any fruit; you want to vent your frustrations out on akka. How is that fair?" Innawagan raved and ranted as much as she could until she was suddenly cut short by a humongous golden hand that sprouted out of the ground and held her suspended in its grip.

"Kakteh! Please don't tell me you were swayed by this woman's ravings?" Pane Nagdombilan exclaimed as he stepped between his brother and Innawagan. "Her ramblings are nothing more than that, ramblings! Her logic doesn't even make sense!"

Pane Kalimangalnuk stared at his brother intently and then turned his gaze to Innawagan. He closed his eyes, took a deep breath, and smiled. "I do hear you kakteh and I do agree with what you are telling me. But I also agree with mavid. I am taking this entire thing out of proportion."

Pane Kalimangalnuk opened his eyes and sighed in relief. "Come kakteh, Talimannog awaits his next challenge," he said as he took his brother by the shoulders and turned him towards the door that leads to Talimannog. "And don't worry mavid, I shall be fair to your beloved akka. I shall give him ample time to rest and some water to drink before I present him with his next challenge."

*****

Taguwasi and Dalawesan had just crossed the Cagayan River and were well on their way to save Innawagan and her brothers. Dalawesan still suffered from exhaustion from his long and arduous search which caused him to fly slowly. Taguwasi being an extremely fast flyer through his very nature could not bear flying at Dalawesan's pace.

To remedy the situation, Taguwasi commanded the wind to carry Dalawesan so that he could match the Lakandian's speed. The only thing the kumaw needed to do was spread his wings and allow the wind to carry him.

"I am ashamed to say that in all my life, I have never flown at such speeds before," Dalawesan said as the exhilaration of their speed excited him. "At this rate, we should reach the lagoon and the caves in less than an hour."

"That means we still have a lot more time on our hands before Taguwasi has to fight," The anito Bago said as he hovered over the back of Dalawesan. "Please tell us more about these manulib creatures that the Lakandian will face."

"I think I told both of you all that I know about them," Dalawesan replied. "One can create rakuhs or rooms of illusion, and the other one can create solid objects made of gold.

"They are strong, and their flesh is far more durable than a normal human's. Hapu Innawagan mentioned something about them using an agimat which is probably where their powers come from."

"Did you see an agimat around their necks or anywhere on their person?" Taguwasi asked as he flew alongside Dalawesan and Bago.

"No. Not really. They wore clothes similar to the Ivatan people from the northern islands, but nothing out of the ordinary." Dalawesan answered.

"Then I guess I'll just have to kill them like I do every other evil thing I encounter," Taguwasi said decidedly.

As they flew over a small Agta settlement, Dalawesan saw someone on the ground looking up at them. "Hapu Alig?" Dalawesan said softly.

"Hapu what?" Bago asked as he didn't quite understand what Dalawesan meant by what he said.

"It's Hapu Alig! She is down there at that settlement," Dalawesan said excitedly. "We should stop by and see if she has any news of our siblings."

A crowd of around five other people gathered around where Dalawesan and Taguwasi landed. At first, they were afraid when they saw Dalawesan, but the second they saw Taguwasi, a fellow Aeta man flying around and landing as gracefully as a bird, all their fears turned to instant curiosity.

"Dalawesan!" Alig said as she waved at them when they arrived. "I'm so happy to see you. Is this him? Is this the flying man?"

"Well, I do fly, so I suppose I am he." Taguwasi greeted

Alig as he introduced himself. "I am the Lakandian Taguwasi."

"My name is Alig. Are you here to help save my siblings from those manulib creatures?"

"I will do my best, that is all I can promise."

"Hapu Alig, I am glad you are safe. Do you have any new information before we head over to the lagoon?" Dalawesan interjected.

"Nothing new, unfortunately," Alig answered. "Though I did see the big red kumaw Ammalabukaw pass by here yesterday. I hid in one of the huts as soon as I saw him in the air. These people were kind enough to take me in when I ran away from our home."

"Ammalabukaw is the kumaw that is in league with the manulib is he not?" Bago asked.

"Agay!" Alig exclaimed. "Is that an anito?"

"Whoa!" Bago exclaimed as well. "She can see me?! Is she Angkang Dian as well?"

"What is that?" Dalawesan asked perplexingly. "She and her siblings are sensitive to the presence of spirits, much like some humans are. Though I am not sure of this Angkang Dian that you speak of?"

"Never mind," Taguwasi interrupted. "It matters not. We need to focus on saving your siblings, that is the main goal."

"You are right Lakandian, I am sorry," Dalawesan

apologized. "If Ammalabukaw is out looking for us, then that means Pane Kalimangalnuk ordered him to find us. This tells me that tension is building between the manulib brothers and our siblings. We should go there at once."

"I would like to help and fight," Alig said as sternly as she could.

"I would advise against that," Taguwasi responded. "Though I do not doubt your prowess in battle, you would unintentionally slow us down. This is a battle between beings with powers and abilities, I need to focus on the fight itself and not worry about your safety."

"Stay here where it's safe Hapu, pray to the Poons to keep us and all our siblings safe," Dalawesan said as he turned towards Taguwasi and signaled him that they needed to go.

Suddenly, a gust of wind came from out of nowhere and lifted the three and carried them northeast towards the lagoon.

*****

Talimannog passed through the sakbawan and emerged in a small empty settlement in the middle of the jungle. There were several huts and a few pinanahang structures laying about. It seemed like it was in the middle of the afternoon where he was, but knowing that he was still inside a rakuh, Talimannog was uncertain.

Anibo. His brother's name suddenly popped into his head as he turned and looked at the rippling distortion in the air. *Where are you? Come on wadi! Show yourself!*

Panic suddenly started overwhelming him as the seconds went by and Anibo was nowhere to be seen. Each second felt like a minute as Talimannog kept running through his memory of the last fleeting moments before he crossed the sakbawan.

He was right behind me! I saw him next to me a few seconds before I reached the sakbawan. He should be here! Were the thoughts that raced in Talimannog's mind. "Anibo! Wadi! Where are you?!" He finally yelled out.

"Your brother fell in the last challenge Talimannog," Pane Kalimangalnuk's voice suddenly came from behind him, startling Talimannog as he turned around.

"Anibo is now with Ammani," Pane Nagdombilan spoke next. "They are trapped in a cave wall, losing their minds as their bodies slowly die of exhaustion!"

This angered Talimannog greatly but knowing that there was nothing he could really do angered him even more. It took every ounce of willpower from the proud warrior not to react to the blatant taunting he received from the arrogant manulib.

"Kakteh, don't be like that," Pane Kalimangalnuk playfully told his brother. "I told Innawagan that I was going to be fair in testing her brothers and so I will."

"Talimannog," Pane Kalimangalnuk said as he turned his attention to him. "You look tired. Out of the spirit of fairness as well as my promise to my wife-to-be, I will let you rest and recuperate before your next challenge begins."

Talimannog looked at the manulib with untrusting eyes as he tried to decipher what form of deceit lurked behind his words.

"Don't look at me like that patepag," Pane Kalimangalnuk said jokingly. "I said I was going to let you rest and so I shall. If you are worried about the twins, then you should set your worry aside. They are alive yes. Are they well? Well, that is left up to you. All you need to do is pass this final challenge."

"And what is the final challenge, if you don't mind me asking?" Talimannog asked.

"All in due time patepag. For now, you should eat and rest. Come and enjoy the meal I have prepared for you." Pane Kalimangalnuk said as he stepped aside and revealed a group of five beautiful women carrying baskets of food.

The women, like the Kalinga headhunters that Talimannog had fought in the previous rakuh, were not real. They displayed no emotion nor did they even blink. Talimannog was taken aback and tried to deduce the treachery behind the manulib's intentions.

"None of this is real," Talimannog whispered under his breath. "Not the food, not the water, nor the women."

"Of course, they're not!" Pane Kalimangalnuk shouted out in laughter. "I am glad to see that you finally understand what it means to be inside my rakuh. But that doesn't mean that the food will not make you feel like your belly is full, or that the water in those jugs will not quench your thirst; at least in your mind."

"But why do this?" Talimannog asked. "To what end?"

"To make sure you are ready for the next challenge of course," Pane Kalimangalnuk said gleefully. "Succeed and you will not only get to see your sister become my wife, but you would also get to save the twins from death as all three of you become our servants."

You spoke of five challenges before," Talimannog said. "This only makes four."

"The last challenge will be the simplest," Pane Kalimangalnuk replied. "Provided you succeed in this one, the next challenge will be a simple oath-taking where you and your siblings pledge your loyalties to us and watch as I marry your sister."

"What is the next challenge then?" Talimannog asked.

But quite suddenly, Pane Nagdombilan picked Talimannog up by the throat and threw him at the false women carrying food.

"What is with all these questions?" Pane Nagdombilan

asked angrily as Talimannog crashed to the ground. "Can't you just appreciate my kakteh's generosity and be grateful? He will tell you what the next challenge is when he is good and ready and not a moment before!"

"You must forgive Kekteh's hotheadedness patepag," Pane Kalimangalnuk chuckled. "He was never known to be a patient man even when we were humans like yourself.

"Now go eat and rest. You may even bed these women if you wish. I can make that happen quite easily" Pane Kalimangalnuk said magnanimously as the five false women set the baskets of food on a table that magically appeared in front of Talimannog. The women then began disrobing in front of the bewildered Talimannog.

Though the manly urge threatened to overtake Talimannog's senses and perspective, his intelligence won out in the end. "As much as what you offer is tempting, I must regrettably decline," he said with the utmost confidence. "I will need to conserve as much strength and stamina as I possibly could to pass your challenge and be of any service to you and my papatwadi."

"Very well said patepag!" Pane Kalimangalnuk said as he clasped his hands together and the five women disappeared into a puff of smoke. "Enjoy your meal and rest. Kakteh and I will wait until you are ready. You never know, this might be the last meal of your life."

*****

Even though he knew that none of the food he ate was real, it did not diminish the fact that it was probably the most delicious and satisfying meal Talimannog had ever had. There was roasted duck and boar meat slathered in a red-brownish sauce that was completely foreign to him. Big grilled eels skewered on sticks, a variety of vegetables and fruits, and large helpings of freshly cooked rice. All of which he ate greedily along with precious mouthfuls of quenching cold water.

Though to the eyes of the manulib brothers, Talimannog was nothing more than a gluttonous human over-indulging himself in food that wasn't even real, to begin with, he was secretly assessing his environment as he tried to guess what the next challenge was.

The settlement itself was surrounded by a thick, unforgiving jungle with no visible paths that led either in or out of the place. This meant that the challenge would be taking place within the settlement which also meant that it would not be an arduous trek as were the previous ones.

The huts and pinanahang structures were situated in a circular formation which told Talimannog that whatever the challenge was, it was going to happen right in the middle of the settlement. *The next challenge is going to be a straight-up fight.* Talimannog thought to himself. *The space is not too big which means my opponents will not be too many unless he means to simply outnumber me. But he mentioned something about fairness so it will probably be five or fewer false warriors that I face as it wouldn't be sporting or fair otherwise.*

The manulib brothers were just standing there as they watched Talimannog eat his fill of the false food they provided. They were unmoving as they stared at him as a predator would observe its prey. Finally, after a hearty meal, Talimannog stood up and spoke to Pane Kalimangalnuk, "You mentioned earlier that you allowed me to rest as well eat to my heart's content. Is that still allowed before I undergo my next challenge?"

"Why yes, of course," Pane Kalimangalnuk answered. "After a big meal such as what you just indulged in, I will allow you an hour's rest. After all, you will need all the rest you can muster for what's to come next. I suggest picking one of the huts to sleep in for that hour."

"As much as I appreciate the hospitality, why do I feel like a dying man being granted a final request?" Talimannog asked rhetorically.

"Because that's exactly what you are Talimannog!" Pane Nagdombilan suddenly snapped back at him.

"Then if that is indeed what you think I am, then would you mind granting a dying man a true final request?" Talimannog asked as courteously as he could.

"Maybe I will, maybe I won't," Pane Kalimangalnuk

answered playfully. "Tell me what your last request is, and I shall consider granting it."

"I wish to see and speak to Innawagan," Talimannog said. "I want to have a private conversation with her for at least half an hour. If you allow me this, then I will forgo the one-hour rest you offered me earlier."

Pane Kalimangalnuk was taken aback by this request. All the while he truly believed that he had anticipated every moment of how this last rakuh was going to play out. But Talimannog's final request had him thinking.

At first, he thought of just outright denying Talimannog's request. But at that point, he also considered the fact that there really wasn't anything Talimannog would be able to do to change the outcome of his fate. Denying him would actually make Pane Kalimangalnuk seem like he was afraid of granting him his request.

"I'll be honest Talimannog, I am actually quite intrigued by your request," Pane Kalimangalnuk finally replied. "Very well then. I shall grant you your final request and..."

"Kakteh!" Pane Nagdombilan suddenly interjected. "Why are you even considering giving this dead man any consideration?"

He really doesn't think I will survive this last challenge. Talimannog thought to himself as soon as he heard Pane

Nagdombilan's words. *My situation is becoming direr with every moment. I need to stall for as much time as I can.*

"Why does it matter kakteh?" Pane Kalimangalnuk replied to his brother. "How does talking to his sister affect us in any way?"

Seeing his brother silenced by reason, Pane Kalimangalnuk turned his attention back to Talimannog. "Being the merciful and considerate manulib that I am, I will grant you your request."

*****

Innawagan had heard everything that was said through the magical pool of water. At first, she couldn't believe what she had just heard. *Am I actually going to see akka?* she thought as she continued to listen to the conversation between Talimannog and Pane Kalimangalnuk. Then she saw her manulib captor look at her directly through the magical pool.

"Mavid, it's time for you to reunite with your akka regardless of how brief it may be," Pane Kalimangalnuk said. "Go through the door to your right and join us."

"Go ahead Innawagan," Ammalabukaw said as he gestured for her to go. "The master summons you."

"May I go with her old friend?" Dundunan asked.

"No. The master said nothing concerning you, so you cannot."

"Don't worry about me Dundunan. I will be fine." Innawagan assured Dundunan as she walked through the door.

Just as it was before when she passed through the door, she found herself in a dark tunnel. Though this time the tunnel was only a dozen feet long and she could clearly see a brightly lit room at the end of it.

When Innawagan exited the tunnel, she found herself in an empty hut. Realizing where she was, Innawagan hurriedly ran out the door and saw Talimannog standing there with his back to her. "Akka!" Innawagan quickly called out to her elder brother as she ran to him.

Talimannog turned and ran to his sister as soon as he heard her call him. "Wadi! Is that really you?" he said as he ran.

Both brother and sister caught each other in the middle and embraced each other tightly. Innawagan broke into tears of happiness as she thought she would never get to see her oldest sibling ever again.

"It's me akka, it's really me!" Innawagan cried out as she held her brother tightly.

"As touching as this little family reunion is, I do have to remind you that your limited time together started as soon as Innawagan entered this rakuh," Pane Kalimangalnuk said. "You might want to start telling each other your farewells as this might be your last chance to do so."

"Let's go into one of the huts wadi," Talimannog said as he pointed to one of the huts. "We have a lot to talk about in a short amount of time."

They entered one of the huts and quickly sat on the floor. Talimannog didn't want to waste a second of their time together as he wasn't actually sure how long the manulib would allow him to talk to his sister.

"Wadi, are you well?" Talimannog couldn't help but ask out of worry and concern for his sister.

"Yes akka, I am well," Innawagan answered impatiently. "But that's not what we need to talk about right now."

"I know, I know," Talimannog replied, as he tried to clear his head and stop acting like a big brother. "Tell me everything that happened to you. Maybe we can…"

"Akka, stop!" Innawagan retorted and cut him off. "I need you to listen to me very carefully. I have set something in motion that might help free us from these beings.

"I've sent Dalawesan off to seek help. I've sent him off to find and secure the aid of the flying man…" Innawagan began as she told Talimannog everything she thought he should know.

*****

Innawagan told Talimannog as much as she could in the short time allotted to them. She spoke of her desperate plan to enlist the help of the flying man. A man for all she knew might not even exist. But knowing what she knew of the manulib brothers, a desperate, farfetched plan was all they really had to pin their hopes on.

"I need you to tell me all you know about these beings," Talimannog whispered to Innawagan. "During your time with them, did you hear or see anything that might help me kill them? Even the most minute detail could help me."

Innawagan racked her memory of Pane Kalimangalnuk's tale of how they came to be. "He said they got their powers from an agimat bestowed to them by an evil spirit," Innawagan said as she began.

"I didn't see any agimat on their person," Talimannog retorted. "Neither necklace, bracelet nor anklet."

"He said the agimat was in the form of a beating golden heart that they swallowed so you wouldn't see it on their person," Innawagan continued. "They also said that the agimat cursed them as well as gave them their powers and unnaturally long life."

"What curse?" Talimannog asked curiously.

"Have you not heard the grumbling in their stomachs?" Innawagan asked surprised. "Ever since the day, they ingested the agimat that gave them their powers, they've never been able to swallow a bite to eat, nor sip a drop of water to quench their thirst. They are cursed with eternal hunger and thirst."

Talimannog fell silent as he took in everything that Innawagan just told him. *To kill them, I need to separate the agimat from their bodies. But how do I even find it if it's inside them?* he asked himself.

The agimat is preventing them from eating or drinking. It is also in the form of a small beating heart. It could be located in their chest or has replaced their actual hearts. Maybe it acts like a barrier that prevents food or water from reaching their grumbling bellies. But even if I was sure it was in their chests, how would I even go about cutting it out?

As Talimannog contemplated the manulib's possible weakness, a familiar yet saddening voice rang out from outside the hut.

"That should be enough time for you two to say what you need to say to each other," Pane Kalimangalnuk yelled out. "Time to come out Talimannog and face your final challenge."

Talimannog stood up and sighed. He had a terrible feeling in his gut that this might be the last time he was able to see his baby sister. "Wadi, I... I have to go." Talimannog said sadly, as he gave Innawagan a farewell hug.

"Don't go akka!" Innawagan cried. "Maybe we can run

and hide."

"No, we can't. We are in his rakuh. There is no place for us to hide."

"Then I am coming with you. We will face this challenge together!"

"As you wish," Talimannog said as he turned and stepped out of the doorway to face his next challenge.

But as Innawagan followed her brother, as soon as she stepped through the doorway, she found herself back in the stone room with Dundunan and Ammalabukaw. "What?!" Innawagan exclaimed. "How did I get back here?"

Talimannog turned around after he felt the sudden absence of his sister's presence. "Innawagan! Wadi! Where is she?" he asked Pane Kalimangalnuk angrily.

"I sent her back of course. We don't want mavid to get hurt now do we?"

Talimannog's heart sank at the thought of not seeing Innawagan again, but he quickly gathered his wits about him and approached the manulib brothers. "How many am I fighting?" he asked Pane Kalimangalnuk as he stood in front of him.

"It seems you've already guessed part of what the next challenge is," Pane Kalimangalnuk said as he smiled at Talimannog's perceptiveness. "But the answer is one. Just one."

"I've killed more than a dozen of your false Kalinga warriors. One doesn't seem quite the challenge. So, what is the catch? Why only one?" Talimannog inquired.

"The *catch* is that you get to fight me!" Pane Kalimangalnuk said as he burst out laughing in glee.

Talimannog felt as though a gigantic shadow had enveloped and swallowed whatever hope he had left. He was hoping to at least pass the challenge and become a servant of these beings which should give him ample time to find a way to assassinate them in their sleep. But facing off against one of them would surely spell his doom.

"How is this a fair challenge?" Talimannog asked and tried his best to keep his composure. "How can I possibly best a being such as yourself? I doubt any of my weapons can even scratch, much less hurt you."

"There is truth in your words patepag," Pane Kalimangalnuk replied. "So, in order to give you a chance, albeit a very minuscule chance of defeating me, I will have kakteh provide you with a weapon made from his golden constructs. These weapons can inflict damage on our flesh. Who knows, maybe the Poons will look favorably upon your plight and provide you with some luck."

"Kakteh, are you sure you want me to give him the actual means to hurt you?" Pane Nagdombilan asked with concern. Though he did not show it, Talimannog was actually thrilled by Pane Nagdombilan's concern about granting him weapons. The manulib's concern proved to Talimannog that the golden constructs can hurt them.

"Do not concern yourself too much about my well-being kakteh," Pane Kalimangalnuk replied to his brother's concerns. "Think about it. What could he really do to harm me?"

Pane Nagdombilan nodded in agreement and stepped forward toward Talimannog. "Tell me human, what sort of weapon would you like to wield?"

"Would it be presumptuous of me to ask for three instead of just one?" Talimannog asked.

"That wouldn't be a problem at all." Pane Kalimangalnuk chuckled. "Go ahead, ask what you will."

Talimannog turned his attention to Pane Nagdombilan and said, "The first thing I need is a kalasag shield to defend myself."

Even before Talimannog could speak again, a golden kalasag shield magically appeared on his left hand. The sudden weight of the shield dragged Talimannog down though he was quick to right himself. *Amazing!* he thought to himself as he inspected the shield.

"Hurry up and ask for the other two!" Pane Nagdombilan exclaimed impatiently.

"Yes, of course," Talimannog responded. "The next weapon I need is a five-foot-long Kalinga war spear."

Just as it was with the kalasag, a golden war spear with

a dual-edged tip appeared in his right hand. Talimannog checked the weight and found it light and easy to wield.

"The last weapon I need is a pinahig bolo similar to mine. It should also come with a scabbard as I might need it as a secondary weapon."

With all three golden weapons at hand, Talimannog stepped back and made himself ready for the fight of his life. He rotated his shoulders and stretched his legs as he waited for Pane Kalimangalnuk to make his move.

"Prepare yourself Talimannog," Pane Kalimangalnuk said as two three-foot-long golden itak swords appeared in his hands. "Now we will truly see if you are a warrior worthy of..."

Pane Kalimangalnuk suddenly stopped and closed his eyes tightly. A scowl came across his face as he opened his eyes and looked at his brother.

"Someone has just entered one of my rakuhs! No, there are two of them! And one of them is the kumaw Dalawesan!" Pane Kalimangalnuk exclaimed.

"Who is the other one kakteh?" Pane Nagdombilan asked dumbfounded.

"I don't know," Pane Kalimangalnuk replied. "But whoever he is, he is a dead man! Will you please deal with him kakteh while Talimannog and myself conduct our business?"

Chapter 16

The Throes of Conflict

Taguwasi, Bago, and Dalawesan had finally arrived at the lagoon. "There!" Dalawesan told Taguwasi. "Through that cave on the left. The small one where not much water is coming out. That is the entrance to the rakuh where Hapu Innawagan is being held."

"Then let's go in there and get her out. Maybe if we're lucky, we can get her out without anyone noticing." Taguwasi said as he commanded the wind to bring them down and into the cave.

As they landed at the mouth of the cave, Dalawesan immediately looked around and tried to find the rippling in the air that marked the entrance to the rakuh. "It's not here!" the kumaw exclaimed. "I remember it being not too far from the mouth of the cave!"

"Let me take a look around," Bago said as he proceeded deeper into the cave. "The cave is long and leads deep into the mountain. I sense the lingering effect of magic that had been cast over a long period of time but that is all that there is, a lingering effect."

"Pane Kalimangalnuk must have closed this rakuh after he found out I had used it to make my escape," Dalawesan said in dismay.

"You mentioned that this was where you exited, am I

right?" Bago asked.

"Yes. I flew right out of here just a few days ago." Dalawesan answered.

"So where did you enter?" Taguwasi asked.

"You're right Lakandian!" Dalawesan exclaimed. "There is another way in. I guess being tired has made my mind addled. We need to go to the bigger cave."

All three of them entered the cave that Talimannog and his brothers along with the kumaws entered before. "Nothing has changed since the last time I was here," Dalawesan said. "You should light a torch before we go in deeper. It will get dark fast."

With a torch in one hand, Taguwasi led Dalawesan and Bago deeper into the cave. He was actually surprised by how fast the light from the outside waned and disappeared only a few moments later.

It didn't take them long before Dalawesan saw what he was looking for, "There! Do you both see the rippling in the very air itself? That is the entrance to the rakuh."

"I see it!" Bago exclaimed. "It is a magical barrier that separates this section of the cave from a completely different section controlled by magic."

"I see it as well," Taguwasi said as he raised the torch he carried over his head to better see his surroundings. "It looks like the same type of rippling you see on the surface of a pond, only this one ripples on the air itself.

"So, what do we do now? Do we just step through?" Taguwasi asked.

"Yes. You will feel a strange sensation on your skin when you pass through. It will feel like you've just accidentally stepped through a giant spider's web." Dalawesan replied. "Pay it no mind and just walk through as you would an open door. I will go first to put your worries to rest," Dalawesan said as he passed through the ripple and disappeared.

Taguwasi was just about to do the same when Bago stepped in front of him. "Be careful and be ready for anything when you pass through. Whatever is on the other side is made up entirely of magic. I cannot see past the barrier, but I sense danger awaits us on the other side."

Taguwasi nodded and stepped through the ripple. Everything felt exactly as Dalawesan described. All of a sudden, his eyes were bombarded with bright blinding light. From the pitch darkness of the cave to which his eyesight had adjusted to earlier, Taguwasi suddenly found himself outside at the bottom of a deep chasm.

"What?! Where are we?" Taguwasi exclaimed as he squinted and rubbed his eyes to adjust to the brightness of his surroundings.

"We are inside a rakuh," Dalawesan replied. "This was where I last saw Hapu Talimannog and his brothers as well as my sister Dundunan."

"This whole place was created with magic," Bago said as he appeared next to Taguwasi. "Everything that you see is real and false at the same time. I don't really know how to explain this to you in terms that you will..." Bago was saying this when Taguwasi suddenly jumped away from him and cut him off.

"Agay! Bago! Is that you?" Taguwasi exclaimed.

"Y... yes. Why do you ask?" Bago asked perplexed at Taguwasi's reaction.

"I can see you!" Taguwasi exclaimed again. "I mean I can actually see you! Completely! You look solid and naked. You have pale skin, and silver-colored hair and your eyes look like they're made of gold."

Bago looked at his arms and body and was astonished to see himself in this form. "Well, this is certainly a surprise," Bago said as he gazed at his body. "I haven't seen myself like this in a very long time. Enkantos are solid, physical beings when we are in Kaluwalhatian, but it would appear that..."

Taguwasi interrupted Bago once again when he placed his left hand on Bago's right shoulder but found out that his katiwala was still ethereal in substance as his hand passed through Bago as it would through smoke or mist.

"That is just rude Lakandian!" Bago snapped at him. "Anyway, as I was explaining before the rude interruption. Apparently, this rakuh has enough magic in it to make you see my true form, which is actually a bad thing.

"For one, me being seen as easily as anybody else means that I can no longer be your invisible agent should you need one. Secondly, this means that whatever type of magical beings these manulib creatures are, they are not to be underestimated."

Taguwasi turned his attention back to Dalawesan, "So what do we do now?"

"Atop that towering rockface in front of you lies a ledge. On that ledge is a golden door called the sakbawan. It will lead us out of here and take us to the next rakuh." Dalawesan answered.

"And what makes you think I will allow you to pass through my sakbawan?" A booming voice suddenly shouted down at them. Pane Nagdombilan suddenly stepped forward at the edge of the ledge and looked at them with malice.

"You have failed Dalawesan," Pane Nagdombilan said. "Two of your masters have already fallen, and your precious Hapu Talimannog is about to meet his doom at the hands of kakteh.

"And in your misguided, inconsequential attempt to save them, the best you could get is the aid of one man and an anito who could do only as much as a stiff breeze on a windy day." Pane Nagdombilan said as he raised his right hand high above his head.

Suddenly, more than a dozen golden arrows appeared above him with the arrowheads aimed directly at Taguwasi and Dalawesan. "I've been wanting to kill somebody for a while now but kakteh wouldn't allow it. Imagine my glee when he finally told me to dispatch the both of you at my leisure and discretion."

Pane Nagdombilan dropped his arm to his side as the arrows rained down at Taguwasi and Dalawesan.

"Move! Scatter!" Taguwasi shouted as he and Dalawesan took to the air and away from the arrows' trajectory.

"What?!" Pane Nagdombilan said in surprise after seeing Taguwasi fly. "The flying man? You are real!"

"I am the Lakandian Taguwasi," he said as he effortlessly flew away from the falling arrows. "And you must be the manulib, Pane Nagdombilan."

The arrows fell harmlessly on the ground. A couple of them passed through Bago as he looked up at the manulib on the ledge.

"It would seem that Dalawesan has been telling you quite a lot during the past few days," Pane Nagdombilan said as he raised both his hands over his head. "But it matters not. You'll be dead very soon Taguwasi."

More than two dozen golden arrows appeared overhead as Pane Nagdombilan aimed each and every one of them at Taguwasi. "Fast and nimble you might be, but I'll make sure you cannot dodge these!"

The golden arrows flew at Taguwasi with deadly intent. But rather than dodge them as he did the first wave, Taguwasi decided to fly up directly at them. Taguwasi, with his arms extended forward ahead of him, began rotating them slowly as he commanded the wind to create a small wind tunnel ahead of him which deflected the arrows away from him.

As soon as the arrows flew away, Taguwasi commanded the wind to take one of the golden arrows and turned it around from its trajectory. Taguwasi stretched out his left hand and made a series of gestures as the wind turned one of the golden arrows around and up toward Pane Nagdombilan.

This caught the manulib completely by surprise. Pane Nagdombilan had to jump back to avoid being killed by his own construct. Though he avoided being struck by the arrow in the chest, the golden arrow did manage to open a small cut near his neck, just over his right clavicle.

"Aaargh!" Pane Nagdombilan cried out as the arrow cut him and he fell flat on his ass. Feeling the sensation of pain for the first time in almost a century, Pane Nagdombilan placed his left hand over his cut and stared blankly at his rust-colored blood.

My blood! He thought to himself. *This is actually my*

blood.

Suddenly realizing he was in an actual fight, Pane Nagdombilan shook himself free from his stupor and looked around for Taguwasi. But by the time he saw him, the manulib suddenly found himself defenseless.

Taguwasi was already flying towards him at an incredible rate with a short bolo in his hand. Taguwasi slashed the blade right under Pane Nagdombilan's neck with so much speed and power that had his neck been the trunk of a coconut tree, that tree would have been cut in half. But fortunately for Pane Nagdombilan, his flesh was made of much harder stuff.

Taguwasi's bolo shattered like a clay pot upon impact, leaving only the hilt intact in the Lakandian's hand. "What in all the realms?!" Taguwasi exclaimed as he looked at the hilt of his bolo.

Though unharmed by Taguwasi's attack, Pane Nagdombilan still found himself pushed back and rolling on the ground by Taguwasi's blow. But by the time he regained his composure, he was only a few feet away from the sakbawan.

Pane Nagdombilan got to his feet and felt perplexed and apprehensive by the whole thing. He didn't know what to make of Taguwasi and didn't know how to proceed. "Stop!" he cried out, hoping to get a better read on his enemy.

"What manner of being are you?" Pane Nagdombilan asked. "You said a word earlier, what was it again?"

"Does it really matter?" Taguwasi answered back.

"The sakbawan!" Dalawesan suddenly cried out as he flew over them. "The golden door! We need to pass through it!"

"Give it to him Taguwasi! Show him the power of your dinatal!" Bago said as he reached the top of the ledge.

Pane Nagdombilan suddenly felt overwhelmed and surrounded. Not wanting to give Taguwasi the means to inflict real damage on his person, the manulib resorted to creating melee weapons instead of projectiles that could potentially be used against him.

In his right hand he created a *binaroy* (sling blade) and on his left was a kalasag shield. He then proceeded to charge and attack Taguwasi who hovered on the ledge, no more than ten feet away from him.

As the manulib charged at him, the Lakandian just stood there motionless with his eyes closed. He concentrated as he gathered the power of the wind and collected its breathtaking might in the middle of his chest.

Pane Nagdombilan was already halfway to Taguwasi when he raised his binaroy high and readied to strike his enemy dead. But still, Taguwasi remained motionless. Wanting to cut the distance between them even faster, Pane Nagdombilan leapt at the last second to add speed and power to his strike.

This is it! He's mine! Pane Nagdombilan thought to himself as he neared his enemy.

But a split second before the golden binaroy made contact with Taguwasi's head, the Lakandian opened his eyes and gave a deafening roar! At that very moment, he released the accumulated strength of his dinatal that slammed against Pane Nagdombilan with the power of a hurricane.

The manulib was still fortunate enough to have had his kalasag raised when the dinatal hit him. Though it still struck him with the force of a hurricane, his golden kalasag had taken the brunt of Taguwasi's power. At that range, being hit by the dinatal would have most likely severed his limbs from his body had it not been for his kalasag.

Nevertheless, Pane Nagdombilan found himself in terrible pain as he tumbled and twisted in the air like a leaf caught in the wind. The dinatal knocked the manulib through the air, passed the length of the ledge, and right through his own sakbawan.

"The sakbawan! We need to pass through!" Dalawesan cried out as he flew after Pane Nagdombilan. Taguwasi and Bago did the same.

*****

Each blow that he blocked with his kalasag felt like it came from a charging *galampes* (carabao). Talimannog was getting worried that one of the blows might break his forearm. He tried his best to counter-attack with the spear he wielded, but Pane Kalimangalnuk was surprisingly skilled with his double itak blades.

"I was honestly expecting a little more from you patepag," Pane Kalimangalnuk taunted Talimannog as he continuously attacked his kalasag. "I have been watching all three of you fight in the previous rakuhs and found you to be the most capable amongst your siblings. Yet here you are, barely holding on to your life."

Pane Kalimangalnuk attacked with a horizontal slash with the itak in his left hand followed by a downward blow with the itak in his right. Talimannog saw this coming and braced his kalasag for the left-handed blow. The horizontal slash bruised his forearm, but Talimannog paid no mind to it. He was far more interested in the downward attack from the manulib's right.

As soon as he saw the right hand raised, Talimannog pulled his right hand carrying the spear back, and awaited the attack. As soon as Pane Kalimangalnuk slashed downward, Talimannog pushed the itak away with his kalasag rather than blocking it outright. Using the strength of the manulib's own attack against him,

Talimannog was able to knock Pane Kalimangalnuk off-balance for a brief second.

With a quick thrust of his spear, Talimannog was hoping to run his spear through the manulib's chest and hopefully strike at the agimat resting where his heart used to be. But all hope faded into nothingness when Pane Kalimangalnuk spun around, effectively side-stepping away from Talimannog's thrust. He continued his spinning movement and followed through with a spinning kick that landed squarely on Talimannog's abdomen and sent him flying through the air and crashing down on a pinanahang.

Talimannog had the wind completely knocked right out of him. He was gasping for air as he held his battered and bruised abdomen. Never in his entire life had he been hit with so much force. As soon as he managed to get some air in his lungs, he felt something rise up in his throat. He spat it out and saw a thick glob of his own blood.

"That was impressive Talimannog," Pane Kalimangalnuk applauded his opponent. "Anyone else might have fallen to your cunning countermove. I was hoping you would see the pattern in my attacks and come up with a counter to it; just to keep this fight interesting.

"I honestly thought it would take you much longer to see it but imagine my surprise when you reacted to it after only two quick successions."

I don't stand a chance against him. Talimannog thought to himself as he cradled his injured abdomen. *He's not even using his powers and he's still beating me like I was a small child. My only chance to survive this is to stall for time.*

They looked genuinely worried when he felt Dalawesan arrive with the flying man. I need to last longer and buy myself and wadi more time. If I can keep them from ganging up on the flying man, the better his chances are of defeating Pane Nagdombilan.

"That's quite enough time to nurse your wounds patepag," Pane Kalimangalnuk said. "Pick up your spear and shield and let's continue."

Talimannog tried his best to stand up straight as he picked up his spear and kalasag. His injured abdomen was causing his torso to bend forward and topple him over. He had to use his spear as a walking staff to pull himself up properly. "I don't suppose you would afford me the luxury of rest?" he asked the manulib.

"I have already granted you more than your fair share of requests and considerations," Pane Kalimangalnuk replied. "I think I would like to just end this farce of a duel now."

As Pane Kalimangalnuk approached him, Talimannog started backing away. *I need to delay the outcome of this fight for as long as I can.* Talimannog thought as he started looking around, trying to find something he could use to last a little longer against a superior enemy.

He waited for Pane Kalimangalnuk to dash forward. As soon as the manulib attacked, Talimannog jumped back and thrust his spear forward. It was a simple feat for Pane Kalimangalnuk to parry the spear away and follow through with a thrust of his own.

Talimannog blocked the forward thrust of the manulib's itak with his kalasag and used its momentum to push him even farther back and create some distance. Though his abdomen still ached considerably, Talimannog did his best to fight through the pain.

He started backing up towards a hut as Pane Kalimangalnuk approached. "Why are you backing away from me?" the manulib asked.

Pane Kalimangalnuk suddenly dashed forward and tried to close the distance between him and Talimannog. But rather than standing his ground trying to block or counter-attack, Talimannog chose to extend his spear forward yet again while simultaneously jumping back to get closer to the open doorway of one of the huts. As soon as he sees that he has passed the doorway's threshold, Talimannog pretended to make his stand from inside the hut.

"That wasn't very smart," Pane Kalimangalnuk commented. "Now you're trapped inside the hut with nowhere to go but to your doom."

As soon as Pane Kalimangalnuk went after him, Talimannog turned and ran towards one of the walls of the hut. Using his kalasag as a ram, he crashed against the bamboo and cogon walls and once again found himself outside the hut. Mustering all the strength he could, Talimannog started running behind the other huts and pinanahang structures.

"Are you seriously trying to run away from me inside my own rakuh?" Pane Kalimangalnuk chuckled. "But I am curious as to what you hope to accomplish with this little plan of yours. I'll play along and try to stalk you as a predator would its prey."

Talimannog ran into another hut and sat quietly on the floor. He poked a small hole in one of the walls to see where Pane Kalimangalnuk was. He spotted the manulib walking towards the very hut where he was hiding and trying to be sneaky as he did so. *He must have seen me come in here.* Talimannog thought to himself. *I need to get out of here through the back.*

Talimannog got to his feet and headed straight to the back window. The windowsill was only a foot up from the floor which made jumping over it a task a child could easily do. So Talimannog thought nothing of it and leapt through. But in the heat of things, Talimannog temporarily forgot about his injured abdomen, which as soon as he leapt, made itself completely self-evident.

He felt as if a muscle was torn forcing him to lean forward as he leapt. The hut itself was elevated three feet off the ground which added an additional level of difficulty to his landing. As Talimannog tried his best to land on his feet, he twisted his left ankle as soon as it touched the ground. He fell chest and shoulder first onto the ground which did not help with the twisting pain in his gut.

Pane Kalimangalnuk, having seen Talimannog enter a hut, approached it as stealthily as he could. He even saw Talimannog's fingers poke a hole through one of the walls of the hut. Though it was easily within his power to simply make the huts disappear, Pane Kalimangalnuk found the cat-and-mouse game to be a welcome distraction from his perpetual hunger and thirst.

As Pane Kalimangalnuk approached the hut, he pretended to not notice the hole made by Talimannog and turned his back to it. Quite suddenly, the manulib swung both his itak blades at the wall effectively shredding it with his strength and ferocity. "Aha!" Pane Kalimangalnuk yelled out as he all but destroyed half the hut with his blades.

But to his surprise, Talimannog wasn't hiding behind the wall. "Why you clever little monkey!" The manulib said in amusement. "Did you jump out the back window?"

With a twisted ankle and a bruised abdomen, it took everything that Talimannog had to get back up and limp behind the next hut. As he struggled to make it to the next hut, he heard the crashing sound of Pane Kalimangalnuk completely destroying the hut he was just in.

He turned the corner of the hut and was safely beyond the purview of the manulib for the time being. *More time! I need more time!* he thought as he reached the entrance to the hut.

As Talimannog was about to enter the hut, he heard Pane Kalimangalnuk call out to him again. "Where are you hiding this time? You do realize that I will eventually find you."

Just then, an idea found its way into Talimannog's head. Just before entering the hut, he picked up two smooth stones at the base of the steps leading up to the hut. He hid next to a wall by an open window that pointed in a direction away from the hut. He placed his kalasag on the bamboo floor as quietly as he could and unsheathed his bolo. He placed the bolo next to the kalasag and began listening intently.

Talimannog heard the crunch of Pane Kalimangalnuk's heavy feet as they crushed the grass beneath it. *Start talking again you pompous arrogant attay* (shit). *I need to hear where you are.*

"Maybe I should just change this entire rakuh into

nothing less than an open plain if you insist on just hiding instead of fighting. What do you think patepag?" Pane Kalimangalnuk shouted out from the other side of the wall that Talimannog was hiding behind.

As soon as Talimannog heard the manulib from the other side of the wall he immediately threw one of the rocks out the window and hoped that it would catch Pane Kalimangalnuk's attention.

"Are you hiding in this hut this time patepag?" Pane Kalimangalnuk asked out loud. "Let's see shall we."

But just as Pane Kalimangalnuk raised his blades and was about to shred the wall hiding Talimannog from him, he suddenly heard a rustling sound from the hut next to the one he was at. Talimannog had thrown the second stone which luckily landed on the thatched roof of the next hut.

"There you are!" Pane Kalimangalnuk exclaimed.

As soon as Talimannog heard the manulib say this and start walking to the next hut, he took his spear in both hands and thrust it through the wall!

Surprised and caught completely off guard, Talimannog's spear struck Pane Kalimangalnuk on the top of his right shoulder and opened up a large gash. "Aaarrrgh!" The manulib cried out in pain as he unwillingly dropped the itak in his right hand.

Knowing he struck a successful thrust against his

enemy, Talimannog pulled his spear back and thrust it at him again. This time the spear found its mark on Pane Kalimangalnuk's right thigh. The tip of the spear buried itself deep into the manulib's thigh muscle and even grazed the femur bone.

Pane Kalimangalnuk cried out in pain again, only this time he took action against his opponent. Though wounded and bleeding rust-colored blood, the manulib was still able to use his right arm and grabbed hold of the spear by its shaft and prevented Talimannog from pulling it back and attacking him with it again. And with his left hand still holding one of his itak blades, Pane Kalimangalnuk swung at the hut's wall and shattered it to splinters.

As soon as he felt the spear held in place when Pane Kalimangalnuk took hold of it by the shaft, Talimannog released his grip on it and immediately picked up his bolo and kalasag. A split second later, he saw something golden pass through the wall as the bamboo and cogon walls of the hut exploded right before Talimannog's eyes. He shielded himself from the flying debris with his kalasag and waited for a second for things to settle.

As soon as the wall between them was gone, Talimannog saw Pane Kalimangalnuk with a face full of rage glowering at him. As terrifying as the sight of Pane Kalimangalnuk's face was, Talimannog wasted no time and capitalized on his brief advantage. He charged at the manulib with his kalasag raised forward in his left hand and his bolo in his right.

He slammed the kalasag squarely on Pane Kalimangalnuk's face and brought his bolo down on the manulib's left shoulder. His bolo bit deep into the trapezoid muscle but stopped just as quickly when it hit the shoulder bone.

Though Pane Nagdombilan's constructs were able to cut through their flesh and muscle, Talimannog, unfortunately, did not possess the strength necessary to cut through bone. The next thing Talimannog felt was the powerful brush of Pane Kalimangalnuk's right arm as the manulib swatted him away like nothing more than an insect.

Talimannog was struck on the left side of his torso which sent him flying a few feet away from the manulib. He crashed on the grass and rolled uncontrollably a few times. He had dropped his bolo and kalasag in the process.

His body was wracked in pain, both from his previous injuries and from his newly acquired broken ribs. He hardly had the strength to lift his head, much less his body. All he could do was open his eyes and look at Pane Kalimangalnuk and pray that his end would come quickly.

Chapter 17

Fallen Brothers

Pane Nagdombilan continued to tumble on the ground even as he passed his own sakbawan. He was out of breath and everything from his chest down to his thighs felt bruised and battered. He had never felt anything as powerful and as painful at Taguwasi's dinatal.

As soon as he stopped tumbling, he tried to sit up, but he was still lightheaded from the attack. *What was that?* he thought to himself. *I'm hurt! I am actually hurt. Maybe this flying man is actually powerful enough to kill me? Maybe he can free me from my torment.*

But when his head cleared, the first thing he saw was Taguwasi flying straight at him with his own binaroy at hand. Knowing how strong Taguwasi was, a blow from his golden binaroy will definitely kill him. Though Pane Nagdombilan yearned for death, the proud warrior in him reflexively created a golden wall between him and the Lakandian at the last second.

What followed next was a loud thundering bang as the binaroy struck the golden wall that protected the manulib. Taguwasi was caught completely by surprise. He didn't expect the sudden appearance of the wall. But the wall itself was small and could easily be circled. But just as

Taguwasi was moving to the edge of the wall, the binaroy in his hand disappeared like smoke, and so did the wall.

The next thing Taguwasi saw was a large fist connecting to the left side of his face that sent him spinning in the air and crashing on the ground. The manulib followed through with a powerful kick to his ribs that sent him back up off the ground and then a two-handed blow to his spine that sent him crashing back down.

Taguwasi was now the one who was hurt and out of breath. Though he felt the same battered and bruised pain he dealt Pane Nagdombilan earlier, Taguwasi was also getting angry. He looked up and saw that the manulib was half a second away from stepping on his head to finish him off.

But at the last moment, just as Pane Nagdombilan did a moment earlier, Taguwasi used his power and commanded the wind to knock the manulib back. Even before Pane Nagdombilan fell back, Taguwasi leapt straight up, commanded the wind to push him forward, and began pummeling the manulib with several blows to his face and body.

Pane Nagdombilan fought back as hard as he could and at the same time decided not to use his powers to produce anything that could be used against him by Taguwasi. What followed next was a fistfight between two exceptionally strong and skilled fighters.

Their fight was savage and brutal, and a glory to behold. Both Taguwasi and Pane Nagdombilan wailed at each other for a good long while with neither man backing up or falling down.

"Why doesn't he use the same power that he used earlier when he knocked Pane Nagdombilan through the sakbawan?" Dalawesan asked Bago as they stayed a good distance away from the combatants.

"His dinatal, though an exceptionally powerful ability also drains a lot of energy from Taguwasi," Bago answered. "Ever since he learned how to harness its power, he has only been able to use it twice in a single day without needing to rest for at least half a day. When he used it earlier, it was supposed to be a killing blow."

"Do you think he can defeat the manulib without his dinatal?" Dalawesan asked.

"Don't forget that even without the use of his most powerful ability, Taguwasi is the Lakandian and the master of the wind," Bago replied.

Having felt the effects of the manulib's punches and kicks, Taguwasi felt confident that he would be able to weather them much better than his opponent. He also noticed that Pane Nagdombilan had stopped using his powers to create weapons that could be used against him. But try as he may, Taguwasi still can't seem to pierce the manulib's skin.

I can try to beat him to death or knock him unconscious, but I sincerely doubt if I can. Taguwasi thought to himself. *I need him to use his powers so I can use his constructs against him.*

When Pane Nagdombilan telegraphed one of his punches, Taguwasi used this mistake to gain him an advantage. Taguwasi ducked under the manulib's left-handed punch which was made even easier because of their height difference. As soon as his arm passed over Taguwasi's head, the Lakandian gave him a powerful uppercut to the ribs followed by a command to the wind itself to lift Pane Nagdombilan off his feet.

Pane Nagdombilan was spinning upward beyond all control. Once the manulib was in the air, his strength meant absolutely nothing. Taguwasi commanded the wind to slam the manulib all over the unnaturally dense jungle that surrounded them.

Pane Nagdombilan had never felt as helpless as he did at that particular moment. He felt his body crash and slam against every tree trunk and branch that the wind carried him to. He tried to grab hold of a tree branch once but the branch itself snapped when he grabbed hold of it.

I need to use my power. the manulib thought. *He is clearly using his which leaves me at a great disadvantage.* Pane Nagdombilan created a golden rope around his waist and on the other end of it, he created a giant barbed arrowhead that buried itself in the ground beneath him effectively anchoring him in place.

As soon as he stopped tumbling and got his bearings back, he created a golden triangular roof over himself and let it drop, shielding him from Taguwasi's wind. For a brief moment, Pane Nagdombilan had time to think and assess his situation. *I can shield myself from his wind powers, but I can't use projectiles against him. He is faster and far more agile than me which means he can easily avoid me if he wished. I need an advantage.* Pane Nagdombilan was thinking when he suddenly had an idea.

In a blink of an eye, the golden roof around him disappeared and was replaced by a large golden fishing net. He flung the net at Taguwasi hoping to ensnare the Lakandian in it. But Taguwasi was far too fast to be ensnared by something so obvious.

With a quick wave of his hand, Taguwasi commanded the wind to blow the net away. As soon as the net fell harmlessly to the ground, Taguwasi was surprised to find the manulib running away from him through a narrow path through the jungle. He immediately flew after him and so did Dalawesan who carried the Anito Bago on his back.

There is no way he can get away from me on foot. Taguwasi thought as he started to catch up to Pane Nagdombilan. The density of the jungle and the canopy above made flying difficult but not completely unmanageable. Even in such close quarters, Taguwasi was still exceptionally fast.

But just as he was about to catch Pane Nagdombilan, a giant golden spear the size of a coconut tree suddenly burst out of the ground beneath him. Had it not been for his superhuman agility, he would have been skewered for sure. "Look out!" Bago had to shout out as he saw the spear come shooting out from the ground.

After dodging the spear, Taguwasi continued to go after Pane Nagdombilan. But after a few seconds of continuing his pursuit, another spear appeared, and then another, and so on. Had the spears been normal sized then it would have been a simple matter of using the wind to take control of them and hurl them at the manulib. But each spear weighed more than a boulder which meant that Taguwasi had no choice but to dodge each and every one of them.

"Keep your distance from me!" he yelled out to Dalawesan. "I'll draw them out, so you don't have to evade them as they come out."

After a while, Pane Nagdombilan started gaining ground and increased his lead with every giant spear that he created. It had gotten to a point where Taguwasi had lost sight of the manulib. All he could do was try to avoid the spears as they came and catch up as best he could, even through the narrow corridor trees that made everything else even more difficult.

As Taguwasi zigged and zagged through the narrow corridor of trees and golden spears that came out of the ground, the Lakandian suddenly found himself in a completely different place when the trees opened up and revealed a vast swamp as far as the eyes could see. The spears had also stopped bursting out of the ground gave him a great sense of relief.

"Where are we?" Bago asked as he and Dalawesan flew by Taguwasi a few moments later.

"This is the swamp where Hapu Ammani fell," Dalawesan answered. "Hapu Taguwasi! Be careful of the giant frogs! They are everywhere in this swamp, and they are dangerous."

"Frogs?" Taguwasi asked puzzled but let it go. "Where do we go from here?"

"There!" Dalawesan answered back as he started flying to the west. "I can see something big and golden a few miles out. That is where Pane Nagdombilan is and that is probably where the sakbawan is as well."

They flew toward the golden thing as fast as they could. At the speed they flew, it would take them only a few minutes to get to it. But as they flew, the croaks from the toads and frogs that littered the swamp became louder and louder.

"That sound," Taguwasi said as soon as he heard the

croaks getting louder. "Those must be the frogs I presume?"

"Yes," Dalawesan answered. "Beware their tongues Taguwasi. They are not normal amphibians. They are as big as dogs."

"Just be careful," Bago cautioned his charge. "Do what you did earlier and keep your distance from Pane Nagdombilan. He is no match for you when you use the wind to keep him at bay."

When they reached their destination, they realized that the golden thing that Dalawesan saw resembled a giant golden anthill almost as big as a hill. Its surface was littered with holes much like a beehive or hornet's nest. It was also where Pane Nagdombilan hid and waited. "What do I do now?" Taguwasi asked Bago.

"Fly around them and see if you can spot the manulib?" Bago answered but was actually more of a speculation than an answer.

"I can see that you've never fought in the wars of Kaluwalhatian," Dalawesan said mockingly at Bago's answer to Taguwasi's question.

"I never claimed I did!" Bago snapped back at the kumaw.

"Keep quiet! The both of you!" Taguwasi said to both of his companions. "I need to focus and find him, and I can't do that with the two of you bickering!"

Taguwasi flew over and around the giant golden mound, trying to find any sign of the manulib. He saw glimpses of movement here and there but couldn't really do anything unless he got closer. Suddenly, from the corner of his eye, he saw something golden streaking toward him; it was a golden arrow like the one Pane Nagdombilan used earlier against him.

He managed to move to his side and dodge it. He commanded the wind to catch the arrow but as soon as the arrow flew past him, it disappeared into nothingness. *He's being more careful with his attacks.* Taguwasi thought to himself. "Keep your distance!" He called out to Dalawesan.

He circled the mound again but still, the manulib eluded him. A few moments later another arrow shot out at him. Taguwasi managed to evade it yet again, but just as he tried to grab onto it midflight, the arrow disappeared. But unbeknownst to him, a second arrow flew out. He barely managed to move his head out of the way to avoid it. The second arrow opened a small gash across his left cheek that greatly infuriated Taguwasi.

Just like the arrow before, the one that cut Taguwasi disappeared before he could catch it. *I need to be faster than them!* he thought as he readied himself and the wind at his disposal. *What am I doing?* he suddenly asked himself.. *Why am I waiting for him to attack me?*

The Lakandian threw powerful gusts of wind through the various holes and openings, hoping to flush the manulib out. A couple of times, one of those monstrous frogs from inside the structure would be caught by Taguwasi's winds and would come flying out, but not once did it come upon the manulib himself.

On and on he commanded the wind to seek out his enemy and drive him out of hiding, but Pane Nagdombilan was one step ahead of him. The manulib would move the walls within the mound to block or redirect Taguwasi's attacks, frustrating the young Lakandian even more.

Every now and then an arrow would come darting toward Taguwasi. Most of the time, the Lakandian would easily dodge and evade these arrows, but on more than one occasion, an arrow would come in contact with his skin and open up a cut or gash.

"Hapu Taguwasi," Dalawesan called out to him. "You are at a disadvantage fighting him from the outside. Pane Nagdombilan is immortal and can keep this up forever if he wanted to."

"So is a Lakandian!" Bago protested from the back of the kumaw.

"But Hapu Talimannog and Innawagan are not," Dalawesan rebutted. "They do not have the luxury of time as these immortals do."

"He is right," Taguwasi said. "I need to go in there and end this."

Seeing Taguwasi begin to descend, Bago leapt off Dalawesan and approach Taguwasi before he went into the golden mound. "Taguwasi, this is dangerous. You have the advantage of keeping him at a distance. Why throw it away?"

"I lost that advantage as soon as Pane Nagdombilan created this… thing to protect himself from me. Besides, Dalawesan is correct in what he said. The people we came here to save don't have much time." Taguwasi said as he began walking into one of the openings into the maze.

"I need to put an end to this, now!"

*****

Pane Kalimangalnuk limped as he made his way to the battered and beaten Talimannog lying on the ground. He had his right hand over the deep open wound on his right thigh as the rust-colored blood oozed out of it. Though he used his right hand to cover his thigh wound, the first wound on his right shoulder prevented him from lifting his arm any higher than his chest.

His face was a mask of rage and deep thought as contemplated how to go about torturing Talimannog before dispatching him to the spirit realm.

"Though I am honestly quite impressed by your

ingenuity in our little skirmish, I am also quite enraged by your insolence in hurting me." Pane Kalimangalnuk said as he loomed over the badly beaten Talimannog. "Though I promised your breathtaking sister that I will spare you and your lives, I am now considering ripping your limbs from your body as I listen to you scream in agony."

*****

"No!" Innawagan screamed as she watched helplessly at what was about to befall her eldest brother. "You promised me you would spare them! You said they could live as your servants! Pane Kalimangalnuk! You promised!"

"I am truly sorry Innawagan," Ammalabukaw said as he too watched what transpired in the other rakuh through the magical pool. "But my master did say that he only considered sparing your siblings only if they passed his challenges."

"But didn't Hapu Talimannog somewhat succeed in this last challenge by injuring the manulib? The objective of the challenge was never really made clear. Can we not plead our case?" Dundunan asked the other kumaw.

Ammalabukaw thought about what Dundunan said and considered its merits. "I suppose you do have a point," he answered thoughtfully. "I can call out to my master, and he will hear me I assure you. But in his state of mind right now, he could choose to kill all of us if I interrupt him."

"Please do it Ammalabukaw!" Innawagan begged and pleaded. "I am willing to risk it if it means saving my siblings. Please, do the honorable thing and let us plead our case to him."

*****

Pane Kalimangalnuk grabbed Talimannog by the back of his neck and lifted him up with his left hand. He put Talimannog's face close to his and stared directly into his eyes. "Though I am wounded by your attacks, I am still strong enough to carry out my threat to you. Tell me... warrior, what would you prefer I do to you before I end you? Would you like to feel what it is like to burn as though you were nothing more than a piece of meat on a spit? Or would you like to know what it feels like to have worms devour you from the inside out?"

Suddenly, Pane Kalimangalnuk was distracted by a voice calling out to him from another rakuh. A voice he personally allowed to be heard by him from anywhere and in any rakuh. "Master! Master," Ammalabukaw called out to him. "Innawagan wishes to talk and plead with you about her brothers. Would you please allow her to speak with you?"

Hearing Ammalabukaw's calls and the mention of

Innawagan's name had an effect on the enraged manulib. An effect that he found annoying yet undeniable. He thought about what Innawagan wanted and what he wanted to do and eventually came to a decision.

He dropped Talimannog on the ground, who curled his body in pain as the manulib stretched out his left hand and opened a hole a few feet in front of him that opened to the rakuh where Innawagan was. "Step forth and I shall hear your plea." Pane Kalimangalnuk said.

Innawagan and the two kumaws passed through the opening and entered the other rakuh. For a brief moment, Innawagan and Talimannog locked eyes with each other and it took a tremendous amount of will for Innawagan not to run to her brother's aid. She knew she had to appeal to Pane Kalimangalnuk through reason and logic rather than raw emotion.

Pane Kalimangalnuk was already emotional with his rage over his wounds. Had she sobbed and begged for Talimannog's life, the manulib might have found it irritating and killed him anyway out of spite. So, Innawagan decided to go the same route she did before and tried to reason with Pane Kalimangalnuk.

"Pane Kalimangalnuk," Innawagan began. "I wish to beg you to spare akka's life and for you to keep your promise to me."

"I promised you I would spare them only, and only if

they or at least one of them successfully pass all my challenges. As you can see, Talimannog failed and as a result, he will be the first to die." Pane Kalimangalnuk said as he pointed to Talimannog on the ground by his feet.

"How did he fail?" Innawagan asked. "Had Talimannog not succeeded by drawing blood from you in your duel? Great manulib, you did not specify the actual terms of your duel and what actually counts as a victory."

"The winner kills the other one!" Pane Kalimangalnuk exclaimed. "How complicated must a duel be?! Two combatants fight until one of them dies! It's that simple!"

"But you said in your promise to me that you would make them your servants should any of them pass your challenge," Innawagan argued. "But if the terms of your challenge were for someone to kill you, then that would go against your own rules. How can they serve you if one of them kills you?"

Innawagan's logic was sound, and this irritated Pane Kalimangalnuk greatly. He had just realized his error and could not refute it. For the first time since Innawagan proposed sparing her brothers, Pane Kalimangalnuk had decided to just forgo reason and act based on what he felt at the moment.

"You are right mavid. As always, you are right," Pane Kalimangalnuk said which made Innawagan sigh in relief. "But I don't care! Talimannog hurt me, so now he dies!"

Pane Kalimangalnuk raised his right foot over Talimannog's head and meant to crush his skull under his heels. Innawagan instinctively dove down towards Talimannog's golden bolo that she had been eyeing as soon as she saw it. Dundunan was about to leap into action to attack Pane Kalimangalnuk as Ammalabukaw was about to attack her.

All these things happened in a span of a second. Time seemed to freeze and extend a few moments longer as everything was about to come to an end. But as quickly as it began, Pane Kalimangalnuk stopped mid-stomp and slowly lowered his feet, and turned his head. Innawagan grabbed the bolo but stopped short as soon as she saw the manulib do the same. Both kumaws stopped as well as all eyes were on Pane Kalimangalnuk.

"Something is wrong," the manulib said as he closed his eyes and listened. "Kakteh?"

*****

Taguwasi entered the golden mound and was amazed and surprised to see that the inside was a series of tunnels and corridors. Once inside, he saw that each tunnel twisted and move in different random directions which explained why sending powerful gusts of winds earlier was so ineffective. The walls redirected them much like how a pinanahang shields those behind it from moderate gusts of wind.

The force behind the walls moving was mediocre at best. Taguwasi was able to redirect the walls that got in his way or were about to squish him with relative ease with his own physical strength.

"I am here Lakandian," Bago said as he suddenly appeared next to him.

"Agay!" Taguwasi yelled out. "By the Poons! Don't just sneak up on me like that! Especially since I can see you as clearly as anybody else in this place!"

"I am sorry Taguwasi," Bago apologized. "I'll make it up to you by finding the manulib for you. I can pass through these magical constructs just as easily as I would any other wall. I'll go find him and tell you where he is."

Taguwasi continued moving through the maze as soon as Bago left. It didn't take long for him to encounter the first of many oppositions. It was a big gray toad with beady eyes staring at him as soon as he made a turn. For a brief second, they locked eyes and stood there motionless. Suddenly, as fast as a blink of an eye, the toad stuck out its long sticky tongue at the Lakandian.

The tongue was aimed at Taguwasi's face when it lashed out. Luckily, being a Lakandian, Taguwasi's reflexes were just as fast as the creature's tongue. He blocked the tongue with his left arm but was surprised at how sticky it was when it latched onto his forearm. The toad retracted its tongue and tried to pull Taguwasi forward. But a Lakandian's natural strength far exceeded that of two or three grown men which was just too much for the monstrous toad.

"Disgusting!" Taguwasi said in revulsion as he stood his ground with the toad's tongue still clinging to his forearm. He raised his other arm towards the creature and commanded a gust of wind that blew the creature away. With its tongue still attached to Taguwasi, the creature only had two choices, to let go of his arm and be blown away by the wind or to cling to Taguwasi until its tongue snapped off. The toad chose the latter.

As soon as the tongue snapped, the toad flew straight to a wall and splattered into a disgusting goo. Taguwasi moved on and ventured farther into the maze. He encountered yet another amphibian as he went, this time in the form of a red and orange tree frog clinging to one of the golden walls. Only this time, he didn't let the creature lash its tongue out at him. As soon as he saw the thing, he commanded the wind to blow it off its sticky legs and slammed it hard against the opposite wall.

This happened a few more times as he went, and the same thing happened with each encounter. Suddenly, Taguwasi heard Bago call out his name. "Taguwasi! Where are you?"

"Here!" he answered. "I'm over here. Follow my voice."

Bago appeared before him a few moments later with a worried look on his face, something Taguwasi would not have noticed had they been anywhere else. "I found him!" Bago exclaimed. "I found Pane Nagdombilan. He is waiting for you in the center of this labyrinth of golden tunnels."

"Good! Can you take me to him?"

"Maybe..." Bago doubtfully answered. "It's one thing to just pass through walls and go to him directly, but it's quite another to guide you through them. I shall do my best Lakandian."

"Just see what you can do to get me there as quickly as you can," Taguwasi said as he started running through the maze of tunnels.

Bago did what Taguwasi asked of him and helped him as best he could in navigating the tunnels. He informed the Lakandian of dead ends that he found as well as warned him of the presence of monstrous toads and tree frogs.

But even with the aid of someone who can pass through walls, it was taking Taguwasi a great deal of time to reach the center. It was sometime after more than fifteen minutes had passed when Bago felt something different in those golden tunnels. "Stop!" Bago suddenly blurted out. "Something is different in this part of the labyrinth. It feels as if the walls of the tunnels themselves are reaching... no searching you out."

"Stop being vague Bago, tell me what's going on?"

There is a presence..." Bago said as he closed his eyes. A moment later, his eyes snapped open as he told Taguwasi, "Run! Run now!"

Taguwasi started running but didn't manage to get very far before the tunnel itself collapsed around him and tried to squeeze him like a piece of fruit sliding down a person's throat. Luckily for him, he was quick enough to extend his arms and legs and prevented the walls from completely constricting him.

"Taguwasi!" Bago yelled when he saw the walls collapse around him. "It's the manulib! He is using the walls like extensions of his skin. He can feel you as you would an ant crawling down your arm!"

Using the wind to push him through the collapsing tunnel, Taguwasi shot himself out like a dart through a blow gun. The wind propelled him several feet away where the tunnel has not yet begun to collapse. But as soon as his feet landed on the ground, he noticed the tunnel start to shift and move which meant it was about to collapse.

Using just his fleetness of feet, Taguwasi began running as fast as he could but was unsure of his direction. "Bago! Where do I go?!"

"Turn left at the next opening!" Bago exclaimed as he passed through the walls as quickly as he possibly could. "Now turn right! Take the next right and keep going straight and follow the tunnel. Take another left here… no wait… right! Go right again!"

This went on for what seemed like forever for the both of them as the tunnels behind Taguwasi started collapsing mere moments after he passes them. Taguwasi even encountered another frog but didn't have time to engage it. Instead, he simply evaded the tongue and left the collapsing tunnel behind him to finish the frog off.

But just like it was earlier when they exited the narrow corridor of trees and exited to the swamp, the labyrinth of tunnels suddenly exited to a low-ceilinged dome no more than a dozen feet in height and around fifty feet in diameter. The ground was a damp muddy landscape with only a few brushes and plants. There were also a few waist-deep puddles scattered around that section of the swamp.

But what really caught Taguwasi's attention was the sight of Pane Nagdombilan running towards him with a large golden war spear! It took the manulib only a few seconds to thrust his spear at the Lakandian who despite being caught by surprise, still managed to sidestep to his left and avoid the spear's tip. "Agay!" Taguwasi exclaimed as he sidesteps the thrust.

Though Taguwasi evaded being skewered, Pane Nagdombilan followed through with his initial attack by swinging the war spear at Taguwasi. The shaft of the spear slammed against the Lakandian's abdomen and ironically knocked the wind out of him. Taguwasi fell and rolled on the mud a few feet away from the manulib. As Taguwasi wrapped his arms around his bruised abdomen, he sees Pane Nagdombilan barreling towards him with the war spear yet again. He had to resort to rolling on the ground away from his charging attacker to avoid the first two thrusts.

When the manulib raised his spear for the third time, he anticipated where Taguwasi was going to be and adjusted his aim. But Taguwasi anticipated this as well and instead of rolling away from the manulib, he rolled towards him and avoided the third downward thrust.

Finding himself beneath the manulib, Taguwasi extended both his arms and shot Pane Nagdombilan with a short yet powerful gust of wind that knocked the manulib back a few paces and gave Taguwasi the distance he needed to compose himself.

"You are quite the warrior flying man, I will grant you that," Pane Nagdombilan complemented Taguwasi. "Even before I became a manulib, I prided myself to be one of the best warriors amongst my people. But I am humble enough to recognize another who might actually be better."

"Your words do me honor manulib, but they will not alter the result of this fight, unfortunately. You will die here I assure you." Taguwasi replied.

"You are half right... Taguwasi was it? You are correct that words mean nothing to men like us. But as to who will be doing the dying, that is up for debate. Especially since I am not alone."

Bago suddenly yelled out to Taguwasi, "Look out! Behind you!"

But it was too late. Several toads suddenly appeared from several different puddles and lashed their long sticky tongues out at the Lakandian. Taguwasi found himself struggling to move as he desperately tried to pull away from the creatures and their disgusting tongues. But just as suddenly as the toads appeared and pinned Taguwasi where he stood, the real danger was flying straight at him.

Pane Nagdombilan had thrown his spear at the Lakandian. Taguwasi noticed the spear coming his way but being unable to use his hands, he was rendered powerless to do anything. All he could do at the last second was move his left leg back to try to evade the spear aimed at his stomach.

The spear did miss his stomach but not him. It struck Taguwasi on the left side of his pelvis, just above his left thigh. He felt the spear tip pierce both muscle and bone and the pain he felt was excruciating. "Yaargh!" Taguwasi cried out as the pain sent shockwaves all throughout his body.

"Taguwasi! No!" Bago cried out as he hurried towards the helpless Lakandian.

As Taguwasi looked down on the spear sticking out of his pelvis, the golden war spear suddenly vanished as though it was never real, though the wound it left was very real including the pain that came with it. When he looked up, he saw Pane Nagdombilan charging towards him with a golden itak in his hand.

I'm dead! Taguwasi thought. *I can't stop him!*

Suddenly, Bago stopped right in front of the charging manulib with his hands raised and yelled for him to, "Stop!"

Out of instinct or reflex, the manulib swung his blade at the anito which harmlessly passed through the incorporeal spirit. "You are nothing anito!" Pane Nagdombilan said with a smirk. "And nothing is all you can do to save him!"

Bago's action bought Taguwasi a good five seconds before Pane Nagdombilan ran straight through the body of Bago and raised his itak for the final blow. But that five seconds gave Taguwasi all the time he needed to clear his thoughts. *Why am I pulling against these beasts?* he suddenly asked himself as he leapt backwards, allowing the tension of all those tongues to draw him closer at a blinding rate.

This simple, yet effective action provided enough slack for Taguwasi to bend his arms and legs. This in turn allowed him to command the wind yet again. His command to the wind was to spin his body around and around and create a small albeit powerful cyclone around him.

The cyclone lifted the toads off the muddy ground as they began spinning uncontrollably with their tongues still attached to Taguwasi. The spinning toads acted like a flail and struck Pane Nagdombilan a couple of times, sending the manulib flying and dropping his itak in the process.

As Taguwasi spun like a top, he felt each of the tongues attached to him loosen its adhesion to his flesh and snap free of him. As soon as the last tongue was gone, Taguwasi stopped spinning and saw Pane Nagdombilan on the ground, trying to get back up on his feet as he shook the cobwebs from his head where one of the toads struck him. Taguwasi also noticed the itak embedded in the ground between him and the manulib.

Though the pain on the left side of his hips still ached and bled, Taguwasi knew he had to capitalize on the situation. With one last command to the wind, Taguwasi had the wind push him forward toward Pane Nagdombilan like an arrow.

He grabbed the itak from the ground, raised it as quickly as he could, and with one precise and powerful swing, he separated Pane Nagdombilan's head from his shoulders!

Chapter 18

Escape

Kakteh?" Pane Kalimangalnuk said again as he felt something terribly wrong going on in the other rakuh. "He's… he is in pain."

The manulib lowered his leg which was about the stomp the life out of Talimannog and turned around. Innawagan, who already had possession of the golden bolo thought about attacking the manulib while his back was turned to her. But when she looked behind her, she saw Ammalabukaw eyeing her with intent and decided to drop the bolo and run toward her brother instead.

"Akka! Akka are you well?" she asked the barely conscious Talimannog.

"I'm … I am alive… but everything hurts." Talimannog whimpered.

"Don't worry akka, it won't be long now. Help is on the way…" Innawagan was saying when she suddenly stopped after realizing that Pane Kalimangalnuk was glowering down at them.

"Yes. Go on! What were you about to say mavid?" the manulib snarled. "Help? There is no help! The only thing you were right about was that it will definitely not be long now! It's time you moved on to the next life Talimannog!"

As Pane Kalimangalnuk raised his foot again to crush

Talimannog's head beneath it, Innawagan jumped on top of her brother and shielded him with her own body. "Stop! Please spare him!" Innawagan cried out.

For a brief moment, the manulib looked down disparagingly on the two siblings beneath his heel. Then that overwhelming sense of dread for his brother came upon him again and at that point, it was all he was concerned about.

"Ammalabukaw!" Pane Kalimangalnuk called his kumaw. "Take them to the other two and make sure they stay there. I need to see to kakteh."

"Yes master," Ammalabukaw replied as an opening to the rakuh where Ammani and Anibo were being held opened up behind them.

"Dundunan, help your Hapu place Talimannog on my back. I will carry him through the opening." Ammalabukaw ordered Dundunan.

*****

Taguwasi landed on the muddy ground rolling and still holding the golden itak in his hand. He was out of breath and a little nauseated after spinning around in his own cyclone a few moments earlier.

"You got him!" Bago exclaimed as he approached him. "You killed the first manulib!"

"Did I?" Taguwasi asked as he tried to stand up. But as

soon as he put some weight on his left leg, a bolt of searing pain suddenly shot up from his hips. "Aaaargh!"

"How is your wound?"

"It hurts Bago! It hurts a lot!" Taguwasi said in frustration. "I know I heal fast, but the spear pierced my hip bone. Standing up hurts like you wouldn't believe!"

"Then don't put any weight on it. You do remember you can fly right?" Bago said mockingly.

Taguwasi rolled his eyes and felt a little embarrassed that he didn't think of it first. Then with a quick gesture from his hand, he commanded the wind to levitate him off the muddy ground.

Suddenly, he and Bago heard a soft gurgling sound coming from the direction of Pane Nagdombilan's head that fell a few short feet from the body.

"I knew it!" Taguwasi exclaimed. "I knew that stinking piece of attay isn't dead!"

Both Bago and Taguwasi hovered over to Pane Nagdombilan and saw his head on the ground with his eyes still moving. His mouth was moving as it made a strange sound. The manulib was trying to speak but since his vocal cords and windpipe had been severed, no actual voice came out of his mouth.

"Look at the body!" Bago said in horror and revulsion. "The fingers are moving!"

"Agay! I've never seen a creature survive decapitation

before," Taguwasi said. "Regardless, I should put him out of his misery. Dalawesan mentioned something about an agimat remember?"

"Kakteh!" A deep thundering voice suddenly screamed from behind them. "What did they do to you?!"

Taguwasi and Bago turned around and saw another manulib standing behind them. "That must be Pane Kalimangalnuk," Bago whispered to Taguwasi. "He looks very upset."

"Indeed, he does, but he's also hurt," Taguwasi whispered back.

"What did you do to Kakteh?!" The manulib screamed again as started limping towards them.

"Unfortunately, your brother had to die for being an attay and..." Taguwasi was answering back with a snarky attitude when bamboo spikes suddenly sprang out from beneath him and impaled him multiple times all over his body. "Urk!" Was the next thing that came out of Taguwasi's lips as blood spewed from his mouth.

"No!" Bago screamed in horror as he saw the Lakandian under his watch just get murdered right before his eyes. "Taguwasi!"

"It is you who needs to die!" Pane Kalimangalnuk said with murderous intent.

"Wait! It's not real Taguwasi!" Bago suddenly exclaimed. "It's like everything in this place. Other than those golden things, everything else is false. I need to make you see them as I do."

Bago placed his hands on the Lakandian's eyes and used his magic to free Taguwasi from the illusion of dying. "There, do you see? Or rather, do you not see?" he asked.

When Bago removed his hands and Taguwasi opened his eyes, the bamboo spikes in his chest, abdomen, and legs suddenly looked a bit translucent. The pain he felt from being impaled lessened to a large degree and up to a point where the pain from his hip wound was far greater. Taguwasi simply moved away from the bamboo spikes that passed through him harmlessly as they did with the intangible anito.

"What was that?!" Taguwasi exclaimed. "I thought I was dead!"

"It's his power," Bago answered. "He creates the most amazing illusions that I have ever seen. Illusions so real that your mind believes them to be and reacts to them accordingly."

"So, what do I do? Do I just close my eyes?"

"The first thing you need to do is take care of him!" Bago said as he pointed to the approaching manulib with a golden itak in his hand.

Taguwasi raised his hand and blew Pane Kalimangalnuk away with a gust of hurricane-force winds. "That won't keep him away for long," Taguwasi said. "So, do I just close my eyes or what?"

"His magic goes beyond just sight," Bago answered. "It beguiles all your senses and even your mind. So, to answer your question, no. You can't just close your eyes."

Suddenly the entire area was engulfed in flame! Taguwasi suddenly found himself burning and eaten alive by fire. Reflexively, he summoned a cyclone to surround him which kept the flames a few feet away from him.

He looked down at his arms and torso and saw his burnt skin bubbling and peeling away. The pain was excruciating!

"Bago! Help!"

Bago used his magic again to free Taguwasi's mind from the illusion. "We need to get out of here to understand Pane Kalimangalnuk's powers as well as their limitations," Bago told Taguwasi. "I saw where the sakbawan is located. We need to exit this rakuh and hide. You need to distract him so we can make good our escape."

Taguwasi summoned all his will and extended his arms to his sides. This expanded the girth of the cyclone which forced Pane Kalimangalnuk to cover up and anchor himself to where he stood. Taguwasi and Bago used this opportunity to fly towards the sakbawan and escape.

"Are you sure we can still pass through that thing?" Taguwasi asked as he flew towards the sakbawan.

"Yes! I can still feel the magic coming from the golden doors," Bago replied. "Just focus on getting through. We need to put some distance between ourselves and the other manulib!"

Both Taguwasi and Bago exited the sakbawan and ended up inside Pane Kalimangalnuk's third rakuh. "Now where are we?!" Asked an exasperated Taguwasi.

"We're inside another rakuh," Bago replied. "But right now, you have more immediate concerns than knowing where we are. We are not alone here!"

*****

Ammalabukaw gently set Talimannog's battered body on the ground at the foot of the wall where Ammani and Anibo were held.

"Akka! Is that Akka?" Ammani cried out when he saw Ammalabukaw, Dundunan, and Innawagan arrive. "How is he doing? Is he alive?"

"He is badly hurt," Innawagan replied as she gathered some water in her hands from the small stream that ran through the middle of the cave and slowly poured them into Talimannog's mouth. "He fought Pane Kalimangalnuk as bravely as he could, and he even managed to wound the manulib. But alas, Pane

Kalimangalnuk was far too powerful for even akka to defeat."

"Then it is hopeless," Anibo muttered in his stone prison. "What little hope we had left with akka is all but gone. Now our only salvation lies with Dalawesan should he succeed in finding the flying man."

"Then do not abandon hope Hapu Anibo," Dundunan said. "My akka has indeed returned, and he brings hope with him."

*****

"Get on that rock," Taguwasi told Bago. And as soon as the anito hovered over the flat piece of rock, Taguwasi commanded the wind to lift the rock off the ground and follow him several dozen feet in the open sky.

"Agay!" Taguwasi exclaimed as soon as he looked down and saw more than a hundred Kalinga warriors looking up at him from across the grassy expanse. "Where did they come from?"

"They are not really there Lakandian," Bago replied. "These beings are just like those toads and frogs we saw in the last rakuh. They may seem real and alive much like everything else you see around you, but they are all part of the vast magical illusion that the manulib created."

"Speaking of the manulib, we should get out of here before he arrives," Taguwasi said. "He is far more powerful than his brother and I need a way to get past his illusions."

They flew in a random direction and went as fast as they could. "Agay! We forgot about the kumaw!" Taguwasi exclaimed as he just remembered Dalawesan. "We left him at the other rakuh!"

"There's nothing we can do for him at this point. I would have asked him to come with me, but the constraints of that golden mount were just too narrow for a kumaw to navigate through. But we need to focus on Pane Kalimangalnuk and what we need to do about him."

"You are right Bago," Taguwasi agreed. "You can obviously counteract his magic with yours as far as shielding me from his illusions. Can't you just keep doing that as I fight him?"

"I can only unravel his illusions one at a time. Each one is different from the others as each one will hurt and kill you in different ways. But in doing so, we will be reacting to each and every illusion and we will find ourselves at a constant disadvantage. How many times can you really endure burning to death or worse before you lose your mind?"

"So, what do we do?" Taguwasi asked frustratedly.

"Right now, nothing," Bago answered disappointedly at himself. "If only there was a way I could make you see what I see inside this place?"

Taguwasi sighed as they flew. "Should we start looking for the sakbawan in this rakuh? Or are there other ways to leave besides the sakbawan?"

"I have seen these ripples in the air as I know you have. Especially the ones we come out from the moment we pass through those golden doors," Bago mentioned. "I believe I've seen others in the last rakuh."

"Try to find some in this rakuh," Taguwasi said. "If we can't fight this manulib, then should at least try to find the people we need to rescue from them."

The vast fields of tall grass were bathed in the bright rays of the midday sun as it was earlier when Talimannog and Anibo were there. Far below them as they flew over the grass, Taguwasi and Bago saw countless Kalinga warriors and headhunters chasing after them and shooting arrows. But from their height and speed, Taguwasi felt relatively safe from them.

But after a few minutes into their flight, the bright blue midday sky suddenly and rapidly started turning dark. It took only a few seconds for the day to turn into an inky night, and a bright perfectly circular full moon appeared right above them.

"This does not bode well!" Bago exclaimed.

"He's here," Taguwasi seconded. "Be ready to snap me out of whatever illusion he comes up with next."

"I'm ready Lakandian," Bago replied. "I'm actually

wondering what took him this long to follow us here?"

"Why don't you ask him yourself?" Taguwasi said as he pointed to the gigantic face of Pane Kalimangalnuk that suddenly materialized in the night sky.

"You are the flying man that the kumaw Dalawesan sought out I presume?" Pane Kalimangalnuk asked them in a voice that rang out like thunder across the vast fields of grass. "Tell me your name flying man, so I at least know what to call you before I kill you."

"I am Taguwasi!" he said proudly. "And this is the anito Bago, and you are the manulib Pane Kalimangalnuk. Now that we know each other, I would like to ask you a question of my own."

"Go ahead Taguwasi, ask away."

"I would like to ask if you are willing to just free the people you are keeping captive so we can avoid any further unpleasantries and just leave each other be?" Taguwasi asked.

Pane Kalimangalnuk burst out laughing and said, "You are quite humorous Taguwasi, and I do admire your candor. But Innawagan is mine and for what you did to my kakteh, I am afraid I cannot just leave you be."

The face of the manulib faded into the night sky as a sudden eerie silence surrounded them. "I guess that's a no," Taguwasi said half-jokingly. "So, what happens next?"

"Listen," Bago whispered. "Do you hear that?"

"Yes… what is that?" Taguwasi asked as he strained his ears. "It sounds like wood splintering or hide being sheared."

"Look down there! Something is happening to those false warriors!" Bago exclaimed.

The hundreds of Kalinga warriors and headhunters began convulsing and writhing as their bones started breaking and their flesh tearing. Some of them started sprouting giant batwings from their backs while others began growing black feathers on their sides.

"They're turning into night creatures!" Taguwasi cried out. "They're turning into aswang!"

Suddenly, something slammed into Taguwasi's back followed by several sharp stabbing pains on his sides. "Behind you!" Bago cried out as a *manananggal* (segmented, half-bodied night creature with bat-like wings) attacked Taguwasi from behind. The aswang buried its sharp claw-like fingers deep into Taguwasi's back and ribs. Taguwasi screamed in pain as the manananggal tore at his flesh.

"Just remember, it's not real!" Bago yelled at Taguwasi.

Bago leapt from the rock he was on and onto the Lakandian's back. He placed his hands on the sides of his head and released him from the illusion.

As soon as Taguwasi was freed, the manananggal

disappeared into nothingness and the pain began subsiding.

"Thank you, Bago. Why don't you just stay on my back from now on, so I don't have to deal with these night creatures."

"I don't think it's going to be that easy Taguwasi," Bago replied.

"What do you mean?" Taguwasi asked puzzled. "Just keep doing what you are doing and..."

"Look at those garudas (half-man, half-bird-like night creatures) coming towards you," Bago interjected. "Do they look real to you?"

"Yes," Taguwasi answered. "But as I said, just keep doing what you're doing and..."

"I already am!" Bago said exasperatedly. "It looks like each aswang is a separate illusion of itself. This means I need to free you from each and every aswang in this rakuh!"

"But there are hundreds of them!" Taguwasi said worriedly. "How are you going to do that?"

"I'm not! Start flying! We need to get away from them!"

With the weightless anito Bago on his back, Taguwasi flew as fast as the wind would take him. Behind him were countless flying night creatures while below him, terrestrial versions of the aswang made multiple streaks on the high grass as they ran after him.

"I can't keep flying forever Bago, I need a destination!"

"I know that Lakandian. Just give me a moment to find a sakbawan or those strange ripples in the air."

After a long aimless flight across the grassy field, Bago finally sensed something not too far from where they were. "There! Turn to your left. I sense something distorted in the magic of the rakuh. It feels like the sakbawan but not exactly the same."

"Where?" Taguwasi asked. "Towards those dark clouds?"

"Yes! Yes, head towards those dark..." Bago was confirming with Taguwasi when he suddenly stopped. "Those are not clouds!"

Taguwasi had to stop as he realized what was directly ahead of them. "There are a hundred more of them! I'm not sure I can fight them all. Is the ripple still far from here?" he asked Bago.

"It's close by," the anito answered. "But to get to it, you will have to go through them."

"If it's that close then I cannot go around them," Taguwasi said as he assessed his situation. "I'm going to have to fight. I need you to jump off as soon as the fight begins and find that exit. Call me as soon as you find it."

"Very well Taguwasi," Bago answered. "I will do my best to find it, just promise me you'll survive this."

Without mincing words, Taguwasi flew towards the

multitude of aswang and other night creatures that awaited him. As soon as he was less than twenty feet away from them, he reached forward and commanded the wind to reach out and grab a few dozen of them and slam them against each other.

What followed next was complete and utter chaos! At this point, Bago had leapt off the Lakandian's back, and as soon as he hovered over the ground, dozens of aswang began attacking him. Luckily for Bago, he was a spirit as every slash from every clawed hand and needle-like tongue passed through him as they would a puff of smoke.

Above the anito, the chaotic battle of Taguwasi continued. He was surrounded from every conceivable angle by manananggal, garuda, and alàn alike. He used whirlwinds to keep them at bay as he used his speed and strength to outmaneuver them and rip chunks off them from their bodies.

One garuda carried a large binaroy sling blade on his person from when he was still in his human form. Taguwasi saw this and grabbed the weapon off the garuda's back and hacked off one of the creature's arms with it.

Having this weapon helped Taguwasi greatly as he was unarmed when he entered the rakuh. He had dropped the golden blade he used to decapitate Pane

Nagdombilan when his brother burned him in the previous rakuh.

With the binaroy in one hand and his ability to command the wind, Taguwasi was able to hold his own against the massive sangkawan of night creatures that assailed him. But as successful as he was in the battle, Taguwasi was as far from invulnerable against the aswang as they were from him. He had a multitude of cuts and lacerations across his body from the few that managed to get close enough to wound him.

At one point, a couple of alàn managed to grab both of his legs as they dragged him down closer to the tall grass where more than a hundred aswang awaited him. He managed to bend over and swing the binaroy across the face of one of the alàn and the neck of the other, effectively killing them. But by the time they released their hold on his legs, he was already low enough for the terrestrial night creatures to pounce on him.

Dozens of needle-sharp fingers started piercing his skin as the aswang started piling on the Lakandian. It would only take a split second for him to be completely overwhelmed and end up as food for the ravenous night creatures. But that split second was more than enough for the quick-witted Lakandian to summon a cyclone around him, much like he did earlier to protect himself. But being that close to the ground, several rocks and other debris got caught in the cyclone's wake and began spinning around him at an incredible rate.

Taguwasi saw this and commanded the wind to grab hold of the rocks and continue spinning them around his person even as he dispersed the cyclone that kept the aswang away. The rocks spun around him so fast that they produced a whizzing sound as they passed through the open air, the blades of grass, and the bodies of every aswang in their path.

Having no cyclone to hold them back, the mindless night creatures moved perpetually forward, trying to get to the Lakandian. But as soon as the spinning rocks made contact with them, flesh and bone began exploding all around Taguwasi. Even the flying night creatures that dove down to get to him were no match for the spinning debris of death that protected Taguwasi.

As the debris both protected Taguwasi and dispatched his enemies, Taguwasi made use of this time to assess his wounds and injuries. His body was mostly covered in blood as most of his skin had slashes and cuts. Even his cheeks, neck, and scalp were not spared from these wounds.

"Bago!" Taguwasi cried out. "Bago! Where are you?"

But Bago did not answer. It was either Bago could not hear him or he could not hear Bago amongst the cacophony of snarls, growls, and that blunt squishing sound the rocks made when they hit a night creature. Suddenly, Taguwasi saw the hovering image of Bago approach him.

"Taguwasi, I found it!" Bago yelled to speak over the noise that surrounded them. "I found the rippling in the air! The exit is near!"

"How far is it?" Taguwasi asked.

"Around a thousand paces in that direction," Bago replied. "Can you fly over there?"

"I think so. I am getting tired though." Taguwasi said.

He and Bago hovered over to where the exit to the rakuh was. Taguwasi continued to spin the rocks around him to keep the night creatures away, but he noticed the velocity of the rocks beginning to slow down as fatigue was starting to get to him.

"How much farther is it?" Taguwasi asked.

"There! It's right there. Don't you see it?" Bago replied as he pointed to an empty section of nothing over the grass.

"I see it! I see the ripple!"

*****

Innawagan was tending to Talimannog's wounds when a strange whooshing sound suddenly came from the other end of the cave. Suddenly, two strange men appeared before them out of thin air. One was a bloodied

Aeta man with numerous cuts and lacerations across his body while the second man was a strange-looking naked man with white hair and yellow-golden eyes that seemed to float a few inches above the ground.

"Is... is he the flying man?" Innawagan asked Dundunan who looked as surprised and aghast as she was.

"No... Hapu," Dundunan answered. "That man is not a man. He is an anito."

"She can see me!" Bago said in astonishment. "Either she is sensitive to spirits, or this place makes me visible to everyone."

"Whoever they are, they are not welcomed here!" Ammalabukaw exclaimed as he opened his wings and charged at the intruders.

"Get away from me kumaw!" The bloodied injured man said as he pointed his right hand toward the charging kumaw. Suddenly a powerful gust of wind blew the large red kumaw back and slammed him against the wall on the opposite side of the cave.

"I am in pain, and I am not in the mood for games!" the wounded man said as he slumped to the ground.

"Taguwasi remember, your wounds are not real, neither were the night creatures that inflicted them upon you," Bago said as he placed his hands on the side of Taguwasi's head.

"They feel real, and they really hurt!" Taguwasi exclaimed.

Innawagan stood with her mouth agape as she saw some of the wounds on Taguwasi's body vanish right before her eyes. "You... you healed him anito!" she said in amazement. "Can you do the same for akka?"

"Unfortunately, I cannot," Bago answered. "Even from here, I can tell that your brother's wounds are real, whereas Taguwasi's are illusions inflicted by other illusions created by Pane Kalimangalnuk."

"If they are illusions, why are some of my cuts still here?" Taguwasi complained.

"Because your mind had believed them to be real far longer than the others. Eventually, your body made real what your mind perceived to be." Bago answered as he removed his hand from Taguwasi's head and approached Innawagan.

Ammalabukaw was about to get up from the ground as he stared at the intruders menacingly when Bago spoke to the red kumaw, "I wouldn't try it again kumaw. Even though he is wounded, you are no match for a Lakandian."

"Stay still old friend," Dundunan told Ammalabukaw. "There is no need for you to sacrifice your life just yet, especially since they have not yet violated your master's orders to keep us here."

Ammalabukaw nodded to Dundunan and kept to himself as he observed the intruders.

Taguwasi stood up and approached Innawagan. "Greetings Innawagan, I am the Lakandian Taguwasi," he said to Innawagan who stared at him with a puzzled look. "I am the... flying man you've sent the other kumaw to find."

"Are you here to rescue us Taguwasi?" Innawagan asked.

"I didn't come here for your amusement so yes," Taguwasi answered back snarkily as he was still annoyed with all the cuts he received.

"How is he?" Taguwasi asked as he looked at the unconscious Talimannog.

"He is badly hurt from his fight with Pane Kalimangalnuk," Innawagan said worriedly. "We need to get him away from here as soon as possible."

"What is going on out there? Who's out there? Why did Ammalabukaw suddenly crash against the wall?" Anibo and Ammani asked from their vertical coffins.

"Who are they?!" Taguwasi asked with surprise.

"They are my other brothers, Ammani and Anibo. They also failed the manulib's challenges and were imprisoned in the cave walls by the manulib.

"Bago, can you get them out?" Taguwasi asked.

Bago placed his hands on each of the brother's heads

which freed them from the illusion of being trapped. After that, it was a simple matter to simply step forward and be free. To Bago's surprise, both Ammani and Anibo could also see him. Ammalabukaw did not like this and tried his best to keep his composure, especially after seeing what Taguwasi was capable of.

"Is akka with you?" Dundunan asked Bago. "Where is he?"

"Dalawesan is most likely still in the other rakuh where the toads are," Bago answered. "He could not follow us through the narrow tunnels made by the other manulib. He should still be there."

"We need to get out of here and find a way out of these rakuh illusions Pane Kalimangalnuk created," Taguwasi said as he motioned for the twins to carry the injured Talimannog. "Bago, you need to find another doorway for us to pass through."

"Wait!" Innawagan interjected. "What of the other manulib; Pane Nagdombilan? We should worry about him the most. Unlike his brother, he has absolutely no qualms about killing any of us."

"He is actually the least of our problems," Taguwasi replied. "Especially since I separated his head from his body when we fought."

Everyone other than Bago suddenly fell silent when they heard this. Everyone had assumed that the manulib were invincible even after Talimannog had inflicted wounds on Pane Kalimangalnuk. But hearing Taguwasi say that he actually killed one was beyond belief.

"Then my master's brother is finally free from his torment," Ammalabukaw said as he approached Taguwasi and the others. "But unfortunately for me, my master ordered me to prevent anyone from leaving. And since you spoke about your intentions to do so, then I must prevent it from happening. Even if it means I have to die."

Taguwasi looked at the approaching kumaw and raised both his hands with his palms up. Two small whirlwinds appeared carrying with them several small rocks that spun around them at an incredible rate.

"Then I shall grant you your wish kumaw," Taguwasi said as he prepared to launch those rocks at Ammalabukaw like arrows and finish him.

"Hapu, please wait!" Dundunan said as she stood between Taguwasi and Ammalabukaw. "Ammalabukaw is a dear old friend of ours. I beg you to spare his life this one time because he cannot help but follow Pane Kalimangalnuk's commands. He owes the manulib a life debt just as Dalawesan and I owe them to Hapu Innawagan and Talimannog."

Dundunan then turned her gaze to Ammalabukaw. "I will beg for your life just this one-time old friend, only because that is what you were to us. But the next time you go against us and our masters, it will be the last."

"You know I cannot defy him Dundunan," Ammalabukaw said. "I must still prevent you from..." Ammalabukaw's words were cut short when a powerful gust of wind came out of nowhere, picked him up and slammed him against the wall for a second time, and rendered him unconscious.

"We have no time for this!" Taguwasi exclaimed. "Bago! Where do we go from here?"

"Here!" Bago answered from inside a small hole in the cave wall barely wide enough for two people. "There is a tunnel here that leads to a ripple. We should go through here."

*****

Anibo and Ammani who helped Talimannog walk were the last to re-emerge from the ripple. They all stood in a circular room with a high domed ceiling where Innawagan was held earlier before.

"Up there," Innawagan said as she pointed up to the domed ceiling. "There should be another ripple in the middle of the ceiling. That was where Dalawesan escaped through to find you."

Taguwasi flew up to inspect the ceiling but found nothing but cold hard rock. "There's nothing here," he said. "Bago, do you see anything?"

"Nothing. There's nothing there," Bago replied. " If there was an opening there before, it is gone now. But there are other doors here. I'll go see if they lead anywhere."

Taguwasi flew down and spoke to Innawagan. "How is your brother?"

"He is drifting in and out of consciousness. We need to get him out of here," she replied. "The anito will not find anything through those doors. I tried going through them before when Pane Kalimangalnuk held me captive in this very room. All of them lead back to this room."

"Maybe Bago will fare better," Taguwasi said. "He is as you said an anito, a being of spirit and magic. He can see through the manulib's illusions and maybe he will be able to see through these doors as well. But while we wait, do you mind telling me what that is?" Taguwasi asked as he pointed to the magic pool.

"Pane Kalimangalnuk created that to allow me to see what was happening to my siblings as they braved his challenges. If your next question is if we can pass through it, then the answer is no. It only shows us the other rakuhs."

"It is only showing us a place with broken huts. Do you know if we can use it to see where Pane Kalimangalnuk is right now?" Taguwasi asked.

"I don't know how to make it work," Innawagan answered. "The rakuh you see there was where akka Talimannog fought Pane Kalimangalnuk."

Bago suddenly came out from one of the doors surrounding the room. "Everyone come! I found a way out! Hurry!"

"Go!" Taguwasi called to the others. "Anibo, Ammani, both of you go first and take your brother with you. Innawagan, you go next and then you kumaw."

Bago led the twins who carried Talimannog down the short tunnel through one of the doors. In the middle of the tunnel was a small, almost unnoticeable opening on the left wall that turned into yet another short tunnel. A dozen feet or so was a ripple. They passed through it and came out near the mouth of a cave.

The sun was out and bathed the entrance to the cave in a warm soothing glow. The twins took Talimannog out and saw that they were back in the lagoon.

"Dundunan go!" Innawagan gestured for the kumaw to go. "I'll follow you next. Just go with the anito."

"But Hapu... you should go first." Dundunan protested.

"Just go. Please." Innawagan insisted to which Dundunan had no choice but to obey.

"Taguwasi! Let's go!" Innawagan called out to Taguwasi who stood by the opening of the doorway.

"You go first," Taguwasi replied. "I'll make sure we're not followed.

Innawagan raced back to Taguwasi and took his hand in hers. "Very well, but please hurry," she said as she ran after Dundunan and exited the rakuh.

A few moments later Bago returned to Taguwasi and told him, "They're out! Let's go now before..."

Suddenly Bago found himself outside the rakuh and inside a perfectly normal cave. He looked behind him and saw the mouth of the cave where the siblings were standing by the banks of the lagoon. *Oh no! I'm outside the rakuh and the ripple is gone! That means Taguwasi is in there alone with...* "Taguwasi!" Bago cried out.

Taong Ganap (Poem)

ᜆᜂᜅ᜔ ᜄᜈᜉ᜔

May mga landas na dapa't kong tahakin
May mga tungkulin na dapa't kong gawin.
Hindi ito batas na isinulat sa bato,
O kaya ay salitang imbi sa pangako.
Kundi mga gawi na ayon sa tama
Para sa nakararami at matuwid.

Naisin ko man na magtampisaw
Sa ligaya ng kabataan at murang lakas
Ang tumahak ng anumang laya
Na hindi inda ang darating na bukas
Walang balangkas ang mga oras
At bukas palad ang hinaharap.

Hindi kayang bulagin ang aking mga mata
At maging bingi sa hinaing ng iba
Kaya't ang nararapat ay tanggapin na kusa
Ang tinig na umaaawit sa puso at isip –
Sasayangin ba ang talino at bisig
Sa daan na masaya at gawaing madali?

Taong ganap ang ikubli ang nasa
At ibalikat ang buhating mabigat
Ngayon pa at ako ang may angking handog
Na magbata ng dalahing hindi kaya ng maliliit.
Taong ganap ang humaharap sa mahirap tanggapin
Matinik na bulaklak ay aking yayakapin.

Chapter 19

Acceptance

Taguwasi stood there confused and horrified at the same time when all the doors in the round room vanished before his eyes. The walls themselves started moving back and the domed ceiling disappeared, revealing a starry night sky and a bright full moon.

Suddenly, the figure of Pane Kalimangalnuk stepped forward from the fading gloom and stood a few feet away from him. Taguwasi instinctively tried to raise his hands and command the wind but was surprised to find them unresponsive.

"What?!" Taguwasi exclaimed as he looked down and saw that his arms from his shoulders down were made of stone.

"Don't bother using your powers flying man, they will not serve you any good now. Especially if you can't use your hands," Pane Kalimangalnuk said as he slowly walked over to him.

"As you can see my wounds and injuries have already healed," the manulib said as he pointed to his shoulder and leg where Talimannog had wounded him earlier. "Whereas I can see that you've sustained more battle wounds since I last saw you."

Taguwasi tried using his legs, but they too had been

turned to stone. Finally, he used his head and neck but all he could summon was a short gust that had no real power to it. Taguwasi had always been dependent on using his extremities to summon and command the wind. But now that he had lost access to them, he found himself powerless and helpless for the second time in his life; the first being when his parents were killed.

Pane Kalimangalnuk stood right in front of Taguwasi and gave him a thunderous slap across his face. Having seen Taguwasi take it and just continue to look at him, Pane Kalimangalnuk spoke again, "Hmm… you have real strength as well as powers. Tell me… flying man, did you gain your powers and abilities through an agimat or some other magical item?"

"First of all," Taguwasi replied. "As I mentioned earlier, my name is Taguwasi so stop calling me flying man. And as for my powers, I will tell you, but I cannot say it out loud. You need to come closer."

Pane Kalimangalnuk humored Taguwasi and leaned forward. As soon as his face was close enough, Taguwasi butted the side of his head on the manulib's left eye and opened up a small cut just below his eyebrow.

"Aaargh!" Pane Kalimangalnuk cried out as he covered his left eye with his hand. "You! You cut me! You actually cut my skin?!"

Suddenly two sharp bamboo spikes shot out from the

ground and stabbed right through Taguwasi's armpits and exited just above his shoulders. "Yarrrgh!" Taguwasi cried out as the pain was beyond excruciating.

They're not real. They're not real. They're not real. Taguwasi kept thinking over and over to himself like a mantra, hoping he could do what Bago was able to do for him to counteract these illusions from the manulib. Suddenly, a small ugly creature with baby-like features came from under the earth just in front of the hapless Lakandian.

"How do you like my *tiyanak* (ghoul in the form of a baby)?" Pane Kalimangalnuk asked. "It is quite grotesque if you ask me. But it does seem hungry."

Without warning the tiyanak leapt at Taguwasi and started sinking its small needle-like teeth into his chest and abdomen. Its teeth ripped through skin and muscles as it began biting off small chunks of flesh off of the Lakandian's body. It was feeding off of him while he was still alive.

They're not real. They're not real. They're not real. Taguwasi just closed his eyes and summoned all his will to persuade his mind to disregard the illusion.

The pain was intense and most of the time, Taguwasi was nearing his breaking point where he just wanted it all to be over. But his will proved much more powerful than his despair. After what seemed like an eternity, just as quickly as it began, the pain began subsiding.

Taguwasi opened his eyes and saw the tiyanak on his chest seemed a bit translucent. Though not as completely free of the illusion as it would be had Bago been there to assist him, Taguwasi seemed to have managed to free himself from the pain. Albeit he still could not free himself from the bamboo poles and return his extremities to normal.

"That is very impressive Taguwasi!" Pane Kalimangalnuk exclaimed, clapping his hands sardonically. "You actually freed yourself from the illusion of pain without aid from your anito friend. But as impressive as your will may be, I simply cannot allow you to continue completely unscathed."

Pane Kalimangalnuk approached him again. The tiyanak on his chest vanished into a puff of smoke. Suddenly and without warning, he drove his thumb deep into Taguwasi's pelvic wound where Pane Nagdombilan had stabbed him earlier with a spear.

Taguwasi cried out in pain yet again! "Yes! That's it Taguwasi, cry! Cry out just as I cry out in pain every day from the curse of perpetual hunger and thirst. And don't even bother trying to block out this pain for everything I am doing to you now and what I am about to do is real!"

*****

Bago hurried to where Innawagan and her siblings were. Bago was panicked in a way that he had never felt before. "Innawagan!" he called out. "Do you see me? Do any of you see me?"

"Agay! *Mangilen!* (Ghost)!" Anibo screamed.

"Hapu, please be calm," Dundunan said. "It is the anito Bago."

"Bago?" Innawagan said as she approached him. "You look different."

"It's because I'm not in the rakuh anymore," Bago replied. "But that is not important right now. It's Taguwasi... he..."

"Where is he?" Innawagan interjected worriedly. "Were you not just with him?"

"I was! And then all of a sudden, the rakuh disappeared and I found myself back out here with you! The ripple disappeared and I couldn't get back to him."

"You need to find another one," Innawagan said. "You can always take the one where you entered from earlier."

"But that route will take far too long to get to Taguwasi, on top of which I doubt I will be able to find my way back to him," Bago replied. "Do you know of any other sakbawan or ripple I can use? Taguwasi will not last long against Pane Kalimangalnuk's powers without me."

"I don't," Innawagan answered. "The only other ripple

that I know of was where Dalawesan escaped from before but that one has already been closed."

"I need your help Dundunan," Bago asked the kumaw. "Do you know where the closest balete tree is?"

"There is one only a short distance north from here. I saw it when we first came to settle here." Dundunan replied.

"Will you bear me on your back and take me there? We need to ask someone for help." Bago asked of Dundunan.

"I am sorry, but I cannot. I can't leave Hapu Innawagan and her siblings here unguarded. Also, akka is still trapped in there somewhere."

"Dundunan," Innawagan said as she stood up and placed her hand on Dundunan's white feathered chest. "Taguwasi and your brother will not survive if you don't help the anito. Please go with him and help him as best you can."

"But Hapu, what about you?" Dundunan sheepishly protested.

"We will be fine. We'll do our best to get back to the settlement and find Alig. But Please go with Bago and save Taguwasi and Dalawesan." Innawagan said as she gave Dundunan a warm parting embrace.

"Yes, Hapu. I will do as you say." Dundunan said.

*****

The beating went on and on for what felt like forever. But being a Lakandian made Taguwasi able to endure it, whereas any other man would have succumbed to death at that point. He felt his face was swollen and several of his ribs had snapped in two. His eyes were but narrow slits given how swollen they were.

"You're still alive, that's good Taguwasi," Pane Kalimangalnuk said as he stepped back from the immobile and bloodied figure of Taguwasi before him. "I must admit that my hands actually hurt from beating on you this much. But since I don't want you to die just yet, I'll stop for now so we can get a chance to talk before I start again."

Even after enduring such pain and torture, Taguwasi kept his mind as calm and as focused as he possibly could. He knew that the only way he could find his way out of his predicament alive was to surpass the physical limitations that the manulib was instilling upon him through his mind.

They're not real. They're not real. They're not real. He kept thinking over and over as he tried to free himself from the illusion. *I cannot die here like this. Sinag needs me as well as everyone else whom I can save from such evil beings. Poong Kedes, if you can hear my prayers, please help me.*

I know now what you meant when you told me that to be a

true Lakandian, I had to forgo my mortal bonds and submit myself to the will of Kaluwalhatian. I thought that I could do good on my own without being beholden to anyone. But I was wrong.

I was wrong to blame you for the death of my parents and Puyang Anag's family. Please grant me the strength and the will to free myself from this creature's magic. Please hear me my Poon.

"I don't think I broke your jaw so you should still be able to converse with me," Pane Kalimangalnuk said as he paced back and forth and inspected Taguwasi. "But if you don't want to talk I can always just continue beating up on you."

The manulib stopped pacing and grabbed Taguwasi by the hair with his left hand and raised his right as he prepared to begin pummeling Taguwasi's face again.

"How... how is your brother doing?" Taguwasi suddenly asked in a weak almost inaudible voice.

This made Pane Kalimangalnuk pause as he released Taguwasi's head. "You are either really brave or stupid for asking such a question of me.

"Having decapitated him yourself, you know that he is either dead which makes you brave for asking, or you know that you've actually failed to kill him which makes you stupid," The manulib replied.

"But I will answer your question. Pane Nagdombilan

lives but has been terribly weakened from his fight with you. I've spent a great deal of time helping him attach his head back on his shoulders which by the way, was the only reason I didn't finish you off earlier than I should have.

"I had to resort to using false creatures to take care of you as well as give me enough time to heal my wounds from Talimannog's surprising prowess in battle."

"How was it that a human such as Talimannog managed to wound you like that?" Taguwasi asked.

"Luck," Pane Kalimangalnuk answered. "Luck and the fact that I tried giving him a fighting chance to placate his sister whom I so desire. Had I wished it, he and all his brothers could have just dropped dead when they were inside my rakuh.

"But their sister wanted them to have a chance and I wanted some sport and entertainment, so I created these inane challenges for them."

As Pane Kalimangalnuk rambled on, Taguwasi was still trying to will himself free from the manulib's magic. He tried his best to seem like he was listening to the manulib's words as he secretly focused on what he was doing.

Suddenly, the Lakandian felt the weight on his arms and legs begin to lighten. Some semblances of feeling started reemerging from his dormant nerves. It started as a tingling sensation at the tips of his fingers which flowed down to his palms, feet, and joints.

Taguwasi knew that in a few short moments, he would regain the use of his limbs and with it his powers. But to what extent, he wasn't sure. His greatest worry was the injury to his arms by the two bamboo poles. Though he knew the cause of the injuries to be an illusion, he remembered what Bago told him about wounds that his mind perceived to be real and had the potential to actually become real.

He doubted that he could move his arms to any great extent which would limit the use of his powers. That was on top of the real injuries he sustained at the hands of Pane Kalimangalnuk. *I don't have a choice but to use the dinatal for a second time. I only hope that I've recovered enough of my strength to stay conscious after I use it.*

Slowly and very carefully, Taguwasi bent his hands ever so slightly as Pane Kalimangalnuk blabbered on. The last thing he wanted was for the manulib to notice that he had regained the use of his limbs prematurely and start attacking him again.

He felt his connection to the wind reconnect as he slowly harnessed its power into his chest. *Almost there.* he thought to himself. *I can feel its power building in me. I just need to avoid drawing his attention for a few more moments.*

"... my power within the rakuh is almost absolute,"

Pane Kalimangalnuk continued to talk. "I can feel and know almost everything, and anyone trapped within as a spider would a fly trapped in its web. I know the kumaw Dalawesan is still trapped in the rakuh with the toads, just as I know that Ammalabukaw is starting to regain consciousness in the other.

"Come to think of it, I think it's time my kumaw killed his old friend Dalawesan," Pane Kalimangalnuk said as he stopped directly in front of Taguwasi and turned to his right. "Ammalabukaw, get up! I am transporting you to where your old friend Dalawesan is. Do me a favor and rip his wings off from his body."

"Manulib!" Taguwasi suddenly cried out. "Why don't you do me a favor and die!"

Without wasting another second, Taguwasi used his dinatal to its full destructive potential. Pane Kalimangalnuk stood only a foot or two away from him which didn't give him enough time to do anything but absorb the full power of Taguwasi's dinatal!

Pane Kalimangalnuk was struck with such an overwhelming force that he was blown off his feet and flew across his own rakuh at such a speed that his whole body made a whistling sound as it passed through the air.

He felt his rock-hard skin start peeling from his very muscles as every piece of clothing he wore was reduced to tatters. He crashed into the stone wall more than a few dozen feet away so violently that it made a sound like thunder and almost every bone in his body shattered.

Blood sprayed from his flesh where bone fragments protruded like thorns. His entire body actually remained embedded in the rockface for a good long moment before it fell on the cold unforgiving stone floor.

Taguwasi felt most of his strength wane as soon as the entirety of the dinatal left his body. Having regained the use of his limbs, he stepped down from the bamboo poles that held him as they became translucent and almost ghost-like in appearance and solidity.

He fell on his hands and knees as he tried to muster whatever strength he had left just to stay awake. "It's done," Taguwasi whispered. "I got him! I got Pane Kalimangalnuk. But I still need to finish him off before regains consciousness or his brother returns."

The crawl to reach Pane Kalimangalnuk's body was long and arduous. Every inch felt like a foot and every foot felt like a yard. Taguwasi knew he needed to sleep and rest but he also knew that the fight was not yet over. To sleep at that point was to die.

The sheer exhaustion complicated by his injuries almost drove the Lakandian stir-crazy. His emotions were running amok in his mind. He was happy Pane Kalimangalnuk crashed against the wall as he did but cursed the distance he had to crawl to get to him.

His broken ribs felt like knives stabbing at him from within his body but at the same time kept him awake to do what must be done. During the entirety of his trek to reach Pane Kalimangalnuk, Taguwasi had cried, laughed, and grunted a good number of times.

Finally, Taguwasi reached the body of Pane Kalimangalnuk who lay flat on the ground face down. *His heart. I need to remove his heart.* Taguwasi thought as he turned the manulib's body over. But as soon as he turned the body over, Taguwasi was shocked to see the manulib still lying face down on the ground.

"What?!" he said in shock and confusion. "I turned him over! I know I did."

Taguwasi turned him over a second time and the same thing happened again! *What is going on? Am I going mad?*

And then he heard it, a low rumbling and churning sound coming from behind him. It was the sound of hunger. It was the sound of a manulib standing right behind him. Taguwasi dropped his head as the body of the manulib in front of him disappeared like smoke.

*****

Unable to follow Bago and Taguwasi into the golden mount, Dalawesan awaited their return or for anything to happen for hours on end. Finally convinced that the two had passed through the sakbawan, the kumaw decided to leave and go back through the way they came. But when he reached the spot where the ripple used to be, there was nothing there, the sakbawan had been closed.

There must be another ripple or sakbawan somewhere else in this rakuh! Dalawesan thought to himself. *There has to be another one!*

Dalawesan had been flying around the endless expanse of swampland for a very, very long time. But since it was perpetually nighttime inside the rakuh, Dalawesan was unsure whether he had been there for hours or days.

He stopped to rest a few times by perching on top of the tallest mangrove trees he could find but his short rests never lasted long. The monstrous toads and frogs were everywhere, and they would attack him as soon as they spotted him. Dalawesan had to fight a few times just to free himself from their long and deadly tongues.

He was tired and his wings felt sore. With each passing hour, hope seemed to leech away from his soul much like how his strength waned with every breath. Suddenly, a ripple appeared from out of nowhere in the open night sky. From out of the ripple suddenly came the figure of Ammalabukaw flying straight at him!

"Forgive me, old friend," Ammalabukaw said as he raised his taloned feet and aimed them directly at Dalawesan's head. "My master had ordered your death!"

Dalawesan had to spiral and dive out of the way at the last second to avoid getting his head crushed by Ammalabukaw's gigantic talons. *I'm not going to win this fight!* Dalawesan thought bitterly. *"I need to get away from him and escape through the ripple he just came from!*

Dalawesan dove down even farther to gain some speed. As soon as he felt he had reached the fastest possible speed he could attain, Dalawesan used its momentum to fly up and towards the ripple.

He was less than twenty or so feet away from the ripple when he saw Ammalabukaw catch up to him from below. The bigger, more powerful kumaw reached up with his beak and tried to bite off one of his legs. Dalawesan was forced to change course yet again just to avoid being maimed.

But just as Dalawesan was rolling away from his attacker, Ammalabukaw managed to grab hold of his underbelly with his talons and ripped off a small chunk of flesh and black feathers. "Aaarrrgh!" Dalawesan cried out as he desperately tried to flee.

"Just give up old friend!" Ammalabukaw yelled as he pursued Dalawesan. "I promise to make it quick and as painless as possible if you let me kill you without putting up much resistance!"

"Why don't you give up and let me kill you quickly?!" Dalawesan retorted as he tried his best to create as much distance between himself and certain doom.

But given his injury and how tired he already was before Ammalabukaw attacked, Dalawesan knew it was only a matter of seconds before his old friend caught up with him again and finished the job. *I can't outrun him, and I can't overpower him. I need to outmaneuver him as soon as he catches up to me.* Dalawesan thought to himself.

He dove and flew close to the surface of the swamp where there was a wide pool of water. He flew as fast and as close to the water's surface as possible. With the bright light from the full moon looming over them, Dalawesan could see his reflection over the surface of the still and unmoving pool.

Another thing that Dalawesan could see was the reflection of Ammalabukaw swooping down on him with his talons outstretched and ready to make that fatal strike. He waited for the last possible second before Ammalabukaw caught up to him. As soon as he saw his old friend directly above him, Dalawesan flapped his wings forward which drastically put a halt to his forward momentum.

Ammalabukaw did not expect this and crashed onto the smooth surface of the water, skimming, and bouncing before finally slowing. Dalawesan was hoping Ammalabukaw would fall in and sink but Ammalabukaw had strong powerful wings that he used to steady himself and began taking flight yet again.

But his little stunt allowed Dalawesan to turn the tables on his attacker. Even as Ammalabukaw began to pick up speed and climb, Dalawesan was flying straight for him from behind. As soon as he reached the bigger kumaw, Dalawesan reached out with his own talons and buried them deep into each of Ammalabukaw's wings.

Dalawesan thought he had the advantage and was about to bite into Ammalabukaw's nape when the bigger kumaw did the exact same thing he did earlier. Ammalabukaw flapped his wings forward to stop his momentum as well as throw Dalawesan forward with the strength of his wings.

Dalawesan fell off Ammalabukaw and started rolling in the mud numerous times. As soon as his world stopped spinning, Dalawesan found himself looking up from the ground with his wings spread open. He was about to get up when Ammalabukaw suddenly crashed right on top of him.

The red kumaw buried both his taloned feet deep into Dalawesan's wings, pinning them to the ground. The bulk of Ammalabukaw's weight was resting on top of him, pinning the rest of him down as well. Dalawesan was going to try to reach up with his beak and tear Ammalabukaw's throat open when the red kumaw suddenly squeezed his right foot tighter over Dalawesan's left wing and broke his cartilage in two!

"Aaarrrgh!" Dalawesan cried out again.

"I'm sorry that it has come to this old friend," Ammalabukaw said as he raised his head for the final blow. "Close your eyes, I will end this quickly."

As Dalawesan looked up at the face of his own demise, something bright flashed from behind Ammalabukaw's head. It was a bright white light which Dalawesan thought to be the light of the moon at first. As everything seemed to slow down to a crawl at the last moment, Dalawesan saw white feathers flapping directly behind Ammalabukaw.

"Get away from Akka you big red cock!" Dundunan suddenly cried out as she buried one of her taloned feet behind Ammalabukaw's neck and another foot on his back. She closed her grip as tightly as she could and severed the giant kumaw's spine at the base of his skull!

The attack was as effective as it was brutal. Ammalabukaw was caught completely by surprise and was unable to react, much less defend himself. He simply rolled his eyes back and died almost instantly.

"Dundunan!" Dalawesan exclaimed when he saw his sister lift Ammalabukaw's massive corpse off of him. "You're here! How did you find me?"

"I had help brother," Dundunan replied. "You are hurt!"

"I will live. Don't worry about me. What of Hapu Talimannog, Innawagan and everyone? What of the Lakandian Taguwasi? Did you meet him?" Dalawesan asked as he struggle to get to his feet.

"Yes brother, I did. Try to relax," Dundunan said as she tried to calm her brother down. "A lot has happened since the anito, and I left. I'll tell you everything I know in due time, but right now we need to wait and hope we were not too late in getting back with help."

*****

"That was an incredible display of power Taguwasi!" Pane Kalimangalnuk said in amazement as he kicked Taguwasi in the back and pinned him on the ground. "Had I been the one you actually used that power on, then I would be at your mercy as we speak."

Suddenly, four stone hands emerged from the ground and grabbed hold of the Lakandian's extremities. The hands lifted him up and had him facing upward while suspended on his back.

"Did you actually think I was unaware of your little ruse earlier?" Pane Kalimangalnuk asked as he walked around the helpless and completely vulnerable Taguwasi. "I told you before that once you are in any of my rakuhs, you are at my complete and utter mercy.

"I know everything that is happening anywhere in my

rakuh. I knew you were breaking free of my first illusion as I knew you were building up this amazing power you used on my kakteh earlier."

Pane Kalimangalnuk balled his right hand into a fist and raised it so Taguwasi could see what he was doing. Slowly, the manulib began opening his fingers. As each finger parted from the other, so did each of the four hands that held Taguwasi's arms and legs.

"It's not real! It's not real! It's not real!" Taguwasi started chanting out loud as he began feeling his muscles stretch and his joints leave their sockets.

"You can try to will yourself free as much as you want Taguwasi, but I doubt you have the time to actually do it," Pane Kalimangalnuk said. "In a few short moments, you will start to feel your flesh and muscles being torn like corn husks. The pain and shock will be so severe you will probably die shortly after. Farewell… flying man…"

But just before the manulib could open his hand completely, a blinding white light exploded right next to him and Taguwasi. The light felt like a powerful wave of pure magic and as soon as it struck Pane Kalimangalnuk, it knocked him back several feet and slammed him onto the ground.

When the light struck the hands of stone that threatened to pull Taguwasi apart, they shattered into a thousand pieces no bigger than the tiniest pebble.

"Taguwasi! I am here!" A familiar voice said as Taguwasi fell to the ground.

"Ba...Bago... Is that you?" Taguwasi meekly asked as his voice barely made it out of his lips.

"Yes! It's me!" Bago responded as he hurried to Taguwasi and placed his hands on the sides of his head. "What has he done to you?"

As soon as Bago freed Taguwasi's mind, the pain in his joints began subsiding. The tearing feeling in his flesh and skin disappeared as a soothing wave of relief washed over him. "I'm hurt Bago. I am hurt very badly."

"Then allow me to heal you Lakandian." A familiar female voice said as a warm comforting light enveloped him.

Taguwasi immediately felt his wounds begin healing, the soreness and aches vanish, and his strength returned to him. He opened his eyes and saw the beautiful, statuesque visage of Poong Kedes standing over him.

"My Poon," Taguwasi said and quickly fell to his knees.

"Arise Lakandian Taguwasi. You've been down in the dirt long enough." Poong Kedes said as she gestured for him to arise.

"Not that I'm ungrateful for your aid my Poon, but I am confused as to why you've come to help me at all. I denounced you the day that my parents were killed and had completely abandoned the notion of serving you."

Taguwasi said with a bit of shame in his tone.

"Yet you still did what is right and defended the helpless against the dark creatures of the world," Poong Kedes said as she shot a look to her left where Pane Kalimangalnuk was on his knees and bound in ropes of bright light. "Creatures like this manulib who uses false magic given to him by a dark spirit in the form of an agimat in his chest."

"My Poon, if you would allow me to speak freely, I would like to apologize for how I reacted when I rejected you and Kaluwalhatian," Taguwasi said.

"The fact that you say this now is apology enough Lakandian," Poong Kedes said.

"I thank you my Poon, but what I am trying to say is... I..." Taguwasi was trying to say but kept fumbling his words.

"Go ahead Taguwasi," Bago said. "Tell her how you feel."

Taguwasi took a deep breath and said, "My Poon, I wanted to say that I now understood what you meant when you told me to be a true Lakandian, I had to break the bonds that hold me to this realm. I understand that I must transcend my humanity in order for me to actually protect humanity.

"Even if that means forsaking those whom I love and putting the needs of Kaluwalhatian above all else. I guess, what I'm saying is that I am ready to be a true Lakandian."

Poong Kedes smiled and had an expression of pride across her face after hearing Taguwasi's words. "By passing the final test, I now know you are ready to be a true Lakandian."

"What test?!" Both Taguwasi and Bago asked in unison.

"The fact that you are willing to forgo all that you are for the sake of others and the will of Kaluwalhatian means that you are now completely selfless. But I do not wish for you to relinquish your humanity Taguwasi, for your humanity is what gives you the heart of a true Lakandian.

"Now that your heart and mind are ready, I believe your body is ready as well. Once I unlock the full power of the Balaang Nakar within your body, you will finally reach your full potential as a Lakandian. Your strength, speed, and stamina will increase but what will truly stand out is the improvement in your unique power to command the wind.

"Over the years to come, your ability will continue to grow in strength as will your other gifts. But for now, I believe you can command stronger and more powerful cyclones and gusts of wind. You can use your dinatal more frequently as it will drain far less energy from you than it once did. And your spirit will be that much stronger. Are you ready for this Taguwasi?" Poong Kedes finally asked.

"Yes, my Poon," Taguwasi answered. "I am ready to be of service."

A bright blinding light suddenly emanated from Poong Kedes' eyes and mouth. The light quickly started to pour out of the goddess' skin which quickly enveloped her entire body. The fifteen-foot deity then knelt in front of Taguwasi and enveloped him in her light-covered hands. The light that emanated from her was so bright that even Bago had to shield his eyes from it.

Suddenly, just as quickly as it started, the light vanished and all that was left was the image of Poong Kedes standing before Taguwasi. "It is done," the Poons said. "How do you feel Lakandian?"

"I feel... I feel, different," Taguwasi said as he looked at his hands and moved his fingers. He closed his eyes and took a deep breath. Almost immediately, storm-like winds rushed toward Taguwasi and entered his nostrils. "I feel... powerful!"

"Now that you are a true Lakandian, it is time I bestow upon you your Raniagad weapon," Poong Kedes said as she reached inside a small white satchel at her side and produced several items. One was a white hunting bow with a golden bowstring running across it. The bow itself looked like ivory with intricate carvings along its surface. Another item was a white pusot with several white shafted arrows with white feathered fletching.

"This is a bow made from gansagat or the wood harvested from the magical balete trees of Kaluwalhatian," Poong Kedes said as she handed the bow to Taguwasi. "This bow will never break and has been infused with the tree's magic. The longer you draw an arrow from this bow the faster the arrow will travel."

Taguwasi took the bow reverently in his hands and drew the string back. He could immediately feel the power of the bow and knew for a fact that only a being as powerful as a true Lakandian could use it.

"This now brings us to the real power behind these weapons; the arrows," Poong Kedes continued as she handed Taguwasi a pusot with seven arrows. "As I have shown you before when we last met, only a true Lakandian can wield these mighty weapons."

Taguwasi slung the pusot with its golden strap around his neck as he unsheathed the arrows from within. The arrowheads began glowing at the touch of his hands.

"Raniagad weapons are the most powerful weapons at our disposal. They can cut and pierce anything in all three realms save for a Hartadem weapon used by the Yawàs and dalaketnon of Kasanaan. These dark weapons were made from the same *punlanag* seeds of a balete tree that had lost its light. So be wary of beings that wield a Hartadem weapon." Poong Kedes said.

"I thank you my Poon, not for just coming to my aid,

but also for the forgiveness you've bestowed upon me," Taguwasi said as he knelt once again in front of the Poon. "I swear to you that I shall be your champion in all the realms and shall do your bidding as best I can."

"That is good to hear," Poong Kedes said. "I must take my leave and return to Kaluwalhatian. Should you ever need my help again, your katiwala will know where to find me. But before I go, would you like me to dispatch this manulib for you? Though I doubt he is of any consequence to you now that you are far more powerful than you were earlier."

"Please do not bother with Pane Kalimangalnuk my Poon," Taguwasi replied. "I would like to finish this myself as I owe him for all the pain and suffering he had caused me."

"Very well. Farewell Lakandian." Poong Kedes said as she disappeared in a flash of blinding light.

As soon as the Poon disappeared, Taguwasi looked around his surroundings and finally saw them for what they were. Everything from the ground under his feet to the brightly lit night sky seemed like phantoms lingering in the real world.

Suddenly, spikes of bamboo sprung up from the ground and went through Taguwasi's body. But just like everything else, the bamboo was nothing more than translucent phantoms.

"I am beyond your powers now," Taguwasi told Pane Kalimangalnuk who couldn't believe what he was seeing. "Your illusions are but ghosts, and like ghosts, they can accomplish nothing more than present themselves but carry no real weight in the physical world."

"No!" Pane Kalimangalnuk cried out and suddenly Taguwasi was engulfed in flames and giant boulders started appearing out of nowhere and began falling on him.

The Lakandian simply looked at them and had a bemused smile across his lips. "Had you used these earlier, I might be dead right now. But sadly for you, it is far too late!"

Taguwasi simply raised his finger and a cyclone suddenly appeared and took hold of the helpless manulib. Pane Kalimangalnuk was slammed multiple times against the rock walls of the cave and then finally on the hard stone floor.

Pane Kalimangalnuk was dazed by the Lakandian's attack but quickly shrugged it off. He decided to physically attack Taguwasi himself and created several doubles of himself hoping that it would confuse him. The manulib along with his seven other doubles rushed at Taguwasi all at once.

But Taguwasi was immune to all of the manulib's illusions at that point and just kept his eye on the real Pane

Kalimangalnuk. The punches and kicks from the false ones simply passed through Taguwasi like the specters that they were.

But when the real manulib did finally throw a punch at Taguwasi, the Lakandian simply ducked and easily evaded it. Pane Kalimangalnuk continued attacking him with several more punches and kicks, but to Taguwasi's newfound speed and abilities, the manulib seemed to move at a snail's pace.

Having had enough of Pane Kalimangalnuk's feeble attempts at attacking him, Taguwasi delivered one quick knee to the manulib's gut that drove the wind right out of him. Taguwasi followed through with a powerful swing with his white hunting bow that sent the manulib flying and crashing on the ground several feet away from him.

"Let's see what a Raniagad arrow can really do," Taguwasi told Bago as he drew an arrow from his pusot. The arrow he drew was shaped like the patak arrows his people use that bury themselves deep into their intended target.

He placed the glowing white arrow on his bow and drew it. He felt the tension in the bowstring rapidly increase. He waited for five full seconds and loosed the arrow. It went through Pane Kalimangalnuk's midsection and exited his back without losing its momentum. The arrow would have buried itself deep in the cave had

Taguwasi not retrieved it using the wind to guide it back to his hands.

The manulib looked at the gaping hole in his stomach and could not believe what was happening to him. Rust-colored blood spewed from the wound as well as his mouth. He looked up at Taguwasi and was about to say something when another arrow struck him in the right shoulder. This time it was shaped like the *palsok* or bladed arrow of the Agta people. This arrow cut through his flesh and bone and almost completely severed his right arm.

This time, it was his turn to cry out in pain as he desperately tried to keep his arm from falling off. "Yaaagh!" Pane Kalimangalnuk cried. "Mercy! Please have mercy on me!"

"Would you have shown me mercy had Poong Kedes not rescued me from your clutches?" Taguwasi said as he drew another arrow from his pusot.

Knowing he had lost and was most likely going to die, Pane Kalimangalnuk had one last scheme to gamble his life with. "The two kumaws are still inside one of my rakuhs. I have closed all the entrances and exits to both of them. The only way they can leave is if you spare me."

"This is where you are mistaken," Taguwasi simply said and loosed his last arrow which was like the barbed *tinanad* arrow. The arrow struck Pane Kalimangalnuk square in the chest, piercing his heart and the tagrakuh agimat that sustained him. The arrow stayed embedded in his chest.

Pane Kalimangalnuk saw the encroaching darkness of death finally come to take him and free him from his torment. In the end, he smiled as he welcomed death's sweet release. The very last thing the manulib saw was Taguwasi approach him, put his foot on his chest, and pull the arrow out.

Taguwasi stood there for a moment and looked at the golden beating heart at the tip of his arrow. "How bizarre," Taguwasi said as the heart slowed, then stopped beating.

"Look at his corpse Lakandian!" Bago exclaimed as the body of Pane Kalimangalnuk began shriveling and decaying right before their eyes.

Taguwasi spat at his corpse and ripped the dead manulib's head off his shoulders.

"What are you going to do with that?" Bago asked a bit disgusted.

"I will place this at one of the entrances to these caves as a warning to anyone to avoid going in," Taguwasi answered. "His rakuhs are still around us even after his death. These caves and tunnels are dangerous to anyone unlucky enough to venture into them."

"We still have the kumaws to take care of though," Bago mentioned. "Oh, and don't forget Pane

Nagdombilan. He is probably still somewhere in here. I suppose we should start looking for any ripples he might have forgotten to close and start looking?"

"Maybe we don't need to," Taguwasi said as he drew out one of his bladed palsok arrows and went to the edge of the rakuh. Using the Raniagad weapon, Taguwasi was able to cut a hole through the rakuh itself and pass through.

"How did you know it could do that?" Bago asked in amazement.

"When I shot the manulib with the first arrow, I saw it go through the boundaries of the rakuh before I retrieved it. That's how I knew that Raniagad weapons were able to literally cut through these realistic illusions."

"Amazing!" Bago said. "You're actually very smart for someone barely three years old. Let's go find those kumaws and finish this once and for all."

Chapter 20

Bertan

ᜊᜒ ᜇ᜔ ᜆ ᜈ᜔

Because of the severity of the injuries sustained during his fight with Ammalabukaw, Dalawesan was unable to take flight which left him at the mercy of the monstrous toads and frogs that inhabited the rakuh. Luckily for him, though he did not want it, Dundunan was there to defend him and fight off the amphibians as they came.

"Dundunan just go and leave me!" Dalawesan cried out to his sister who circled above him.

"Don't be ridiculous!" Dundunan yelled back. "I am not letting any of these things anywhere near you! Taguwasi will be with us soon. Poong Kedes said she will make him even more powerful than he already is." Dundunan said as she dove down, grabbed one of the toads headed for Dalawesan, and killed it.

Suddenly a strange tear appeared in the night sky as if someone took a dagger and just cut a hole through the fabric of space. "Dundunan, look! Up there!" Dalawesan said when he saw the tear.

From the tear flew out the kumaw's deliverance in the form of the Lakandian Taguwasi. "He's here!" Dundunan cheered.

*****

Anibo and Ammani created a makeshift stretcher from some branches and vines that they gathered close by and carefully placed Talimannog on it. "You need to take akka back to the settlement as soon as possible," Innawagan said as she gave him a sip of water from an old coconut shell she found near the lagoon. "The sooner you can take him home the better, just so you can care for him."

"But what about you wadi?" Anibo asked. "Are you not coming home with us?"

"Not just yet. I want to stay here a little while longer and wait for the kumaws and Taguwasi," she answered.

"Then you don’t have to wait too long Hapu," Dundunan's voice suddenly said from within the cave.

"They're back!" Ammani exclaimed as both kumaws and Taguwasi flew out of the cave along with the ghostly presence of Bago.

Innawagan jumped up and warmly embraced Dundunan as soon as the kumaw landed next to her. Dalawesan walked right next to Talimannog who was laying on the ground and sorrowfully bowed his head next to the wounded Talimannog.

"I am so sorry Hapu that I couldn't stop this from happening to you," Dalawesan said shamefully.

"There's no need to feel sorry my friend," Talimannog said as he placed his hand on Dalawesan's head. "I'm actually overjoyed that all of us are here, alive and somewhat well."

Innawagan then approached Taguwasi and wrapped her arms around him as well. "Is he dead?" she asked. "Is that monster dead?"

"Yes. He's gone," Taguwasi said as he showed her the decapitated head of Pane Kalimangalnuk tied around his waist. "He will trouble you and your family no more."

"And what of his brother?" Ammani asked. "What of Pane Nagdombilan?"

"The other manulib still lives and is probably in hiding," Bago answered.

"I will go back in there and hunt him down," Taguwasi said. "How is your brother doing?"

"Akka is very badly injured," Innawagan replied. "We need to get him home and try to save him."

"Oh! I almost forgot." Bago suddenly said. "Dundunan, do you still have the *tambadon* leaves I attached to your leg?"

"Yes! I forgot I had those as well."

"Tambadon?" Taguwasi asked, puzzled as to what Bago was saying.

"Tambadon leaves are the leaves of the balete trees in Kaluwalhatian," Bago replied. "If ground up and mixed with water, they are able to heal almost any sickness or injury. I took some with us when Dundunan and I went to Kaluwalhatian to seek out Poong Kedes' help."

Innawagan bent down and found a small pouch tied around Dundunan's right leg. When she opened it, she saw three glowing leaves in the shape of a heart. The leaves glistened and changed colors as she looked at them. "I can use this to heal akka?"

"Yes. Just grind them up, mix them with water, and have him drink it." Bago replied.

"While you do that, I will return to the caves to find and kill Pane Nagdombilan," Taguwasi said as he handed Pane Kalimangalnuk's head to Anibo. "Please take this and place it near the entrance to the lagoon as a warning. The rakuhs still exist even after his death which makes these caves a very dangerous place for weary travelers seeking shelter."

*****

Taguwasi returned to the caves and searched the rakuhs and found no trace of Pane Nagdombilan. He often returned there over the next few weeks just to see if the manulib ever went back but his searches always ended in disappointment.

Taguwasi stayed with Innawagan and her brothers in their settlement just to be near the caves he often visited and searched. Alig was reunited with her siblings a few days later as were Sinag and Puyang Anag when

Taguwasi started to miss his own family and decided to pick them up and took them to Innawagan's settlement.

In the few short months that both families were together, love had blossomed between Taguwasi and Innawagan. Sinag, who helped nurse Talimannog back to health also fell in love. The lives of everyone in the new bertan they formed were full of bliss during their brief stay near the lagoon. As the weeks gave way to months and no trace of the manulib had been found, a sense of happiness and security had started to take root amongst the members of the bertan.

But their time of peace and prosperity quickly ended on the night of the dual weddings between Taguwasi and Innawagan and Talimannog and Sinag. On the afternoon of their wedding presided over by Puyang Anag, a band of Kalinga head-hunters attacked their settlement during the ceremony.

The band was led by Naisaganam, a Kalinga chieftain who led a group of exiled warriors that often raided Agta settlements on both sides of the Cagayan River. But what really set them apart from any typical headhunter party was that they were all armed with golden weapons ranging from spears, bolos, and axes.

Armed and dangerous as these fearsome warriors were, they were of no consequence to a Lakandian like Taguwasi. What the Kalinga expected to be a grueling battle ended up being a short-lived massacre of their entire band. Naisaganam was the last Kalinga left alive by Taguwasi who asked him to tell them where Pane Nagdombilan was hiding in exchange for his life.

But by the time Taguwasi reached the Kalinga camp, the manulib had escaped yet again. Deciding it was just too dangerous for them to stay there, the bertan decided to move farther west and settled near a small piece of land near a branch of the Cagayan River.

*****

"And we've been living here ever since," Innawagan concluded the tale just as the sun was beginning to rise.

"Wait," Kidul interjected. "What happened to Pane Nagdombilan? Did you never hear from him again?"

"Not to this day," Taguwasi answered. "I go to the caves every now and again, but I still can't find him. I've visited Kalinga villages up and down these mountains, but no one has ever seen or heard of him."

"That was an amazing story," Lumalindaw said as he stood up and stretched his entire body. "Now that I know of this manulib, I shall hunt for him as well. If I ever find him and get rid of him for you, I'll be sure to let you know."

"Does that mean you'll return here and tell us?" Anibo asked as he rubbed his sleepy eyes.

"I'll just shout it out into the empty sky, I'm sure you'll hear it," Lumalindaw said and chuckled.

Puyang Anag had awakened and stepped out of her hut. She approached the group and said, "Have none of you slept all night?"

"No Hapu," Sinag said as she too stood up and stretched. "We had just finished telling Lumalindaw our story."

"And will you be staying with us a little longer Lakandian Lumalindaw?" Puyang Anag asked.

"Unfortunately, I cannot," Lumalindaw answered. "I need to continue my search for Muwan and to be honest, I have already stayed longer than I planned as it is."

"Then I suggest going farther west just past the Abulog River. My old friend told me last night of a cursed woman who lives in a crystal cave," Puyang Anag suggested. "Whether she was cursed or she's the one doing the cursing, I am uncertain. But I hope it can lead you to where you need to go to find the one who cursed you."

*****

A few hours later, after loading some food and supplies in a small basket around the neck of Kolago the bannog, Lumalindaw and Kidul were saying their farewells to Taguwasi and his bertan. He gave a warm hug to each person and mounted Kolago. Just before he gave the command to take off, Taguwasi flew to his side.

"I hope to see you again Lumalindaw," Taguwasi said. "I am really happy to have met another Lakandian."

"So am I," Lumalindaw replied. "I am sure we will see each other again. Sooner rather than later."

"Especially when the first true Lakandian comes. But until then, I hope you find this Muwan and break your curse so you can finally be with your family. Farewell Lakandian." Taguwasi bid goodbye.

"Farewell Lakandian. Kolago! Mikkayyab!" Lumalindaw said and flew to the west.

Ibalon Seas (Map)

Epilogue

He's been on this boat for almost two weeks. Before that, he's been on the run and hiding in caves and underground rivers for the last few months. His hunger knows no bounds but his longing for his long-lost brother is the one pain that ails him the most.

The sun had just set as darkness was starting to cover the vast seas near the eastern shores of the Ibalon kingdoms. And just like the nights that came before, Pane Nagdombilan was aimlessly adrift at sea.

He had just emerged from the berk of the small *biroco* sailboat he had stolen from a fishing port in Dingalan when something big suddenly slammed onto his vessel. At first, he paid it no mind thinking it might have just been a dolphin or some other fish that accidentally struck the boat. But when a second and more violent bump shook the boat, Pane Nagdombilan sprang up and produced a large golden harpoon in his hand.

"Whatever you are, you're dead!" The manulib cried out as he scanned the dark waters surrounding him.

At first, nothing moved on the surface but white frothing waves that glistened in the light of the rising moon. And then he saw it, around thirty or so feet away, and heading fast towards him was the largest shark's fin he had ever seen!

The shark moved so fast that it reached his boat only a few seconds later. The shark leapt out of the water and seemed even bigger with its gigantic manta-like wings on its sides. Pane Nagdombilan recognized the beast as a *pating na pakpakan* or winged shark, and he only had a second to do anything before the beast crashed onto his biroco and sink it.

The manulib instinctively increased the size of his golden harpoon by three times and threw it directly at the flying shark. His harpoon struck the beast's underbelly and sent it flying back with the force of his throw.

Blood gushed freely from the creature's wound as it sank into the ocean. It didn't take long before a strange frenzy started happening below the surface of the water. The waters turned and churned as several fins started appearing around where the pating na pakpakan sank.

Thinking that the danger had passed and the creatures beneath the waves had satiated their hunger, Pane Nagdombilan started to relax. But the moment he started to sit on the bow of the boat, a creature far deadlier than anything the sea could produce, rose from the waves and boarded his biroco.

The manulib couldn't believe what he saw at first glance. He had heard of the merfolk that populated the seas and of the beautiful *sirenas* (mermaids) that seduce fishermen and sailors alike. But that being in front of him screamed of death and danger the second he saw her; the being was called Magindara of the Lalad. She was a dalaketnon and one of the remaining five.

She was a beautifully sublime woman with a thin narrow face, jet black eyes with green iridescent pupils. Her lips were bold but darkly cold like the sea at night. Her top half was naked and covered in black tattoos. But what made Pane Nagdombilan mistake her for a sirena was her bottom half which had been transformed into the tail of a shark by Gat Yawà Asuang himself.

The only piece of clothing that she actually wore was a thick dark leathery belt around her waist. And on that belt was a *minasbad* sword with an intricately carved pommel in the shape of a shark's head sheathed in a black marble-like scabbard.

"How dare you kill one of my children!" Magindara said with her beautiful face contorted in rage.

"Your children? That shark-like thing tried to eat me!" Pane Nagdombilan retorted and produced a golden itak in one hand and a kalasag shield in the other. "Let's see if you bleed like your children, shall we?"

Pane Nagdombilan charged at Magindara and tried to cut her in half with his golden itak. But as soon as he moved in to attack her, the dalaketnon's face shifted from outrage to calm and a somewhat happy expression as though violence actually gladdened her.

What happened next happened so fast that Pane Nagdombilan wasn't really sure how it came to be. Magindara drew her Hartadem blade and cut the golden itak in half even before it could come close to her. She then swung her weapon around and made two quick slashes at the manulib's kalasag and cut it down to size.

Pane Nagdombilan couldn't believe it. He never dreamed that there was anything in the world that could do that to his magical constructs. He was about to create another weapon when Magindara lopped off both his hands!

"Aaargh!" the manulib cried when he looked at the stumps where his hands used to be.

"You're not human," Magindara said calmly as she picked up one of Pane Nagdombilan's severed hands from the deck of the boat and licked the blood dripping from it.

"You were human once, but magic had altered you somehow," she continued. "Tell me how you came to be, and I might spare you."

"Agimat... An agimat..." Pane Nagdombilan answered with a noticeable quiver of fear in his tone.

"And who gave you this agimat and why?"

"A mamaw... his name was Munduntug. He said he would give me and my kakteh power to avenge our people from bandits in exchange for our service."

"And what service was that?"

"To find those who sleep in the mountains and tell him or others like him of their locations." Pane Nagdombilan answered.

"I don't know this mamaw specifically, but he obviously wanted you to find the Likum. Probably to gain favor with the Yawàs. Well, did you find any?" Magindara continued to ask as her interest was piqued at the mention of the Likum.

"N…no. We searched for almost a century but never found one."

"Then I see no reason for you to exist," Magindara said as she raised her Hartadem and prepared to kill the manulib.

"Lakandian!" Pane Nagdombilan blurted out in a last-ditch effort to save himself.

Magindara stopped mid-strike and lowered her weapon at the mention of Lakandian. "What about them? What do you know of the Lakandians?"

"It was a Lakandian called Taguwasi who killed Kakteh right in front of me," the manulib replied.

"And why in all the realms would this Taguwasi spare you if you were there?" Magindara asked a bit suspicious about the circumstances of his tale.

"I… I… was in hiding," Pane Nagdombilan said as he

bowed his head in shame. "I was afraid. Especially when the Poon showed up..."

Magindara's eyes widened in surprise. "A Poon?! Now, this is information that can save your life. Start talking!"

~ The End ~

Other books in the Alamat Book Series:

The following books are available on **Amazon.com** in eBook, Paperback, and Hardbound copies

ALAMAT: BOOK 1

LAM-ANG

ALAMAT: BOOK 2

LUMALINDAW

Available in the Philippines on **Lazada** and **Shopee** through **Milobytes Hobbies**

Milobytes Hobbies

For more information on the **Alamat Book Series**, visit us at www.alamatbookseries.com

www.ingramcontent.com/pod-product-compliance
Lightning Source LLC
LaVergne TN
LVHW090257210926
848480LV00001B/55

* 9 7 9 8 2 3 0 8 0 4 7 4 1 *